NOT YOUR CINDERELLA

KATE JOHNSON

CONTENTS

ACKNOWLEDGMENTS

Thanks must go to:

The Naughty Kitchen, as ever, for cheerleading, advice, beta-reading and wine. For saying, "Sure, you can write a Royal Wedding book, edit it, format and publish it in four months. Easy," and looking at eleventy-million cover ideas. Alison May, Annie O'Neil, Immi Howson, Janet Gover, Rhoda Baxter and Ruth Long, you rock.
Jan Jones, also for cheerleading, beta-reading and suggesting wedding selfies.
The friends and family who endured me turning into Random Facts Girl: Royal Family Edition (aye but it won us that pub quiz, didn't it?)
The RNA Cambridge Chapter, especially Lucy Sheerman, for fact-checking a few things for me (why don't maps show benches? It's just silly not to).
Prince Harry & Meghan Markle, who announced their engagement and reminded me of a book I once started about a younger brother of the heir to the throne...

PART ONE

CHAPTER ONE

Clickbait.com: Is Prince Jamie the world's most eligible bachelor?

Yes, and here's why:

1. *His grandmother is the Queen of England, and his father, Prince Frederick, will be King some day.*
2. *Jamie is a man who knows how to serve his country: as a captain in the royal regiment of the Coldstream Guards he served two tours in Afghanistan.*
3. *The further away he gets from inheriting the throne, the more chilled out he is. Born fourth in line, after the birth of his niece and nephew he's dropped to sixth, and does a lot of charity work.*
4. *He's super smart: he graduated UCL with a First Class Honours degree in Computer*

Science ten years ago, and now he's been accepted in the PhD program at the world-famous Cambridge University.

5. *His hair. Come on, have you ever seen a man with hair that thick and wavy and totally run-your-hands-through-it-gorgeous? We want to know what products he uses!*

Next article: 23 ways you're eating avocado wrong!

"I dunno, you young people, always sexting and texting."

Clodagh looked up from her phone. One of the regulars stood at the bar, drink empty.

"I wasn't texting, and do you even know what sexting is?" She hurriedly shut down the animated gif of Prince Jamie's hair blowing in the wind, and put her phone facedown behind the bar. "I was actually doing very important research. For… my… night school course."

His smile said he didn't believe her for a second. "All right, love. Have it your way. Get yourself an education and a better job, don't stay in this dive for the rest of your life. But while you are here," he added, sliding his tankard onto the bar, and Clodagh rolled her eyes.

"Another pint of Abbot?"

"Please."

Jamie's sister was shouting silently at him. She was angry; he could tell by the pink spots on her cheeks. Victoria hated those pink spots. Hated her complexion being anything other than peaches and cream. She took a make-up artist quite literally everywhere with her. Jamie hadn't seen his own sister bare-faced since she was about fourteen.

"James William Frederick Henry," he made that bit out by lip reading, "will you…"

The rest was lost over the noise of his headphones, but Jamie could more or less figure out the gist. *Take off those bloody headphones before I...*

"...rip them off your bloody head!" she finished, as he paused his game and slipped the headphones down over his neck.

"So sorry, Vicky. Didn't hear you."

"Do *not* call me Vicky." She smoothed down hair that didn't need smoothing.

"You used to prefer it."

"It's common." The greatest insult from Victoria. "Put down that... that bloody thing, will you?"

Jamie looked at the controller in his hand. It was customised, given to him on a factory tour before they'd even gone on sale. "This bloody thing is a prototype and therefore wholly unique. I soldered a bit of circuitry on it, you know," he added proudly.

Victoria sighed as if he was the most tormenting creature in the universe. "Yes, we know. Most thrilling day of your life. It's a bit of wire, Jamie. You're sixth in line to the throne."

Yes, and I know which fascinates me more. Sighing, Jamie took his lovely noise-cancelling headphones off completely. *Goodbye silence, my old friend.* "Was there something you wanted, sister dearest, or do you just hate Lara Croft?"

"You're so lame. Vincent's looking for you. Says it's time to get ready."

Oh, bollocks. Jamie knew he ought to remember what he should be getting ready for, but he'd been so absorbed in the sidequest he'd been playing he'd forgotten the time. And now... oh yes. Bugger. Here was Vincent with the red tunic of the Coldstream, which paired with the blue riband of the Royal Victorian Order usually made him look like a macaw. Vincent's assistant Graham was busy laying out the medals, badges and random bits of gold braiding so beloved of these occasions.

"Her Highness requested it specially," said Vincent before Jamie could speak.

His gaze flew to his sister, who smoothed down her elegant and un-peacockish dress, which did not clash with her own blue riband, and said, "He means Isabella. She wants everyone in dress uniforms, especially the godparents," she added pointedly, and Jamie tried to look like he totally remembered he was becoming a godparent for the fifteenth time today.

"Nearly had to get Granny to invent something for Anthony until someone remembered he was in the TA for about five minutes." She marched to the door. "Could be worse, remember Anthony wanted to be a Highlander," was her parting shot.

Great. Well, she was right, at least he wasn't in tartan.

"I'll be infested with magpies," he said, taking off his sweatshirt. His nice comfortable sweatshirt in its nice plain shade of blue with its nice picture of the Death Star on it.

"No, sir, the falconers have been out," said Vincent, who Jamie suspected as having had his sense of humour surgically removed some time ago.

"Of course they have. All right." Jamie stripped off his t-shirt and Vincent took it as if it was radioactive. Jamie gave him a bright grin, because annoying Vincent with his geek t-shirts was one of his favourite things. This one just said, 'It's not magic, it's science!' which was fairly tame compared with some of his collection.

"Don't lose that," he warned as he kicked off his jeans. "Put it with the others."

"Sir, I have never lost your laundry," Vincent said in wounded terms, handing Jamie his special seamless controlling underwear. No one wanted a visible reminder he was a human male under his impeccably tailored uniform trousers.

Vincent and Graham gave every indication of not noticing their boss was naked, which always impressed the hell out of and annoyed Jamie in equal measure.

"Yeah, but I can just imagine how many of them will end up in 'storage'," he said darkly.

"If this is the case, sir, you can only blame your new bedder," said Vincent with distaste, handing Jamie his undershirt.

"She's not going to be doing my laundry," said Jamie. "I've got a washing machine."

Vincent and Graham stared at him, more shocked than they had been when they discovered the tattoo Jamie had got in Afghanistan.

"Whatever for, sir?" said Vincent, recovering first.

For mixing cocktails, what do you think? "Well, because washing by hand is a bit of a faff," he said instead.

The two men gaped at him. Jamie smiled at them and held out his arms. "Now remind me," he said. "Trousers go on over my head, right?"

"Arms up," said Clodagh, patiently holding out the little jumper.

"No!"

"Hollee. Put your arms up."

"No!" Hollee thrust her arms out instead.

"Christ's sake, it's like dressing an octopus."

Hollee slapped her hand over her mouth. "Umm! Naughty word!"

Clodagh took the opportunity to ram the jumper down over her niece's head and reach through the sleeve for her hand.

"Mummy! Auntie Sharday said a naughty word!"

"Shar, don't fucking swear," said her sister, and turned back to her phone.

The coffee shop was overcrowded with buggies and playing a different music from the mall outside. The clash was not helping Clodagh's temper.

"I'll think about it if you stop calling me Sharday."

"It's the name Mum gave you."

Clodagh opened her mouth to repeat the argument she'd been having for years, then held her tongue. What the hell was the point? She gave Hollee a grimace of a smile and yanked on her hand. Hollee screamed as if Clodagh had dislocated her shoulder.

"Should've put your arms up then, shouldn't you," she said.

Hollee started shrieking and slamming her hands on the table. Clodagh felt the eyes of everyone else in the overheated coffee shop turn on them.

"Jesus, Shar, I just asked you to put her jumper on," said Kylie, grabbing her bawling daughter, who kicked and flailed and knocked over her white mocha latte. "Why is that so difficult?"

Because your child is the spawn of Satan, thought Clodagh, but she'd come to blows with her sister often enough over her choice of babydaddy. "When's Mum getting here?"

"Dunno. She had to go pick up Tyler, but you know that's just because Whitney don't wanna talk to that bitch teacher about his ADHD."

"Tyler has ADHD?" asked Clodagh.

"Yeah, well she says he has but you know he's just been a little shit since Jayden left. Fuck's sake, Hollee, I am trying to Instagram. Shar, can you get me another coffee? And some stuff to wipe this up with? Cheers babe."

Clodagh, glad of the excuse to escape the screaming toddler her sister was ignoring, got up to queue at the counter and promptly got stuck there for twenty minutes when her mother whirled in with an indiscriminate number of her progeny. As Clodagh tried to collate a sensible order, which was impossible since at least two of the children refused to drink anything but Red Bull which the cafe thankfully didn't sell, her mother started up the litany of complaints that never ceased.

"...so I just turned around and said, well, it's not my fault you can't give a proper diagnosis, so she turned around and said, I don't give the diagnosis, you have to get the Head Psycho to do it—"

"Ed Psych," murmured Clodagh, who had dealt with a few in her time.

"Yeah, like Nevaeh saw that time, so I said so when are you going to do that and she just gave me this, like, smug look and turned around and said she didn't 'believe there was a case for referral', so I just turned around and said—"

"Don't you get dizzy?" Clodagh said.

"What?"

"All that turning around."

Her mother stared at her blankly, then launched into, "No, only when I've got one of my headaches. Did I tell you about my headaches, babes? Like, oh my God. This new doctor, right, he doesn't even speak English, I don't think he understands what a migraine is. Like yesterday he just turned around and said..."

Clodagh nodded and smiled, and thought about the library book on Mary Seacole she had sitting in her shoulderbag, and ordered another white chocolate bloody latte.

"Here." A glass of champagne appeared in Jamie's line of vision. "You look as if you need this as much as I do."

He took it, not darting out of his hiding position behind a curve of the Grand Staircase. "How did you know I was here?"

Olivia winked. Of course she knew, it was where he

always hid. "How do you know I wasn't just trolling for hiding bachelors?"

"Because you've cast your eye over every bachelor in this place and rejected them all out of hand several times."

She shrugged. "Back atcha. Plus I saw Melissa Featherstonehaugh out there in a revolting little excuse for a hat, so I knew you'd be lurking somewhere."

She leaned against the balustrade, facing back into the Grand Hall, and Jamie laughed out loud when he saw the bottle of champagne she had hidden behind her back. "Be an angel and take that off me."

He did, but not before topping up his glass. If Melissa was out there, he'd damn well need it. They'd barely had any sort of fling at all, but the papers had caught a whiff of it and started planning the wedding, and poor Melissa had rather bought into it all.

"I told you to break it off nicely with her," Olivia warned.

"I did! I was very nice. And gentle. And kind." And all the things he always was when a girl started seeing crowns and sceptres. "And yes I did ask her not to go to the tabloids."

"Who did she send?" asked Olivia, because Melissa would never risk contacting them directly. Far better to send an intermediary with a 'scoop'.

"I dunno. She has quite the coven."

"Yes, you've slept with most of them. It really is a terrible habit, Jamie. Try shagging girls who won't go to the tabloids."

"What, you mean imaginary ones?" Jamie drained his champagne and poured some more. "Besides, I'm on quite good terms with most of them." He'd needed to be. Two of them were his fellow godparents to Isabella's offspring. "Lucinda barely squeezed the baby before she passed her to me earlier."

"I see the vomit sponged off nicely," Olivia said, and yawned discreetly.

"Don't be ridiculous. Vincent had a spare uniform upstairs."

This time Olivia laughed. "Ah, Vincent. Is it the Boy Scouts or the SAS who are always ready? I don't suppose he's got a pair of flat shoes, ladies' six, has he? My feet are bloody killing me."

Jamie glanced down at her heels, which were towering, exquisite, and probably cost more than the GDP of a small country.

"I wouldn't put it past him. Oll, why do you wear those things if they hurt so much?"

"Same reason you wear a dress uniform that makes you look like a Christmas tree."

Jamie straightened his immaculate red tunic with its hastily replaced blue riband, and tried to ignore the lingering scent of baby vomit which Vincent assured him was hardly noticeable.

"Believe me, I'd have been happier in a t-shirt."

Olivia groaned. "One of those stupid science ones."

"Excuse me, they're very clever science ones." He'd got a new one last week with the periodic table on it, which made him very happy even though he wasn't much of a chemist. "You laughed at the Pluto one."

"Only because I didn't understand it. Oh, Christ." Olivia suddenly ducked behind the staircase with him. "Bunty Twistleton," she added by way of explanation.

"Ah." A swift mental picture came to Jamie's mind, of a red-faced young man with sweaty palms and a tendency to place them where they weren't wanted. "Still got over-friendly hands?"

"Swear to God, one of these days I'm going to break his bloody arm. Oh God, he's seen me." She suddenly fixed her full attention on Jamie, which was terrifying since Olivia was one of the most intimidating people he'd ever met, and that included his grandmother. "Oh Jamie, darling, you say the naughtiest things," she purred. "Tell me again."

Jamie leaned in and told her the naughtiest thing he knew. "Jailbreaking an iPhone isn't that hard."

Olivia gasped in mock outrage and playfully batted his shoulder, as behind her the shape of Bunty Twistleton loomed. "Remember the first time we did it," she said, and Jamie fought to keep a straight face.

"Was it your first time?" he asked her. "Come on, be honest with me."

"Um, excuse me, Lady Olivia, er… oh, Your Royal Highness."

Bunty bowed, very correctly but very tiresomely. Olivia rolled her eyes at Jamie and draped her arm around his neck.

"Not to be impolite, Bunty, but shove off, would you? Jamie and I were having a private moment."

Bunty turned even redder, mumbled an excuse and tripped away.

"What a dull little bore," Olivia said.

"You've got to stop doing that," said Jamie, because it was at least the fourth time this season she'd used him to get rid of an overzealous suitor.

"And he has a tiny penis. Oh God no," she added at Jamie's appalled expression, "I didn't. Serena told me. Well, she says she got it from Finty but who knows?"

"Olivia."

"She was very flattering about you, by the way."

"Olivia."

She sighed gustily and used her arm around his shoulders to balance herself as she eased off her shoes. "All right, I'm sorry, but it works. Until that chap off *Poldark* agrees to marry me I've got far too many offers and men don't take 'I'm not interested' for an answer. Such is misogyny, darling. The only time they back off is when you tell them you have a boyfriend."

"I am not your boyfriend. Look, even Granny asked me the other day if we were, and I quote, 'walking out'." She'd never asked that about Melissa or Serena or any of the others.

Olivia snorted. "Is that what they called it in her day? What did you tell her?"

"I told her I loved you like a sister—" possibly more than, he thought, because Olivia never threatened to rip his headphones off "—and had about as much expectation of marrying you."

Not that he expected the Queen believed it, but he was guiltily aware that the rumour mill had had him and Olivia on the brink of an engagement since they were about four years old. Every time someone snapped a picture of him and Olivia together, one of the tabloids ran some kind of speculation on their wedding date. One had even gone so far as to photoshop poor Olivia into Jamie's mother's wedding dress.

"They will want their gossip. I mean little what's-her-face's christening—"

"Lucy, her name is Lucy," Jamie said in exasperation. The poor child had barely left the Bow Room. Her face was still wet from the baptismal font. "You're her godmother."

"Darling, I've got eight god-children. Can't blame me for not keeping them straight. I think I should get a new assistant, just for that."

"I have fifteen godchildren," Jamie reminded her, but kept to himself that he relied upon his private secretary to remind him of their birthdays.

"Show-off. Anyway, I meant a royal christening is one thing but it's Isabella's baby, darling, she's so far down the line of succession you'd run out of bullets before you got to her."

"She's eighth," said Jamie, "and ugh."

"What I meant is no one really gives that much of a damn," said Olivia. "Your dad's going to be king one day. People want to see you get married. You're a proper heir."

"Ed is the proper heir," Jamie said wearily. His brother had been born second in line to the throne, his sister third, and now they were both married and starting families Jamie was quite happy to be bumped further down the line of succession.

"You just need to find someone suitable, with an unembarrassing history, decent fertility, and very good hair, and marry her and everyone will be happy and remember why they pay for you in the first place," was Olivia's advice. "Not me," she added automatically.

"Sure. A snap to find the perfect woman who can actually cope with all this bollocks, and happens to love me in return."

"I'm sure she's just around the corner," said Olivia, and they both peered out into the reception room to come face to face with Melissa Featherstonehaugh.

"Not her," Olivia said automatically, and once again, Jamie was in agreement.

Lee was there when Clodagh came home. She slipped past him as fast as she could, ignored Hanna's pointed, "Hey, been shopping then?" and shut herself in her bedroom.

It wasn't large; the bed took up most of it. Clodagh sometimes thought she should get a smaller bed, but then she reminded herself she was only here temporarily, and it'd be someone else's problem soon. *Soon.*

She put the bag with a bunch of Hollee's baby clothes down on the floor. Kylie had waited until they were all in attendance before making the big announcement that she was expecting a boy this time, and as an afterthought did anyone want all this pink stuff Hollee had grown out of. No one did, so Clodagh had brought it for the charity shop.

Did people still buy baby clothes in charity shops? Her sisters all shopped in Primark, and a lot of the charity shops around here sold much more upmarket second hand clothes. Maybe someone else would have it. One of the student unions had advertised a collection for refugees and—

Raised voices came from outside. Lee shouting at Hanna again. Hanna mumbling back in Polish, which always infuriated him.

She'd only known Lee a few months, but one look had told her who he was. Clodagh had grown up surrounded by men like that. Her mother had wasted years on men like that. She didn't have to know Lee to know who he was.

She heard a thump, and flinched. *You should go.* Hanna always claimed she'd tripped over something and that was Clodagh's fault for being a messy cow, but Clodagh knew the marks a man's fists left as well as the ones his words did.

Fear made her hands shake, but resolution had her unplugging her hefty bedside lamp, the heaviest thing she could find, and holding it clear in front of her as she eased open the door.

"Everything all right?" she said, taking in Hanna cowering on the sofa with her hand to her face and Lee glowering over her, his fists still curled. He swung on Clodagh, who tensed.

"No, babe," he told her. "My stupid girlfriend tripped again, didn'tcha Hanna?"

Hanna nodded and glared at Clodagh. "Yeah. You're so messy."

There was nothing to trip over.

"Whatcha got there?" Lee asked, eyeing the metal candlestick and the wire Clodagh had wrapped around her hand, plug swinging.

"Nothing. Just a lamp that wants fixing."

"I'll do it."

"I can manage."

"I said—"

Clodagh swung the lamp like a baton. "I can *manage*, thanks."

They both glared at her.

"You working tonight?" Hanna asked.

Clodagh nodded. Thank God, away from this horrible little flat for a few hours.

"Good," said Lee, eyeing her menacingly. "There's no privacy when you're here."

"I pay my half of the rent. I'm entitled to my half of the space."

"Unless you want to join us?" Lee stepped towards her, lazily swinging his fists. Clodagh gripped her lampstick so hard her fingers hurt. "I like… dark meat." He gave a low, suggestive chuckle.

"You come any closer and I will hurt you," Clodagh said. Anger made her eyes burn with tears. God dammit, she *did* not want to cry in front of him.

He took another step closer, leering mockingly, and Clodagh forced herself to take a breath. Her jaw clenched, and it was hard to get the words out.

"Touch me and I'll wait until you're sleeping then come in with a knife or my nail scissors or my own *teeth* and cut your balls off, do you understand?"

He came closer, she swung the lampstick, he made to catch it and she jabbed with her fist. Clodagh was out of practice but Lee was a coward, and he jerked back at her show of force.

"Ugly black slut," he said, and Clodagh's teeth bared themselves at him. But he backed off, which was the important thing, and headed for the front door. "I wouldn't fuck you anyway."

"Glad to hear it," she said through sharp breaths, as he slammed the door and stomped off down the cheap, noisy stairs.

Clodagh waited until her muscles let her move, then crossed the room on shaky legs to the door, where she slid the deadbolt across. "You okay?" she said to Hanna.

"He does love me," Hanna said, and Clodagh tried to keep from laughing bitterly.

"Yeah. Sure he does."

"You can't have him! You steal him and I'll find you and I'll cut you…" she trailed off into Polish.

"You can keep him, love," Clodagh said. "Put some ice on that," she added, and went back into her room, locking the door as she did.

She leaned against it, shaking, and looked around. Shit. This place was tiny and heating was terrible and the cafe downstairs was noisy and smelly, but they had unsecured wi-fi and it was a short walk into town, which saved on bus fares.

Slowly, she uncurled her clenched fingers from the lampstick and set it down. Plugged it in. And started to do her sums, once again.

She mentally counted up what she'd got left in her account and how long she had until payday. If she left now she'd default on the rest of the month's rent, but she could probably cancel her direct debit and maybe go into hock on a new place, just for a month. Assuming she could find a new place. Cambridge was Cambridge, after all, and it was a seller's market. She'd learned the hard way that students got the cheapest accommodation in a university city.

Her phone bleeped with a message. "*4got 2 tell u Nevaeh want doll purple NOT pink!!! every1 has pink gud luck hun!!!!!!*"

Whitney. *Shit*. So many bloody birthdays, and her sisters wouldn't take 'I can't afford it' for an answer.

Clodagh would bet good money purple was an impossible-to-find colour for this particular doll. And it *had* to be this particular doll.

"Will do my best," she texted back, and set to gathering her most valuable and treasured possessions into a bag she could leave at work. Hanna was the spiteful kind, and God only knew what Lee would do if he could break the lock.

That done, she sat down on her bed, tried to ignore the blaring gameshow Hanna was watching, and opened the property app on her phone.

CHAPTER TWO

Historygal Blog: All The Work, None of the Rewards

If I'm honest, that title could correspond to about 90% of my blog posts. But anyway. Since I'm a woman who is striving (Oh, so striving) to study history at Cambridge one day, I've been delving into the history of women at Cambridge.

It's not long, nor is it pretty (insert your own actress/bishop joke there).

Cambridge was founded in 1209, but there were no colleges admitting women until 1869, when Emily Davies founded Girton College. Hussah for Emily Davies! But while her students were allowed to study, sit exams and have their results recorded, none of them were awarded a degree. Female students didn't achieve parity with males until 1947. Nineteen-forty-frickin-seven!

Think about that for a moment. Despite doing exactly the same work as the male students, they got none of the reward...

"It's the Master's Lodge, Your Royal Highness," said the bedder, who'd nervously admitted to being called Lenka, "so it's the finest the college has."

"It's got three bedrooms, sir," said Major Peaseman, who'd never allowed Jamie to call him by his first name, "and more importantly a study."

"It's very secure," said Geraint, who didn't care what he was called as long as Jamie let him do his job, "there's a garage at the porter's lodge which we'll have manned twenty-four seven, a door direct to the college over there, and the team and I will occupy the rooms overlooking the garden."

Jamie looked up at the Elizabethan building, its windows leaded and its herringbone redbrick carefully preserved, the late roses blooming under the windows and the gargoyles at the edges of the roof, and said, "It's beautiful."

Lenka beamed. Peaseman checked his official binder. Geraint checked lines of sight.

The house had its own garden, beautifully tended, with mulberry trees and an abundance of roses. In the summer, when term had ended, the Globe put on Shakespeare productions here. Jamie wondered if they'd still go on doing so when he'd vacated for the holidays.

"I will show you around, Your Royal Highness," Lenka said. She produced a large ornate key and unlocked the door.

"That'll need to be changed to a more secure lock," said Geraint, who'd said the same of every property they'd looked at.

"He means in addition," Jamie assured the bedder, who looked somewhat alarmed at the idea of someone chiselling through the old oak to put a modern lock on it. "Something discreet, right Geraint?"

Geraint frowned in response.

"This furniture will have to go," said Peaseman,

wrinkling his nose at the shabbiness of the old dark bookshelves and faded velvet sofas.

"I like it," said Jamie, who was fairly ambivalent but could see Lenka was very proud of the place. "We can sort out furniture later, Peaseman."

"There is a kitchen: will Your Royal Highness be bringing your own chef?" asked Lenka.

Peaseman looked at him enquiringly.

"No, I can manage by myself. I did when I was at uni the first time," he reminded them.

"Bloody nightmare, you being in Halls," Geraint muttered.

"I just want some privacy," Jamie said.

"Your Highness has privacy at Kensington Palace," Peaseman said politely.

Yes, along with pretty much every other member of my family. "But Kensington Palace is rather a long way from the Cambridge Faculty of Computer Science," Jamie pointed out, equally politely.

He allowed Lenka to show him around the pleasant little house, while Peaseman made notes on everything and Geraint's sharp eyes assessed even more.

Two weeks, he thought. Two weeks and this will be mine. Just mine. Not an apartment in a palace I share with my parents, my brother and sister and about a million tourists every day; not a five minute drive from my grandmother; not even anywhere near Peaseman.

He'd negotiated a weekly meeting with Peaseman, who would remain based at Kensington. The freedom from daily meetings with his private secretary was so tantalising it nearly made his mouth water.

Geraint, of course, would remain with him, as he'd remained with him since the day he'd left Eton. Geraint had organised Jamie's security when he went to UCL and had, in fact, been one of the reasons he'd been allowed to live on campus in the first place. Geraint had

19

accompanied him to Sandhurst, where he'd scared the bejeesus out of people whose job it was to scare the bejeesus out of everyone else. He'd been an essential part of Jamie's security detail when he'd done his stint in the Army, in the Navy, and in the RAF. Jamie hadn't even had to ask if Geraint was coming with him to Cambridge.

"I think we'll need drones," Geraint said, as they went back outside. The sky was so blue. Spotless, offset by a few waving rosebushes. It was paradise.

"No drones."

"We'll need to make sure no one else has them," Geraint said. "All these computer types about, I don't trust them."

"Geraint, I'm one of those computer types," Jamie said, dizzy with excitement. It was like Christmas as a child, the anticipation almost too much to bear.

"All the more reason not to trust you," Geraint said darkly.

Jamie squared his shoulders. "Lenka, it looks wonderful. I'll be delighted to move in. Shall we say the twenty-fourth? Excellent. Major Peaseman will talk about the details with you."

There was a sudden flurry of 'Your Royal Highnessing', which Jamie stopped with a raised hand.

"I will be moving in," he said pleasantly, in the voice he'd learned at Nanny's knee and honed at Sandhurst, "on the twenty-fourth of the month. I will be bringing my own desk and computer equipment in addition to my personal effects. The rest is up to you to negotiate, Major. Geraint, I leave the security details in your capable hands. Lenka, would you be so good as to direct me to the nearest pub, please?"

"Pub?" said Geraint, a vein throbbing on his forehead.

"Short for public house. A hostelry, inn, bar, licensed

to serve intoxicating liquor for consumption on and off the premises," Jamie explained, enjoying himself. "Who's on today? Cutter? Farquerson?" Those two liked a drink. Or at least, they could give a decent facsimile of people enjoying a drink whilst remaining alert to danger at all times.

"Khan and Morris, Your Highness."

Even Geraint was Your Highnessing him now. Jamie didn't care. "Khan and Morris, then. Give them a ring, will you? Lenka, what was the name of that pub?"

Clodagh was still shaking a bit when she reached the Prince's Arms that afternoon. Bloody Hanna and bloody Lee! She'd called the police on her way to work, more in hope than expectation. Hanna would answer the door, tell them she'd tripped over something her flatmate had left out, ask which 'anonymous caller' had tipped them off, make up some reason she and her boyfriend had been shouting, and send them away. If she didn't press charges there wasn't much they could do. Not today.

But maybe tomorrow. Maybe the next time.

Clodagh pushed into the warmth of the pub, noise hitting her like a wave. Smiled in a distant way at whoever said hello to her. Got behind the bar, swung open the big door into the cellar, and dumped her heavy bag in the corner.

"What you got there?" asked Oz, glancing up from where he was changing a barrel.

"Oh, just some overnight stuff." Keep it vague, that was what she'd told herself. Don't get pushed into making up lies.

"Going somewhere nice?"

"No, just got back from my mum's." That was true, at least. She'd been bitching about it all last week.

"Ah. Nice time?"

"Yeah, not bad." That was a lie. She'd shared a

bedroom with a seven-year-old niece who watched cartoons in bed. "I mean… you know. Family." She rolled her eyes at him and hung up her coat. "Where d'you want me?"

Oz didn't react to the line. He'd heard it too often. "Top bar, my love. Kronenbourg will just be a minute."

She expected a queue when she got there, but the regulars were all facing away from the bar, watching as a couple of men in black looked around the place with blank faces.

"What's going on?" she asked Stevo as he sipped his bitter.

"Dunno. These two fellas just came in and started poking about. Marte asked what they were after and they took her aside. Reckon they're spooks."

"Nah. Mafia, innit," said Paulie. He groped blindly at his packet of pork scratchings, watching the two men as if they were in a movie.

"Cambridge mafia? You right in the head there, boy? They're just having you on."

The men bantered back and forth, exchanging conspiracy theories in voices quite loud enough to carry. Clodagh glanced back at Oz, who'd just come back out of the cellar.

"Don't ask me," he said. "They're talking to Marte." Marte was the manager appointed by the brewery, hoping to take over as landlady one day, so Clodagh supposed that made sense. "Probably cellar inspectors."

"It's spooks, I'm telling you," said Stevo, plonking down his empty tankard with finality.

"Spooks? In the Prince's Arms? Do me a favour. Same again, Stevo?"

"Please."

That was the thing about the Prince's Arms. The regulars might be a scruffy lot but they paid their tabs, they didn't get into fights, and they treated her with some respect. They were half old men who'd been drinking there forever, and half students spending more than they could probably afford on lager whilst arguing about the principles of robotics.

The wallpaper was fading, the drinks menu was limited and there was an entire corner of the lounge bar dedicated to the conker tournament that had been run for thirty years by the previous landlord, but Clodagh had definitely worked in worse places.

By the time she'd poured Stevo's pint and added it to his weekly tab, the men had conferred with Marte one more time and left. She came back to the bar, looking somehow pale and flushed at the same time.

"What's going on?" asked Clodagh, the three of them congregating in the narrow corridor between the two bars.

"Cellar inspectors?" said Oz.

"Did you ever see cellar inspectors in black suits?" Marte twisted her hands. "Well, you'll see."

Clodagh frowned. Oz groaned. "Not strippers, Marte!"

"No," she said, an odd look on her face. "Not strippers."

"What, then?"

Marte peeked around into the top bar, which had gone somewhat silent. "See for yourself."

The entirety of the top bar seemed focused on the small party entering the pub. Sound came only from the bottom bar, where football ebbed and flowed from the TV in the corner.

"Evening," said a voice which sounded oddly familiar.

A slight murmur of 'evening's chorused back. Marte pushed Clodagh out into the bar, where she stood frowning and then suddenly gaping at the man on the other side of it.

He seemed unaware of her scrutiny. "I'll have a pint of..." he perused his choices. "Carlsberg, I think. Lads?"

The two large men behind him had gazes that seemed to drill into Clodagh's brain. "Tonic and lime," said one of them.

"Two tonics and lime, please."

Prince Jamie looked up at Clodagh then, smiling his white-toothed, open, friendly smile.

Clodagh gaped at him some more. His hair really was as thick and wavy as it looked on TV. The eyes that twinkled at his cute niece and nephew shone greenish-hazel in the pub's dingy lights. He had really long lashes, like a cow.

Oh God, I just compared a member of the Royal Family to a cow.

"And maybe some crisps? Do you have prawn cocktail?"

Clodagh nodded. She had no idea. He wore a Pac Man t-shirt.

"D'you want," someone said, and she realised it was her, "Schweppes or Fevertree?"

"Schweppes is fine," said one of the men in black.

"Slimline," said the other.

"One regular, one slimline," said the prince, still smiling at her as if she was an ordinary person and not one whose brain had leaked out of her ears. Pac Man had a crack down the middle of his vinyl printed face.

"Clodagh!" snapped Marte from behind her. Louder, she said, "One Carlsberg, was it, sir?"

"Your Royal Highness," corrected Oz from her other side. "Prawn cocktail?" He placed a packet of crisps carefully on the bar. The crackle startled Clodagh, who moved her gaze from Prince Jamie's patiently smiling face to the condensation ring an inch from the crisps.

"I'll clear that up," she said. "I'm so sorry."

"Don't worry about it," said the prince, but she was

already stumbling off to find the paper towel, her hands shaking like anything.

What the hell? What the actual hell? Prince Jamie in the pub? Prince Jamie, youngest son of the Prince of Wales, grandson of the *Queen* for God's sake, was out there ordering prawn cocktail crisps. And lager. Which she still hadn't poured.

She emerged again with too much paper towel, started scrubbing the bar, and watched Oz pull a pint of beer. He set it down, eyeing her with amusement, and went to the till.

"While you're there," said the prince, too quiet to be heard over the increasing murmur of voices, "a round for everyone?"

Oz paused. One of the men in black slid over a credit card.

"And yourselves, of course," Jamie added. He took a sip of lager. "Ahh. Gentlemen, shall we find a table?"

With that, he sauntered off to a table in the conker corner. *He really does have amazing hair.* Clodagh watched him peer closely at the conkers in their neat mounts and read the comic poems Stevo's father-in-law had composed about the winners of each annual tournament.

"I'm going mad," she said out loud.

"Yeah. I thought that when I first saw the conkers," Marte said. She chucked Clodagh under the chin. "Come on, Clo, never seen a royal before?"

"Er, no," Clodagh managed.

"Really? The Princess Royal opened the new swimming pool last year."

"Duke of York did prize-giving at my sister's college," Oz put in.

"He's starting at Lady Mathilda, isn't he?" said Paulie.

"What, the Duke of York?"

"No, fathead, Prince Jamie. Summink to do with computing, I don't know. It was in the papers. Here, pass us the papers."

Mechanically, Clodagh did just that. Computer science, wasn't it? A PhD? The gifs from the clickbait article danced dizzily in her head. Prince Jamie giggling at something his nephew said. Prince Jamie in full military dress. Prince Jamie with his grandmother, the Queen.

From under her hair, she watched him take a sip of his lager and smile at something one of his bodyguards said. He glanced around with a bland smile on his face.

His gaze lingered on the group of students trying to ignore him.

Then it moved on.

"Well, this place is a dive," said Khan.

"It's not that bad," said Jamie, still fascinated by the conkers. There were poems attached to each one, in rhyming verse, telling the story of the match as if it was an epic battle.

"Laddie, I've been in nicer places in warzones," said Morris.

"It's authentic. So many pubs these days are all the same. Gin bars and hummus on the menu. Look, there's a whole verse here about soaking it in vinegar."

"How often," said Morris, "do you go to pubs?"

"As often as you let me," Jamie said, which wasn't often enough. "Look, this place has actual students. Maybe I'll make friends with them. You know, friends? People you have things in common with and choose to spend time with?"

"Like Lady Olivia?" said Khan slyly.

Yes, like Lady Olivia. Who, as Jamie had often been at pains to point out, was the only one of the eminently suitable young moppets Nanny Barkatt had chosen for the royal nursery all those years ago he was still in touch with.

"Olivia is one of my best friends," he said evenly, "but she doesn't give a fig about coding. She has no idea why my shirt is funny," he added, looking down sadly at Pac Man and the two ghosts. *I see dead people*, ran the caption.

"That's because it isn't," Morris said.

"You people," said Jamie. He looked around at the bunch of old men clustered around the bar and the students huddled at a couple of sticky-looking tables, and smiled. He was older than a lot of the students, for sure, but that girl there had a *Game of Thrones* t-shirt and that guy there had his laptop open with lines of code streaming by. These were his people.

"Scuse me," said one of the regulars from the bar. Jamie glanced up, a ready smile on his face. He smiled at everyone so much it sometimes hurt to stop. "Are you Prince Jamie?"

"Indeed I am. Nice to meet you. What's your name?"

"Er," the man clutched his pint and looked slightly panicked. Behind him, his mates egged him on. "I'm Stevo. Er, there was a thing in the paper about you."

"Was there?" said Jamie, trying not to let his sarcasm show.

"Yeah. Page 23. Look."

He thrust a local paper at Jamie, who allowed Morris to take it and smooth it out on the table. The two men would have already checked it for half a dozen visual signs of contamination before it even got within five feet of Jamie.

"Ah, yes. Royal pubs of Cambridge. 'Which one will Jamie the student choose?'"

"It even mentions us!" said Stevo proudly, and Jamie dutifully scanned the page until he found it. It wasn't hard; much had been made of the pub's moniker.

"The Prince's Arms, Lady Mathilda's Passage," he read, to an accompanying snigger apparently the regulars hadn't grown out of. "'Despite its royal name, there's little to recommend this spit & sawdust pub down a dingy backstreet near the Faculty of Computer Sciences, except perhaps its location. We expect the prince would prefer a more bustling environment like The Eagle on nearby Bene't Street, the location where Watson and Crick announced their discovery of DNA.' Well."

He looked around the pub, where the regulars and the students alike wore expressions mixing pride and shame. The carpet was scuffed and thinning, the ceiling sagged, and the wooden panelling had been repainted so many times the original grain was invisible.

"No mention, I see, of Rosalind Franklin in that article," said Jamie, and got no response.

The manager, or landlady or whoever she was, watched him warily. The lad who'd served him raised one pierced eyebrow. The girl who'd frozen frowned a bit and picked at a thread on her sleeve, not looking directly at him.

Jamie raised his voice and said, "I'm sure The Eagle is wonderful, but I rather like it here. So cheers."

He raised his glass, and everyone else did the same.

"In fact I think I'll stay for another," he said, even though he had to take several rather large gulps of his pint to justify that.

"Don't overdo it, laddie," muttered Morris.

"Where's your sense of adventure?"

"I left it in Sarajevo."

Jamie grinned as he got up for another drink. Neither Morris nor Khan had got more than a quarter down theirs.

One of the students got there before him, ordering a lager top and trying to look as if she wasn't waiting for Jamie to stand next to her. She was the one in the *Game of Thrones* t-shirt, her glasses framed in chunky blue, her hair pinned into a bun with a couple of pencils.

"Yes, sir?"

Slightly to his annoyance, it was the frozen girl who served him. Eyebrow Guy was filling the lager top with lemonade.

"Another Carlsberg, please."

She nodded and reached for a glass, not quite meeting his eye.

"There's a plaque to her," she said to the lager tap.

"Sorry?"

"Rosalind Franklin. In the Eagle. It's newer. In the middle bar. Don't sit there though, people will interrupt you for photos."

"Occupational hazard," said Jamie. She still hadn't looked at him.

"Excuse me," it was the *Game of Thrones* girl, "are you really doing your PhD in Computer Science with us?"

He smiled at her. "Yes, I'll be starting soon. What's your area of study?"

"Interactive analytical modelling," she said.

"Oh, that's cool. I read a paper on that earlier this year. Professor Khattak, I think."

Her eyes lit up. "He's a tutor on this course!"

"Yes, I've heard. I'm really excited to work with him. What's your name?"

"Ruchi Sarkar." She held out her hand, then hesitated. Jamie took it before she could get embarrassed and start curtseying or something.

"Nice to meet you, Ruchi. I'm Jamie."

"That's three-seventy. Shall I put it on your tab?"

He glanced aside at the barmaid. "Yes, please. And Ruchi's too."

The barmaid gave him a weirdly assessing look, but nodded and went to the till as Ruchi tripped over her words trying to thank him.

"No problem. Now, are you using queuing theory in your modelling?"

He went back to Ruchi's table with her, which had the added bonus of making Morris annoyed at the change in arrangements, and continued to talk with her about measuring and calculating the behaviour of the various elements of computer systems.

She could talk the hind leg off a donkey when it came to computer science, which was fine by Jamie. The others were in a similar vein, every single one of them happy to discuss algebraic subtyping or grammatical error correction in non-native English, but when he asked them where they were from or what they did when they weren't studying, they clammed up, stammered, spilt their drinks.

"These are my people," he said to Khan as he slightly unsteadily left the pub two hours later.

"Yes, sir."

"I mean who cares about titles and royal bloody christenings? Ruchi had this brilliant theory about—no, it was Zheng who said it—about how Jon Snow is going to defeat the White Walkers using wildfire, because it's not magic, it's science, and all the stuff that's actually made a difference in *Game of Thrones* has been about practical applications of science."

"Yes, sir." Khan opened the car door for him.

"Apart from the Red Witch and… no hang on it doesn't work as a theory, does it?"

"No, sir."

"You have no idea what I'm talking about, do you?"

"No, sir. Hour and a half to get home, sir. Don't forget to strap in."

Jamie laid his head back against the headrest. Tonight had been fun, the kind of fun he just didn't get to have often. The first time he'd been a student he'd mostly hung around with the same crowd he had as a kid. Nights out at Chinawhite and Mahiki, private jets to Monaco, It Girl models giving him the eye. He'd always felt more like he was pretending to have fun than actually having it.

The closest he'd come to this kind of comradeship was the army. After all, he'd pretty much been bred to stand on ceremony and lead people, and he'd made some good and genuine friends there. But still…

…sometimes he really just wanted to talk about computer games and why Sheldon from the *Big Bang Theory* probably wasn't all that smart.

Rosalind Franklin. Of course, around here she was probably better known than elsewhere. Funny how that was the only thing the starstruck barmaid had found to say to him. He supposed it took all sorts.

Jamie yawned. Hour and a half until home. He found himself smiling. "When I live here, I'll be home now," he said.

"Sorry, sir?"

He replayed that. "I mean in two weeks' time I'll be home in five minutes."

There was a slight pause from the front seat. "Yes, sir. Perhaps try to get some rest." More pointedly, "There's water in the cooler."

Jamie cracked open a bottle and closed his eyes. *Ten days. I can wait ten more days.*

I can't live here another day.

Hanna hadn't managed to get into Clodagh's room, but she had thrown out all her food and broken her favourite mug. She and Lee were having noisy make-up sex when Clodagh got home, late, after she'd got tired of the regulars speculating on their royal visit and called last orders. Thumps and groans came through the wall.

Fed up, Clodagh thumped back. "Everything okay in

there? Sounds like someone's choking."

Lee called back something Clodagh only caught half of. That half was bad enough.

She checked the lock on her door, jammed a chair under the handle, and shoved her earbuds in, cranking the Hamilton soundtrack up to top volume and wondering what the founding father would have done in these circumstances.

The next day Hanna more or less behaved as if nothing had happened and she and Clodagh were great friends. Bleary with tiredness, Clodagh escaped to the library, where she nabbed a desk and sat making notes on her next module.

Her sisters thought she was mad to try to get into Cambridge. Her mother thought she was daft even trying to get an education. "I worked in a shop all my life," she'd say to Clodagh, "and it never did me no harm."

"You worked in a shop four times in your life, none of them for more than a year," Clodagh pointed out.

"Well, maternity leave, innit? Takes a lot of work looking after six kids and I didn't get no help from Little Miss Brainy, did I?"

Clodagh had stopped bothering to reply to this. She'd done as much raising of her younger siblings as her mother—probably more—and had learned a long time ago that asking why her mother didn't, yanno, stop having babies, wasn't a useful thing to say.

"You'll understand when you have kids," Sharon would say.

"If, Mum, *if* I have kids." Privately, she thought it was bloody unlikely.

Clodagh tapped her pen on her book and realised she'd been staring into space for ten minutes.

Right. Witchcraft and the Civil War, witchcraft and the Civil War…

Imagine what her mum would say if she heard Prince

Jamie came into the pub last night. Probably get on the first train into town and work her way through the gin menu while she waited for him to come back.

"You should marry him, Clo. Good-looking fella, innit? All that lovely money. Our Kylie's been after her own flat that long, just imagine! Where do they all live, in Buck House?"

Or worse, she'd come onto him herself. Christ, imagine having Prince Jamie as your stepdad! He was only—Clodagh looked it up on her phone—yeah, he was only a couple of months younger than Clodagh herself, not that the age gap would stop Sharon Walsh if she had her sights on a new man. After all, the last one had been slightly closer to Clodagh's age than her mother's.

Witchcraft and the Civil War, witchcraft and the Civil War...

If he came back into the pub, Clodagh would have to apologise for her frozen-rabbit impression. No doubt he thought she was completely witless. He'd come back in, and she'd have warning this time because she'd know what the bodyguards were for, and she'd be composed and friendly and professional. She'd smile, and get his drink, and as she handed it over she'd say, "By the way, I'm so sorry for my behaviour the other day. I was just a bit startled and I'd been having a bad day—" *No Clo, he doesn't care about your day,* "—I was startled and reacted weirdly and I'm so sorry, Your Highness. It won't happen again."

Wait, was it Your Highness? The bodyguards had called him Sir. Was that a military thing? He'd been in the army for ten years or so. Maybe she should ask. Should she? Maybe asking was rude and you were meant to know this, like maybe they taught it in schools or something. Only not the shitty sink school Clodagh had been to, where the only thing you really learnt was how to smoke behind the gym and give a blowjob in the toilets…

"Excuse me? Miss?"

Clodagh jerked awake in the middle of Cambridge Central Library, a woman in glasses standing over her. *Oh God, please don't let me have fallen asleep. Please don't have been obvious…*

"I know the Civil War can be a bit boring," the woman said, looking over Clodagh's history module, "but you were snoring loud enough to interrupt the kiddies' storytime."

CHAPTER THREE

She didn't see the prince for a couple of weeks.

He'd joined Lady Mathilda College and moved into an undisclosed location which had to be, as Clodagh understood it, within a ten mile radius of Great St Mary's Church. Since this radius also included every other student at Cambridge, it didn't narrow things down very much.

Clarence House reported that the prince was settling in and enjoying his studies and would be undertaking light royal duties for the foreseeable future. Clodagh didn't know what exactly 'light royal duties' might entail. Cutting the odd ribbon at the opening of a shopping centre? Polo matches every now and then? Polishing a few tiaras?

She kept her head down, read pages of her textbooks in the pub, typed up essays on the library computers, and tried to avoid Hanna and Lee. They were going through a honeymoon phase now anyway. They always did after he'd hit her. Clodagh knew the pattern like she knew her own face.

She finished a particularly boring module on the

Chartist movement, checked out a much more interesting book on Rosa Parks and gave herself a few days off studying. Then, one damp day in October, the pub door opened and a large man in a black suit came in.

He was followed, slightly nervously, by some of the students who'd been here at the start of Michaelmas term. Ruchi with the funky glasses and Hunter the cocky American and the Chinese boy with the stutter whose name she couldn't remember. A couple of others. And then Prince Jamie.

Clodagh made a point of being disinterested.

Hunter was the one who strolled up to the bar, as the others spread out over a couple of tables. He was probably the most socially competent of them all, but he had that air about him, like he called girls 'chicks' and said things like, "I'm not sexist, but…"

Clodagh smiled professionally at him as she marked her place in the book and set it aside.

"What can I get you?"

"Howdy. I'll take three pints of lager, three pints of that warm stuff you call bitter and one vodka and orange."

Clodagh ignored the 'warm stuff' comment she'd heard a variation of from every American she'd ever met in a pub, nodded and moved to pick up a glass. She'd been told to upsell if people asked generically for 'a lager' but with students she didn't bother. Whatever was cheapest was usually fine with them.

She hesitated at the tap though. What if she poured cheap beer and the prince didn't come back again?

Oh, fuckit, Clo, not like he'll be a regular here anyway. He's only here slumming it with his new study buddies before he pisses off somewhere fancy for some decent champagne.

Cooking lager it was then. She poured three pints, then reached for a different shelf for the beer glasses.

"Why the different glass?" enquired Hunter.

"What?"

"It's a different shape glass for the 'bitter," his fingers made the inverted commas, "than for the 'lager'."

Clodagh looked at them. Yep, tall and narrow for the lager, shorter tulip shapes for the beer. "No flies on you," she said, and started pulling the first bitter.

Hunter waited for her reply, then when none was forthcoming, "Yeah, but why though?"

Clodagh shrugged. "No idea. Maybe it tastes different in a different kind of glass."

"It's 'cos proper beer doesn't need fancy glasses to taste good," piped up Stevo from his corner of the bar.

Hunter took a lip-smacking pull of his lager. "This is proper beer."

Stevo just snorted and turned back to his pint of bitter and his incomprehensible conversation with Paulie about how badly Spurs were playing this season.

"Hey, do you know, Your Highness?" Hunter said, and Clodagh only spilled a bit of the beer she was pulling.

She glanced up as Hunter explained the question to the prince, who'd sidled up without her noticing. "Why's it one kind of glass for your lager and another for your beer? And what is the difference anyway?"

"Colour, taste, method of production, temperature," she said without thinking.

A slight pause. She mentally kicked herself for replying.

"Is that so?" asked Hunter. "What is the method of production?"

Clodagh, who was more or less repeating what an old boss of hers had said when she'd asked the same question, shrugged. "I don't know."

Hunter gave her a look of satisfaction. Of course, if she had known, he'd have pushed until he found something she didn't. *Wanker*.

"Do you?" Prince Jamie asked him.

Clodagh blinked.

"What? No, man, I'm a scientist, not a… brewer."

"Brewing is science," said the prince reasonably. "Chemistry at the very least. There may well be something in the shape of the glass," he held two up to the light to compare them. "As with red and white wines. Perhaps the lager is in a narrower glass to create a smaller surface area to maintain the lower temperature?"

Clodagh found herself smiling as she poured the third pint.

Hunter said, "Well, it's better cold anyway," and took two glasses over to the table.

"We do have trays," Clodagh said.

Prince Jamie winked at her and expertly gathered up the remaining four pint glasses in one go.

"Rosa Parks, huh?" he said, even though she'd put the book on the back of the bar. And then, under his breath, he started singing the *Horrible Histories* song about her as he turned away.

Clodagh gaped like a landed fish. Again.

"I think it's to do with the, what-d'you-call-it, effervescence," Jamie said when he went back to get Ruchi's vodka and orange.

The barmaid raised her eyebrows. His heart had sunk a little when he'd walked in and seen her there, because she was the one who'd behaved like a frightened rabbit last time he was here. Only, maybe she wasn't. She certainly seemed to have found some backbone from somewhere. Probably dealing with Hunter W Carmichael III, who thought he was God's gift to women, science, and the universe.

"Effervescence?"

"Yeah. I mean, lager is supposed to be… fizzier, for

want of a better word, than beer. Stands to reason that a smaller surface area will allow less of it to evaporate. Whereas with an ale, you don't want it fizzy…"

"Therefore you do want some of it to evaporate," she said as he trailed off. She made a face as if she was considering that. "Could be. Or maybe it's just tradition."

"Maybe it is," he said, and paid for the drinks with his grandmother's face.

Most of his conversation with his fellow students conversation on this, the first Friday of their first term as postgrads, was about the course, the tutors, and the sheer overwhelming amount of work they were expected to do.

Forty hours a week, that was what he'd been advised. Lab work, individual research, seminars, tutorials and the like. It was a full time job, he'd been told. There wouldn't be much time for partying any more.

Jamie had nodded sincerely and tried not to laugh his head off at the idea that forty hours was a full working week and that he ever went out partying if he didn't have to. He'd never done less than sixty hours a week for the last ten years; even more since he'd left the army. He'd had to apply for special dispensation to carry out his royal duties, which had been drastically reduced. "For Christ's sake, your grandmother is the Queen," Olivia had said. "Get her to tell them to cut you some slack."

"No bloody fear," said Jamie, who'd never run to his granny for help in his life and wasn't about to start now. "Won't be a proper doctorate if I don't take it seriously."

His phone bleeped. Peaseman, reminding him he had his weekly meeting on Saturday. Jamie had tried to talk his secretary into coming to Cambridge for, say, one weekday lunch meeting a week, but the good major had insisted this was impossible, so Jamie had to go down to Kensington Palace for it instead, where his entire family could bug him about why he couldn't just accept an honorary doctorate like his father had done.

Beside him, Ruchi whooped with sudden laughter and he abruptly tried to tune back in to the conversation.

"…and then he said, 'Actually can you help me with *Call of Duty*, I'm stuck on #YOLO mode and I can't restart from a checkpoint!'"

Laughter rippled around the table.

"Seriously, what does he even think YOLO means?" Ruchi said.

"I didn't know it had that mode," Jamie said. "Ugh. I'm so behind on my gameplay."

"You only get it when you've completed the ordinary play," said Micah, who was specialising in game development. "But I could probably hack it for you."

"No, I'm bad enough at it as it is. There was this one level… I can't remember, but I died so many times, it was just embarrassing."

"Especially for a real soldier!" said Ruchi, then coloured as if she'd gone too far.

Jamie laughed to show her he wasn't offended, and to hide the memories of Helmand from himself. "Exactly! If my old sergeant heard about it he'd never stop laughing. Right." He made to stand up. "Is it my round?"

"Oh, dude, I was going to get the last one." Hunter passed him a twenty, which wasn't really enough. Jamie took it with a smile anyway.

The minute you stop being generous is the minute people ask what their taxes are paying for…

He made his way to the bar, noting as he did that the place had filled up. Geraint and Cutter were minding him tonight, and Jamie found, as he usually did, that the crowds parted somewhat for him in their presence.

The guy with the eyebrow ring served him this time. He had a Kiwi accent, and Jamie was entertaining himself trying to work out if it came from the north or south island, when the girl with the Rosa Parks biography leaned over.

"Nucleation," she said.

"Sorry?"

"The process of creating bubbles in lager. It's called nucleation. They etch designs into the bottom of the glass to trap oxygen and promote seeding. To keep the head of the lager frothy," she explained, reaching past the Kiwi for a Stella Artois glass with a stem and tilting it to show Jamie the base.

"And I guess giving it a stem helps keep your warm hands away from your cold beer," Jamie hypothesised.

"Just like with wine," she replied, smiling, and Jamie blinked at the sight of that smile.

The girl carried on serving her customer, joking with him about raising the price of the beer now they had royal patronage, darting glances at him from under her hair. Curly hair, brownish, lighter than her skin. He watched her hands as she gave the customer his change and turned to pull the cask beers for the Kiwi. Good, capable hands with short, unvarnished nails. A cheap watch on her left wrist. No rings.

You shouldn't be noticing whether she wears a ring.

Jamie mentally shook himself and took the lagers back to the table, handing Zheng the shandy he'd asked for in a whisper, and setting Ruchi's orange, no vodka, down in front of her. He wanted to ask the girl behind the bar how she knew about nucleation, but she was serving someone else when he went back for the other drinks, and after half an hour talking about security metrics with the other postgrads, he'd forgotten.

The weekend passed with a busy Saturday shift in the shopping centre and another busy shift in the pub. Word had got around about Jamie's visit to his namesake pub, but the Prince's Arms remained empty of its main

41

attraction that weekend.

Sunday was Clodagh's day for catching up on sleep and TV, but this weekend Hanna and Lee were being pointedly smoochy in the living room, so she walked to the pub anyway, sat nursing a Diet Coke all afternoon, and made some progress with the next module on her course.

This time, she was determined to get it in on time. She'd forfeited too many course fees by missing deadlines before, and her tutors were getting sick and tired of her excuses. The first time, Whitney had suffered pre-eclampsia and been sentenced to bed-rest, requiring Clodagh to take care of her on a constant basis. The second time she'd welched on the deadline had been when Scott had some drugs planted on him—at least, that was his story—and she'd spent months and months researching and pleading his case until she'd wondered if she should be studying law instead of humanities. The third time she'd just run out of money and had to work every hour God sent instead of studying…

Well, anyway. Clodagh had given up trying to explain why it had taken her ten years to get the basic qualifications most people got by the time they were sixteen. She was on the home stretch now. A year or so more on this course and she'd have enough credits to apply for an actual degree. Hopefully. Maybe.

October dragged on, with Hanna and Lee getting steadily less cosy and Clodagh glad of any excuse to get out of the flat. Her property search threw up hideously expensive flat-shares in impractical parts of town, and the couple of times she found somewhere she thought might work, someone had always pipped her to the post.

Prince Jamie came back to the pub once or twice, as pleasant and friendly to her as he was to everyone. This was fine by Clodagh, who didn't want to be forever known in his memory as the Frozen Rabbit Girl.

Oz asked her one Tuesday if she could work a private party on Wednesday in place of a friend of his who'd had to pull out at the last minute. The hours were long, involving both serving and clear-up afterwards, but the pay wasn't bad. She said yes, and got out her smart black trousers and good white shirt.

By the time the party ended the shirt wasn't so white any more and Clodagh's face ached from smiling at people who pointed and laughed at the red wine stain on her chest. It wasn't even her fault; some posh bird had got into a shriekingly loud argument with her boyfriend and thrown her glass in his face. But her aim was bad and the catering company only paid for the cleaning of their own uniforms.

Three am, plates and glasses packed away and the agency vans driving off, Clodagh huddled into her coat and calculated how long it'd take her to walk home. The buses didn't run this early, and besides there was some terribly long and drawn out construction work going on near Midsummer Common that made a bus journey slower than walking.

"Nice to meet you," she said to the last girl leaving, then watched her slip on a wet leaf on the bottom step of the stoop, flail wildly and smash her arm into the spike of the metal railings guarding the building from the street.

For a second there was silence, then the girl—Becca, maybe?—let out a scream.

"Okay, let me have a look," Clodagh sighed, but Becca wouldn't even let her touch her arm. Blood started running out of her sleeve. Clodagh could see how torn the fabric was, and didn't really want to see the flesh below it.

She looked around, but at three o'clock on a Wednesday morning there wasn't a soul to be seen.

"Okay, I'll call an ambulance," she said, and held

Becca's good hand until it came. Sitting there on the step, she tried to distract her, like she'd always distracted her siblings from childhood hurts. She told Becca the story of the time Whitney had fallen off the swings and cut her lip, and had been such a martyr to it she'd bandaged her whole head and insisted on a week of school. It had been bloody annoying at the time, but she could make it funny now.

Becca insisted Clodagh came with her to the hospital, which she could really have done without, but the girl was clearly frightened and alone and in pain, so she could hardly say no. She sat with her in A&E, tried to smother her yawns, and when they were finally released into the cold pale dawn, asked in vain hope which way Becca might be headed.

"Cherry Hinton," she said, which of course she would, because it was nice and close to the hospital and also completely the opposite direction of the one Clodagh needed to go in. "You?"

"Arbury." A good half hour bus ride on the best of days.

She hugged Becca goodbye, took a phone number she'd never call, and waved her off on a bus which, of course, arrived before her own.

She was chilled to the bone by the time it turned up, and if she hadn't found a seat she might have committed murder. The bus chugged on through the dawn light, and she leaned her head against the window, earbuds in, hood up, almost dozing off before the bus stopped and the driver announced this was the end of the line. Clodagh blinked at the street outside.

"Oh, Jesus," she muttered, and wondered why that raised a smile until she realised they were on Jesus Lane. Great. Another ten minutes walk, fifteen maybe, in the freezing dawn air.

Clodagh got off the bus, so tired she felt drunk, and

trudged halfway up Victoria Avenue before the cold and the tired and the smell of wine and blood and disinfectant got too much and she flopped onto a damp bench at the corner of Jesus Green, tears overwhelming her.

Thursday she had a lunchtime shift at the Prince's Arms. She had to be at work in... oh God, five hours, and she couldn't bear it. Back home to the cold, frightening flat she was forced for now to call home, snatch a few hours of sleep if Hanna wasn't being spitefully noisy, and then get up and spend eight hours being cheerful to men who began sentences with phrases like, "The trouble with young people these days..."

"Hey, are you okay?"

She sniffed loudly and looked up. Three men stood looking down at her, all of them somewhat large and wearing black head to toe, like burglars, one of them even wearing sunglasses for Christ's sake. *Oh my God, is there really a Cambridge mafia?*

Then he took off his sunglasses and black beanie and a load of thick, soft, wavy dark hair sprang out, and once again Clodagh found herself looking into Prince Jamie's face.

"Wait, I know you," he said. "From the pub, right? Rosa Parks and nucleation? Are you hurt?"

She blinked at him. Yes, she hurt, in her cold toes and her sore shoulders and her aching soul, but she had no idea what he was talking about until he gently reached out for her arm.

"Did you cut yourself?"

Clodagh looked down. The sleeve of her cheap parka had a rusty red bloodstain on it. *Great, that's not going to sponge out.*

"No. I mean, it's not mine. I mean... I was helping someone. She's fine, it was just a couple of stitches and tetanus shot, but..."

Jamie squatted down in front of her. His black clothing was running gear, she realised, the darkness of it relieved by changes in texture and weird seaming. Reflective strips ran in patterns along his torso and legs. He hadn't shaved, and his jaw was dark with stubble. She'd never seen him unshaven before. Apart from that first time in the pub he'd always dressed smartly, was always well-groomed.

He's in disguise, she realised. This was him being incognito.

"You don't look okay," he said, peering close. "You look frozen."

"It's cold out," she said, as if he might not have noticed. Actually, with all the technical cleverness going on in his clothes he might not have.

"That's because it's barely daylight." His eyes peered carefully at her. Hazel, she thought. Changeable in the light.

They took in more details than she wanted him to see.

"Are you an early riser," he asked, "or haven't you been to bed yet?"

Clodagh thought about lying, but she was too cold and too tired. "The latter," she mumbled. "I was working," she added defensively.

"What, at the pub? Must've been a hell of a lock-in," he said. He got to his feet and held out his hand. "All right, come with me."

Clodagh stared at his hand. He wore technical-looking gloves, which probably kept his fingers much warmer than the old cheap fleece pair she'd forgotten to bring anyway.

"What?"

"You look colder than Queen Elsa," he said, and glanced at his watch. "Must be nearly lighting down time by now. Come on. I know where we can get a cup of tea and a bacon sarnie."

Clodagh wanted to say no, she was only ten minutes from home, and she didn't go off for bacon sandwiches with strangers, even if they were of the blood royal, and she had no idea what lighting down might be. The sun was pretty much up by now.

But then her stomach rumbled audibly and Jamie smiled, lines bracketing his mouth, and she heard herself say, "Okay then."

She took his hand, stood, and followed him and his blank-faced bodyguards across Midsummer Common. The grass was wet with dew, remnants of mist hanging low over the land, and the only other people around were other joggers, dog walkers, and the occasional cow.

"Still can't believe there are cows in the middle of the city like this," Jamie commented, as Clodagh tried not to notice how fit he was in his close-fitting running clothes.

"Bloody traffic hazard," muttered one of the bodyguards. Unlike Jamie, they wore bulky jackets, which probably concealed firearms.

"They can't get onto the road," Jamie said. "There are those, what d'you call them. The gaps in the fences."

"Squeeze gaps," Clodagh said, and he glanced at her in surprise. "They're open lower down so people in wheelchairs and buggies can get through, but they're narrower higher up so bikes and livestock can't." Dammit, there she went again with the random facts. No one liked Random Fact Girl.

Jamie's eyebrows quirked. "Squeeze gap. I'm impressed." He smiled at her.

Clodagh glanced at him, then away again. He had a very nice smile.

From the river sounds began to drift through the mist. People shouting, but not in an angry way. Rhythmic, as if instructions were being given. Someone shrieked and laughter rose up.

"Told you not to tangle the oars!" came a bellow, but

it didn't sound like much of an admonishment.

It was the rowing teams. Clodagh had walked past the river more times than she could remember, but she'd never really had the time to stop and watch them. Some smaller boats were on the river, young men and women in sports gear and bobble hats attempting to control them.

"Each and every one of them hoping to be a Cambridge Blue," Jamie said.

"You're not tempted to join them?" Clodagh had some hazy idea that one of his cousins had rowed for Oxford. His brother, Prince Edward, was always being photographed on a horse or a bike or running with a rugby ball.

"Are you kidding? I've got no desire to throw myself into a freezing river every morning before breakfast. If I wasn't cruelly forced into it," he quirked an eyebrow at his bodyguards, "I wouldn't even go out for a run in the morning."

"I think if you end up in the river you're doing it wrong," said Clodagh vaguely, and he laughed.

"This is very true. I'll settle for watching the Boat Race from the warmth and comfort of my own living room, thank you."

"But you'll be cheering the pale blues?"

He looked offended. "Of course! So much as a word of encouragement for the Other Place and I'd be sent down."

Jamie led her towards Midsummer House, and for a moment her heart leapt because that place had Michelin stars, didn't it? Did they open at sparrow's fart for tea and bacon sandwiches? Maybe they did, if you were a prince. But then he took her past it, across Peterhouse Bridge, and down a lane towards a building facing the river. *Not Michelin-starred bacon, then.*

From the road side it looked like an ordinary house,

but as they went down the side of it, the view changed. It had large pale blue garage doors on the ground floor, a concrete slope down to the water and a balcony above, with large windows looking over the common. One of the boathouses, which she was more used to seeing from across the water.

An older man with a thick parka and faded Lady Mathilda College scarf nodded at them.

"Your Royal Highness. Changed your mind about joining us?"

The prince's eyes sparkled. "Maybe I have. I think I should probably have a bacon roll and a cup of tea while I think it over, though."

The coach rolled his eyes and laughed. "You've been thinking it over for weeks. You owe the Lard cupboard a fortune," he said.

"I promise I will go direct to..." Jamie hesitated, "the shop and get some of everything."

"Oh yeah, I can just see you in the local Morrisons," said the coach, but he waved them cheerfully inside.

The garage doors didn't conceal cars, but racks of carefully stacked rowing boats and oars. Like the college scarf, the oars were green with blue stripes along them. A blackboard on one wall was headed "Lighting down/up times October" and lists of times that roughly corresponded to sunrise and sunset scrawled below it.

Lighting down, Clodagh thought. *Can't just call it 'sunrise', can they? Cambridge has to have special names for everything.*

One bodyguard preceded them through the door at the back of the boat room or whatever they called it. One waited for her to follow Jamie before bringing up the rear. They did it so smoothly probably no one would notice the formation if they didn't know who these men were.

They went up a flight of stairs and into a room with

those huge windows overlooking the common. Jamie went over to a kitchenette, but Clodagh stood staring at the view. The Common was spectacular in the early morning, mist wreathing the trees and cows looming like minotaurs. From below, she could just about make out the sounds of the rowers in training.

You didn't get mornings like this any other time of year. *"Where are the songs of spring? Ay, Where are they?"* she murmured.

"Think not of them, thou hast thy music too," said Jamie, and she jumped a little. "You like Keats?"

She was fairly ambivalent about the romantic poets in general and Keats in the specific, but since she'd always like autumn, that poem had stuck in her head. "He's okay. I did a module on him for... for school," she fumbled, not quite willing to admit to someone doing a PhD that she was doing an Access course because she didn't even have any GCSEs.

The prince stood in the kitchenette, frying pan in one hand and a pack of bacon in the other. He'd taken off his snug jacket and underneath he wore a *Star Trek* t-shirt. "Yeah, he goes on a bit. But then I was never one for poetry. Not bright enough."

"Says the man doing a PhD at Cambridge."

He shrugged. "There are different types of brightness. You, for instance, just quoted one of the lesser-known lines of a poem most people only know the first line of, and you also know about nucleation. Are you a chemist?"

Clodagh shook her head. She wanted to say she was a historian, but she wasn't, not yet. You probably had to at least have A levels to say things like that. "No, I just looked it up. Plus I've worked in bars and pubs a long time, so..."

Jamie nodded. "Do you..." He frowned. "I'm so sorry," he said. "I've just realised I don't know your name."

He glanced up at her from under his hair, eyes bright and curious, and suddenly Clodagh didn't know what her name was either.

"Should I... guess it?" said the prince politely, putting down the frying pan he appeared to be about to cook her breakfast in.

Oh God, he thinks I'm an idiot again. "Call me Clodagh," she managed. "Clodagh Walsh."

"Clodagh? That's unusual." He turned away to light the hob. "Irish?"

"Yeah. My grandmother. It was her name." She didn't elucidate further.

"That's nice. We recycle names like mad in my family. We've all got the same middle names, after Dad and Granny. How clever my grandcestors were to choose names that could be feminised or... masculinised? Anyway, it saved me from being an Alexandra in Granny's honour."

"Jamie's a nice name though. I mean, I forget, you're actually Prince James, aren't you?"

"Yes, but Jamie, please, and drop the 'prince'," said the prince, slicing some butter into the pan. It sizzled hotly, the smell making Clodagh go a bit weak. "I didn't actually check, Clodagh. Bacon sandwich for you? Ordinary bacon, ordinary bread? Might be able to scare up some eggs..." he added, peering into the fridge.

"Bacon sandwich would be amazing." She should help. "Look, let me do it."

He glanced back over his shoulder at her, eyes dancing. "I can cook, you know."

Crap, she'd insulted him. Clodagh opened her mouth to apologise, but Jamie was grinning at her.

"The bacon goes in the toaster, yes?"

"I had a roommate who actually did that," said one of the bodyguards, a Scostman by the sound of it, who had taken the only chair where he could see the window and the door at the same time.

"Fire hazard much?" said Jamie. "You can sit down, you know."

Clodagh looked between the three of them and realised this comment was aimed at her. "Oh. Sure. Um, isn't there anything I could do?"

An almost invisible look passed between the prince and his bodyguards. "Sure," said Jamie, "you could make the tea if you like."

Grateful for something to do in this weird interlude, she filled the kettle and set about finding mugs. The kitchenette was small and she nearly bumped into Jamie more than once. *Oh God, imagine jostling him with the frying pan and then he'd get burnt and it'd be my fault. Isn't that treason? Would I go to jail? Do we still have capital punishment?*

It was weird, making drinks for people without getting paid for it. She almost said that out loud, but then realised it'd make her look as if she wanted to be paid, which she didn't. Because that would be weird. He'd invited her, after all.

"Who's Queen Elsa?" she asked as the kettle boiled. She knew there were other kingdoms in Europe but couldn't have named a ruling monarch if her life depended on it.

He didn't look up from buttering bread. "Not a Disney fan?"

Clodagh blinked. "Elsa from *Frozen*?" *Of course, you idiot. Who else is literally frozen?*

"Yep." He hummed something she thought might have been *Let It Go*. "You know it?"

"Dude I have like five nieces, of course I know it."

Jamie glanced up at her from under his mop of hair and smiled. "Mine's a little young for it, but you wouldn't believe the number of little girls I see in Elsa dresses when their parents drag them along to meet me."

"Well, she is a queen. I suppose it makes sense."

He grinned at that. "I shall have to tell them they outrank me." He started singing, and the Scottish bodyguard groaned.

"Just wait til he starts doing the gestures too."

Jamie made a grandiose flourish, and Clodagh found herself laughing at him. He laughed back, eyes bright, and flipped the bacon in time to his singing.

"I thought it might've been, like, the Queen of Denmark or somewhere. Sweden."

"The Queen of Denmark is Margarethe II," said Jamie, apparently without having to think about it. "And Sweden currently has a king. His name is Carl XVI Gustaf, and yes the order is important. His consort is Queen Silvia. No Elsas I can think of. They do have a granddaughter called Estelle, if that helps."

"Any Annas?"

He cocked his head. "Not that I can bring to mind. Loads of Annes, obviously, in my ancestry, and Annemarie my sister-in-law, of course, but Annas... a Russian or two, I think."

By then she'd warmed up enough to take off her coat, and that did seem to startle Jamie into nearly burning himself.

"Jesus Christ," he said sharply, and the two bodyguards immediately snapped to attention, hands delving inside their jackets. Clodagh froze, but then Jamie let out a huff of what might have been laughter. "I thought that was blood."

Clodagh looked down at the wine stain. "Oh. No. Red wine. I was working at a party, you see, and someone threw it at me. Well, not at me, but she missed and I got it. So yay, now I smell like a wino."

Jamie flipped the bacon. "Must've been some party if you're still up at this hour."

"Well, it was, but that's not… one of the other girls hurt herself, so I went with her to A&E. I should've been home hours ago." She couldn't smother a yawn at the thought.

Jamie looked appalled. "Oh God, am I keeping you up? Should I let you go home?"

She was so tired it took her three tries to pick up a teaspoon, but Clodagh said, "No, it's fine. I don't really want to go home."

That was a stupid thing to say. The attention of all three men snapped to her.

"You'd rather enjoy our company?" Jamie said after a tiny pause. He said it lightly, but there was a clear undertone there.

"Yes, of course. I don't have bacon at home," she added, trying to match his tone for lightness.

"Well, for this we shall be thankful to the Lady Mathilda Lard Cupboard," he said, checking the bacon and turning off the heat.

"The what?"

"The Lard Cupboard." He waved at the general kitchen area with the frying pan. "It's what they call it. I forget why. Probably because if you fall in the river, a generous coating of lard will keep you warm."

He slid the bacon onto the buttered bread, added an egg, squidged a second slice of bread on top and sliced the whole messy thing in half. Holding out the plate to her, he bowed his head. "Your breakfast, madam. Or is it dinner?"

"I don't honestly care what you call it," Clodagh said, and he grinned as he piled up the rest into a mountain of delicious unhealthiness.

The Scottish bodyguard tucked in with gusto. The other one, who Jamie had called Khan, ignored the food. "Aren't you hungry?" Clodagh asked, and he looked at her as if she were a statue who'd just spoken.

"Allah forbids," he said, and Clodagh felt like an idiot.

"Right. Sorry. I just thought…"

He winked at her. "Nah, I'm messing with you. I'm just keeping my hands free. Never know if you're going to make a sudden move on His Highness."

Jamie, his mouth full, just rolled his eyes.

She ate one round, and then at Jamie's urging another. Khan made them all more tea. The room was warm, the sounds coming up from the river rhythmic, and she was full of food. And safe. Hell, if she wasn't safe with royal bodyguards who would she be safe with?

Clodagh could barely remember the last time she'd felt this content…

She was woken by someone yelping, "I'll be stuffed, you're Prince Jamie!"

Sofa. Sunshine. Smell of bacon. Somewhere, someone was shouting, "Stroke, stroke," for reasons hopefully known to them.

Oh crap, she'd fallen asleep at the rowing club. The boathouse. The… whatever it was called!

Hurriedly, she sat up and fought her way out from under the coat someone had draped over her. The Scottish bodyguard, who she thought might be called Morris, glanced at her, and evidently considered her less of a threat than the Australian woman in rowing gear exclaiming how much she adored the Royal Family.

Clodagh checked her watch. She had just over an hour to get home, shower, change and be back at the pub on time for her shift. She got up, shoving her arms into her coat.

"You're leaving?" Jamie said, looking her over. "Stay a while. There's no rush."

"There is. I have to be at work by twelve."

His thick dark brows drew down. "But you worked all night."

"Yes. Different job. Um, thanks for the bacon and tea and things." She tripped over her own feet and Khan steadied her before she could fall into the prince. "Thank you. I'll see you, um, around, I guess."

"No, wait. I'll take you home."

"You don't need to, it's really close."

"I'll walk you there."

Clodagh opened her mouth to complain, but he was already putting his jacket on. The Australian girl watched them in bewilderment.

"Clodagh. You've been up all night and had two hours' rest and I would be derelict in my duty if I didn't at least see you home. If you fall in the river or get hit by a flying oar I'll never forgive myself," he added.

I don't want to you see how crappy my flat is. "Sure, okay. But I have to run, like now, or I'll be late."

Jamie shrugged. "Ready when you are."

They left the boathouse, the sun properly up now and glinting prettily on the river. Clodagh tried to get her bearings; she'd cut past the boathouses many times but never actually been inside one, and she ended up halfway along Kimberley Road before she realised she was going the long way.

"Look, I'm sure if you call in to work they'll understand," said Jamie as he walked along beside her.

I am being walked home by a prince. This is so weird I might be dreaming. Clodagh pinched herself discreetly and said, "At this short notice? They'll not be able to get anyone in. It's hard enough during the day."

"Yes, but... surely it's a health and safety issue? You've had no sleep—"

"I've had a couple of hours." And tonight she could sleep all she wanted, because she only had an evening shift on Friday and no pressing essays to turn in.

"That's not enough," Jamie said and Clodagh, too tired for patience, snapped.

"Well, it'll have to be. Look, I'm sorry, Your Highness," she stopped walking and so did he. "I don't have any option. I have to pay rent, the electricity is due this month and I've barely managed my course fees this year. I have to go into work, because they pay me by the hour and I need every penny I can get, okay? I don't have a safety net. I don't have anything to fall back on. I am only one skipped shift away from homelessness."

Jamie swallowed. Behind him, the two bodyguards looked tense. Oh hell, did they think she was going to wallop him? Clodagh took a step back.

"All right. Fine. I'm sorry," said the prince. His hands came up in a gesture of appeasement. "I didn't… I didn't understand. I apologise. Would you like me to explain to your boss why you're… no. Okay. Let's go."

They walked in silence for a bit. Clodagh felt a bit sick. *I just yelled at a member of the Royal Family. Oh shit. This probably* is *treason.*

"I'm sorry," she said after a few excruciating minutes. From a window somewhere came the sound of a violin. Purcell, maybe. She'd done a module on that, too.

"Not as sorry as I am," replied the prince gently. "I shouldn't have pushed. Please, accept my apology."

He held out a hand to her. This time, it was ungloved. Clodagh swallowed, and took it.

The touch of him shocked her. His fingers were chilly, he didn't try to crush her hand and his palm was soft, but none of that was what made her stop and stare, jolted, up at him.

He touched her hand, bare skin to bare skin, and this was something she'd done countless times with countless people, but somehow it felt like the first ever time a human being had actually touched her.

Jamie's hand held hers, and he looked down at her and their eyes met, and his looked incredibly green, the green of Midsummer Common at sunrise, the green of the sea, the green of forever, and she couldn't look away. His lashes were long, his brows thick and glossy, and there was a small freckle just under his left eye.

They held hands, not shaking them, standing still and alone on a deserted street in an empty city, close and getting closer, electricity building between them.

I know you. I know you, now, and I always have and I always will.

She breathed him in, the closest thing in the world to herself. There was no one else around.

Then the violin screeched and with a pop like a bubble bursting, the real world slammed back into place around them. A passing car blared out hip-hop, and a phone rang somewhere and an accusatory voice from behind them said, "Oi, you're blocking the pavement."

Clodagh looked round, astonished to find anyone else in their private universe, and found a woman with a large pram and several shopping bags glaring at her.

And Clodagh realised she'd been standing opposite the Co-Op on the corner of Milton Road holding hands and staring at Prince Jamie like a fucking idiot.

Morris or maybe Khan said, "Sir? Miss?" in a tone that said they were acting really weird and could they knock it off, please?

She snatched her hand back, face hot, and scurried out of the way of the woman with the buggy, who glared and barged past, taking with her the last remnants of the moment that had expanded to fill everything Clodagh knew.

"I'm sorry," she stammered. Why was she always apologising to him?

His hand followed hers, as if it wanted to catch it and keep it hostage, and then he shook it off as if it was full of electrical charge, and gave her a flicker of a smile.

"Don't be," he said, very softly, his eyes still on her

face. He looked puzzled, as if he couldn't work out what had just happened. Then he put on his sunglasses, and she couldn't see the changing shades of his eyes any more.

"I should—I just live—I should go." She flapped her hand in the direction of her flat, which made it look as if she lived in the Co-Op. "Thanks for the... bacon," she said, and turned. Thanks for the *bacon*? Jesus Christ, Clodagh. Get a grip.

They were following her, she realised as she waited on the traffic island for the lights to change. The two bodyguards, neither of them huge but giving an impression of massiveness, flanking Jamie, in his technical sports gear and sunglasses like any student leaving the boathouse after a training session. He was watching her, although how she knew that she couldn't say.

She crossed the road, rounded the corner and felt in her bag for her key. Her fingers shook, and she told herself that was just because she was so tired.

It took two tries to get the key in the lock, but she managed it, and the last thing she saw before she closed the door was Prince Jamie of Wales standing on the pavement with his hands in his pockets, watching her.

CHAPTER FOUR

Historygal blog: The little known story of how Edward VIII nearly married a divorced commoner and abdicated!

Bear with! Yes, I am talking about the Queen's father and yes, this is all true. We're all familiar with the beloved Queen Mum, Freda Dudley Ward, later Queen Winifred. We all know they met in an air raid shelter during the First World War, while he was still the Prince of Wales and she was still married to her first husband, from whom she was living a discreetly separate life.

But here's the story of the woman he almost *married; and who would have led to his abdication. Why? Well, let me tell you about Wallis Simpson…*

"Now what's this your PPO has been telling me about some girl?" Olivia said, throwing herself onto the back seat with no warning. Well, he knew she was getting into the car. He didn't know his personal protection officers had been blabbing about him.

"Why yes, I do think that went well," said Jamie,

fastening his seatbelt. He was proud of his hands for not shaking. "Great turn-out and I was especially pleased to see the improvement Sergeant Drayton has made."

"Yes, yes, whatever. He's walking with a frame, it's a medical miracle, I'll say a rosary for him." Her hands fluttered impatiently at him.

"You're not Catholic."

"Jamie!"

He looked out of the window to give himself time. Smiled and waved at the crowds outside the clinic. A man in a wheelchair saluted him.

He thought he saw a girl with bouncy brown curls and a wide, pretty smile, but when he looked again it was a total stranger.

When Jamie turned back to Olivia he was composed. "You don't believe everything the PPOs tell you, do you? Which one was it this time?"

"The sexy one."

"Oh, that's helpful—"

"The Indian one."

"Khan? His family is from Pakistan, actually, and your mother really would disown you if you brought home a Muslim boyfriend." The Duchess of Allendale was the sort of person who began sentences with things like, "I'm not a racist, but…"

Olivia smoothed her skirt. "It's 2017, darling, I can date who I like. And speaking of dating…?"

The car paused at a junction. With the privacy screen up, no sound came from the front of the car. Jamie stared at nothing, then said, "I'm not dating anyone."

"Seeing, shagging, whatever. Semantics. Jamie, I'm your oldest friend. Spill."

"There's honestly nothing to spill. I'm not seeing anyone. I haven't got time."

That part at least was true. He'd cut his royal duties to the bone, but there was no way he'd miss a visit to the military veterans charity both he and Olivia were patrons of. It had been doable after his weekly meeting with Peaseman, and he'd also been asked to do an afternoon tea with young carers in Stoke, which was where they were currently headed. Tomorrow he had a hospital opening, a meeting of former Land Girls and then, if he was lucky, he might be able to catch up on some of the reading he'd missed this week while he was sitting in a boathouse watching a pretty girl sleep.

He should have woken her the minute the plate slipped from her hand, but instead he'd caught it and tucked a cushion under her head. She hadn't stirred when he lifted her feet onto the sofa or covered her with her stained jacket. She was clearly exhausted, and Jamie had been too ashamed of his own privilege to go back to the pub that week.

And too shocked by that moment on the street. Benjamin Franklin with his key and his kite had nothing on that moment. Jamie was amazed they hadn't blown every electrical circuit in the city. For a brief eternity, it had felt like they were the only two people in the world.

He didn't know what to think about that.

When Vincent dressed him for this event Jamie had looked at his pristine white shirt and asked idly what would happen if red wine got on it.

"I'd fetch you a new one, sir," came the smooth reply.

"No, I mean if you didn't have a new one. If you had to clean it. Is it hard?"

Vincent gave him a long-suffering look, explained that the shirt would never be snowy white again, and then under duress supplied a list of products he relied upon for the royal linen.

"Not everyone has the luxury of a new shirt every time one gets dirty," said Jamie, shame curling inside him at the profligacy.

"Not everyone is photographed by the international

press every time they go outside, sir," Vincent replied, adjusting the knot of Jamie's tie.

I am only one skipped shift away from homelessness. Did she mean that? Was her life that precarious? How had a bright girl who knew Keats and hummed along to Purcell ended up living in such a crappy flat—one cracked window had been covered with newspaper for so long all the print had faded—and moonlighting as a waitress to make ends meet?

She'd mentioned course fees. And there'd been that book she hadn't quite hidden behind the bar. Was she a student? How did she ever find time to study with all that working going on? Didn't she have a student loan?

Jamie told himself there were a million reasons why Clodagh might be short of cash and none of them were any of his business.

Except that when he closed his eyes he saw hers, staring up at him, wide with shock. Pale brown, maybe amber, bright and clear even when she was dead on her feet. Her lips parted with surprise, her mouth full and lush. Her hand in his, jolting him like they were both made of pure electricity.

Morris and Khan hadn't said a word to him about it, but he knew they'd noticed. They'd probably have reported it back to Geraint, who'd be busy compiling a dossier on Clodagh Walsh, a girl he'd met three times and spoken to very little and whose hand he'd held, for a lifetime that lasted less than a minute.

"Oll, when I'm seeing someone you'll be the first to know," he said, and closed his eyes.

Pale brown, maybe amber.

He opened them again. "What's the name of the charity this afternoon?"

"Caring Hands, and don't change the subject," said Olivia.

"There is no subject," said Jamie, and ignored her

until she gave up.

Clodagh didn't see the prince for a week or two, during which Hanna and Lee's relationship cycled back into arguments and slammed doors and bruises that weren't quite concealed by make-up. Clodagh twice drummed up the courage to talk to her flatmate, but was met with scorn and a flurry of what sounded like abuse in Polish.

She took extra shifts at the pub as much out of desperation to get out of the flat as for the cash.

The first week after the boathouse incident, she came into the pub to find the staff nudging each other and the regulars making jokes about flowers and chocolates. "Who's brought who flowers?" she asked, and Oz burst out laughing.

"Maybe this is what royalty does instead of flowers," he said, handing her a paper bag.

Royalty? Oh hell, what had he brought her? And why? Clodagh looked around, but there was no sign of the prince or his interchangeable protection officers.

"Maybe it's money," said Marte.

"Or a tiara," said Paulie.

"Nah man, I bet it's some kinky sex toy."

"Sex toy? You shagging the prince then, Clodagh?"

Clodagh tried to block out their whoops of laughter as she opened the bag. It wasn't a tiara, or money, or a sex toy. It was two small bottles with colourful labels. And a note. "I am reliably informed," it told her in beautiful handwriting, "that these are best for red wine and blood stains. Hope you're well. Jamie Wales."

Stain remover. "He's sent me stain remover," she said, and smiled for the first time since she'd seen him.

The staff and the regulars looked at each other in consternation. "Now that is kinky," said Oz.

Hallowe'en found her pinning up the tattered decorations the Prince's Arms had had for donkeys years and listening to the older regulars complain about how American the whole thing was.

"Actually Hallowe'en is firmly British," she said, preparing to bring out Random Facts Girl and launch into what Oz called her Samhain Monologue.

"What? No it's not. We didn't do this when I was a kid," said Paulie.

"We had Mischief Night when I was," said Stevo.

"Nah, that's for Bonfire Night," said Paulie.

"Bloody isn't. It's Hallowe'en."

"Bloody is!" Paulie shook his head, his Bradford accent getting stronger. "Bloody southerners."

"Well, go back up north, then."

Clodagh had heard the argument too many times to count. Paulie was adamant Yorkshire was the best place to be from, but equally adamant he wasn't going back.

The pub began to fill up. Marte had hired a band to play and put up a few posters and the clientele ebbed and flowed with pub crawlers in costumes of varying quality. Clodagh, who'd been raised with the 'wear black tights and draw a cat nose with Mummy's eyeliner' type of costume, always appreciated the home-made over the shop-bought, of which there were more every year.

"Anyway, it's all trick or treating now," said a man Clodagh knew only as John the Milk. He waved his empty pint glass at her and she nodded and picked up a clean one.

"Yeah, and try getting them to do a trick!"

"Can't, mate, you'll have the PC brigade on you. 'Want to see a trick, little girl?' Just imagine."

"Never did us any harm."

"When were you a little girl?" said Clodagh, and they all laughed.

The conversation moved on. She served John the Milk, then Paulie, and then the students came in, noses pink from the cold, talking excitedly about some computing thing that was quite literally a different language. Hunter the American was dressed somewhat incongruously as Luke Skywalker. Zheng had a t-shirt that said, 'Go, ceiling!' There was a vampire, a mad surgeon and half-hearted ghost.

Ruchi came to the bar. Her t-shirt said 'Error 404: Costume Not Found.'

"Cute," said Clodagh, fetching the lager glasses for the boys. "I don't get Zheng?"

"Oh, he's a ceiling fan."

Go ceiling. Clodagh had to laugh at how terrible that was. "What are you having?"

"Red wine, I think, then I can pretend it's blood." Ruchi leaned forward. "And then spill it on Hunter, who said earlier my talk on system modelling was 'quite good for a girl'."

Clodagh felt her eyes get big. "Why is it some men confuse being a massive dick with having one?"

Ruchi laughed uproariously. "That's brilliant. What are you?"

Clodagh groaned and looked down at her tight, itchy polyester dress. "For some reason Oz was in charge of the costumes. I think it's meant to be a sexy vampire. It was that or sexy witch. Or a sexy... I want to say pirate?" To be honest there was little to tell them apart.

"Was there an option not to wear a polyester minidress?" Ruchi said, looking her over with an expression that said she was glad it was Clodagh and not herself.

"Nope." At least she'd had enough advance warning to find a pair of normal tights to wear under it, instead of the fishnets Oz had been so hopeful of. And Clodagh didn't expect sexy vampires usually wore trainers, but she was going to be on her feet all night and she had to walk home, too.

There had been a wig, but Clodagh had just grabbed a

handful of her wild corkscrew curls and asked Oz sweetly how she was meant to fit them all under the damn thing, and he'd backed off.

"Oh well. It's just for one night. And at least you're getting paid."

Clodagh repeated that to herself several times throughout the night, when a customer spilt a pint of beer on her, when another grabbed her arse as she was collecting glasses, when she went too close to the speakers just as a guitar screeched with feedback.

"I'm getting paid," she muttered when a large werewolf came up to the bar and snarled at her, his fingers ending in claws that dripped fake blood.

"I'm going to eat you, little girl," he said, and at that point Clodagh's blood did run cold because the voice belonged to Lee, who wasn't supposed to know where she worked.

"Are you sure it won't sweat off?" said Jamie, as the make-up artist applied the last false eyelash.

"It doesn't sweat off Elphaba every night," she replied.

Jamie's eyebrows went up, which was a weird sensation since the face in the mirror didn't have eyebrows in the same place as his own.

"You work on *Wicked*?"

"I have done. This is the same brand they use. Close your eyes now, and don't breathe in for a moment."

She squirted some stuff onto his face that reminded Jamie vaguely of the fixative glue he'd sprayed on pastel paintings as a child in art classes.

"You look amazing, darling," said Olivia, as he opened his eyes.

"Not as amazing as you."

She preened a little. It had been her idea to dress as Victor and the Corpse Bride, her little joke on the rumours everyone liked to spread. Jamie had agreed, mostly because Olivia was the one planning it all and he didn't have to go very far. Also, as a major plus point, he was almost unrecognisable under the professional make-up job. So long as Geraint and the team could lose the paparazzi tail, he could probably get out of the car as just another anonymous Hallowe'en reveller.

Tonight's team consisted of Morris and Cutter, and Olivia had cajoled them to add dark sunglasses to their usual black outfits so they could pass as Blues Brothers. As it was a party night, Geraint and Farquerson would be following them in the car, with the others ready as usual for back-up.

All this had been explained to Jamie in his weekly security briefing. He'd nodded and managed to take on board the particulars, whilst wondering at what point in the evening it would be best to mention the Prince's Arms and how long he might persuade Olivia to stay there.

Because his student friends would be there, of course. Not because of a girl with amber eyes and very curly hair. Nope.

They hit the Lady Mathilda party first, of course, out of courtesy. University dignitaries looking uncomfortable in their costumes, and students who hadn't met Jamie yet, trying to suck up. After that it was a party one of Olivia's schoolfriends was throwing. Jamie kept an eye out for Clodagh amongst the waitresses, but she wasn't there.

A small group of people he vaguely knew gathered around them, people it was hard to hide his identity from. People who kept taking pictures. They straggled on to a couple of bars, one of the more upmarket pubs, and then someone suggested a club.

Jamie looked at Olivia. One of the many things they'd admitted to each other over the years was that neither could stand clubbing. Here was their chance to escape.

"Sure, we'll follow you," he said. "In the car. You know the PPOs, always so protective."

They agreed happily and tottered off down a street filled with costumed partiers. The car seemed blessedly silent as Jamie shut the door and watched Olivia trying not to smear make-up on the seats.

"Home, James?" she said, because she'd never grown out of thinking that was funny. "Or do you know a watering hole where we're terrifically unlikely to run into Serena Armstrong-Whitely?"

"As a matter of fact," said Jamie, checking the eerie slanted eyebrows drawn on his forehead, "I do."

The Prince's Arms was busier than he'd ever seen it. A duo in the corner played popular hits, some of which even had a slightly Hallowe'en-ish slant to them, and he spotted his fellow postgrads occupying a corner table crammed with glasses and discarded costume items.

"Ooh it's such a dive," said Olivia admiringly, adjusting one tattered lace glove. "I love it."

"To yourself," Jamie muttered, pasting on his usual smile. The place had been decorated somewhat half-heartedly for Hallowe'en, the lights dimmed, and people were enjoying hamming it up in their costumes. He smiled as he saw his PhD supervisor, Dr Carlow, dressed as a mad doctor. "Go and sit down with those people and be nice. Tell them not to give me away."

Olivia beamed at him and passed him a fifty. Like a lot of people he knew, she had no real concept of how much things cost.

"White wine spritzer, darling. Hello everyone, I'm Olivia. I believe we have a friend in common…"

Her voice faded away as she made herself comfortable next to Zheng, who looked at her like she was made out of cupcakes and rainbows and puppies.

Jamie threaded his way to the bar. "Hi! White wine spritzer and... actually I'll just have a shandy," he said, mentally adding up the drinks he'd already had and getting somewhat fuzzy answers.

It wasn't Clodagh serving him but one of the other girls, who'd whitened out her complexion to match her vampire outfit, and added fake blood too. He saw Clodagh—his pulse leapt up although it had no right to —looking somewhat fed up in her tacky costume, serving a guy in a Steppenwolf t-shirt and werewolf mask.

How do you drink in that? he wondered. How did he even make himself understood?

Clodagh didn't glance his way. She served the customer, took his money and gave him his change without a single smile.

Maybe she was one of those people who didn't like Hallowe'en. Or maybe she was fed up of being harassed about her sexy costume. He watched her tug at the skirt, sigh, and move onto the next customer, who was one of the old regulars, not in costume. She found a smile for him, but it didn't reach her eyes.

Frowning, Jamie went to sit down with his friends. But this time he wasn't distracted from Clodagh by computer talk, partly because Olivia kept changing the subject. They were clearly all enthralled by her, which was the effect she tended to have, and she soaked up the attention, batting him on the arm when his wandered back to the bar.

Clodagh had cheered up a bit now, he thought, laughing and smiling with customers and posing for a photo with the other girls. But it was a smile that only lasted until the werewolf went back up to the bar.

Jamie didn't recognise him at first, because he'd taken the mask off. But he still had the claw hands, and the Steppenwolf t-shirt he probably thought was funny, and he leaned over and said something to Clodagh that made her jaw go tight.

Jamie was on his feet before he could think, and a hand on his arm pulled him back.

"Sir?" muttered someone, and he looked round to see Cutter in his Blues Brothers shades.

Jamie looked pointedly down at his arm, and Cutter let go of him. But the point had been made. *Don't do anything rash.*

He dug out a banknote as he approached the bar, despite having half a pint left.

"Clodagh! Great costume. Could I have another pint, when you're ready?"

She glanced at him, irritated, then paused and looked again.

"'Scuse me mate," said the werewolf, a beefy guy with a red face. "I was here first."

"I do apologise," said Jamie politely. "I'll wait."

He gave them both a beaming smile which was probably terribly at odds with his eerie make-up, and waited for the werewolf to finish whatever he was trying to upset Clodagh with. He'd bet the guy would back off once he got an audience, and he was right. The werewolf picked up his drink and stalked off back to a group of rough-looking guys, and Clodagh let out her breath slowly.

"Pint of Carlsberg?" she said, as if nothing was wrong.

"Please," said Jamie. "Are you okay?"

"Yep. Apart from this stupid costume." She didn't look up.

"Was he bothering you?"

She shrugged in a way that was almost convincing. "He was just being a prick about the," she waved a hand at her short skirt and exposed legs. "You know."

"Sure. He was being a prick earlier, too."

"I suspect he was born a prick. Three seventy, please."

"Clodagh." He reached out to touch her hand, and she drew it back sharply.

"Don't." She closed her eyes momentarily. "I... look. I don't know what happened the other week. I was..." She let out a gusty sigh. "I was overtired and acting stupid and I just got..."

She still hadn't made eye contact with him. Jamie realised she hadn't had to look all that closely to recognise him, which was something everyone at his table kept doing. *She knows me.*

"...confused," she finished, looking unsatisfied with the answer.

"Confused."

"Or something. I'm sorry if I embarrassed you. You were really kind and I was really weird and—"

"You weren't weird." What happened was weird, but she clearly didn't want to talk about it. "No apology needed. I..."

Someone else came up to the bar, and Jamie sighed. It was too busy to talk to her properly here. "I'll talk to you later," he said, handing over a tenner and taking his drink away before she could give him any change.

He sat down, took his phone out of his pocket and hesitated for a moment. Then he glanced over at Steppenwolf and nodded to himself as he sent a text to Geraint.

The band had played a dark, eerie version of Rockwell's *Somebody's Watching Me* and it kept snagging in Clodagh's brain as she walked home. Of course, even this late there were still plenty of people around, their costumes and fancy make-up jobs flagging in the heat of so many old, low-ceilinged pubs and party venues.

Jamie's make-up didn't flag, she thought as she

passed a vomiting Harley Quinn. Probably got a pro in to do it. Or maybe his girlfriend had done it for him. Whoever she was, the girl with blue skin and a tattered dress had looked stunning, and the way she kept touching Jamie on the arm was terribly proprietorial.

More than once Clodagh had felt the Corpse Bride's gaze on her. "You're welcome to him, love," she muttered as she cut through Christ's Pieces with its faintly glowing blue paths.

It was quieter here, away from the pubs and clubs. Clodagh didn't usually head through the parks at night but this was a faster route and she'd bargained on there being more people around.

The song bounced around her head as she glanced over her shoulder. No, she was being paranoid. Nobody was watching her. There was a guy fifty yards behind her but so what, there was a guy fifty yards ahead, too.

The itchy feeling between her shoulder blades was all Lee's fault. How he'd found her, she didn't know, because she'd deliberately never mentioned the Prince's Arms to either him or Hanna. Maybe he'd just been in there on the off-chance.

Thank God he'd left the pub. Wherever the hell he'd gone, he hadn't been in the pub at closing time. Neither had Jamie, he and his gorgeous girlfriend having vacated when the band finished, probably for a posher party. Or maybe just to go back to whatever palatial little bit of Cambridge he called home, where they'd shag royally.

How do royals shag? she wondered. Politely? Wearing tiaras? Insisting their partners call them 'Your Royal Highness' throughout?

She laughed quietly to herself, and a man dressed as a zombie leered at her.

Clodagh felt in the pocket of her cross-body bag for her keys, transferred them to her pocket and kept her hand in there, slotting the cool metal between her knuckles the way she'd been doing since she was a teenager.

Bet Jamie's girlfriend has never keyed a mugger in the face, she thought darkly as she passed a couple snogging on a bench. A taxi passing on Emmanuel Road illuminated them and she picked up the pace to leave the ill-advised darkness of the park for the comparative busyness of Short Street.

She relaxed a little as she navigated the roundabout and headed up Victoria Avenue. This was the home stretch, and as long as she ignored the bench where Jamie had been so kind to her that morning, she'd probably get home without imagining too many more ridiculous things.

She felt irrationally angry with him. How dare he be so kind, so considerate, and how dare he touch her hand like that when he had a girlfriend? A girlfriend he'd never introduced to her—although she'd been getting on well his his PhD friends, who were clearly a cut above.

Muttering under her breath, Clodagh crossed the road and rounded the corner, flipping up her hood against the cold and the leers of late-night partygoers. There was still a party going on in one of the pubs nearby. Sound thumped out, music and laughter reaching her on a tide of cigarette smoke.

She really hoped Lee wasn't there when she got home. He'd creeped her the hell out earlier, making sleazy comments about her outfit, and racist ones about why she wasn't as white as the other vampires. She'd entertained fantasies all evening of smashing a glass into his face.

The lights were on upstairs in the flat, which meant someone was in. Clodagh sighed, and let herself in the front door. She could hear Lee shouting from the top of the stairs. The flat door must be open. Well, this was just swell.

Clodagh steeled herself and started up the stairs. Her fist clenched hard around the keys splayed between her fingers. She'd punch him if she had to. If he laid a finger on her she'd have the police on him. Might report him anyway for hate crimes—

"The fuck?"

The flat had been totally turned over, furniture on its side, clothes thrown everywhere. Cushions ripped apart, the TV smashed. Her bedroom door had been kicked in, the cheap plywood splintered. Oh God, it wasn't Lee, it was a burglar! Clodagh stepped back, feeling for her phone, and made to creep back down the stairs. Maybe a neighbour would let her in to wait for the police.

But before she could turn around Lee came crashing out of her bedroom, his face red with fury. Spittle flecked as he advanced on her, snarling.

The one and only time she was glad to see him!

"Were we robbed?" Clodagh said, and he snarled at her.

"Where is she?"

"Who? Hanna? I don't know—"

"You know, bitch!"

"I don't! I've only just got home, what… happened…"

It dawned on her far too slowly. They hadn't been burgled. Lee had done this, because Hanna had left. *Finally*.

"Lee," she said carefully, looking around at the wreckage of her crappy flat and holding tightly to her keys in her pocket, "were we burgled?"

His face went purple. "Who you calling a fucking burglar? Where's Hanna?"

"I don't know. She was here when I left." Clodagh started moving backwards.

"Bitch, you helped her escape!"

"I didn't—"

Lee darted sideways, and she flinched, but then he grabbed a small table with a broken leg and hurled it at her.

"Jesus!" Clodagh ducked, but it caught her arm and knocked her off balance. She crashed into the doorway, reeled and turned to run as he came after her.

He grabbed her by the arm, bellowed something she didn't understand, and shook her like a wet rag. Clodagh swiped at him with her keys and that infuriated him further, his big hand letting go of her arm to clutch at his face and his other hand coming up to hit her, hard, right in the eye.

She felt herself fall, unable to stop it, grabbing helplessly at the wall and finding no purchase. The stairs rushed up to meet her, hard, and she tumbled down, a dozen points of impact before she came to rest, crumpled on the cheap lino outside the downstairs flat.

Lee bellowed something at her but she couldn't quite take it in. Her head rang, her vision blurred, and a sharp pain shot up her leg.

Then the front door crashed open and a Blues Brother flew in.

Clodagh passed out after that.

CHAPTER FIVE

"So that's the girl you like," Olivia said as they left the pub, swaying slightly.

"There is no girl," Jamie said automatically.

"There's so a girl! The one with the hair." Olivia mimed lots of curls with the hand she didn't have tucked into his arm.

"Most girls have hair," Jamie said, trying not to think about Clodagh's.

"You know the one I mean. That werewolf guy was hassling her and you were a knight in shining armour. Don't pretend you weren't, I saw you."

The werewolf guy had been twice Jamie's size and mean with it. He'd still happily have punched his lights out, given half the chance.

Except he wouldn't, because princes didn't punch people. No matter how much they deserved it.

"I'd step in if I saw a guy like that hassling anyone," he said nobly.

"But especially someone you fancy."

He sighed. "Look, I think she's pretty. We've hardly spoken. I barely know her."

I know what she looks like when she laughs and when she sleeps and when she's angry.

"I'd go for it if I were you," Olivia said as they rounded the corner of Bene't Street. "You're a handsome prince, Jamie. She's hardly going to say no."

Jamie frowned at her. He'd never knowingly used his position to get girls, and anyway, the sort of girl who just wanted to say she'd slept with a prince held no attraction for him. But he was horribly aware that there was no separating Jamie from the prince. Everyone knew who he was.

If he came on to a girl, any girl, would she say yes because he was a prince? Would she be scared to say no? Would Clodagh?

"Do you ever use your title to get guys?" he asked Olivia.

She snorted. "Darling, it's a bit different for me. I don't usually tell them for a while. Never quite know if they're after the house and the money and all that."

Of course it was different for her. Outside of their limited social circle Olivia wasn't all that well known. People might think she looked a bit familiar and the sharper-eyed readers of a certain type of magazine might recognise her, but if she wasn't with Jamie the general public didn't usually put two and two together.

Cutter and Morris took them to the gatehouse, bid them goodnight and watched them totter across the lawn to the front door of Jamie's little house. Well, it wasn't that little, but to someone who'd grown up in a palace it was like a doll's house. He loved it.

"Little drinky?" said Olivia, tossing her hooded velvet cape onto a chair.

Jamie shrugged. "Let me wash this bloody make-up off and I'll be right with you."

Olivia extended her hand and admired the illusion of bones painted onto her arm. "Whiskey?"

"Splash of water." He headed up the stairs, discarding clothing as he went. Off with the make-up, using some special remover the make-up artist had thankfully left behind, and on with joggers and t-shirt.

He never got to wear clothes this comfortable in front of anyone else. Granny had Rules about what constituted casual wear around any of her homes—which technically was all the ones Jamie had ever lived in— and jogging bottoms were not part of her vocabulary.

She was on the phone when he came downstairs, frowning. "Jamie, it's Geraint. Says you weren't answering your phone. Something about… something you asked him to do?"

Damn, he'd left it in the pocket of his costume. He took Olivia's from her. "What's up?"

"Benson followed Miss Walsh, sir, like you asked."

Something uncomfortable tightened in Jamie's stomach. "Is she okay?"

The tiniest of pauses. Jamie didn't know what his face was doing but it made Olivia's eyes widen.

"He's on his way to hospital with her now, sir—"

"What?"

Olivia grabbed his arm. Her weird blue cartoonish face was creased with concern.

"She's not badly hurt, sir, so don't worry, and the police have taken care of Mr Cunningham—"

"Police? Geraint, what the hell happened?"

He found himself moving towards the hallway, grabbing his jacket and swearing at his running shoes as he tried to pull them on one-handed.

"Where are you going?" said Olivia.

"There's no need to come, sir, we have the situation under control."

"Geraint." Jamie tried to hold on to his patience. "Tell me in words of one syllable exactly what happened and yes, that *is* an order."

He was already outside, striding across the lawn. Geraint began explaining things, his voice infuriatingly calm. Benson had followed Clodagh home as instructed, seen her safely into the house, heard shouting and then a scream and series of thumps. He'd broken down the door to find Clodagh crumpled at the bottom of the stairs, and the Steppenwolf guy standing over her. "Steppenwolf said she slipped, sir, but Benson said if she slipped then he's the King of the Belgians." Benson had taken him out—Geraint did not elaborate as to how—and called the police and an ambulance.

"Where is she?"

He was inside the gatehouse now, the control room set up with monitors showing every angle of his house and the street outside. Geraint and three others were there.

"She's perfectly safe, sir—"

"Is it Addenbrookes? I need you to drive me."

"Sir, that's not appropriate—"

"Fuck appropriate," Jamie said sharply. "You know why she's hurt?"

"Because a drunken bully attacked her," said Geraint, infuriatingly calm.

"No, because of me. Because I got involved with her. I made her breakfast. I interrupted her fight with that guy. Now he's taken it out on her and it's my fault she's hurt."

"Jamie, you're not making any sense," Olivia said. He hadn't even realised she'd followed him.

"That guy? Beating her up in her own flat? He's her boyfriend, Olivia, who else would he be?" Christ, she'd told him she didn't want to go home, that morning in the boathouse. She'd sat there with blood on her sleeve and told him some story about someone having an accident, outside freezing herself to death at dawn because she didn't want to go home because that arsehole was there.

"And I interfered, didn't I? I tried to stop him creeping on her and he went home and waited for her and threw her down the stairs."

Silence. Jamie had tears in his eyes, angry frustrated stupid tears, because someone was hurt and it was his fault.

Olivia broke it. "It's not your fault," she said, and held up a hand to stop him replying. "But I see why you must go." She handed him his phone. "Do you want me to come with you?"

She was still in costume. Midnight had come and gone. "No, you stay here. Get some sleep."

She nodded and said in her Lady Olivia of Allendale voice, "Geraint, I believe His Highness requested the car be brought round."

Geraint had been with Jamie in Afghanistan when they rescued a family being held hostage by insurgents. From the look on his face, he'd rather be back there now facing them than Olivia.

"My lady," he said stiffly. "Sir."

She gave Jamie a hug, whispered, "Now tell me you don't like her," in his ear, then trailed back to the house like a ghost.

The drive should have taken ten minutes. They got there in seven. Geraint had Benson in his ear telling them how to find Clodagh, and Jamie nearly ran down several people in his haste to get there.

And there she was, sitting on a bed with a paper sheet on it, still wearing that stupid bloody vampire dress. Her eyes were closed, one of them swollen and purple, and there were scrapes and bruises on her arms and legs. Her right ankle looked gruesome, twice the size of the left and the colour of damsons.

"Clodagh." He hadn't meant to sound so anguished.

Her eyes opened, one of them not fully. "Oh," she said. "We keep meeting."

"I came as soon as I…" He reached for her hand and she looked down curiously as he took it. It wasn't electricity he felt this time, but a jolt of shame. "Clodagh, I'm so sorry."

"Hmm? My head is killing me."

He peered closer. "Did you hit your head?"

She blinked a bit. "Maybe. I don't remember. This man says he works for you."

Benson gave Jamie a speaking look.

"He does, and he's getting a raise after tonight," Jamie said firmly.

Right then the doctor came in, a tired-looking man not much older than Jamie. "There are too many people in this room," he said.

Jamie looked at his PPOs, who turned to go. Geraint looked like he really wanted to say something, but kept silent.

"Are you the next of kin?" asked the doctor, and Jamie panicked.

"Why? How bad is it?"

"Oh, not too bad." He showed Jamie an X-ray, as if that was something he knew how to read. "Clean break. We'll get it in a boot, six weeks, should be fine. No walking for you," he added sternly to Clodagh, who nodded dazedly.

"Does she have a head injury? She couldn't remember." Jamie's thumb stroked Clodagh's. Her nails were torn and the back of her hand grazed.

"Yes, a concussion. There's no skull fracture or swelling, just a bump that will take a little while to heal. You'll need to keep a close eye on her for the next forty-eight hours. No need to keep waking her through the night, let her sleep but do be aware for these signs." He handed Jamie a leaflet. "The rest are just bumps and bruises. You're a lucky girl," he added to Clodagh, who looked up at him blearily.

"Yeah, so lucky to be thrown down the stairs," Jamie said. He hadn't asked if Benson had shot and killed Steppenwolf. He hoped not. Jamie wanted him to suffer.

The doctor looked between Jamie and Clodagh. "It's been reported to the police?"

"Yes. My… colleague took care of that."

The doctor shook his head as he bustled about. "Hallowe'en. Drunks and idiots."

"She's neither."

Jamie didn't snap at people very often. No one in his family did. They didn't need to. But every now and then when he was tired and angry, out it came. Olivia said it was a tone of voice that reminded her he was descended from men who ruled their kingdoms with swords and nooses.

The doctor stopped what he was doing, looked Jamie over and appeared to see him for the first time.

"Forgive me," he said. "I didn't recognise you. Your Royal Highness."

"Would you have insulted my friend if you had?"

The doctor paled, but rallied. He fitted Clodagh's ankle with a thick kind of boot that let her toes stick out, and gave Jamie a set of instructions on how long she had to wear it and what she could do in it, which wasn't much, apparently.

He checked her eyes and her head again, then announced she was free to go, so long as Jamie, "or perhaps someone else," could keep an eye on her for the next couple of days. Jamie wondered if the man thought he had special flunkies for this kind of thing.

He dispatched Benson to find a wheelchair while Clodagh sat on a chair in a waiting room and yawned.

"Where are you going to take her?" Geraint asked quietly. "There are a few hotels—"

"Hotel? Don't be ridiculous. She's coming home with me."

Geraint's mouth got very thin. "Sir. This is highly inadvisable. You hardly know her."

"I know enough." Jamie shoved a hand through his hair, which needed a wash after all the product the make-up artist had applied. "And don't tell me you don't have a full dossier on her."

His security team compiled dossiers on pretty much everyone he spent time with. They'd checked out all the students in his lab and all the staff too. They knew more about his friends than he did. Jamie was pretty sure they'd run background checks on everyone he'd ever slept with, but he'd never asked because he really didn't want to know.

"Of course, sir. Standard procedure."

"And? Is she dangerous, violent, anti-monarchist?"

Geraint looked like he'd swallowed a toad. "No," he said, and the 'but' hanging there was enormous.

"No? Good, then. She can stay. You can't seriously tell me you'd leave her alone in this state? She clearly can't go back to her flat."

They looked at Clodagh, who was purple with bruises and grey with tiredness. Well, but maybe she did have somewhere to go. A friend or relative nearby, perhaps. Jamie sat down beside her and said, "Where do you want us to take you?"

"What?" She still seemed dazed. Jamie had suffered a concussion once as a teen, falling off a horse. He remembered virtually nothing about it but the headaches and nausea that followed. The accident itself had vanished from his memory.

"You can't go back to your flat. It's not safe or secured. Is there somewhere you can go?"

Clodagh looked at him like she was having great trouble remembering who he was. "Um. My mum, I suppose. Can you take me to the station?"

Jamie glanced at Geraint. "Where does your mum

86

live?"

"Uh, it's in, it's near… it's in Essex."

"Where in Essex?"

She rubbed her face and winced when she encountered her black eye. "Harlow."

Probably only about thirty miles away, but still thirty miles too far. "Clodagh, it's the middle of the night. There aren't any trains. This isn't a Journey song."

She blinked a few times. "I'll wait at the station. It's fine. Where's my bag? Or I could get the Megabus…"

"Your bag is in the car, and you are not waiting at the station, or getting the Megabus." He didn't even know what what was. "Isn't there anyone closer?"

She thought about this for a while. Benson came back with the wheelchair and Jamie helped her into it.

"I can go to the pub," she announced triumphantly.

"Do they have rooms?" It really didn't seem like the sort of pub that had rooms.

"No, there's a settle in the top bar though—"

"No," said Jamie frankly. "Do you even have a key?"

"Oh." Her face crumpled. "I don't have anywhere else to go. Do you think they'll let me stay here?"

He wanted to hug her. He wanted to hold her close and tell her everything would be all right and he was going to take care of her. Yeah, she'd love that.

"I have a spare room," he said. "It's up some stairs, I'm afraid, but it's yours if you want it. And Olivia will be there, just in case you were worried about being alone with me."

Clodagh looked confused. "I can't," she said.

"Sure you can. It's no skin off my nose."

"But you're…"

"A friend," said Jamie firmly. Apparently the only one she had.

Clodagh woke with a splitting headache and absolutely

no idea where she was. The bed was comfortable, the room large, and her handbag sat on a chair near the window. The place looked old, with an exposed beam running above the window, and uneven walls. The only door was heavy and old, the kind that ought to have metal studs in it. Propped near it was a set of crutches.

It was really unlike her to get drunk and hook-up with a random guy she couldn't even remember the next day, but it seemed the most likely explanation. At least until she tried to sit up and pain shot up her leg.

Oh. The crutches must be hers.

Clodagh pulled back the covers and stared at the big padded boot on her right leg. Her unvarnished toes stuck out the end. She wiggled them experimentally, and then tried moving other bits of her foot until she located the source of the pain in her ankle bone.

A flash of memory hit her. Lee, throwing her down the stairs, yelling at her and looming over her…

Well, that explained the headache and the ankle boot, but not the surroundings. Clodagh thought she could remember a hospital, and maybe… no, she must have imagined Prince Jamie being there.

She glanced at her bag. Her phone might give her a few clues. Swinging her damaged leg out of bed, she attempted to stand, and promptly crumpled with a yelp of pain.

Damn that hurt! Tears came to her eyes and she grabbed her leg above the cumbersome boot, as if that would stop the pain.

From the other side of the old wooden door came footsteps, rushing up stairs and along a creaky corridor. "Clodagh?" A knock on the door. "Are you all right?"

Okay, that sounded like Prince Jamie. This was getting weirder and weirder.

"I'm okay," she said. "I just… um…" Fell out of bed. Ugh, like a child. "I stumbled. I'm okay."

Well, she would be if she could manage to get up. Her ankle hurt too much to move a lot and it was so bloody cumbersome.

"Can we come in?" asked a female voice. Right. Jamie's girlfriend. "Are you decent?"

Clodagh looked down at herself. She was still wearing her bloody Hallowe'en costume.

"Not really," she sighed, "but you might as well."

The door opened, and she looked up to see a prince of the realm standing there, frowning.

"Do you need a hand?" he asked.

Humiliated, Clodagh nodded. He took her hands, and she braced herself for the spark she'd felt before, but all he did was pull her to her feet—well, foot—and let her fall back onto the bed.

"Takes a while to get used to, doesn't it?" said his girlfriend as Clodagh tugged futilely at her skirt. It could not be seemly to show this much leg to a member of the Royal Family. "I remember when I broke mine years ago. Spent most of my time lying on the floor like a tipped over tortoise."

"You spent most of your time sitting on the sofa watching TV and ringing a bell for service," Jamie said.

She giggled elegantly. "Bardfield kept trying to hide it. I mean really, what is the point of having a butler if one isn't to be waited upon?"

Jamie cast Clodagh a sideways look. "Would you like a bell?" he asked without much enthusiasm.

She briefly entertained the fantasy of being waited on by a prince. "Actually, I'd settle for knowing where I am," she said. "I seem to… have… forgotten a few things."

"Ah. Yes." Jamie ran a hand through his hair. By the looks of it, he'd been doing that all day. "They did say you might lose a bit of memory, be confused. How's your head?"

"Splitting."

He nodded and glanced at his watch. "Time for some more painkillers." He handed her a glass of water and pressed a couple of pills out of their packet. "If they don't help, tell me and I'll call the doctor. How's your vision? Any blurriness? Double vision? How many fingers am I holding up?"

"Two," said Clodagh, as his girlfriend said, "For heaven's sake, Jamie, she asked where she was, not for a full medical exam. This is Jamie's house, darling. It seemed the most sensible place to bring you. Your flat is not habitable, apparently."

The look of distaste on her face said it might not ever have been.

I'm in Prince Jamie's house. I'm actually in a royal residence. I'm in the house where royalty lives.

Holy shit.

Mistaking her look of shock, the girlfriend went on, "The boys went round to see what they could salvage for you, but it was all quite ripped up, I'm afraid. There are some bags with some clothes in, and if there's anything in particular you want them to look for I'm sure they can."

Clodagh looked where she pointed. Two plastic bags sat on the floor by the wardrobe, apparently all that remained of her possessions from the flat.

"Well, getting out of this dress would be a bonus," she muttered. Louder, she added, "Thank you for bringing me here. And for... um, I can't actually remember most of what happened but I think one of your guys rescued me?"

Jamie nodded, his expression darkening. "Your... the man who attacked you is in police custody. Unfortunately, Benson didn't kill him."

"Imagine the fuss if he had, darling. Now, we're crowding poor Clodagh, who I'm sure just wants to get some rest. The best thing for a concussion is sleep. Do you need anything?"

They both peered anxiously at her, the little charity case they'd picked up. They looked like something out of a glossy magazine. So polished and beautiful. Jamie, wearing thick-rimmed glasses and a *Big Bang Theory* t-shirt and still managing to look regal, and his girlfriend in a cashmere cardigan that probably cost the same as Clodagh's rent for six months.

Oh Christ, her rent…

"What is it?" said Jamie, coming closer. "Clodagh? Are you all right?"

"I have nowhere to go," she gasped. "I… I was supposed to be looking for a new flat but I couldn't find anywhere I could afford, and oh God, I can't work like this," she looked down at the heavy boot on her leg, "where am I going to go?"

"Nowhere," said Jamie firmly. "You'll stay here. As long as you need to."

The girlfriend opened her mouth, then shut it again.

"I can't do that," Clodagh said, aghast. "I can't impose on you like that!"

"Nonsense. Of course you can. I have three bedrooms and I'm only using one of them. There's a second bathroom along the corridor. The wi-fi is very fast and the coffee maker is almost usable."

He said the last with a faint smile. But he was just being kind, Clodagh knew. He didn't really want her underfoot, getting in his way and being all common.

But what was the alternative? Going back to her mum's? With Whitney living two floors down and Kylie in the next block and Tony still at home and the twins constantly bitching at each other? With the constant soap operas, both on TV and in real life, the neighbour whose music was as loud as it was terrible, the woman upstairs who screamed at her dog whenever it barked, which was constantly? With her five nieces and two nephews and Peppa bloody Pig and Lego underfoot…

She rubbed her face, which hurt. "I'll go back to my mum's as soon as," she said. "Just let me get used to the crutches and I'll be out of your way."

"It's no problem—" Jamie began.

"You've been very kind," Clodagh said firmly. She suddenly felt quite appallingly tired. "But I don't want to impose."

Prince Jamie narrowed his eyes a little, but he said, "Look, why don't we leave you to rest? I have a lecture later but Olivia has promised to stay in so if you need anything," he handed her handbag over, "give one of us a buzz. Can I have your phone?"

"I won't tell anyone I'm here," Clodagh promised quickly.

He smiled. "I'm not going to confiscate it. I'm going to program our numbers in."

Dazed, she handed it over and watched a member of the Royal Family put his phone number into her contacts while she desperately tried to remember if there was anything embarrassing on there he might see by accident.

"Ooh what a nice picture," said Olivia, peering over his shoulder, and Clodagh panicked until she clarified, "On your wallpaper. King's College?"

"Oh." Clodagh relaxed a little. "Yes. When it snowed last year."

"Mmm. So picturesque. I have a picture of Allendale House in the snow somewhere. Mummy put it on the calendars this year. Very beautiful, but maddeningly impractical. Bloody dogs made such a mess everywhere. Oh, I've just thought, would you like me to call the pub and tell them you won't be in?"

"I'll," Clodagh began. If she told them she wouldn't be in for a while they'd probably hire someone else. "I'll do it." She'd tell them she'd be off for a few days, because surely by then she'd be able to stand and walk a bit. If she put her weight on one leg she could probably stand behind the bar.

Only not if she went home to her mum's. It was just under an hour by train, but she had to get to and from the station at both ends, which would mean leaving the pub no later than about 10pm to make the last train. Impossible.

Jamie handed her phone back. "I'll see if I can find you a charger for that," he said. "Get some rest, and when you're ready come down and have something to eat. Give one of us a shout and we'll help you with the stairs."

They turned to go, and then Jamie hesitated and looked back at her.

"The police will want a statement from you, but maybe not until you're feeling better. I can probably get someone to come round and take it." He paused, then added, "He can't hurt you any more, you know. You're safe here."

Clodagh could only stare after him as he closed the door.

CHAPTER SIX

Olivia was giving him a Look. She'd been giving it to him since he'd brought Clodagh home in the middle of the night, and she'd only stopped while they were in Clodagh's room with her.

"Stop it," he said as they reached the bottom of the stairs.

Olivia grinned. "I can't," she said.

"Yes, you can. You are an Altringham of Allendale, you can school your expression to whatever you want."

"And right now I want to give you big cow eyes and make fun of you because you *like* her," Olivia said.

He rolled his eyes and flopped down on the sofa. "Are we schoolchildren? Teasing each other because of who we fancy?"

"Firstly, you went to Eton, so there were no girls for you to fancy, and secondly: Aha! You do fancy her."

I do. "I don't. I think she's pretty, and I like her perfectly well as a person, but that's not the same as fancying someone."

"Stay as long as you need to, Clodagh," Olivia mimicked. "Let me give you my phone number,

Clodagh…"

"Oll, stop it."

It was silly, because he was allowed to have a little crush on someone, wasn't he? It didn't mean he was going to do anything about it. He and Clodagh were very different people with little in common but a postcode, and besides right now she was hurt and vulnerable and he refused to take advantage.

He opened his mouth to say as much to Olivia, but the glint in her eye stopped him. She'd just tell him he was protesting too much.

"Fine, think whatever you like," he said, and picked up the textbook he was supposed to have finished reading last night. "I'm just helping out a friend. I'd do the same for you if your boyfriend beat you up."

Olivia gave him a look that said no boyfriend would ever dare.

"Have you read the dossier on her?" she asked.

"You know I haven't." He paused. "Why? What's Geraint been telling you?"

"Not a thing." Olivia looked innocent. "I asked Davood."

"Who?"

"Davood Khan. Really Jamie, you don't know their first names?"

"Not unless they tell me. They're personal protection officers, not mates. And I don't want to know. If there's anything really important she'll tell me."

Olivia laughed as if at a private joke. "I bet she won't. Jamie…" She trailed off, looking suddenly serious. "Look. I would love to tell you that your personal life is your own business, but we all know that's not the case. I can just imagine the tabloids if you take up with a mixed-race barmaid from Essex."

"Well then, it's a good job I'm not, isn't it?" Jamie said, trying to concentrate on his textbook. But Benson's words from earlier this morning kept echoing round his head. 'I wouldn't let a dog live in a flat like that.'

Olivia reached out and touched his arm. "Just be careful, darling. For all we know she might have staged this whole thing simply to get in your house."

Jamie snapped the book shut on his thumb. "Oh, sure, she got her boyfriend to throw her down the stairs just so she could see what kind of toilet paper I use. Don't be ridiculous, Oll."

"I'm not! Don't you remember that girl who faked a broken leg just to get in a photo with Edward? And Victoria had someone feigning mental illness or something, didn't she?"

"PTSD," Jamie sighed. "Yes. All right, I take your point, but I was there with her in the hospital with Clodagh. I saw the X-ray. She hasn't faked that part. And besides, what on earth was the likelihood of me inviting her to stay? I don't do that with everyone I meet who's broken their ankle. I'd fill up Buckingham Palace."

"So why did you?" asked Olivia. "Ask her to stay?"

Jamie thought about Clodagh sitting there on that hospital bed, looking so small and fragile and broken. He'd seen people in much worse states. Hell, he spent half his time in hospitals and convalescence wards.

Because when she touched my hand, something happened that I can't explain and I need to get to know her better so I can prove to myself it doesn't mean anything.

"I just did," he said, and refused to be drawn any more on the subject.

Clodagh hadn't meant to go back to sleep, but she did anyway. The room was in semi-darkness when she woke, horribly thirsty and desperate for the loo.

This time she took it more carefully, not really willing to be found by the prince and his perfect girlfriend on the floor in a puddle of her own wee. The crutches had been left closer to her bed, and she used one of them to support herself as she hopped along the corridor in search of a bathroom.

The upstairs corridor was lined with shelves containing leather-bound books of the variety which could only be called 'tomes'. A window at one end held a bust of a moustachioed gentleman and the stairs at the other end had exposed wooden beams hung with oil paintings.

A door stood partly open to a bedroom with a fabulous leaded bay window, overlooking a rose garden artfully lit by Victorian streetlamps. It was pin-neat and impersonal, with only a couple of complicated-looking textbooks by the bed to give a clue that it was actually occupied.

Clodagh didn't dare venture inside. It would be a terrible thing to be caught snooping. What if she were accused of stealing?

The bathroom was the next door along, clearly recently and expensively refitted with a rolltop bath and those tumbled marble tiles that were meant to look ancient. The towels were fluffier than a Persian cat. The soap was probably made from real rose petals. Even the toilet paper was luxurious. It was thicker and more quilted than Clodagh's own duvet.

Those tiles probably came from Pompeii, thought Clodagh glumly, recalling the mildewed grouting at her old flat.

She recoiled from the sight of herself in the mirror. One eye purple with bruising, her hair a tangled mess, a livid scrape on her arm resulting in a mess of dried blood. She washed frantically at the sink, casting longing looks at the shower over the bath. Probably not wise to risk that when even standing upright was a liability.

Back in her room, she hauled the plastic bags onto

the bed and looked through them. A few changes of underwear, some t-shirts and leggings, a pair of jeans she probably couldn't fit over the padded boot on her leg. After some internal debate and a quick Google on her phone—Jamie was right, the wi-fi was fast—she removed the boot in order to get dressed. Her ankle was swollen up and an even worse colour than her eye.

"Well, at least you don't need to worry about Jamie finding you irresistible," she muttered to herself as she fastened the boot back on. Her hair was a snaggled, snarled mess, tangled round the studs that marched up her earlobes. The one thing from her past she'd held on to were those piercings, and they were still causing her grief.

Clodagh did the best she could with the comb in her handbag and thanked her own foresight in hiding her good conditioner in there too, where Hanna couldn't spitefully nick it or wash it all down the sink.

The stairs posed a problem. Steep and winding back on themselves, with a carpet runner and stair rods that were just begging to snag her crutches and send her headfirst into some priceless artwork.

Clodagh chewed her lip for a while, then remembered the time her brother Scott had broken his leg playing football and had to go up and down stairs on his bottom. Well, it wasn't dignified, but neither was going A over T all the way down.

Inevitably, Olivia appeared when she was halfway down, foot in the air, blowing her hair out of her face and scowling at the world in general.

"Oh, there you are, darling." Jamie's girlfriend looked immaculate, dark hair gleaming, skin peachy pale, posture perfect. "I heard you moving about. What a clever way to get down the stairs. Shall I take those for you?"

She took Clodagh's crutches without waiting for an

answer, slotting her arm in and hopping experimentally. She managed to look elegant even while doing that.

"Lord but these are exhausting," she said. "Mind you, probably marvellous for toning one's bingo wings. Not that you have any, darling. All that pulling of pints has toned you up beautifully. I'm so glad you found something to wear. I was going to try ordering you something but do you know, Cambridge doesn't have Amazon Prime Now. It's like living in the middle ages. All these advances in technology and you still have to wait twenty-four hours to get anything delivered. Ugh."

She gave a theatrical shudder then reached out and helped Clodagh to her feet at the bottom of the stairs.

"Now. Are you hungry? Cup of tea, maybe? Or coffee? I think the machine here might run to a cappuccino."

"Tea is fine," said Clodagh. Of course Prince Jamie had a machine that made cappuccinos. "And I could eat, but I don't want to put you to any trouble."

"None at all, darling, none at all! I mean I'm a terrible cook but I could probably whip up a sandwich or something. Jamie's out, by the way. Lecture or lab work or something. What can I get you?"

Memories of a certain bacon sandwich came back to Clodagh. "It's fine. I can make my own."

"No, you can not! You're a guest here. You don't make anything. You sit down, relax, recover, and let us take care of you."

The stairs had led right into the living room, a handsome space with exposed beams and a beautiful brick chimney. There was a large bay window with leaded panes looking out onto a rose garden, and one side of the room had no wall between the beams, so that a large dining table and even larger inglenook fireplace were visible. *I've lived in flats smaller than that inglenook.*

Olivia fussed over settling her on a large leather Chesterfield, asked if she'd like the fire lit, placed some magazines at her elbow, and wandered off to make her something to eat.

Clodagh looked around. She wasn't much of an expert, but she reckoned probably every item in this room was more valuable than everything she'd ever owned in her entire life.

A small sob escaped her when she realised that pretty much all she owned now was her phone and the clothes she wore. There was the bag she'd left at the pub, of course, with a few keepsakes and important documents in it, but aside from a ring she'd been given on her twenty-first birthday there was nothing in there valued at more than about twenty quid.

She glanced at the watch on her wrist, which had been cheap when she'd bought it off a dodgy stall in the market and utterly worthless now it had a smashed face.

A book lay facedown on the side table, bits of coloured paper sticking out of it. The title on the spine was incomprehensibly long and complex, full of what Clodagh assumed to be computing terms.

The price was visible. It retailed at nearly forty pounds.

Clodagh looked from it, to her watch, and burst out laughing.

"Darling, are you all right?" said Olivia when she came back in, carrying a plate.

Clodagh nodded and swiped at her eyes, trying to calm her giggling fit. "Sure. I just noticed this book cost nearly forty quid."

"Did it?" Olivia said with absolute disinterest.

"That's half a shift's pay for me," Clodagh explained, and watched Olivia's perfect face dissolve into shock.

"But… that's impossible! Isn't there a minimum wage?"

"Yes, and I get paid it," Clodagh said.

Olivia gaped at her.

"What do you do?" Clodagh asked politely.

"Oh... PR. More or less run the Allendale PR myself... Seriously, you make eighty pounds a shift?"

Clodagh nodded patiently. "I'm guessing that's closer to your hourly rate?"

Olivia looked baffled. "I have no idea, darling, I'm salaried. Eighty pounds? I'm floored, darling, I really am. I genuinely didn't know you could live on that."

Clodagh snorted. "You more or less can't. Did you see my flat? No, well you didn't miss much. I kept trying to move out but I couldn't find anywhere else I could afford. It's expensive around here."

"Yes, I know, when my sister came here Daddy bought her a flat and it was way above the national average." Olivia didn't seem to really realise what she was saying. Clodagh attempted to keep smiling. "Well. I'm so sorry, it's terribly rude of me to pry like that. Here. I made you a sandwich."

It was plain cheese. Wondering how it could take anyone ten minutes to make a plain cheese sandwich, Clodagh accepted it and took a bite. There wasn't even any butter in it.

"Is it all right? I'm so terrible in the kitchen, really darling. Oh, I was going to fetch you a drink. What would you like? Tea or coffee, or there's some orange juice or some cans of fizzy pop... I don't suppose you could have a cheeky G&T, could you?"

Right now that sounded amazing, especially with her mouth full of dry bread, but Clodagh thought of the painkillers she'd downed and shook her head.

"Probably not. A can of fizzy pop would be nice, though."

It was real Coca Cola. Not the fake supermarket-branded stuff her mum bought, which always tasted weirdly of cardboard. Clodagh drank half of it in one go, and Olivia promptly brought her another without asking.

She curled up on the sofa, elegant as a Siamese cat. "Now, you must tell me all about yourself. Jamie's mentioned you once or twice but he hasn't told me an awful lot and I'm terribly nosy. Where are you from? Did you grow up around here?"

Clodagh was saved from trying to explain Harlow to her by the sound of the front door being opened and closed again. Through the open wall to the dining room she saw Jamie entering from what was presumably the front hallway, taking off his jacket and setting down a laptop bag.

"Clodagh!" His face lit up with a smile that was the most genuine she'd seen from him. "You're up. How are you feeling?"

She shrugged. "Okay, I guess."

"Head any better? And your ankle? Here, it'll be better if you elevate it." He fetched a footstool for her and placed her ankle on it as if she was made of glass.

"Painkillers are doing the trick. No need to take me back to A&E."

"I am glad," he said, and seemed to mean it. "Has Olivia been taking care of you?"

"I made her a sandwich," said Olivia proudly.

"Miracles never cease. Did you put butter in it?"

Olivia's face fell comically. Jamie laughed.

"You have other talents," he said. "Clodagh. Would you like some proper food? I'm starving."

"You had a massive lunch!" Olivia protested.

"Yes, and then I worked off all the calories by exercising my brain. What would you like for supper? I had a food delivery yesterday so the place is quite well stocked. Some weird Hallowe'en cupcakes I didn't order, but that's online grocery shopping for you."

"I was only telling Clodagh how you can't get

anything delivered quickly here," Olivia complained, following Jamie into the kitchen and apparently forgetting Clodagh couldn't do the same. "I mean, you have to go out to the shops. What's that all about?"

"I think it's what normal people do, Oll."

"Ugh. How awful. 'Outside'."

Jamie came back in, rolling his eyes. He had a package of chicken in one hand and a pizza box in the other. "What do you fancy?" he asked Clodagh. "The chicken will take a while to roast, or I could maybe make a risotto? Or a curry? I saw a recipe the other day for Korean chicken, but I haven't tried it yet. Or there's good old pizza. I have some pepperoni slices to go on it, if you like. And a salad, or chips. Or pasta? What do you like?"

Clodagh felt her eyes get big. She wondered if Jamie knew what an embarrassment of riches he'd just presented her with.

"Yes," she said.

"Yes to what?"

"Any of it. All of it. Yes, please."

He laughed. "I do like unfussy eaters." He gave Olivia a severe look as he went back into the kitchen.

"I'm not fussy! I just don't like things that are too spicy. Or brown. Ugh, brown food."

"Brown food?" asked Clodagh, to be polite.

"You know. Chips. Sausage rolls. Chicken wings. Those sorts of buffets you get where everything is the same colour."

The sort of food I've eaten every day of my life.

"Ignore her, she's a snob and a half," said Jamie, coming back in. "I'll do chicken. Do you like barbecue sauce? I can do some chips with it and a bit of salad to keep Her Ladyship happy."

"You're hilarious," said Olivia as she sat down beside him on the other sofa. "I'm going to go home soon, and eat proper food, like people in proper cities have."

"Proper food from a proper takeaway?" Jamie teased, and she bashed him on the shoulder. "Stay for supper if you like. There's plenty of food, not that you ever eat much."

"Fat girls don't keep jobs in PR, darling. If I have so much as one chip I'll be up at five for the personal trainer, instead of six."

"You should try rowing," Jamie said, glancing at Clodagh and giving her half a smile. "Good all-round workout, so I hear."

"And not as early as five am, either," Clodagh said, glad to finally have something to add to the conversation.

"And cold and wet, ugh, no thank you. I shall stick to a nice clean warm gym, thank you very much."

"Closest Olivia ever gets to rowing is the Henley Regatta," Jamie said. "Apart from that time you were cheering from the boathouse," he added with a sly wink.

Olivia pursed her lips. "I shall say nothing," she said, "except that it's true rowers to have amazing personal fitness. And speaking of fitness, Clodagh, have you seen the PPOs?"

"The...?"

"Personal protection officers," Jamie said. He picked up the control and switched on the huge TV. "Olivia fancies one of them."

"Can you blame me, darling? Have you seen his eyes?"

Jame made a gesture that seemed to convey he could see nothing special about the man's eyes, and also that he was supremely disinterested in his girlfriend's crushes.

Olivia turned to Clodagh. "So gorgeous. His name is Davood. Don't you think that's a sexy name?"

"I guess," said Clodagh, who had absolutely no

opinion on it whatsoever. Watching these two was like watching a sitcom.

"Your mother would disown you," Jamie said, flicking through the onscreen guide. "Remember when you said you thought Idris Elba was hot? She went into conniptions at the very thought of having non-white grandchildren."

"Yes, well, sometimes Mummy lives in the nineteenth century," Olivia sniffed.

"Actually," Clodagh began, and they both turned to look at her. "Um, wasn't there a black queen at one point? I mean, she was descended from a Portuguese family who had African ancestry or something?"

"Really? Who was that?"

Your great-great-great-and-some grandmother. Oh crap. Random Fact Girl strikes again.

"Queen Charlotte, the wife of George III. It's said her ancestor was a Moor, and that she had African features. By the American one-drop definition, that would make her black."

"And me, too?" said Jamie, cocking his very white head.

"I suppose so. I mean it's just a theory, no one knows for sure, and I don't suppose we ever will."

"Gosh, aren't you exciting and exotic," said Olivia, nudging him. "I'll remember that next time Mummy comes over all Lady Catherine de Bourgh. 'Are the shades of Allendale to be thus polluted?'" she declaimed, one hand to her brow.

"Your family is ridiculous," said Jamie, getting up to go into the kitchen.

"Hello, pot, kettle!"

His head appeared around the doorway, a wicked glint in his eye. "What? Apparently the kettle *is* black."

Olivia rolled her eyes at Clodagh. "Ignore him. Do you remember the fuss when Edward got married?

Annemarie is lovely, but there were an awful lot of people complaining he should have married an English girl. Good God, I remember my mother trying to concoct some absurd plot to get me in his bedroom in my underwear."

"Christ, did she?" said Jamie from the kitchen.

"Yes. Oh come on, Jamie, she'd send me off to be one of the Marquess of Bath's wifelets given half a chance. Do you want a hand in there?" she called through.

"No," came his firm reply. "Clodagh, do you like blue cheese dressing?"

"Probably," said Clodagh, who had never been given much choice about what she might and might not like to eat.

"Choice is a luxury," Clodagh's grandmother used to tell her, and as she thought about the insane amount of food Prince Jamie had on offer, she could only nod.

CHAPTER SEVEN

Jamie made sticky chicken with barbecue sauce, and chips with salad and half a dozen types of dressing to choose from. He put on *University Challenge* and bickered with Olivia over the answers, whilst Clodagh drifted gently into a food coma.

She woke some time later under a blanket on the sofa, the room silent and empty but for a strange woman sitting on the sofa, reading a book.

"Um?" said Clodagh.

The woman gave her a polite smile that went nowhere near her eyes. "I'm Martins. One of His Highness's PPOs. He asked me to stay here tonight as a chaperone."

Clodagh tried to sit up, her head throbbing anew. "Why, does he think I'll jump him or something?"

Martins shrugged. "He just thought you might be more comfortable knowing there was another woman around."

Right, thought Clodagh, more comfortable and less likely to make up allegations about him. "That's very kind," she said, attempting to stand. "Where is His

Highness?"

"Gone to bed. He has a full day tomorrow. He said if you give me a list of what you need—toiletries, clothes and so on—I can get them for you tomorrow."

Clodagh thought about the parlous state of her finances, and nearly laughed.

"Yeah, sure. Think I'll go to bed now, if we're talking about silly dreams."

Late the next morning after the best night's sleep she'd ever had, she sat in bed checking her bank account on her phone and working out what she could afford to spend. There were some toiletries in the bathroom, all of them brand new and unopened. Clodagh decided it wasn't freeloading if she was expected to use them. But she needed clothes and shoes and underwear, and she might be able to get some of those things from charity shops but certainly not all.

She gave Martins a carefully planned list of items and shops that might stock them cheaply, and added anxiously, "I can't pay you back immediately because I haven't got enough in my purse, but if you can take me to a cashpoint I probably can."

Hopefully. If she went into her overdraft. Again.

Martins gave her a slightly odd look, but nodded and handed her over to Phillips, another female PPO who had the same air of professional detachment. She sat in the living room, reading the newspaper, while Clodagh tried to work out what was going to be the least expensive thing to eat from Jamie's extensively-stocked kitchen.

There were four types of mustard in the fridge. Who needed four types of mustard? And why did a man living alone need one of those huge American style fridges, with two doors and an ice dispenser?

She amused herself counting the different types of pasta in one cupboard—ten, including wholewheat and gluten free—and varieties of culinary oil on a shelf in the walk-in larder.

"Olive oil, light olive oil, extra virgin olive oil, chilli oil, sesame oil, truffle oil—ew," she added as she took a sniff.

"Mostly that's for dressings," said Phillips, and Clodagh nearly dropped the bottle. Which would have been mortifyingly expensive.

"What?"

"Truffle oil. You add it to dressings and drizzle it into soups and things. It's more of a garnish than a cooking oil." She shrugged. "A little truffle goes a long way."

Clodagh carefully replaced it. "I can't say I've tried it. Isn't that the stuff pigs hunt out?"

Phillips nodded. "And dogs. It's ridiculously expensive."

"I won't go near it."

"I'm sure His Highness won't mind."

"I wouldn't appreciate it," Clodagh said, backing out. Her ankle hurt a little less today, but she was keeping as much weight off it as she could all the same. The faster it healed, the better.

She'd already had to call the card shop in the Grafton Centre and the catering agency she sometimes worked for, to tell them there was no way she could make her weekend shifts. That had been painful. She hadn't quite got up the courage to call Marte at the Prince's Arms yet. Maybe after she'd put in a call to the CRB about disability allowance and sick pay when you had a zero hours contract…

"His Highness did say if you wanted to order anything in, that was fine. A takeaway," Marte clarified. "Some places do Deliveroo around here, or perhaps one of us could go out for something."

Was she mad? Okay, Prince Jamie clearly had a very extravagant household budget, but sending out for lunch? It was ridiculous.

Clodagh made herself a cheese sandwich, remembering the butter this time. She only put on a little, because you had to make butter last, and this was the real stuff too, no fake margarine rubbish. Fancy cheddar, no own-brand 'mild cheese' bollocks for a prince, and bread sliced so thick you got about half a dozen slices to the loaf.

"So this is how the other half live," she said to Phillips, who looked over her tatty leggings and t-shirt and said nothing.

Mid afternoon, a knock came at the door, and Phillips answered it. Clodagh twisted over her shoulder to see her looking at an entry cam before she opened the door, to admit another of the PPOs—how many were there?— with several large carrier bags from John Lewis.

"You get fun looks going round the lingerie department by yourself," he announced cheerfully, extending the bags to Clodagh with a flourish. He was Asian, and had nice eyes. Maybe this Davood Olivia had been goading Jamie with.

"What's this?" she said, eyeing them without taking them.

"Things you might need. Don't worry, Lady Olivia made the order, I just picked things up," he added, holding out another bag, this one with toiletries in it.

Tentatively, she took this one. Everything in it was top of the range. Dread mounting, she looked through the other bags, which had been set on the sofa next to her.

She saw cashmere, or at least what she thought was cashmere. A label peeking from a pair of jeans held a brand name she'd only seen in magazines. There were sets of lingerie, the type that came on hangers and had a ridiculously high cost-per-inch ratio. A silk nightie, with delicate lace trim.

Fishing in the bottom, she found a receipt, and nearly threw up.

No, these must be for Lady Olivia herself. Clodagh felt relief wash over her when she realised this, coupled with embarrassment. Of course they weren't for her!

"Where's my stuff?" she asked, looking up at the two bodyguards, neither of whom held Primark or charity shop bags.

"That is your stuff. Lady Olivia ordered things yesterday when she realised what you didn't have. She took some of the sizes off your clothes to get them right."

Clodagh felt her face burn at the thought of Jamie's girlfriend seeing just how crappy her clothing choices were, let alone how much fatter she was.

"If they're not right I'm sure I can exchange them," said the male bodyguard, glancing at his colleague.

"Exchange them," Clodagh said, looking at the cashmere and silk and lace. "Exchange them for what?"

"For the right sizes?" said the PPO, as if there might have been another answer he hadn't figured out yet.

Yes, there is another answer. Exchange them for what I asked for. For what I can afford.

Carefully, Clodagh put down the bags of clothing that cost more than she'd earned last year, and stood up. "Would it be possible," she said, "for you to give me a lift to the station?"

The two PPOs exchanged glances. "The station, ma'am?"

"Yes. Actually, there's a bus stop on Emmanuel Street, I think, or does the guided busway go to the station?" She hadn't used it yet. Not much point when you could walk everywhere.

"Why do you need to get to the station?" asked Phillips.

"Because I don't think there's a bus to Harlow. There

might be a coach, if you can take me to the bus station on Drummer Street. I don't know if the Megabus goes there directly."

"Harlow, ma'am?"

They both looked at her with identical bland expressions. Gone was the woman who chatted about truffle oil and the man who joked about lingerie shopping. They were as expressionless as mannequins.

"Yes," said Clodagh, lifting her chin. "Harlow. I'm going home."

Jamie's head was full of the conversation he'd been having about games as factorisation systems when he scanned his retina and keyed in his code to get from the Lady Mathilda buildings into the Master's Garden. Damn convenient having the door there like that, although it would have been more fun if the old walkway direct from the Master's House to the library was still there. He glanced up at the floating door halfway up the wall of his house. Today, it was sealed up, and only offered a minor curiosity as one used the back stairs from the study, but—

"What is it? What's wrong?" he said, as Geraint crossed the lawn to meet him.

"Nothing's wrong, sir—"

Jamie narrowed his eyes. Geraint hated being read by anybody, but Jamie had known him too long and had been too well-trained in body language.

"All right. Miss Walsh has left, sir."

"Left?" Not to go shopping, by Geraint's face. "Where? When? Why?"

"She wanted to go home, sir. No, not to her flat, that's still not habitable—"

"Was it ever?" Jamie muttered, striding to the house to drop off his laptop bag.

"—she's gone home to her mother's house. In

Harlow," he added, with some distaste.

"Harlow?"

"Yes, sir. Harlow. It's a new town in Essex."

"I know what it is," said Jamie, who'd opened a new hospital ward or primary school or community centre there once. Maybe. Might've been Stevenage. Or Luton. Hard to tell them apart sometimes.

He shoved open his front door, chucked his laptop bag into his study, and ran his hands through his hair as he tried to think. Paused when he saw the mound of shopping bags on the sofa.

"What's all that?"

"Well," said Geraint, as Jamie moved cautiously closer, "we believe it's the reason why she left, sir."

What? He'd asked Oll to order Clodagh some new things, since she had pitifully little left from her old flat. He'd told her not to go over the top, since Clodagh probably wouldn't appreciate being treated as a charity case, but then Olivia's idea of high street was basically Harvey Nichols.

He stopped when he saw they were from John Lewis. Good old John Lewis. Hardly expensive. The bastion of the middle classes.

Inside was a collection of casual clothing, some lingerie he tried not to look too closely at, some boots and a pair of trainers. None of it was expensive. In fact when he looked at the clothes Olivia had picked out, most of them were very practical, especially for someone who had to wear a large medical boot thing on her leg.

Had Clodagh been hoping for something pretty? Damn, was she insulted by all this practicality? Or worse, was she after designer labels? Maybe she really was a gold-digger. Maybe she really had staged this all to get expensive presents out of him. Maybe he'd totally misjudged her.

"Who was with her today?" he asked, and Geraint radioed Phillips to come over. She was a sensible woman, formerly of the Royal Military Police. Maybe she'd said something to upset Clodagh.

"She got very upset when Khan brought the shopping back," Phillips said. "It didn't seem to be what she was expecting."

Jamie sagged onto the other sofa and glared at the pile of shopping bags. Dammit. How had he read her so wrong?

"With respect, sir, I think Lady Olivia might have… misjudged," Phillips went on.

"You don't say," Jamie muttered. "Well, take it all back, then—"

"I think she was expecting something more like this," Phillips went on, taking a crumpled piece of paper from her pocket and handing it over.

The handwriting was rounded and loopy, the kind teenage girls wrote Valentine's cards in. There was a list of very few items, each one with an estimated price next to it: *Multipack knickers (£2), multipack socks (£2), bra (less than £5), flat shoes/sneakers (less than £5), vaseline lip balm, (80p), facial moisturiser (£4)…*

Jamie thought he'd experienced shame before, but he'd never felt this awful hollow sickness. His face burned, his fingers curled into fists, and his vision blurred as he stared at Clodagh's list.

He folded it carefully into his pocket, then carefully picked up the top item in the nearest carrier bag. A lingerie set, made of lace scraps and costing nearly a hundred pounds.

Under that, another set, and another. A cashmere cardigan with a three figure price tag. Skincare products in packaging that didn't betray their pricing, except to discreetly proclaim they certainly cost more than £4.

He found the receipt and read it silently. There wasn't

a single item on here that cost less than the whole of Clodagh's careful little list.

He looked up, and met Phillips' gaze.

"I'll bring the car round, sir," she said.

Jamie had never subscribed to the idea that crossing the border into Essex meant taking one's life into one's own hands and defending oneself against an army of pikeys and chavs and whatever the tabloids were calling them these days. Having visited some ravishingly pretty parts of the county and met some terribly proud Essex-born flag-wavers at his brother's wedding, he wasn't about to knock the place.

But it was hard, driving into a town like Harlow.

The trees lining the road from the motorway couldn't quite disguise the Brutalist neglect of the place. Tower blocks winked at him through gaps in the sparse foliage. Christmas decorations flickered and flashed, even though Hallowe'en had barely passed. The roundabouts, of which there were a multitude, appeared to have had their signage nicked. Christ, the place even had a greyhound track.

He somehow wasn't surprised when one of the towerblocks turned out to be their destination. Washing hung from some of its balconies, tattered England flags fluttered limply from others, and most of them bristled with satellite dishes. A dog barked incessantly somewhere.

"I'd advise against leaving the car, sir," said Geraint from the front seat.

"Geraint, I survived Helmand Province, I can survive a council estate in Harlow," said Jamie.

"Sir, you got shot in Helmand Province," said Geraint.

"Actually it was shrapnel," said Jamie, but he took his PPO's point. A gang of youths passed, two bull terriers straining and snapping at each other in their midst.

"Oi! I said fucking stop it or I'll kick your fucking ribs in!" yelled one of the kids, and Jamie's hand was on the door handle before he could stop himself.

It wouldn't open. "Dammit, Geraint, unlock it! I'm not a child."

"No, sir, you're a prince of the realm and you don't get involved in private disputes," said Geraint.

"He was threatening that dog."

"I'll call the RSPCA. In the meantime, I suggest you call Miss Walsh and ask her to come down."

Jamie hated Geraint for being right. He got out his phone, called up Clodagh's number, and sat staring at it for ages. Crap. What was he supposed to say?

He opened a new text message instead. "*Hi Clodagh, it's Jamie.*" Duh, like she didn't already know that. "*I got home to find you'd gone. I do hope I didn't do anything to offend you...*"

No. Ugh. Coward's way out.

"*I got home to find you'd gone. I'm very sorry I offended you. Please come back to Cambridge because...*"

...because what? Because he missed her? Because he didn't want her living here? Because...?

"You may not need to call her, sir," said Phillips. "Look."

A figure emerged from the dark recesses of the tower's entrance, walking backwards and limping on a cumbersome boot, tugging something large out of a lift. A pushchair. A small child wearing a Spiderman costume ran out after them.

Jesus Christ, Clodagh had kids?

This time Geraint didn't stop him leaping out of the car, probably because he knew Jamie would have broken the window to do so.

"Clodagh?"

She froze. Jamie tugged on his beanie hat, hunched into his hoodie and checked he was wearing his glasses. Behind him, he heard one of the PPOs get out of the car.

Clodagh looked up, slowly. Despite his disguise, she still recognised him immediately. "What are you doing here?"

She had her hair scraped up into a plastic clip and wore a padded jacket with a cheap fake fur trim to the hood. The bruises on her face had been covered, inadequately, with make-up.

"I was…" Might as well be honest. "I was looking for you."

She crossed her arms across herself defensively. "Why? Tyler, come back here."

"But I want cherry Coke!"

"I want doesn't get," Clodagh said, and started walking, slowly, holding onto the pushchair for support. Jamie thought she was coming towards him, but she turned as soon as the concrete path let her, and veered away towards the road. "Come on, stay close. And stop playing with them fag ends." The path was littered with them.

"Auntie Shar, you're being so slow!" the child cried.

Auntie. The boy wasn't hers. Was the baby? He peered inside the pushchair, where a child swaddled in pink peered suspiciously up at him and sucked ferociously on a lollipop.

"My apologies," Clodagh muttered. She glanced back at Jamie, who stood watching. "Was there something you wanted?"

"I…" He made himself move, caught up and walked beside her. She glowered at him as he flipped his hood up. "I wanted to see if you were all right."

Clodagh gave him an incredulous look. "Well, here I am, all right. You know, us plebs have these things called 'phones'. You could have just called me."

"I suppose I could."

"Or got your butler to send a telegram," Clodagh muttered.

"I don't have a butler."

"Royal herald, then."

"Clodagh. I wanted to see you. Face to face."

"Why? Forgot what a black eye looks like? Tyler! What have I told you about roads?"

At her sharp shout, the child in the pushchair started crying. Clodagh glared at Jamie as if this was her fault, and started rocking the pushchair.

"What are you doing out this late with children?" Jamie asked. At this time of night, his niece and nephew were usually fast asleep, or at least that was what their nannies said.

"Hollee couldn't sleep and Tyler wanted cherry Coke," Clodagh said.

"Should he be drinking Coke at his age?"

Clodagh dealt him a look. He wasn't sure if she agreed with him or not.

"No, but my sister is an idiot and he's a little fucking brat and basically if he doesn't get what he wants he just screams the place down. He's already woken Hollee," she said, indicating the baby who had calmed down a bit, "so I said I'd take them out for a walk, get some fresh air."

"You shouldn't be walking. Where are your crutches?"

"Keisha and Neveah are playing Star Wars with them. Which is fun, because they both want to be Rey because they're both girls. Nobody wants to be Kylo Ren for some reason, not even Zayn, despite, and I quote, 'having a willy'. It's a far cry from when I was a kid and everyone wanted to be Han Solo and nobody wanted to be Princess Leia."

Jamie tried to process this. "I always wanted to be Luke Skywalker," he said, "but Ed usually got there first because he was blond."

"How fun for you," she said crisply. "Bet you had the proper lightsabres and everything."

Jamie had been given one signed by Mark Hamill for his fifth birthday. He did not volunteer this information to Clodagh.

"Why did he call you Auntie Shar?" he asked, and didn't imagine her stiffening.

"Um. Family nickname." Her shoulders hunched over. Not something she wanted to talk about.

"Look, I'm sorry about the clothes and things," he said. "I asked Oll to order you some stuff and I did tell her not to go over the top. I didn't think you'd appreciate it."

Clodagh snorted. "Sure, that stuff is probably cheap to you."

"Yeah," said Jamie simply. "It is."

Clodagh frowned uncertainly at him.

Jamie shoved his hands in his pockets. Pockets in a garment that had cost three times the total of the items on her shopping list. "I don't really have the same concept of money you do. I thought what Olivia bought you was reasonably priced." She snorted again. "I didn't even know you could get clothes as cheap as the ones you asked for."

Mulishly, Clodagh said, "You looked at my list?"

"Phillips showed me. I thought you were mad because none of the things I'd got you were expensive enough."

There was a silence, then Clodagh burst out laughing. "Not expensive enough? Jesus Christ, Jamie."

"Auntie Shar, don't swear!" shouted Tyler.

"Sorry," she wheezed. "Not expensive enough? That's brilliant. Did you think I was expecting, like, ballgowns? Tiaras? Bespoke, I dunno, glass slippers or something?"

Jamie shrugged, shoulders hunched over. "I don't know what I thought. I messed up. I'm sorry."

"Actually, your girlfriend messed up. You just paid for it."

"She's not my girlfriend." The denial came automatically.

"Could've fooled me."

"Could've fooled a lot of people. She's still not my girlfriend."

They walked in silence for a moment, or at least as near to silence as Hollee and Tyler would let them. A car, low-riding and pumping out hip-hop, slowed near them.

"Oi, Shard! That you babe?"

"No, I'm her evil twin Petunia," Clodagh yelled back.

"Where the fuck you been?"

Jamie glanced down into the car. The speaker wore three gold chains, had an unintelligible tattoo on his neck and wore enough nylon to spark a house fire.

Shard? What the hell kind of nickname was Shard? Because she was so sharp? So cutting?

"Somewhere less shitty than this, that's where I've been," Clodagh said, and in the glare of the sodium streetlamp she looked terribly weary.

"Too fucking good for us? You always was a stuck up twat," said the driver of the car, and sped off.

"See, Tyler doesn't tell him off for swearing," Clodagh said, starting to push the pram again. "Double standard. Christ, I hate this place."

"Then leave," said Jamie.

"Sure, leave. With all that money I have saved up, and all those prospects I have? Look at me, I can hardly flipping walk."

"That's temporary—"

"And the reason I can't walk," she went on, as if he

hadn't spoken, "is because the only place I could afford to live was in that shi—that *shirty* little flat with a Polish nail technician and her *flip*tard of a boyfriend, who threw me down the stairs when she wasn't available to be abused. You think I lived there by choice? Choice is a luxury, and I don't have it any more. I'm back in this crab bucket of a place."

"Crab bucket?" said Jamie, somewhat reflexively because his brain was processing that Lee Cunningham wasn't Clodagh's boyfriend after all.

"Yeah. You never put a lid on a bucket of crabs, because if one tries to climb out the others just pull it back in." She made a yanking motion with her hands. "You don't escape places like this. Not for long, anyway. Tyler! Wait for me."

They'd reached a parade of shops. Clodagh thrust the pushchair in Jamie's direction, said, "Hold onto that, the brake's broken. I hear you're great with kids," and disappeared inside a convenience store after her nephew.

Jamie glanced around and saw Phillips a few feet away, pretending to smoke a cigarette. She'd slipped on a casual jacket and was doing a much better job of blending in than he was. She nodded at him, then resumed gazing around in apparent aimlessness.

He looked down at the occupant of the pushchair, who was probably about two years old, wearing a hot pink Puffa jacket and sparkly wellies. On her head was a tiara with blue plastic gemstones in it. Her ears bore gold rings. The lollipop she was sucking had left a pink sticky mess all around her mouth.

He was kind of rubbish with kids, truth be told. Sure, there were nicely staged photo opportunities of him playing with Alexander and Georgina, and according to Khan the odds on Annemarie giving birth to a boy and calling it James were pretty good. But he never had a clue what to say to children, especially ones too small to talk back coherently.

"And have you come far?" Jamie asked her politely.

The child's face crumpled. "Mummy!" she cried.

"Ah, Mummy will be back soon," he said, bobbing down and smiling encouragingly. "She's just taken young Tyler in for some inadvisably sugary drinks, or maybe she hasn't because I'm not sure if she's Mummy or maybe Auntie Shar? Or Shard? Is she?"

"Mummeeeeee!"

"Yes, um, I'm sure she'll be here soon," Jamie said desperately. He fumbled for his phone. "Look! Wouldn't you like to play with this? It's all shiny."

Hollee immediately grabbed for it, all sorrow forgotten. She jabbed delightedly at the screen.

"Don't drop it, it's a prototype," he said, and looked up in relief to find Clodagh exiting the shop with Tyler, who slurped noisily from a drinks can.

"Why am I not surprised?" she said, tucking a bag under the pushchair. "Don't break it, Hollee, it's expensive. And it's not yours. You might never get it back," she added to Jamie.

"A small price to pay for silence."

Clodagh groaned as she took the handle and turned the conveyance round to head back to the tower block. "She's done nothing but cry since I got here. If it's not her it's one of the others."

"How…" How to put this? "How many are there?"

"About seventy, or maybe that's just how it feels. Charlene has three, Whitney has three, including Tyler here, and this little snotball belongs to my sister Kylie, who is expecting a boy in a few months time. So that makes seven, soon to be eight, and those are just the ones actually related to me. Apparently my brother Scott has a new girlfriend who has three kids, so I'm sure we'll have the joy of their presence soon too. And Tony's bloody shady about his love life, so I wouldn't be surprised if there's a bun in whatever oven he's been sneaking off to see."

Jamie became aware he was staring. "You… do you all… live together?"

"Yeah, kinda. In a couple of blocks, anyway. Scott and Charlene are over in Spring Hills, and yes, those are really the names my mother gave her twins. It was the eighties. What can I say."

"Jesus," muttered Jamie.

"You want Jesus, he's over there," she said, pointing to a building that looked like a community centre but whose signage proclaimed it to be a church.

He couldn't think of anything to say after that. He walked with her back to the bleak tower block she apparently now called home, trying to find a way to tell her she didn't belong here and failing because there was no way he could make that sound anything other than patronising and privileged.

All of a sudden Clodagh lunged at her nephew, who Jamie hadn't been paying much attention to.

"Give me that phone!"

Hollee started crying in the pushchair. Jamie remembered he'd given her his phone, and now Tyler had it, and he was dancing away from Clodagh who was incapable of following properly with her broken ankle.

"No! I'm talking to Granny!"

"That's not your granny," Clodagh said desperately, as Jamie realised with a kind of comic horror who he was talking to.

"Shit shit shit—" Jamie made a leap for the kid, who twisted away from him.

"Don't swear," Clodagh said. "Tyler, give me the phone."

"No!"

"It's not yours. It belongs to my friend here. Please give me the phone."

Tyler listened to something from the phone and giggled. "It's my Auntie Shar. No I dunno." He peered up at Jamie. "Are you Jimmy?"

No one called him Jimmy, but maybe with a very posh accent it might sound like…"Yes! Yes, I'm Jimmy. Jamie. Can I have my phone, please?"

Tyler frowned, listened to something else, then said, "'kay," and handed it back.

Swearing under his breath, Jamie grabbed it and pressed it to his ear. It was sticky. "Granny? I'm so sorry. My friend's kids were playing with my phone, I didn't realise they'd dialled it…"

His grandmother hooted with laughter. "Jamie, really. I wondered what on earth was going on."

Well, thank God she was in a good mood. "I think he thought he was dialling his granny… I'm so sorry."

"No, it's all fun and games. I needed something to smile about after the Diplomatic Reception, it was dull as dishwater this year. How's Cambridge?"

"Oh, it's…" Jamie glanced around at the tower blocks, the orange streetlights and the woman in the fur-trimmed Puffa laughing at him, "great. You know. Dreaming spires and all that."

"Isn't that Oxford? Oh… I've got to go, darling, Grandpa can't find his slippers. Do call me soon."

And she hung up. Jamie pressed his hand to his face, eyes squeezed shut.

"That wasn't Granny," said Tyler.

"No, love, it was someone else's granny."

"She talks funny. Is she a nimmigrant?"

"Uh," said Clodagh.

"Yes, she's from Germany," said Jamie, uncovering his face. He met Clodagh's eye and she grinned, which forced a laugh from him. "Yes, well. That's something he can dine out on when he's older."

"You bet." Clodagh looked like she was going to say

something else, but then her phone rang, and she answered it, her smile fading. "I'm outside. Well, I can't walk very fast, can I? No, she's still awake. I dunno, Kyles, I'm not the baby whisperer."

She talked a bit more, looking more and more tired with every word. Five siblings, seven nieces and nephews, all claustrophobically cooped up in a building with badly-spelled anti-immigrant graffiti on the wall.

"I've got to go," Clodagh said to Jamie, and gave him a bit of a smile as she pushed the baby towards the front door.

"I'll help you—"

"Trust me, you don't want get in a lift that smells of piss. And you really don't want to get caught up with my whole... family... thing. Go back to Cambridge, study your computers, be a prince, eat four kinds of mustard. Have a nice life."

And with that she walked away, heavy on her injured leg, not turning back to look at him.

CHAPTER EIGHT

The text came twenty minutes after she left Prince Jamie standing there on the cracked pavement outside the tower block. She'd peered out through Tony's bedroom window, but the big black car had already left by the time she reached her mum's flat.

"*Which one was your favourite?*"

She blinked at her phone. Which what? Which of her many irritating family members? Which contestant on the terrible talent show her mum and sister were watching? While she tried to work it out, her phone buzzed again.

"*Mustard, I mean. Dijon is nice in sandwiches but you've got to have American for hot dogs.*"

Clodagh stared at her phone. On the TV, someone began slaughtering an Adele hit. "*What kind of sandwich has mustard in it?*" she typed, slowly.

"Mum, this is rubbish, put *Geordie Shore* on," said Whitney, and Clodagh winced.

"No. You know I won't have that rubbish on."

"But all my friends—"

"I don't care about your friends. It's—what is it,

Shar?"

"Manipulative bollocks," Clodagh murmured. "Edited to create drama. Neither reflective nor indicative of real life." Her phone buzzed again.

"*The best kind, obvs. Good with ham.*"

"Yeah, and it's cruel to all them kids. What must their mums think?"

"*I noticed you had three kinds of that.*"

"*I like the honey-roasted one. Olivia will only eat organic.*"

Whitney muttered under her breath about how it was called reality TV after all.

"*And the turkey ham?*"

There was a pause. "*Okay don't laugh at me.*"

"Who you texting?" Whitney wanted to know.

"Uh, someone from the pub." Clodagh angled her phone away. "About going back to work."

"Thought you was staying here?" said her mum, not looking away from the TV.

"Yeah just until I get things sorted," Clodagh said absently as her phone buzzed in her hand.

"*The college cat likes turkey ham.*"

Clodagh stifled a laugh. "*You buy turkey ham just for a cat? They don't have Whiskas where you live?*"

"*You laugh, but my dad used to grow a certain kind of apple just because the horses liked it best.*"

"*How the other half live,*" she texted back, and immediately regretted it.

This time the pause was longer. Then an animated gif of Scrooge McDuck swimming in gold coins popped up, and she couldn't quite contain her giggles.

The next day dawned far too early. Clodagh had given up trying to sleep in her old room, where her single bed had been replaced with a child's bunk for whichever grandchildren happened to be staying at the time. Right now it was Nevaeh, who hadn't forgiven Clodagh for failing to get the purple doll she wanted for her birthday and played noisy videogames all night.

Clodagh had decamped to the living room, where she'd been woken in the middle of the night by Tony stumbling in, smelling of weed. This at least made a change because the living room, despite her mother swearing blind she'd given up the fags, always smelled of stale smoke. Then again neither the curtains nor the carpet had been changed or cleaned since Clodagh could remember.

She barely seemed to have got back to sleep when Nevaeh came charging in to put some horrendously noisy cartoon on the TV. Asking her to turn it down resulted in a tantrum. Whitney arrived to retrieve her, complained that Clodagh hadn't given her breakfast, and set off having a loud slanging match over the phone with someone who might have been her new boyfriend.

Clodagh, her head splitting, reached for her painkillers and found the packet empty.

"Mum, where are my painkillers?"

"Oh, I had a… you know," her mum mimed 'period pain', "and I couldn't find any paracetamol, but yours've got codeine in 'em, haven't they love?"

"They did," Clodagh said pointedly, which set her mum off into a sulk. *She's letting you stay here for free. Don't be bitchy.*

Her ankle hurt after yesterday's ill-advised exercise. Getting more painkillers—which wouldn't have codeine in them this time—would involve more exercise. *No Amazon Prime Now here, either.* What would Lady Olivia think of this place?

Her phone buzzed. Ugh, if it was Charlene asking her to take the kids to school she could—

It was a photo of a grumpy-looking tabby cat eating a piece of ham.

"*Should I call him Bernard, or Matthew?*" Jamie asked.

She thought for a moment, then typed back, "*Call him Bustopher Jones.*"

"*Because he's remarkably fat?*"

Clodagh grinned. Probably, Jamie was referring to the original TS Eliot poems, and not the touring production of *Cats* which had come to the Harlow Playhouse when Clodagh was a kid, but that didn't matter right now.

"*Because he's the Lady Mathilda Street cat,*" she replied, and Jamie replied with an applauding emoji.

Most of her nieces and nephews were of school age, although there permanently seemed to be at least one of them excluded or off sick or kept home because of some dispute or other. Today it was Zayn, the youngest of her sister Charlene's three kids. Char launched into a long-winded and complicated explanation of precisely who at school he was being kept home to avoid, but Clodagh tuned out after the fourth, "And then she turned around and said," and asked the kid if he wanted to watch *Paw Patrol*.

It had been a big hit last time she'd babysat Zayn, but apparently now he was six he'd grown right out of it. Hollee, the baby of the family at two and a half, was quite happy with *Peppa Pig*, but Zayn declared it 'for babies and girls,' which made Hollee cry.

Clodagh looked desperately at the clock. Far too early to start drinking.

"I don't suppose you'd go and get me some more painkillers?" she asked her mother, who was scowling at a collection of DVD covers with the wrong discs inside.

"Shar, I'm busy. And Scott's bringing over Kayleigh in a minute. She's got chickenpox."

"I thought they vaccinated against that these days?" Clodagh said.

"Yeah but Kayleigh's mum don't believe in vaccines. Says they cause… what is it?"

"Immunity," Clodagh said. "That's what they cause. With a side effect of life."

Her mum frowned at her. "You don't half come back funny from Cambridge," she said. "Anyway. How long you staying for?"

Clodagh looked at the blankets and pillows she'd folded on the sofa, which were now being used by Zayn to make a pillow fort, and said, "Just until I find a new place."

Eventually she got the bus into town, just to get away from Zayn's determined tormenting of his cousins, on the flimsy pretext of buying calamine lotion. Poor Kayleigh was covered in chickenpox blisters, which she kept scratching at and bursting, in a manner which upset little Hollee and made Zayn point and laugh. She was pretty sure he was tickling her whenever Clodagh turned her back.

"Take Holls with you, will you babes?" said her mum, and Clodagh agreed, if only because the pushchair had storage space so she wouldn't have to carry any bags.

She put her earbuds in and her hood up and limped to the bus stop. Walking hurt like she'd been kicked with every step, she found herself standing up and jostled on the bus, and then Hollee decided to have a tantrum and try to get herself out of the pushchair before they'd even got inside the shopping centre.

Clodagh knew she shouldn't bribe a toddler with sweets, but she did anyway because it shut the little screamer up for long enough to go and buy some proper painkillers.

"Want one!" Hollee said, as she watched Clodagh pop the capsule of sweet, sweet codeine out of its packaging.

"No. These are for grown-ups."

"Want one want one want one!"

Clodagh swallowed them dry, tried to count to ten, lost her patience at three and snarled, "Shut up, you little shit!"

An older woman walking past snapped, "No wonder she behaves like that if that's the language you use," and three teenagers sniggered at her.

Clodagh's fists balled up. She turned to yell at the woman, then caught sight of herself in a shop window.

Pramface. The screaming baby, the cheap parka, the bruised face, the snarl, the scraped back hair. She'd basically turned into the thing she feared the most. Give her a pair of giant gold hoop earrings and the transformation would be complete.

Right then her phone buzzed in her pocket. Probably Mum, after something from the shops, or one of her sisters begging for a school pick-up.

"Hunter the American wants to know if the 'hot barmaid' will be in the pub tonight. Whatever do I tell him?"

Jamie. Of all the places to conjure him up, the shopping centre in Harlow was probably the least likely. *He probably has shops closed specially for his private perusal*, she thought, formulating her reply as she shuffled slowly towards a coffee shop with free wi-fi.

Slowly sipping the cheapest thing on the menu whilst Hollee made a mess of a muffin, Clodagh slowly typed, *"Tell him Maja only works Saturdays, and Tania is gay."*

"I will," he replied, *"but I think the correct reply is, 'She's moved back to her mum's.'"*

Heat flashed through her—*Jamie thinks I'm hot?!*— and then she remembered her reflection in that window. *"He wouldn't call me hot if he saw me right now,"* she typed, then deleted it without sending. *"Tell him he's a sexual harassment case waiting to happen,"* she sent instead.

"*Ruchi already told him. She says she's going to create a computer virus and call it Hunter.*"

Clodagh laughed at that. Hunter seemed to think that being a Cambridge PhD student made him more important than everyone else he spent time with, which was interesting since most of the people he spent time with were also Cambridge PhD students.

One of whom was a prince. She'd forgotten that while he was texting her.

"*Would it pop up on your screen uninvited and ask you patronising questions?*" she asked.

"*Yes. And it would keep going until it found something you didn't know and ridicule you for it.*"

"*But when you asked it the answer it wouldn't know either, because that kind of knowledge is beneath it.*"

"*It would then,*" Jamie went on, "*tell you to be flattered it is interested in you.*"

Clodagh groaned. "*That's not just Hunter—*" she backtracked, "*the Hunter virus, that's pretty much every man who comes into the Prince's Arms.*"

There was a pause, and Clodagh sipped anxiously at her coffee. She'd gone too far.

Then, "*Men are arseholes. All of them.*"

"*Even you?*"

"*No. Not me. I'm a prince among men.*"

She groaned out loud and sent him an eye-rolling emoji.

"*Ask anyone. They'll tell you Jamie Wales is an absolute prince.*"

"*He's an absolute something,*" she replied, and got a laughing emoji in response.

Finishing her coffee, she got up, and her phone buzzed again. Eagerly she picked it up, but this time it actually was her mum.

"*can u go aldis need babywipes.*"

Clodagh pinched the bridge of her nose. Babywipes she could get anywhere. The pound shop if Mum didn't want to spend Boots money. She began to reply, when her phone buzzed again.

This time it was a photo of a long shopping list, with the caption, "*& these ta.*"

Clodagh muttered a few uncomplimentary things under her breath, sighed, and typed back in the affirmative. She used up a bit more of the coffee shop's bandwidth looking up the bus route to Aldi, and then from Aldi back home. It involved a lot more walking than she was really happy with, but at least she wasn't sitting at home listening to Zayn and Kayleigh torture each other.

In the supermarket, she filled the tray below Hollee's pushchair, then started balancing things on top of the folded canopy because there were no baskets. She had to concentrate so hard not not knocking it off that she didn't see a trolley coming towards her. It, almost inevitably, hit her ankle.

"Look where you're going," snapped the man pushing it as pain shot through Clodagh despite the padded boot.

Clodagh bit back her retort and moved on. Five minutes later, as she was checking the list again, the same thing happened.

"Ow," she said pointedly this time, gesturing to the large, padded and very visible cast on her ankle. A can of beans fell off the pushchair and rolled under a display.

"Sor-*ry*," said the woman with the trolley, looking anything but. "If you wasn't looking at your phone you'da seen me."

Clodagh stared at her phone, willing a cheerful text from Jamie to arrive. It did not. Then again, phones couldn't send messages to places that didn't exist, and Jamie probably didn't even know what Aldi was.

Hollee started crying at the check-out, which harassed Clodagh into forgetting she was supposed to pack after she'd paid, which meant the person behind her jostled her and her ankle, tested to its limit, let out such a crackle of pain she sobbed out loud.

"God, don't over-react," muttered the girl behind her, and Clodagh snapped.

"You see this?" she said, pointing to the cast. "You think this is some kind of fashion statement? You see these too?" She pointed to the bruises on her face. "I'm not just fucking clumsy with the eyeshadow, love, I got pushed down the stairs three days ago and I broke my ankle and I have nowhere to live and this place is a shithole and if you don't stop crying, Hollee, I'm going to abandon you in the fucking car park!"

A slight hush fell. Clodagh realised her voice had risen to a scream.

"You're still blocking the queue though," said the cashier, and Clodagh snarled at her.

But she paid, with cash she'd never get back from her mum, and packed her groceries and hobbled outside in search of a bench to collapse on.

There were none. And even if there had been, a handsome prince would never turn up to rescue her again.

She leaned against the wall, trying to get the weight off her throbbing ankle, and spent a few minutes trying not to cry. Then a hand touched her arm, and she looked up to see a woman in a hijab peering at her in concern.

"There's a charity does accommodation for victims of domestic violence," she said. "You can call them freephone. Do you want me to look up the number?"

For a second Clodagh stared at her. Then she gathered her wits and said, "No, it's okay. He's not… I'm staying at my mum's. I'm okay. I just… had a…"

"Bad moment?" guessed the woman.

"Yeah. Bad moment. Thanks, though. You're the first person today who hasn't just yelled at me. Like any of this is my own choice."

She gave a bit of a smile. "Some people don't know how lucky they are. Okay then. If you're sure."

Clodagh reassured her she was, and watched her take her shopping back to her car. Then she straightened up and went in search of the bus stop.

CHAPTER NINE

"Jamie!" Annemarie enveloped him in such an enthusiastic hug he worried she'd go into labour several months prematurely. "It's so good to see you. How is Cambridge?"

"*Het is goed, bedankt*," he said, and she laughed, sitting carefully back down on the striped sofa in her Kensington Palace living room.

"You're still trying to learn Dutch?"

"Hey, trying? I started trying the minute Ed said he was going to marry you. I did my whole official visit there in Dutch."

Annemarie made a rocking 'kind of' motion with her hand. "I was there, Jamie. You didn't really."

"Well, I tried."

"You're very trying." That was Edward, wandering into the room and straightening his tie. He'd just flown home from Wales, where he'd been visiting old colleagues and people his team had rescued from Snowdonia, and to Jamie's irritation, he looked immaculate in a suit five minutes later. "Are you ready?"

Jamie glanced down at his suit, which as far as he

could tell was identical to the other three suits Vincent had laid out then decided against. "Yep. Let's go and watch a crappy film."

"Hey, it might be all right. It's got that guy Annemarie likes, the one off the kid's show…"

"That doesn't narrow it down much. Or is there only one kid's show in your nursery?"

"If Nanny Christensen had her way there would be none," Annemarie said, getting to her feet and pausing for a moment, looking pale.

"Are you all right?"

"I'm fine. The baby is having fun with my sciatic nerve."

Nanny Christensen was waiting with the children, both hyper-excited at being allowed to stay up past bedtime. Little Alexander was in knee socks and shorts —because despite it being November he wasn't allowed to wear trousers until he went to prep school—his sister in a velvet party dress. They walked slowly out to the car, chattering nineteen-to-the-dozen, and Jamie watched the careful way Annemarie bent over the back seat as Georgina was fastened in.

"It's worse than last time," Edward confided in a low voice as they went forward to the second car. "She's had physio and acupuncture but it's not doing a lot of good. I don't think she'll be out much after this."

"I don't blame her." Annemarie had made public appearances right up until the last weeks of her first pregnancy, but retired much earlier when she was expecting Georgina and now it looked as if she'd be spending the next few months doing precious little.

"Then again, I think three children is enough," Jamie added cheerfully, and Edward looked as if he was going to say something, then thought better of it.

"Well, three was good enough for Granny," he said.

Annemarie had elected to travel with the children and

Nanny Christensen in the carefully adapted seven-seater Range Rover Sport Ed's family usually used. Jamie watched his brother sprawl out in the back seat of their own Range Rover and sigh in happiness.

"I'd forgotten what having room to yourself in a car felt like."

Jamie laughed. "Ed, you arrived by yourself last week in a Bentley for the football. I saw you."

Edward shrugged unrepentantly. "If a man can't go by himself to the footie, what can he do?"

"Especially when he's the president of the FA," Jamie added idly. Not that either of them were ever alone, not really. There was always a PPO and usually a secretary or assistant of some kind. Which was why Cambridge was so refreshing… "Did you win?"

"No! Two goals ruled offside but he let Kane's through, and then the jammy sod scored another in the 93rd. 93rd! I'm going to lobby for extra time goals to be disqualified."

Jamie nodded seriously, then said, "I have no idea what you just said."

His brother rolled his eyes. "Yes, well, memorise and repeat, because when someone asks you, you'll need to sound like you know."

"Bloody 93rd," Jamie repeated obediently. "Kane offside! Grr." He shook his fist for good measure, and Edward laughed. "All right, but you count to ten in binary," Jamie dared him.

"I am quite happy to say I can't," Edward said cheerfully.

The film was the premiere of an adaptation of a popular children's TV show. Jamie had ended up escorting Annemarie and the children to watch some of it being filmed whilst Edward was off in Syria or somewhere getting shot at. "Not sure which of us got off the lighter," he'd confided after his return.

141

Jamie, who'd been shot at quite a bit in Afghanistan, considered the screaming excitement of the children and the banality of the filming process, and said, "*Comme-ci, comme-ça.*"

The car slowed as it reached Leicester Square. Jamie rolled his shoulders, watched Ed checking his hair in the mirror, and peered at himself. Tie wonky, hair already a mess. Vincent would despair.

Still, at least it wasn't raining. Jamie recalled the first time he'd gone to a premiere, excited to meet filmstars, and the shampoo used to clean the carpet had frothed everywhere in the rain. Vincent had been livid.

"Ready?" he said as they pulled up.

"I was born ready," Edward quipped.

I bloody wasn't, Jamie thought, but kept that to himself as the door opened and his smile switched itself on automatically.

He and Edward stood side by side, smiling and waving at a sea of flashing cameras. Jamie's grandmother had related to him once how when she was his age, walking down a red carpet meant crushing spent flashbulbs under her shoes. It was still, she said, an improvement on today's culture of snapping pictures of everything on your smartphone.

Edward turned back to help Annemarie out of the second car, then lifted out Georgina as Nanny Christensen brought Alexander round. Professionals even at the ages of four and two, the children stood beaming for the cameras. Audible cries of, "Aww!" floated across the hubbub.

Then they started forward, and the Your Highnessing began.

"Your Highness, is it a boy or a girl?" "Your Highness, did you save any refugees in Syria?" "Your Highness, how's your new school, buddy?"

They smiled and waved some more and ignored the

paparazzi as much as possible. But then it was the turn of the general public, these days mostly just a sea of smartphone camera flashes and hands reaching out across the metal barriers.

"Prince Jamie, ohmigod I love you!"

"Your Highness, can I get a selfie?"

"Oh my gawd, should she be wearing heels like that when she's pregnant?"

Jamie shook a few hands, posed for a few photos, caught Georgina as she ran towards him and swung her into his arms.

The camera flashes nearly blinded him. Little Georgina rubbed her eyes, making a face.

"She looks tired, it's too late for her to be out!" said one woman near Jamie.

"Are you looking forward to a new brother or sister, sweetie?"

"You should be raising the child gender-neutral and let them decide for themselves," someone else shouted, and Jamie stepped smartly back as someone shouted abuse at them.

"Let's go and see what Mummy's doing," he said loudly to Georgina, taking her back to Annemarie.

She was holding Alexander's hand and talking to the public, smiling in a way that didn't in any way betray the pain she'd been in as they left the palace. Her heels weren't even that high, Jamie thought as he carried Georgina over, to awws from the crowd.

Someone asked her a question in Dutch, which Jamie only half understood. He'd made an effort to learn his sister-in-law's language when it became clear she was going to become part of the family, but she'd given herself whole-heartedly to Englishness and rarely spoke her mother tongue. Even on visits home she spoke English to the public, keeping Dutch for formal state occasions.

Jamie wondered idly what his family would think if he married a foreign princess and devoted his life to her country instead of his own. Annemarie was admittedly a minor member of the Dutch royal family—only a countess, as she'd told him many times—but her allegiance had apparently upset some of her senior relatives.

"You look so cute with her!" cooed a woman holding up a small boy over the metal barrier, and Jamie smiled automatically down at Georgina. Her attention was, however, taken by the star of the movie, who'd just appeared to a great roar of excitement.

"Put me down!" she cried, and he did, letting Edward take over.

"When are you going to settle down and have some of your own, Your Highness?" the woman with the little boy asked.

"Oh, not for a while," Jamie replied easily.

"Yes, but you're getting older now. Past thirty. Tick tock!"

Fuck off, thought Jamie, but he said, "Well, it's Victoria's turn first, surely?" which was a rotten thing to do because it set the woman off into speculations about how long Victoria had been married and why there weren't any children yet.

Jamie moved off, smiling and waving and shaking hands and posing for selfies until at least he was at the entrance to the cinema, away from the screaming hordes. Various celebrities were having their pictures taken in front of the film's logo, and he was swept ahead of them all as a priority.

Even celebrities gushed over him. *Christ, I'm tired of all this*, he thought, smiling and agreeing with one veteran actor that not every movie one made needed to be Oscar fodder.

"So long as it pays the bills. Not that you need to

worry about that, eh, Your Highness?"

Jamie, who'd once been the subject of a week's furious opinion pieces because he'd been photographed drinking expensive champagne on a yacht, just smiled a bit more. The fact that the champagne had been provided by the yacht's owner and not paid for by the Privy Purse didn't seem to make any difference. He'd had to wear conspicuous high street labels for months after that, just to ram the point home.

Not that Clodagh would agree that any of his choices had been cheap.

Annemarie made her way over with an over-excited Georgina, and he had to pose for photos with them. Then with Alexander when he came racing up. Then again with Edward.

When Annemarie muttered from the side of her mouth, in Dutch, "I'm going home after this, my back is fucking killing me," Jamie nearly sighed with relief.

"I'll escort you," he said, glancing at his watch. He was supposed to be staying at the palace tonight, but he could probably be back in Cambridge before the film was even over. Back for a pint and a smile from Clodagh

—

No. Bugger.

Feeling slightly flat at the thought of not seeing her, he followed Annemarie's entourage through the cinema and straight out to the back where the car was waiting for them.

"Isn't that the guy from the film?" he said, as a tired looking man ahead of them stripped off his tie and collapsed into a car of his own.

"I don't think I've ever been to a premiere where the stars don't leave before the start," Annemarie replied.

She was quiet in the car, eyes closed, head back. Jamie drummed his fingers on his thigh, then got out his phone, switched it to silent, and opened Clodagh's last text message.

"*Please help me. I need to talk to someone sane. I've just taken my neiflings to a film premiere.*"

Her reply came back quickly. "*Please tell me it was a Quentin Tarantino.*" Followed by, "*Neifling is a nice word.*"

He laughed silently. "*Yeah. Ed's furious. Said they shouldn't learn about blood-spatter until they're at least seven.*"

"*Right now I'd kill for some fictional violence. It's been kid's TV here all day long. Why is it SO bright? And SO high-pitched?*"

"*Right? Imagine eighty minutes of that, trapped in your seat, surrounded by the press.*" He wondered if there had been any decent swag at this screening. Usually it was a bottle of water and a paltry amount of popcorn, but once he'd got an action figure and Victoria still used the little handmirror she'd got from some premiere years ago because she fancied the actor on the back of it.

Clodagh sent a gif of a cat leaping away from a cucumber in horror. "*The cat is me. The cucumber is the film. Tell me what it was so I can be ill the day my lot want to go see it.*"

He was mid-text when they arrived back at the palace, smiling over Clodagh's assertion that too much *Peppa Pig* made her want to eat bacon. Trying to think of a way to offer her a bacon sandwich that didn't sound rude or suggestive, he looked up to find Annemarie watching him with interest.

"Quite the conversation you're having there," she said.

Jamie's cheeks heated. "Just a friend," he said, putting his phone away. "I didn't want to disturb you. How are you feeling?"

Annemarie's expression said she wasn't fooled by the

change in subject. "Tired, and wondering why I thought a third child was a good idea," she said, as he helped her out of the car. "Are you staying here tonight?"

"Yes. No." He wanted to go home, and home wasn't here any more. "What am I doing tomorrow?"

She shrugged eloquently. "I don't know. Major Peaseman will tell you. I have child refugees and Edward has soldiers."

Jamie ran a hand through his hair. "I have homeless. I think. In... I want to say Coventry?" Was that closer to Cambridge, or here? Dammit, he'd end up staying here anyway. Cambridge wasn't on the way to anywhere.

"Has Edward talked to you about the Royal Variety?" she asked.

"No, why? You're doing it this..." he trailed off, realising. Annemarie was retiring from public life very soon, and the Royal Variety Performance was due to be filmed in three or four weeks.

"I don't think I can manage sitting still for that long," she said. "And then the meet and greet afterwards... no. Tonight was more than I could take."

"Maybe Vicky and Nick could go?" Jamie asked hopefully. His grandmother rarely bothered these days and as his mother positively loathed the whole thing his father wouldn't go alone. He and his siblings had taken it on over the last decade or so, occasionally relieved by an aunt or uncle. Jamie usually got off lightly, being the only single one of the bunch.

"Victoria was very clear that she had another commitment," Annemarie said drily, and began ticking off relatives on her fingers. "Thomas is in Afghanistan, Anthony is in New Zealand, Isabella is still on maternity leave, The Duke of Kent flatly refuses and the Penelope has her medical treatments starting then."

Ah yes, Aunt Penelope and her never-ending litany of medical complaints. He hoped this one wasn't serious.

They usually weren't, but sooner or later her hypochondria was going to catch them all out.

"He wants you to go with him. Just like you did the first time, he said. The two boys together."

Yeah, when he was eighteen and thought it was all fun and exciting and that he'd get to properly meet Girls Aloud...

"I'll think about it. See what Peaseman says."

He walked Annemarie to her apartments, refused her offer of a nightcap and kissed her cheek.

"Is there a girl?" she asked, before she shut the door.

"A girl?" Jamie said stupidly. *Her name is Clodagh and she likes bacon and musicals about cats and hates children's TV.*

"You were smiling at your phone. Or is it a boy?"

Her expression was innocent.

"You're being very Dutch," Jamie said, shaking his head and stepping back. "*Slaap lekker.*"

"*Slaap lekker*," Annemarie said, closing the door with a thoughtful look on her face.

CHAPTER TEN

Historygal blog: Anne's Seventeen Little Hopes

My mum has six children. When I tell people that, their eyes go wide and their heads tilt to one side, as if they're wondering whether to send a package of condoms or birth control pills to her house.

Six kids wasn't always considered unusual. At a time when infant mortality was terribly high, you might pop them out in the hopes that some might survive infancy. In the 17th century over 12% of children would die in their first year, and a whopping 60% before they reached adulthood; and that's if you were lucky enough to have a live birth.

Just think about that for a minute. All that pushing and screaming and hoping and praying, and there's a 60% chance the child will never live to see children of their own.

Queen Anne was the last of the Stuarts. And not for want of trying: history has recorded at least seventeen pregnancies, and yet she died, as it's dustily noted, 'without issue'. Here's the story of those seventeen little hopes…

Googling Clodagh would be wrong. It felt wrong, anyway. Of course, there was nothing to stop him reading the meticulously compiled dossier his security team had already compiled on her, which was probably so comprehensive it'd tell him her favourite brand of shampoo and what her first word had been, but Jamie never read those things out of principle. It felt like spying.

Looking her up would be the same, despite a general consensus in the lab last week that everyone did it. "We don't all have James Bond to do it for us," Hunter had said to him.

"Bond is MI6. It's 5 who compile information on subjects within the UK," Jamie replied absently, then felt their eyes on him. "I mean… I don't read them. Look, why don't you just talk to the person you fancy? Find things out that way?"

"Talk to girls?" Zheng said, horrified.

"Boys don't talk to geek girls, unless to insult them," Ruchi said sadly.

"She might come across as normal, and then turn out to have dumped her last three boyfriends for leaving socks on the floor," Hunter said.

"Then don't leave socks on the floor," Ruchi said.

He'd left them to it and concentrated on his work. Or at least, tried to. Now, in the back of the car on his way to Corby—not Coventry, as it happened—the temptation to look her up was almost overwhelming.

He put his iPad down, folded the cover over determinedly, and picked up the report on the charity he was going to visit.

Clodagh was woken by two small children giggling and whispering, but before she could see what time it was, they'd thrown themselves onto the sofa. The sofa Clodagh was trying to sleep on, under a duvet that concealed the ankle she'd freed from its boot last night.

"Jesus fucking Christ!" she yelped, throwing both kids off as agony exploded through her. One of them crashed into the coffee table and started wailing. The other one shouted, "Granneeee! Auntie Sharday said a bad word!"

You chuck a small human onto a broken ankle and tell me what words you'd fucking say, Clodagh wanted to shout, but her breath was robbed by the pain.

"My leg hurts!" wailed whichever one had landed on the coffee table.

Not as badly as mine, Clodagh thought, trying to sit up and failing because moving her leg at all was agony.

"What is going on out here? What's all this shouting?" yelled Clodagh's mother from the corridor. She stormed in, a vision in cheap pink satin and leopard print. "Who started it?"

"Auntie Sharday!" said Nevaeh, the little snitch, as Kayleigh wailed and sobbed on the floor.

Sharon Walsh gave her daughter a frankly disbelieving look, which was encouraging at least, and knelt down by Kayleigh. "All right, where does it hurt?"

By the time she'd ascertained that Kayleigh wasn't about to die and didn't have any bones sticking out and didn't even need a sticking plaster (apparently, they had Olaf the snowman on them and were, therefore, to be greatly desired), Clodagh's ankle had downgraded from Nuclear to Agonising, and she managed to pull the duvet back to look at it.

"Eurgh!" shouted Nevaeh, pointing, and Clodagh was inclined to agree.

Her ankle joint had been swollen and bruised before, but now it had a massive goose-egg above the ankle bone and was as ripe and purple as a plum. Very carefully, she tried to wiggle her toes, and a sob of pain escaped her.

"Jesus, Shar! Is it supposed to look like that?"

Clodagh shook her head and managed, "I don't think so."

"You was limping a bit yesterday. Was you supposed to walk that far on it?"

Bit late to ask that now! Clodagh bit down on her own lip to keep the retort inside. Instead she said, "People kept hitting it with their trolleys in Aldi."

"Seriously? I'd've given them what-for."

"I did. Made no difference. And Kayleigh, look, I'm sorry I knocked you over, but you just landed right on my ankle and it really hurts, love, all right?"

"Mine hurts worse," Kayleigh said immediately, lower lip jutting out.

"Don't think it does, love," said Sharon. "I'll get you some paracetamol, babes," she said to Clodagh, who thought that would be about as effective as an Olaf plaster, but nodded anyway.

Her mum made the kids sit on the floor to eat their cereal, which they did with their noses three inches from the TV. When Whitney arrived to take Nevaeh to school she looked at Clodagh, still in her pyjamas on the sofa, and said, "Wish I could lie around all day like you, Shar. I've been up since six."

"So have I," Clodagh said, and tried moving her ankle again. It was still unsuccessful.

"Yeah, but you ain't even dressed yet." Whitney herself was dressed like the Tammy Girl icon of Clodagh's pre-teens, in high-waisted jeans and a cropped polo-neck that revealed a belly-piercing. It didn't suit her, and it made Clodagh feel old.

"Sharday's a raspberry, leave her alone," said her mum, wrestling Nevaeh into a coat as Tyler and Destiny shed theirs and flew into the living room. "Mind Auntie

Shar's ankle!"

The kids both peered at it and went, "Eurgh!" and laughed.

"What? You was walking around yesterday." Whitney pushed past her offspring and came into the room, peering down at Clodagh. This close, her perfume was overwhelming.

Whitney patted her hair, which had been braided tightly across the hairline. The roots were dark, the ends frazzled blonde. She had thick black eyeliner and spiky lashes, her lips pink and sticky. Clodagh thought she might have seen this particular look on an intensely annoying girlband, and from it she deduced that Whitney was on the hunt for a replacement for Tyler's father, Jayden.

"Ew," she said, looking at Clodagh's ankle. "Is it supposed to look like that?"

"No," said Clodagh.

"You should get to the doctor's then, babe." With that sage advice, her youngest sister swept away her children, leaving Kayleigh behind to scratch at her chickenpox spots and glare at Clodagh.

"She's right,"said Sharon as she picked up the kid's cereal bowls.

"And how'm I supposed to get there?" There was a surgery not far away, but Clodagh wasn't even sure if she could stand, let alone walk, right now. And besides, she thought, looking down at the limb that was beginning to look like something from a cartoon, the GP probably would take one look at it and send her to A&E.

"I'll give Scott a ring. He can give you a lift."

Scott, who did cash-in-hand building work for a mate, took a while to respond, then even longer to agree to give his sister a lift to the doctor's surgery.

"No, the hospital, Mum. The hospital," Clodagh repeated, and then a three-way argument began with her mother stating it wasn't that bad and Scott complaining the traffic round the hospital was really bad and the parking was extortionate.

"Just drop me off, then," Clodagh said through gritted teeth.

Right then her phone buzzed. Jamie. Oh, thank God. "*I never asked what you're studying.*"

Dammit, dammit. All her coursework was done by email, but her registered address for the course was Hanna's flat. She'd have to change that, if she could get on someone's wi-fi. Her mum's had been cut off and they kept trying to nick the neighbours'.

"*A Levels,*" she replied bluntly, in no mood to be cute.

"All right, Shar, Scott's coming to pick you up about ten," said her mother, putting the phone down. "Which means half past, 'cos he's always late."

"He's not my real dad," piped up Kayleigh.

"No, he's not," agreed Clodagh, finding herself tapping out another text to explain. Why did it bother her so much? Oh yeah, because he was doing a PhD in Computer Science and she didn't even have GCSE Maths.

"*I want to study history. At Cambridge. Which probably sounds stupid when I'm 31 and have no A Levels, but there you are, that's the goal.*"

Jamie replied, "*It's a good goal. What's your area of interest?*"

"*Social history. Well, women's history. That's what I blog about. Did you know Queen Anne was pregnant at least seventeen times and was not survived by a single child?*" How's that for Random Fact Girl? "*Mostly women overlooked by history, especially women of colour. But that can wait for the masters degree,*" she added flippantly.

"*Clodagh Walsh, MPhil. Has a nice ring to it. That*

154

explains your rando Rosalind Franklin knowledge. And where's your blog?"

"Sure, why not go for the PhD if we're looking at impossible dreams. And not telling you."

"Why impossible?"

She laughed out loud, then assured her mum she was just looking at funny cat videos.

"You'll use up all your data," said Sharon. "The Singhs changed their password. I'll see if anyone else is unsecured…"

"Er, how much is your PhD costing?" Clodagh texted.

There was a short silence. Then the prince replied, *"Good point. There are grants, you know."*

"Yes, for very exceptional people."

"You're very exceptional," he replied, and she wasn't sure what to say to that.

"Peaseman's going to love you," said Khan as Jamie got back in the car.

He groaned. His private secretary didn't come on every royal visit, and Jamie was beginning to wish he had this time. "I know. What the hell was I thinking?"

"Geraint won't be too pleased either," said Morris.

"Whatever day it is, I'm busy," Khan added.

"Yeah, me too."

Jamie had spent the day with a homeless charity, doing everything from food and laundry to walking the streets speaking to rough-sleepers and visiting families in squats and temporary accommodation. He'd listened with sympathy but no real surprise to the stories that had led people to these sorry states, from failed businesses to domestic abuse. One woman told him she'd been raped four times since she began living on the streets. Another showed him pictures of her child who'd died because the ambulance couldn't find the squat they were living in.

And somehow he'd found himself agreeing to sleep on the streets for a night to highlight the plight of the homeless.

"Why does it have to be in winter?" Morris said.

"Well, if it was in July the point would be rather negated," Jamie replied, waving through the window until they'd passed the crowds. He stretched, his muscles protesting. He'd gone for a run this morning in Kensington Palace Gardens with Ed and his security detail, but Ed was in much better shape and had set a somewhat punishing pace.

"Gotta run fast, little brother, or the paps'll catch us," he said, despite there being no evidence whatsoever of anyone with a zoom lens in the vicinity. They'd run right past a family taking pictures of the palace, but Edward was as accomplished at disguising himself as Jamie.

No, that wasn't quite right. Ed had been the one who pointed out that what they were in public was the disguise. A costume, perhaps. A sharp suit, bespoke shirt, subtle tie. Clean-shaven, hair as tidy as possible (he always gave Jamie a severe look at this point), polished handmade shoes. An impeccable overcoat in the colder months.

They were never officially seen in sports gear other than polo uniforms—and since Jamie was a terrible player this wasn't a problem—and by some mutual accord their smart casual outfits wouldn't have shamed a 1950s churchgoer.

Running gear, sweatpants, hoodies and especially t-shirts were non-U. Jamie had added a variety of hats to his repertoire, from a Kangol beanie to a NY Nicks baseball cap, and of course his glasses helped enormously.

Speaking of which… He got out his contacts case and popped his lenses out. Glasses on, tie off, much better.

His phone lay still and quiet on the seat. Olivia had

texted earlier and his heart had fallen irrationally when he'd seen it wasn't Clodagh.

Googling her would be bad… but she had told him she blogged about overlooked historical women. Women of colour, too. And that Queen Anne quip. Maybe…

He found way more results than he'd expected to. Some were clearly American, so he skipped on past those. Many of them listed the name and credentials of the author, so he could discount those too.

By the time he thought he'd found her, the car had just turned onto the M11. But halfway through a blogpost about Mary Seacole, his phone buzzed. Clodagh!

"What was the name of the doctor who treated me at Adam Brooks?"

Buzz. *"I mean Addenbrookes. Stupid autocorrect."*

Jamie frowned. Maybe she needed to pass it on to her new doctor in Harlow. *"Can't remember. I'll see if Benson knows."*

He opened the privacy screen and asked Khan to call through to Benson.

"Ta. The PAH system won't sync with Cambridgeshire, *of course*, so he can't access my X-rays."

"Your GP can't do it?"

Clodagh took her time typing a reply. More than once the 'typing' bubble disappeared, as if she'd deleted without sending.

"Are you OK?" Jamie sent.

Khan replied with the doctor's name. Thank god for Benson's good memory. Jamie asked for the spelling and texted it to Clodagh, but her reply had already come through.

"I'm fine," she sent, then immediately, *"No I'm not. Ankle got worse. Long story."*

Got worse? How could it get worse? Wasn't it just a

simple break?

"*What happened? Tell me.*"

In fits and starts, she told him she'd done too much walking and then a kid had jumped on her ankle in bed and she'd ended up back at A&E. A longer wait followed this, and Jamie watched the passing road signs with increasing anxiety. Should he tell Morris to keep going onwards to Harlow?

"*They've realigned the bones. I have to wear a plaster cast. Can't bear weight on it at all. Stuck on Mum's sofa for weeks. All because some impatient cow thought I was being too slow at the check-out in Aldi and my horrible step niece or whatever the fuck she is thought I'd make a good trampoline. I hate this place. I hate everyone.*"

Immediately that was followed by, "*Sorry. Just a bit fed up. Not looking forward to the next few weeks.*"

Weeks of her millions of nieces and nephews demanding fizzy drinks and *Peppa Pig*. Weeks of not being able to escape, even to the shops. Weeks of no one doing anything for her—because Jamie got the very clear impression it was Clodagh who did things for her family, not the other way around.

Weeks of her soul being chipped away, bit by bit, until the bright, funny girl who made jokes about cats and learned about nucleation and wrote those smart, clever blogs had disappeared completely.

"Don't turn off," he said to Morris. "We're going to Harlow. Call Lenka and have her make up the second bedroom. No ifs or buts."

To Clodagh he texted, "*I'm half an hour away. Don't go anywhere.*"

Well, what the hell was she supposed to make of any of this? From cat jokes and kids' TV to meeting her at the hospital?

Again?

At least she didn't have a concussion this time. She'd tried to explain to the staff at this hospital that she didn't remember most of what happened at the other hospital because of her concussion, which had led to a misunderstanding about being checked for a concussion now, and all the while her ankle throbbed so badly she couldn't think straight.

Now, with it reset—after a lecture about not letting people hit her with trolleys, as if she'd done it on purpose—and a hard cast on, she was trying to make her way on crutches back to the entrance. God, this was hard work. Slow-going.

And her memories of this place were probably the worst she had. She'd nearly told Jamie that, and deleted it just in time.

She spotted an empty chair and made towards it, so she could sit down and ask Jamie what the hell he thought he was playing at. But then two men came towards her, and one of them was Jamie in his geeky glasses and before she knew quite what was happening he was hugging her.

"Are you okay?"

She thought she heard a snigger from his PPO but when she looked up the man's face was entirely neutral.

"Sorry. Of course you're not okay." He held her by the shoulders and peered at her face. Clodagh had been trying not to cry most of the day, and she'd failed several times, which probably showed. "Does it hurt very much?"

She shrugged. "No, but the anaesthetic hasn't worn off yet. I have some more painkillers." And if her mum nicked them this time there'd be another Walsh in the A&E.

"I'm so sorry."

"It's not your fault."

He sighed. "I know, but it feels like it is. Come on."

He walked her slowly out to his car, the prince and his bodyguard, and no one paid the blindest bit of notice. Clodagh supposed people had other things to worry about in an A&E department. While she'd been inside, darkness had fallen. Had it really been all day?

All day, and the only person who'd contacted her was Jamie.

"I was going to call my brother," she said. "For a lift." Although it would be nice to be escorted in Jamie's luxury vehicle, at least when she was awake enough to appreciate it.

"Well, now you don't have to." He opened the door for her himself. The seats inside were the sort of leather that looked buttery and soft. The carpet was thicker than anything Clodagh had ever had in her home. Even the damn lighting was good.

She sighed, and got into the car, which took a bit of doing. Unsure what to do with the cumbersome cast, she tried to rest her foot on the floor, but the PPO did something to the seat and a leg-rest popped up.

There was enough leg room in this car to have a leg-rest, and inches to spare. Between the front and back seats was a privacy screen. The wood trim gleamed expensively at her. It even smelled nice.

This car was probably worth more than her mum's entire block of flats.

Jamie got in at the other side, and fussed over her comfort as the car set off. It was so smooth and quiet she had to check the scenery to be sure they were moving. *Shame it's such a short journey.*

"Now, okay," he said, as they turned back onto the main road. "I have a proposal, and it might sound a bit mad, but hear me out."

Clodagh looked at him blankly.

"Would it be accurate to say you're not enjoying

living here?"

She gave a hollow laugh.

"I'll take that as a yes."

"You can take it as a hell yes," Clodagh said.

"Right. You'd rather be in Cambridge."

"Well, obvs. But in case you hadn't noticed," she gestured to her cast, toes peeping out from the end with their unvarnished nails, "I'm a bit of a raspberry right now."

"Raspberry?"

Bloody new towns and their stolen rhyming slang. "Raspberry ripple. Cripple. I can't work right now, which means I won't be getting paid, which means I can't afford anywhere to live. Not that I could before all this." She rubbed her face. "That flat was a shithole, but it was all I could afford. Trust me, I'd have moved out if I could find anywhere."

And now it looked like months and months on her mum's sofa, until her ankle healed and she could look for a new job. Mum had talked about disability allowance, but Clodagh knew that kind of thing never kicked in immediately, if it kicked in at all.

"Well, then." Jamie took in a deep breath and blew it out. "That's why I'm offering you my spare room."

Oh, that anasthetic must be having a weird effect on her. "I'm sorry, I thought you said—what did you just say?"

"Would you like to stay with me? The bigger spare room, Olivia had it last time. It'll give you time to recover and work on your qualifications, and get some advice about the application process. And you can feed Bustopher if I'm not around."

He gave her a smile that looked... hopeful?

Clodagh stared blankly at the flawless leather of the seat arm. Hadn't she read somewhere that this stuff came from cows kept inside so their hides wouldn't be marked by scars from barbed wire or branches?

"I can't," she said. There was no way she could afford to live with him. "Did you miss the part about me having no job?"

"I'm not asking you to pay rent. Look, the day-to-day living costs aren't going to change that much with one extra person living there. It's no skin off my nose."

"But…" Clodagh didn't know how to say it. "I can't."

"Why not?" asked Jamie, reasonably.

They were passing Aldi now. It glowed in the darkness, car park full, people visible by the large windows packing up their cheap groceries.

She wanted to tell him she couldn't stay with him, that it felt like charity, that she had her pride, that it was demeaning. She wanted to tell him she would make her own way, but her own way felt short and bleak and somewhat circular. She was always going to wind up back here, in this crab bucket.

As the huge luxury vehicle cruised easily round the roundabout, Clodagh saw a young woman, a teenager really, pause at the crossing with a baby buggy and a toddler. *Pramface.*

"See that girl," she said, and Jamie peered past her to look. "With the kids?"

He nodded, and looked at her quizzically.

Clodagh's fingers came up to fiddle with the row of small hoops in her ear. "When I started secondary school, there were three hundred girls in my year. When I left, there were two hundred and fifty. Some had been excluded, some had left… and about twenty were doing exactly what she's doing."

Jamie twisted back to look at the girl as the car glided past. She was probably sixteen or seventeen, her hair pulled back and a row of gold hoops in each ear. She looked tired and angry as she jiggled the buggy. She looked pretty much like Clodagh at that age, and like her mother had before her.

"I used to look at girls like her and promise myself I'd never be one," she said, staring at her reflection in the smooth black TV screen facing her. No braids, no frosted lipbalm, no spiky eyelashes. Only the earrings to give her away.

"And you're not," Jamie said cautiously.

She nearly told him. She nearly opened her mouth and told him she was Sharday Walsh, and if he didn't know who that was then she'd educate him—

—and then she thought about the exposed beams and herringbone brick of the Master's House at Lady Mathilda College, and about the soft bed and the rainforest shower and the endless array of food and the superfast wi-fi, and the Cambridge students, so bright and shiny and full of potential, and how she could be one, really actually be one if she swallowed her pride and took this chance.

She was a smart girl, and she'd made some stupid choices. Saying no to this would be another one of them.

This could be my shot.

"No," she said firmly. "I'm not. And I will never be. Just because I was born here doesn't mean I've got to stay here."

Jamie's slight frown turned slowly to a smile. "So that's a yes, then?"

"It's a hell yes," Clodagh said, and he reached out to shake her hand.

There it was again, that jolt of electricity, that sense there was no one else around. That look in his eye like he knew her, and always would.

Clodagh snatched her hand back. "I'm not going to sleep with you," she said, and in the soft lighting she saw Jamie's cheeks go pink.

"Right, well, good, because I wasn't expecting you

to." He cleared his throat. "Ahem. Okay. Right then. Um. Do you have things you want to pick up?"

Clodagh nodded without enthusiasm. There wasn't a lot, but it was hers, and she'd work out later how she felt about asking for help buying new stuff.

The Range Rover came to a graceful halt in front of the towerblock. "You can't come up," she warned Jamie. "I haven't told them about you. I'll never hear the end of it."

He raised his hands in surrender and pressed a button on the console under the privacy screen. "Khan, could you go up with Miss Walsh, please, to collect her things?"

"Sir."

She heard the soft thud of the front car door closing, and then hers was opened, and the PPO who was apparently called Khan helped her out and steadied her on her crutches.

The lift was graffitied and stank of stale piss. Clodagh didn't look at Khan as it creaked to a halt and she led him down the badly-lit hallway to her mum's flat, letting herself in with the key.

The TV was blaring, as usual, and kids were squabbling over what to watch.

"I hate fucking *Paw Patrol*!"

"Granny! Callum said a bad word!"

"Callum, don't fucking swear."

Clodagh winced, and thanked God Jamie had agreed not to come up.

"Mum, it's me."

Her mother came out of the kitchen, tugging down the too-tight t-shirt she was wearing. It said 'Diva' in rhinestone letters. "You took your time! Thought you was just going for... who's this?"

Sharon Walsh, never one to ignore an attractive man, perked right up at the sight of PPO Khan. She fluffed her

164

hair, thrust out her bosom and smiled girlishly.

"A friend, Mum," said Clodagh, suddenly tired beyond belief of her mother. *She's doing her best. She does her best.* She'd been telling herself that all her life. Did that mean this was really as good as it got?

"He's come to help me pick up my stuff."

"Your stuff? Why, where're you going?"

She'd thought about this on the way up. "I had an offer of a spare room. Back in Cambridge." It wasn't a lie.

"Spare room?" Her mother waggled her over-plucked eyebrows at Khan. "That what they're calling it these days?"

"No, he's… you know, whatever." She swung past on her crutches, heading for her old bedroom where the carrier bags of her belongings had been stored. Half their contents were missing.

"Where's my stuff?" she asked Nevaeh, who shrugged sulkily. "Nevaeh. Where's my stuff? My blue sweater and my scarf and that grey tunic? And my red bra? Where are they?"

"Callum's wearing them," said her mother from the hallway.

Muttering swearwords, Clodagh swung back out, into the living room, where Scott's stepson Callum was indeed wearing several of her things, including a bra that sagged off his chubby shoulders, and a scarf he was waving like a feather boa. "Very funny, Callum, now give me back my stuff. Now."

Callum ignored her and carried on wiggling his bum to a Beyoncé song on the TV.

"Callum! Now! Give it to me or I'll take it off you myself."

"No! You're not my mum!"

Her patience cracked like a gunshot. *I'm leaving this place, and I never want to come back.*

165

Clodagh hopped closer, penning Callum in the corner of the room, and he glared sullenly up at her. She leaned down and said in a low voice, "Give me back my clothes right now or I'll beat you to death with my crutches."

Callum burst into tears. Clodagh reached for him, and he started throwing clothes at her.

"Now look what you've done!" her mother said. "Callum's on the spectrum, you know."

He damn well wasn't. They'd had this conversation at least three times. Clodagh had seen the Ed Psych at every school her siblings and nieces and nephews had attended, and the only thing wrong with any of them was laziness and spoilt entitlement.

"The only spectrum he's on," she said, "is the arsehole one, and if you say one word about vaccines—"

"Vaccines cause autism," piped up Kayleigh.

"*No they fucking don't.* Tell your mother to read a sodding book for once in her life, would you? Khan, would you get my stuff for me, please?"

"What is wrong with you?" said her mother, glaring. "Why are you being like this?"

"Because I've had enough," Clodagh said, as Khan silently gathered up scattered items of clothing from a suddenly mute Callum. Clodagh realised that as he bent forward, his gun brace was visible.

"Enough of what?"

"Of this. Of you. Of the crab bucket."

"The fuck are you talking about?"

"This is my shot and I will not give it up." She tried to calm herself. "This is my chance to get out of here and be something different." *To not turn into you.*

"Oh, yeah, little miss clever, innit. Always superior to the rest of us."

"At least I want to be better," said Clodagh, and at a nod from Khan, swung out of the flat.

"Well don't expect me to take you back when he

chucks you out," her mother screamed, and Clodagh slammed the door shut.

She was trembling slightly as they waited for the lift, the PPO carrying her pathetic few bags of belongings. Ancient graffiti on the lift doors, not quite obliterated by cleaning or resprays, still said *Pakis out.*

"You okay?" he said, and she nodded, not quite trusting herself to speak without bursting into tears. "Family's tough," he added.

"Yeah."

They stepped into the lift. "You and the prince can swap war stories."

"Oh yeah, I'm sure his mum screams at him all the time. I'm sure he gets stuck sleeping on the sofa and woken up by *Peppa* bloody *Pig* at 6am whenever he goes home."

"No, but he does have the entire world watching everything he does."

She glanced up at him. There had been warning in that statement.

Suddenly the girl looking back at Clodagh in the dull reflection from the lift wall looked younger and scrappier, hair in tight braids across her scalp, eyes spiky with mascara—

"You've read my file," she said.

He acknowledged that with a tilt of his head. "The highlights."

Clodagh lifted her chin, and looked at the person she was now. "And?"

Khan shrugged. "He won't care about your background," he said, as the lift ground to a halt and the doors opened on the concrete forecourt. The Range Rover gleamed expensively under the orange sodium lights.

"Really?"

"No. But the rest of the world will."

167

PART TWO

CHAPTER ELEVEN

The smell of melted cheese and garlic hit Jamie as he walked through the door, and his stomach growled in response. The downstairs lights were on, and he could hear Clodagh's uneven footsteps as she hobbled around the kitchen in her new walking boot. After three weeks, her ankle had begun to heal well, and she'd been allowed to replace the heavy cast with the much more practical boot—so long as she promised to keep the weight off and stay clear of Aldi.

"That smells amazing," he said, tossing his jacket on the seldom-used dining table and going through the living room, where the coffee table was set with paper napkins, wineglasses and a bowl of Wotsits. He grinned. She had him down to a T by now.

"Couldn't get Dominos to come out this late, but I made stuffed crust."

Jamie blinked at her. "Made it?"

"Yeah." She came out of the kitchen, bottle of red in hand, smiling at him. Her hair was pinned up, she had on leggings and an oversized sweater and she looked absolutely gorgeous. "Found a recipe online." She

171

chewed her lip. "I hope it's okay. It'll just be a couple of minutes."

Jamie knew he would eat it even if it was terrible.

"How'd it go?"

Jamie groaned. "As well as can be expected." The Royal Variety Performance, over for another year. He flopped onto the sofa and poured them both a glass of wine. "Cheers. I mean it's always a bit of a curate's egg, isn't it?"

Clodagh nodded, sitting down at the other end of the sofa and propping up her ankle on the stool he'd found for her. "Some dodgy comedian and a popstar you've never heard of."

"And the obligatory American who doesn't really know what they're doing there."

"But heard the word 'royal' and said yes because they thought they were going to marry you," she teased.

Jamie thought back to said obligatory American. "Well, that would be fun, but I don't think he swings that way."

Clodagh laughed, as the phone in her pocket pinged a timer. "Food's ready."

"I'll get it."

He slid the pizza stone out of the oven onto a wooden board and grabbed the slicer.

"Who was the musical this year?" she called through as he slipped the dough balls onto the plate warming in the bottom oven.

"Er…" he stood there in the middle of the kitchen, plate in each hand, trying to remember. "You know, I couldn't even say."

"Clearly memorable, then."

"Yeah. I was hoping for Hamilton, but what can you do?"

She made a noise he couldn't identify. "You know Hamilton?"

"Of course I know Hamilton. It's not all chamber music and *Zadok the Priest* round our way, you know."

"Have you seen it?" She sounded wistful.

"No. Haven't been in America since it opened. Heard good things though." More than good things. He actually desperately wanted to get tickets for the London show, but even if he did there was no guarantee he could actually make the date, booked a whole year in advance. He'd never forget the Crowded House tickets he'd looked forward to so eagerly, only to have Peaseman override him with a state visit to, of all the ironies, New Zealand.

"Cirque du Soleil were on though," he said as he carried the food in, "and they're always good."

"Yeah, I like them."

Jamie put the serving platters down on the coffee table and watched Clodagh poke at the pizza, which looked kind of messy but pretty edible. Was it seriously only three weeks she'd been here? It felt like forever. It felt like it should be forever.

She'd been hesitant at first, not wanting to make a mess or cause a fuss, and Jamie realised she wasn't just nervous about imposing on him, she was ashamed of her lack of knowledge. She didn't really know how to cook, not properly from scratch, and she was puzzled by a lot of the ingredients in the fridge and the larder. He had to admit, some of them were a bit weird. If someone had told him ten years ago he'd have opinions on harissa paste, he'd have been baffled.

Jamie had made a game of buying new kinds of mustard, just to see Clodagh's incredulity.

She'd introduced him to crisp sandwiches and cheap, knock-off Pot Noodles from the pound shop, and he'd taught her how to make bolognese without using a jar of sauce. She'd told him about the *Game of Thrones* books she'd had to wait for at the library, and he'd downloaded the boxset of the TV series. She'd scolded him for wasting water and energy when he did his laundry, and he'd learned that the only thing she was willing to spend good money on was decent conditioner for her hair, which explained those glorious curls.

She'd sit there in the evening combing some coconuty stuff through her hair and Jamie discovered he had a new favourite scent.

And now every time he walked through the door it felt so damn good to know Clodagh would be there, experimenting in the kitchen or clattering down the stairs with her hair in a towel, or sitting on the sofa, exclaiming over whatever she'd just found on Netflix.

I am so into you.

"Pizza okay?" she said, and he realised he'd just been holding one slice in the air after his first bite. He took another one. Actually, it was good.

"Pizza's great," he said, and smiled with pure happiness. "Everything's great."

"You're looking well," said Paulie as Clodagh stumped up behind the bar.

"Apart from the whole cast on my leg thing?" she said.

"Apart from that. Doesn't she look well, Stevo?"

"Yeah, great," said Stevo, one eye on the football showing in the other bar.

Clodagh smiled and pulled Paulie's pint. She felt well, actually, which wasn't a surprise given how good her life had been lately. No worrying about money. No freezing cold flat with a lumpy bed and weird stains on the wall. No horrible flatmate.

Jamie didn't behave like a prince—not, she had to admit, that she'd really had any thoughts on what a prince would behave like in private. She'd honestly expected him to have more domestic help, but apart from

Lenka who came in to clean and change the beds a couple of times a week ("He says he can do them himself, but he's a prince! And it's my job!") he looked after himself pretty well.

Having a nearly unlimited budget helped, of course. Jamie blithely told her to put whatever she wanted on the online supermarket order, but Clodagh still erred on the side of caution. And two days after she'd moved in, Lady Olivia had whirled up, all air kisses and swishy hair, and tossed a couple of glossy carrier bags on the dining room table.

"My sister is clearing out a load of clothes and she's about your size, Clodagh, so I wondered if you wanted them? Not sure quite what you're going to do about that cast, mind you. How do you get clothes over it? And don't your toes get cold? Ooh, I know, ski socks! Shall I see if I have any?"

Clodagh wasn't really fooled by the charade, but she appreciated the effort. Some of the clothes still had their labels on.

Jamie and Olivia looked anxiously at her, as if she'd reject the offer, and the words 'gift horse' and 'mouth' came to her mind. She swallowed her pride, and said thank you.

It would be easy, really easy, to get used to this kind of lifestyle, she realised. Sure, she was working on her last couple of assignments—amazing how decent rest, lack of stress and gentle encouragement helped her progress—to get the baseline qualifications she needed to apply to university, and Jamie was coaching her on the application process, so she wasn't being totally idle. She'd written more essays and blog posts in the last few weeks than in whole years combined. And she'd learned to cook, so there was a skill-set she could utilise, sort of.

But she'd made herself go back to working in the pub as soon as she was able, leaning on a crutch to keep the weight off whenever possible. It might be a horrifyingly small amount of money to someone like Lady Olivia, but it was Clodagh's own horrifyingly small amount of money, and she could save it for the first time in her life.

She looked up as the door opened, and in came Martins, one of Jamie's female PPOs. The security staff were cordial to her, as they were to everyone, but remote. Clodagh couldn't quite shake the feeling they disapproved of her presence.

Martins was followed by the usual Friday night crowd of postgrads, including Jamie. He looked at the bar before anywhere else, and his gaze warmed as it fell on her. Clodagh smiled back without realising.

"D'you want a drool bib?" whispered Oz in her ear, and she jumped.

"Shut up. He's a friend, that's all."

"Yeah, right."

No one knew she was living with Jamie. They'd agreed to keep it quiet. Jamie usually came and went through Lady Mathilda College's admin building, which backed onto the Master's Garden. The Range Rovers left straight from an anonymous looking garage round the back of the college. Clodagh had been nervous about using the gatehouse, where the PPOs dwelt with their many cameras, but no one seemed to pay her the slightest bit of notice. She'd learned what time the walking tours went past, and avoided them, and drew no attention.

"Good to see you back at work," said Jamie, smiling in a way he never did on camera. A genuine smile, she'd come to realise. A smile that meant he was actually happy, and not just presenting a cheerful face for the public.

"Good to be back. Haven't seen you in a while," she said, and he grinned wider at her.

He didn't walk home with her, but left before the

others. He'd explained to Clodagh that this was so no one could follow him, although there was usually a PPO with a car only a few minutes away, should he need to make an escape.

To her surprise, Khan did stay, taking a stool at the end of the bar, making long work of a tonic and lime and pretending to watch the football. Even when the match finished, he stayed.

"Don't you have a home to go to?" Oz teased, and Khan replied calmly, "Not yet."

When Clodagh fetched her other crutch to hop her way home, Khan slid from his stool, handed her the crutch and followed her out. Oz looked between the two of them and laughed.

"Ah, so it wasn't the prince you were smiling at," he said.

"Let him," murmured Khan as Clodagh opened her mouth. "People believe what they want to."

"Don't you mind?" she asked, as they went out into the cold November air. The Christmas lights were already up, shining picturesquely against the old buildings. "That he thinks we're, you know."

Khan shrugged. "Not really. Why would I mind?"

"Well, because we're not. I mean... do you have a girlfriend? Boyfriend?"

"That's a very personal question."

"Pretending to be someone's boyfriend is a very personal thing."

He smiled at that. Olivia was right, he was handsome, but Clodagh didn't fancy him in the slightest.

She was beginning to have a slight inkling as to why, and she wasn't sure she liked it.

"I'm not pretending anything. I didn't make the assumption. And besides. The way you and him talk to each other, look at each other? Won't take long before someone makes the connection."

"What connection?" Clodagh's cheeks heated. "There is no connection!"

"You live together. You're friends," said Khan placidly.

"Oh." Yes, of course. Yes, just friends. "Yeah, right, I mean… you're right." They didn't want people to know Clodagh lived with Jamie. Not that there was anything going on between them, but people would assume there was. "Do… does his family know I live there?"

A fractional pause. "He—" Jamie was always 'he' in public, or 'our mutual friend'— "made it clear to his family that he wanted to keep his private life private. We report nothing that happens inside these walls," he nodded to the anonymous wall Clodagh now knew bordered the Master's Garden. "Unless it's a threat to security, of course."

"Of course."

She was still thinking about what Khan said as she let herself into the house and locked the door behind her.

"Clo?" Jamie's voice came from the right, his study. It was a glorious room with mullioned windows and floor-to-ceiling bookshelves. Jamie's computer equipment took up several tables in the middle of it. There was a whole separate staircase leading from it to his bedroom.

"Yeah." She hung her coat in the cupboard and took off her ordinary shoe, swapping it for a carpet slipper. The floors were slate in the kitchen and got pretty chilly underfoot. The toes on her right foot, despite the thick sock she wore inside the walking boot, were frozen. "Thought you'd have gone to bed?"

"No, I had an idea," Jamie said, "I just wanted to note it down." He appeared in the doorway, hair even more dishevelled than usual, and blinked at her from behind his glasses. "And then I, er, started playing Minecraft."

She smiled fondly. "You're such a geek." She headed

towards the kitchen. "Was it your idea Khan should walk me home?"

"Yes. Hope you didn't mind," said Jamie anxiously, following her. He'd changed into jeans and one of his endearingly dorky t-shirts. "I just… last time you walked home alone…"

Clodagh looked down at the padded boot on her ankle and shuddered. The bruises had faded, the bone was healing, but the look on Lee's face as he'd thrown her down the stairs—that would never go away.

"Yeah," she said shortly. Then she looked up, and found a smile for him. "No, it was nice. Thanks. Except now Oz thinks he's my boyfriend."

She waited, gauging his reaction as she flicked the kettle on. Jamie's brows went up, and he said, "Oh," in a voice higher than usual. His gaze flickered down to the floor. "Really? That's weird."

"Is it? I mean, people will probably think he's the one I'm living with."

"Right."

"So it takes any suspicion off you. I can just be friendly to you like anyone else who comes in the pub. It's a sensible idea."

"Yes. Yeah, sure. It is." Jamie looked up, and smiled at her, and Clodagh wondered why she was waiting for him to say something else. "And he probably thinks it's hilarious, Khan, right? Not that there's anything hilarious about being your boyfriend, I mean anyone would be lucky, but I mean…"

The kettle flicked off, and Clodagh turned to drop a teabag into her mug. "You want a shovel? Keep digging," she said lightly.

But she didn't feel light, as she finished making tea and took it into the living room to watch half an hour of TV before she went to bed. She felt… disappointed, and she didn't like why.

"This is the only place I've been where all the glitter didn't look out of place."

Jamie smiled at the petite woman with the glossy hair and sparkly dress. She was dressed more conservatively than she did on *Strictly Come Dancing*, but he figured there was some contract clause that they had to wear sequins at all times, or risk disqualification.

"It's not even the grandest room in the palace," Jamie said. "You should see the White Drawing Room. It's just over there," he waved vaguely. "Not sure why we call it White, it's mostly gold. There's even a gold piano."

The dancer's eyes grew wide. "Really?"

"Well, gilt anyway. Painted with cherubs and the like. Claw feet. As a child I thought it would chase after me on them."

She smiled. "Maybe you should think of it dancing instead."

Jamie thought of the three-legged grand piano attempting the tango and laughed out loud. "What a brilliant idea! I'll remember that. Thank you."

She beamed, and looked to be saying something else, but Jamie was led away by an aide.

"She's very pretty," said his mother, materialising behind him. Jamie tried not to jump.

"Well, they all are. Haven't you seen the show?"

"Every week, darling." The reception had been her idea. "My money is on Debbie McGee. Have you seen her legs? Extraordinary. Wish mine looked like that. But do be careful, darling."

"I'm not going to start doing the splits." Jamie was not one of life's natural athletes. He'd been taught to dance, of course, they all had, so he wouldn't embarrass himself at state occasions, but he'd embarrass the hell out of himself on *Strictly*.

And royals didn't do things they knew would

embarrass them.

"I don't mean the splits," his mother said, eyeing the dancer, who was now talking to one of the charity guests. "I mean the girl."

Jamie knew exactly what she was implying, and he resented it. He put on a quizzical expression.

"French dancers were what nearly did for your great-grandfather," she said.

"But they didn't," Jamie muttered, because Great Grandpa had been safely married off to someone suitable the minute he started to get too serious about someone unsuitable, "and she's not French."

"Her nationality isn't important," she hissed as an aide came to lead her off somewhere else. "You know what is."

Yes, yes, of course. She was a dancer. She shook her bum in sequins on prime time TV. She wasn't minor royalty, like Ed had married, or aristocracy like Victoria had married. His cousins had married military officers and bankers and the exceptionally well-educated children of very rich foreigners.

"The Crown Princess of Sweden married her personal trainer," he muttered under her breath.

"Indeed, sir," murmured the aide at his elbow, and Jamie swore under his breath. "If you'll follow me, sir…"

He chatted and laughed and applauded the obviously carefully planned 'impromptu' performances, and just when he'd had enough of being festive and cheerful the guests were guided away. He went back to the ante-room where his mother was changing into her carpet slippers and handing her earrings to a dresser.

"I'm tired just watching them," she said. "Do you know, I've just been invited to watch the filming of the Christmas special?"

"How exciting. Will you go?"

She sighed. "I don't know. It's a big chunk of time and one is so busy leading up to Christmas. We'll see if things can be rearranged. Thank you for doing the Royal Variety, by the way. Edward didn't want to go by himself."

"No problem." Jamie rolled his shoulders and tugged at his bow tie. His eyes felt dry from wearing his contacts too long. "Where's Vincent?"

"He popped out to fetch some antacids for your father. Apparently Jeremy has run out."

Concern shot through Jamie. His father always seemed to be in such good health—but then, wasn't that the image they all presented? "Is he okay?"

"Oh yes, you know how he is, sneaking naughty little snacks in." She put a hand on his arm. "It's all right, Jamie. The doctor says it's nothing to worry about."

But he did worry. He worried as his father strolled in and assured him he was fine, he worried as Vincent let him change out of his gladrags to go home, he worried as Peaseman updated him on his schedule next week.

Term ended this Friday, which meant he'd have to work hard tonight to get the term-end report he'd promised his PhD supervisor. He'd missed a seminar today, which had been damn awkward to get out of, but in the end Peaseman had managed to persuade the speaker to hand over her notes for Jamie to study.

In the car on the way home he read the speaker's notes and emailed her a few questions. Tomorrow he'd have a full day at the lab, and then on Friday too, despite everyone else planning to skive off and go to the pub early.

Where they'd get to talk to Clodagh, and watch the way her teeth flashed when she laughed, and admire the muscles of her arms as she pulled a pint, and smile at the very thought of her.

"Oh God," he groaned, head falling back against the

seat rest. This, *this* was why it had been a bad idea to invite her to live with him. Sure, he wasn't going to do anything about it, but it was there now, and he couldn't ignore it.

And here she was, allowing Khan to pretend to be her boyfriend. He should have asked Benson, who was gay, or Phillips or Martins, who were female. Not Khan, who was young and handsome and personable.

The car parked up in the garage at Lady Mathilda College and Jamie made his way across the softly-lit rose garden to his front door. It wasn't late, but it was cold and dark and lights were on in the living room. Through the old leaded windowpanes he could hear faint music.

Clodagh went across the room and turned up the volume on the radio. Well well. A closet Ed Sheeran fan.

He walked in to the chorus of *Sing*, toeing off his shoes and hanging up his jacket quietly, watching through the dining room as she danced to the beat.

He'd spent the afternoon with a dozen professional dancers, and here was Clodagh balancing on one crutch, eyes closed as she sang along, and he knew who he'd have given the perfect score to.

He wandered closer, watching her, and leaned against the doorway, as she yelled, "Sing!" and then, to his astonishment, rapped the whole middle eight.

"You can rap?" he said, and she spun on her heel, losing her balance and stumbling. Jamie darted forward to catch her, and for a moment she was in his arms, breasts heaving, lips parted, and oh God he wanted to kiss her.

She straightened, and he stepped back, and she turned the music down. Jamie drew on ten centuries of breeding and thirty years of living to keep his expression politely neutral.

"Course I can rap," Clodagh said, tugging at her

sweater in a way that drew his gaze to her thighs. "All black people can."

Jamie opened his mouth, then shut it again. Clodagh grinned at him, then she tilted her head and said, "You said you like Hamilton?" Jamie nodded.

Clodagh took a breath, then she launched into the show's signature song, *My Shot*. It was a hell of a tour de force, Alexander Hamilton's cry of ambition. A bright, eloquent boy born to the most desperate of beginnings, burning with the desire to better himself. He even wanted a scholarship to King's College, for God's sake. And from this he'd risen to become one of the most influential men in the early days of America.

And Clodagh not only knew this and understood it, but rapped it better than the soundtrack.

I am so into you.

She broke off at the point where the company joined in the song, her chest heaving, and reached for her drink.

"That was amazing," Jamie said into the sudden silence.

Clodagh shrugged, her gaze dropping. "Told you, all black people can rap."

"Don't try that on me. Where'd you learn to do that?"

She shrugged again, and headed towards the kitchen. "Mis-spent youth." She snorted. "Not much to do but hang around listening to music and memorising it. I went with a guy once who wanted to be a rapper, so I got a lot of practice."

"He ever make it?"

"He made five years for armed robbery." She quirked an eyebrow at him as she set a plate in the sink and glanced at her watch. "I have to go. Work."

He nodded, a little discomfited by her rendition of the song. "Me too. But of the not-leaving-home variety." He had a night of making notes and writing reports.

Clodagh nodded and plucked her phone from the

charger. "See you later," she said, and hobbled off to fetch her coat. A minute later she was gone, and Jamie made himself sit down at his desk and open the email today's speaker had just sent him.

He glanced at the iTunes icon on his desktop. He had the Hamilton soundtrack, but he wasn't going to listen to it. He was going to work.

He wasn't going to sit here thinking about the first time he'd met Clodagh. It was hardly the battle of wits from the song. She'd stared dumbly at him and he'd talked to the other bartender. Not exactly the stuff of ballads.

But then that day on Midsummer Common, that morning, when she'd looked so helpless and he'd just tried to be kind and somehow, somehow she'd turned the tables on him. *A bright, eloquent girl born to the most desperate of beginnings, burning with the desire to better herself...* That was how they'd met. Really met. That was when he saw Clodagh Walsh for the first time.

When she held his hand and the whole world went away.

Jamie realised he'd been staring into space for five minutes. He straightened up, nudged his glasses back onto the bridge of his nose, and read his emails.

And then he put the damn soundtrack on anyway.

CHAPTER TWELVE

There was an end-of-term spirit amongst the students tonight, despite officially having two more days to go. Clodagh served their drinks and laughed at their jokes and tried not to think about the way Jamie had looked at her when she'd rapped that stupid song. What was she thinking?

Sure, Hamilton had risen to greatness, married above his station and become instrumental in the founding of the United States, but then he'd been shot dead in a duel and left his wife—and sister-in-law, if the musical was to be believed—heartbroken at his loss. Hamilton was loved by powerful women. Clodagh was… a roommate. People like Jamie didn't date people like Clodagh, they dated people like Lady Olivia.

Olivia was the daughter of a duke. Clodagh didn't even know who her father was.

Crab bucket.

"You seem pensive," said Khan as he walked her home.

"No, I'm just…" Clodagh curled her cold toes in their walking cast. "Hey, you've read my file. I live with a prince and I'm a nobody, aren't I?"

"Define nobody."

"I'm an illegitimate barmaid with no education."

"You're still somebody."

They walked in silence a while longer. Clodagh shivered; the temperature had plummeted. The forecast talked about snow next week.

"Can I ask you something?" Khan said, and she looked up in surprise.

"Sure."

"When I get an evening off, can I take you out somewhere? A drink, or a meal?"

Clodagh stared blankly at the street ahead. Khan was asking her out on a date? Jamie's bodyguard was asking her out? This was surreal.

"I mean, you say no and that's fine, I won't bring it up again, but—"

"Yes."

"Really?"

"Yeah." He was nice, he was good to look at, and God knew she'd be safe with him. "Yeah, why not? You know which days I work. Let me know."

He smiled, tentatively at first, and then wider. "Cool."

"One condition though. I can't keep calling you Khan. What's your first name?"

"Davood." He held out a hand for her to shake. It was bare, so she stripped off her glove to shake it. His fingers were cold, but there was no spark from them.

Spark isn't everything. Spark is dangerous.

"Nice to meet you, Davood." They'd reached the gatehouse now. "Call me."

Jamie's office door was shut when she went in. She took herself directly to bed, not wanting to speak to him for reasons she didn't care to identify.

Christmas gathered pace once December arrived, and Jamie's break from studying was crammed full with official engagements. He ping-ponged between the Home Nations and near Europe, every other day on a plane or long train, every day full of smiling and polite conversation and half a dozen different suits that all looked the same to him, every night a grand hotel or palace or some other exquisite lodgings he was too tired to even notice.

There were Christmas lunches and dinners and drinks receptions, so many of them that by the time the extended family lunch rolled around he never wanted to see a Christmas pudding again.

"And everyone wants to do their own bloody twist on it," complained his cousin Isabella as they made their way along the Marble Hall, along with anyone else within three degrees of cousinship of Her Majesty. "I've had saffron turkey, spiced turkey, roast goose, roast partridge, three bird roasts, five bird roasts…"

"Sprouts with chorizo, devils on horseback in a *salad*," her brother Anthony added, scandalised.

"A salad? With Christmas dinner?"

"You should see the vegetarian options," Anthony said glumly. Jamie had a dim recollection he was dating a model with ever-changing food habits.

"I'd be happy to never see a roast turkey ever again," Jamie said, but of course that was what he was served. He wore the silly hat and read out the daft jokes and endured mostly polite conversation from his second and third cousins. There was always one who couldn't quite conceal their disappointment that his great-grandfather hadn't abdicated, as everyone had said he would, leaving his stuttering younger brother—their great-grandfather—to inherit the throne.

"Can you imagine?" said the Duke of… well, Jamie couldn't remember where. "King B-B-B-Bertie?"

189

"I used to stutter," Jamie said, and the table went quiet.

"Yes, darling, but the CBT helped you to stop, didn't it?" said his mother, ever the social smoother. "And the foundation is doing terribly well. Dr Cressing tells me they're doing a documentary on it for the BBC."

"How is Dr Cressing?" asked his Aunt Penelope, who had recovered well enough to eat a hearty dinner but not well enough to eat a single bite without telling everyone in gory detail about her treatments. "Oh, no wine for me, I'm on medication," she said smugly to the footman.

"Wine, please," said Jamie, earning a dark look from his mother.

He survived the family lunch, kissed his grandmother goodbye as she prepared to travel to Sandringham, and checked the time.

One more appearance this afternoon, taking presents to sick children, and then he was meeting Olivia for a Christmas drink at some preposterously trendy bar. And then home, where if he was lucky he'd be able to catch Clodagh at the pub. Or at home. He smiled at the thought.

"Something amusing?" That was Victoria, sneaking up on him.

"Nope. Just a joke someone told me. Enjoyed your lunch?"

She grimaced. "Yes, but greedyguts here ate too much and now all the paps will think I'm preggo." She kissed his cheek. "See you on Sunday."

"Bye."

He passed on his good wishes to Annemarie, who had been spared today's lunch but would be expected to attend Sandringham over Christmas, and headed off to the children's hospital. Two hours later, changing out of the suit a small child had thrown up on and into what looked like a perfect replica, he waited in the car outside the bar Olivia had chosen while Geraint and Morris checked the interior.

"Bad news, sir," said Geraint as he came back to the car.

"What?" Olivia wasn't there? The place was considered unsafe?

"Miss Featherstonehaugh is present with Lady Olivia."

Jamie groaned, even as a text came through from Oll: "*Sorry. Couldn't stop her. Want to postpone?*"

Jamie drummed his fingers. Melissa was... well, she'd been a mistake, to put it plainly. She'd always been part of his social circle but he'd been slightly put off by her desperation to please, like an eager puppy. Avoiding her only made the desperation worse. Eventually, at someone's wedding, he'd had too much to drink and given in to her advances.

One night, and she was practically planning the wedding. Jamie had been as polite and gentle as he could with a raging hangover, but she refused to take no for an answer. He'd eventually invented some emergency and had Geraint rescue him, and avoided her ever since.

"*I can tell her you're not coming and meet you in Cambs?*" Olivia suggested.

Grateful, Jamie texted back in the affirmative, and the car pulled smoothly away from the club. Clodagh usually had the night off on Wednesdays, so she could join them for a drink. That would be...

Well, Olivia would get ideas about him and Clodagh, but he could probably weather that.

The house was empty when he arrived home. No music, no food cooking, no smell of coconut from the bathroom upstairs. Jamie called the gatehouse, where Phillips was on duty. "Did Clodagh go out?"

There was a slight, a very slight pause. "Yes, sir."

"Oh." He wondered where. She hadn't mentioned

any friends in the city. "Did she say where?"

"I don't believe so, sir." Another pause. "Khan is with her."

"Oh, good." He knew Lee Cunningham was behind bars—he'd been persuaded that a Guilty plea was in his favour, thereby sparing Clodagh a court appearance—but he still got uneasy about her being out by herself. Because of her ankle, he told himself, and almost believed it. "Lady Olivia is coming up. We'll go out for a few drinks."

"Very good, sir."

Olivia, when she arrived— "So sorry, darling, I couldn't drop bloody Melissa. Said I was going home and she bloody followed me. Had to invent a work crisis and dash off,"—suggested the Prince's Arms for a drink, so she could catch up with Clodagh.

"Apparently she's out," said Jamie.

"Oh." Olivia, like so many people he'd been raised with, could fit all the vowels into that one short word. "What a shame. Still, we'll have a nice night, eh?"

They did, Olivia using her contacts and sheer ebullience to get them a table at Midsummer House, and then drinks at various places on the way back home. The city was in fine festive mood, free of students but full of tourists and revellers, and more than once Jamie posed for photos with well-wishers.

He resisted the urge to text Clodagh and ask where she was and with whom. It was none of his damn business. He should have asked more about her friends, and then he'd know.

And later, after they'd called it a night, after Olivia had thrown her high heels into the smaller spare room and curled up for a gossip on the sofa, her feet on Jamie's lap 'because they'll swell if I put them down, darling,' the front door opened and Clodagh came in.

Jamie put down his wineglass and called out jokingly,

"What time d'you call this?"

She came in, across the darkened dining room which was currently stacked with various gifts Jamie had to wrap and take to Sandringham.

"You didn't need to wait up." Her gaze fell on Olivia. "Oh. Hi."

"Hello, darling. I was expecting you to be around! It's a shame, you could have come for dinner with us!"

"Ah. Maybe next time."

She was quiet. There was an odd look on her face. "You okay?" said Jamie. Fear gripped him. What if Cunningham had—no, Cunningham was behind bars, but what if one of his friends had found her? What if the girl, Hanna, had found her? "Khan did stay with you, didn't he?"

"Davood? Yes, of course. What kind of date would it be if he didn't?"

It was one of those moments when nothing seemed to happen for an extraordinarily long time, and the entirety of it wrote itself onto Jamie's memory for good. He remembered how he sat there, twisted sideways to look at Clodagh as she stood in the darkened dining room, Olivia's feet in his lap. He remembered the tiny beginning of a giggle from Olivia, as if she thought Clodagh was joking, and then the sound it turned into when she realised that wasn't the case.

And he remembered the way Clodagh's chin jutted, as if defying him to ask if it was true, if she was joking, if he'd misunderstood.

"A date?" he heard himself say. "As in… a date?"

"Yes. With drinks and dinner. Just like your evening."

Hollowness spread inside him. The wine tasted sour in his mouth. "We weren't on a date."

"No, of course not."

She turned away, walking back to the hall cupboard to put away her coat and scarf and shoes. Olivia touched

Jamie's arm, her face full of sympathy. He shook his head rapidly.

"Did you have a nice lunch?" Clodagh asked from the hallway.

Olivia raised her eyebrows when he failed to answer. "Lunch? At the Palace?" she prompted.

"Oh. Oh, yes. Very nice." He couldn't remember a single thing about it. "Did you?"

Clodagh gave him an odd look as she came back toward the living room. "I had a sandwich here," she said. "While I wrapped some presents." She hesitated. "Mum asked me to go home for Christmas, so I said yes. After all, you'll be away."

"Sure," said Jamie. Even though she was clearly on the outs with her family, she'd prefer to go home than—no, stop it, Jamie.

"Right. Davood's offered me a lift. He's going home for Christmas."

"With you?" Olivia asked.

"No, to his family. In London. Hence the lift." She went into the kitchen and Jamie gulped some wine.

"It's just one date," Olivia said in a low voice.

"Was it a good date?" Jamie called through, and hated himself for even asking. Olivia thumped him.

"Yeah. He's nice. Funny. Tells a good anecdote. Some of them might even have been true." She came back, and paused at the foot of the stairs, water glass in her hand. "Well, night then. See you tomorrow."

"Night," said Olivia, and Jamie mumbled something similar.

As Clodagh's uneven footsteps thumped up the stairs, he leaned forward and poured a very large glass of wine.

"Jamie," said Olivia.

"Shut up. I know. Shut up," he said, and took a big drink.

"Maybe it's for the best," she said.

"Yes." He drank some more.

"He seems nice. He'll be good to her."

"Yes," said Jamie viciously, draining his glass. Khan —Davood – would be good to her. Jamie wouldn't have asked him to look after Clodagh if he thought otherwise. They'd make a handsome couple.

They could go out anywhere without people taking their picture and speculating on their future plans and when they'd get engaged, married, start having babies. Without commenting on their outfit choices and hairstyles and changes in weight. Without being scrutinised and magnified and objectified and—

It was for the best. Clodagh wouldn't want that anyway, wouldn't want the whole circus. He didn't want to do it to her.

"Jamie?"

I just really like her.

He wanted to cry. Instead, he got up and fetched more wine.

Clodagh lay in bed and listened to them. Jamie had put music on, that nineties band he liked so much. Crowded House. He'd talked about them before. They hadn't been very popular round Clodagh's way. Maybe things were different for Prince Jamie and Lady Olivia.

They hadn't been on a date, but they might as well have been. Cosy on the sofa like that. The rumours were probably true. Jamie might not think he intended to marry Olivia, but he would, one day. He'd marry someone of his class—or as close to it as one could get, when one was anointed royalty. Someone who didn't have an excruciating family and a past that would make the tabloids explode with vicious glee. Someone who understood why there were so many kinds of mustard.

Her date with Davood Khan had gone well. As well as she might have expected, anyway. Clodagh hadn't exactly been on a lot of dates. But he was nice, he was funny, he was kind and she felt very safe with him. All those were good things, right?

And when he'd asked if he could kiss her goodnight, she'd said yes, and hoped for the best, and it had been… okay, really.

He'd asked if she'd like to go out again, and she'd said yes, because it was time she stopped mooning over a man she couldn't have and spent time with one she could. Yes. Going out with Khan was a sensible idea.

She turned over. Crowded House were singing *Don't Dream It's Over*, which was so horribly appropriate she cried herself to sleep.

CHAPTER THIRTEEN

Arrivals at Sandringham were arranged on a strict schedule. Not for the first time, Jamie considered it weird that an event focused so closely on the nuclear family should be at the same so formal. He had the schedule, printed and laminated by one of Peaseman's minions, and he also had a million reminders on his phone. Not that he needed them. Nothing really changed at Sandringham.

He was allowed to arrive on Christmas Eve after his cousins, and for once permitted to drive his own car. The wail of a baby greeted him as he went inside, stripping off his gloves. His luggage was taken from him and a comment murmured that he'd be in his usual room. Well, that was something. He'd half an expectation of being banished to the servant's quarters, because his room was needed for a married couple.

Before she'd married Nick, Victoria and Jamie used to arrive together. But she had precedence now, being married. Jamie had still been allowed to arrive later than his cousins—despite two of them also being married, and Isabella with the baby now—but he morosely

197

predicted a demotion any day soon.

"Come on, droopy-drawers, smile," Victoria chivvied him, as he set out presents in the Red Drawing Room. "It's Christmas!"

Jamie nodded. "Sure is."

"Something wrong?"

He'd woken with a terrific hangover on Thursday, and had to go about his crammed schedule as if nothing was wrong. Clodagh had been out when he came home, and he'd gone to bed before she finished work. Friday he'd hardly seen her, and then he'd spent Saturday with his parents before going through the stupid charade of arriving separately here today.

She'd be on her way down to Harlow now, in Khan's car, probably teaching him to rap along to Hamilton. They could do one of Eliza and Alexander's duets together.

He was trying not to think that she'd been alone in the house last night. Because what if she hadn't been alone? What if she'd invited Khan in? He could hardly object; the man was in his employ after all, it wasn't as if she'd just asked someone in off the street. And then they'd be shagging all over the house, in her bedroom and by the fire in the living room and on the kitchen table, oh God—

"Jamie?"

"I'm fine. Hangover," he lied, blinking to try and clear his mind of the image of his bodyguard and Clodagh together.

"Ah. Don't let Granny see."

"No. Right."

The first thing his grandmother said to him was, "Jamie, dear, what's all this I hear about you and dear Olivia? Are we to expect an announcement?"

"What? No. Still no, Granny." He eyed the decanters on the sideboard. Too early for a drink?

"Well, you looked jolly cosy the other night. The picture was all over the papers."

Ugh. Yes. One of the well-wishers on Wednesday had snapped a picture of him and Olivia, just as she'd leaned close to whisper to him, "That guy has his fly undone," so it looked like she was kissing his ear and he was smiling about it.

"Just one of those angles. You know how it is. Olivia is still just a friend."

"Still?" the Queen asked wistfully.

"Still," he repeated firmly.

They opened presents after tea that evening, the traditional mix of cheap and cheerful. Granny hooted with laughter at the light-up singing Santa earrings he'd found for her, and he accepted with good grace his brother's gift of a picture book entitled *Hot Guys With Kittens*.

Jamie wondered if Clodagh had found the present he'd left for her on the coffee table. He wondered if she'd appreciate it. It had been so long since he'd bought a serious gift for someone that didn't involve half a dozen employees and consultation of a diplomatic textbook that he had no idea if his judgement was sound or not.

She sent him a text on Christmas Day. It had a cheerful Santa emoji, but was otherwise not particularly personal. He replied in kind, then got back to the intense schedule of church and meals and greeting well-wishers and more church and more meals, changing clothes so many times he was up and down the stairs like a jack-in-the-box.

He looked at her text again before he went to bed. Slightly drunk, his thumb slipped and scrolled back to the miserable message she'd sent him all those weeks ago from the hospital. "*I hate this place. I hate everyone.*"

"Sometimes, I'm right there with you," he said, and fell asleep to tortured dreams of Alexander Hamilton making love to Clodagh.

"How'd it go?" asked Davood when he picked Clodagh up on Boxing Day.

She fell back against the car seat with a groan. "Well, I was greeted with the words, 'You're not still wearing that thing, are you?' when I walked in the door," she gestured to the walking boot, which still had at least a week to go, "and it went downhill from there."

"Yikes."

"Yep."

Occupying that weird space between not being forgiven for her outburst but still being an integral part of the family, Clodagh had spent forty-eight hours checking her watch. Her mother had been cordial, but not warm. Her sisters had ignored her unless she was useful for watching the kids. Everyone had made jokes about not jumping on her ankle because it was made of glass and she'd fall apart, which had started out unfunny and got worse.

The turkey was too big for the oven, took too long to cook and most of the adults were pissed as newts by the time it was served. Clodagh's presents for her nieces and nephews—nieflings, she remembered Jamie calling them, with a pang—had been torn into and evaluated critically before being forgotten about in favour of something shinier. Kylie had forgotten to buy Clodagh anything, Whitney claimed she couldn't afford anything, and both her brothers gave her socks.

Joke's on you, she'd thought as everyone laughed at their lack of imagination. Socks were something she actually really needed.

"How about you?" she asked.

"Well, we do our main gift thing at Eid, so we're

mostly in it for the tinsel and cheesy movies," Davood said. "*Home Alone. Muppet Christmas Carol. Elf*, obviously."

"Obviously. We had to watch *Cinderella* this year. The live-action one."

Davood made a slight face.

"I can't even tell you if it was any good because the kids squabbled all through it and I had to run out to the shops for carrots because, you know, there's a million things on the plate but if you don't have carrots it's all ruined."

He laughed.

They passed a house so covered with random flashing crap it made Clodagh's temples throb. "Also there was a screaming fit because we only had plain lights, and not those flashing emergency-vehicle blue ones that are all the rage round here."

"Yeah, what's up with that? I keep thinking it's the police. It's like being back at work. Speaking of, did you see the Boss?"

Clodagh's face flamed a little. "Jamie? No, why would I?"

"I meant the Queen. Nice speech, I thought. Slightly pointed mention of some of her grandchildren 'beginning to choose partners' though. Did you notice the photos?"

"On her desk? Yeah. I'd be well pissed off if I were him."

The Queen had the wedding portrait of her oldest son Prince Frederick and his wife Louisa, who had celebrated forty years of marriage this year, and of Victoria and Nicholas, who'd done a Commonwealth tour, and of Edward and Annemarie and their children. There was no picture of Jamie. Probably unbalance the table to have a single on there.

"Or the others." Davood shrugged. "I mean, she does

have eight grandchildren, and there was no mention of Princess Isabella's daughter."

"True." Apparently all families had their favourites.

"What's so special about first-borns, anyway?"

The first one is always special. The memory, as unwanted as it had ever been, stabbed her like a knife.

"I mean," Davood began. Then he glanced at her face and winced. "Shit. Sorry. I wasn't thinking."

Clodagh sucked in a breath. "Don't be. It was a long time ago. I was someone else then."

He nodded, and changed the subject to his favourite terrible Christmas songs. Clodagh leaned her head against the cool glass of the window and watched the ugly Christmas lights flicker and flash as they passed by.

She dozed for most of the journey, having spent two sleepless nights on the sofa again, and woke to Davood shaking her arm. "We're back."

She opened her eyes. It was fully dark now, the bulk of Lady Mathilda College a familiar and welcome sight against the night sky. She took a deep breath and let it out.

"You okay? I'm sorry I said…"

"It's fine," she assured him. "I only…"

I saw the pictures of Jamie and Olivia in the papers even though I tried not to look, and I know it's probably nothing, that they really are just friends, it's just…

…what if they're not?

"Is everything okay between you two?" Davood asked.

"Yes. Yeah, it's fine," she said distractedly.

"Does he know we went out?"

She nodded, still staring at the dark walls of the college. She could just make out the little light of a security camera above the gatehouse door.

"What did he say?"

She shrugged. "Nothing." He'd been weird though.

Because she was dating his security guard? Because she was dating anyone? Did he not see her as the kind of girl who went on dates? Didn't he think she was desirable enough? Did he even see her as anything other than a lame duck to be rescued?

"Nothing at all?"

"I… kind of interrupted him. With Olivia."

An infinitesimal pause, then, "Ah."

"Yeah. You reckon the rumours are true?"

Davood said nothing, until she swung round to look at him. In the darkness, she couldn't see much of his face.

"I wouldn't believe everything you hear," he said. "Go on, get inside, I don't have my own parking space near here. I'll see you soon."

He leaned across, but instead of kissing her on the mouth he kissed her cheek, and she smiled awkwardly and got out of the car.

The PPOs in the gatehouse greeted her with seasonal wishes and told her Jamie had arrived home that afternoon. She set off across the lawn, trying not to feel like a kid who'd been caught skiving off school, and let herself in.

"Jamie?"

"Clodagh. Happy Christmas."

"Happy Christmas."

He had a log fire burning and a video game paused on the big TV. From here, all she could see was the back of his head as he slouched on the sofa. She couldn't see Olivia anywhere. She put away her outdoor things—no impeccably tailored size eight coats in there, or glossy high heeled boots—and started through the dining room, pausing as she saw the gift she'd left for him still there, unwrapped.

Slowly, she went into the living room. Jamie appeared to be alone, a hamper from Fortnum and

Mason open and raided on the table. Curled up on the hearth rug was the cat they called Bustopher.

Sitting on the coffee table was the present he'd left addressed to her.

"Good Christmas?" she said warily, sitting down on the other sofa.

Jamie sprawled on the sofa in sweatpants and a *Star Wars* t-shirt with mince pie crumbs on it. His glasses were smudged and his hair looked like he'd been pulled through a hedge backwards. He resumed gameplay, not even glancing at her.

"Yes, marvellous," he said politely. "And you?"

"Oh, fabulous. As usual."

"Not full of nosy relatives asking when you're going to settle down and get married, or small children doing their best to break priceless Victorian tree ornaments, or two church services, or five outfit changes a day?"

Clodagh raised an eyebrow. Well, if that's how he wanted to play it… "Turkey wars between my mum and her friends," she began, ticking things off on her fingers, "which means she has to get the biggest one she can even though it doesn't fit in the oven, so I have to saw it in two with a blunt breadknife. Ten adults, one of whom announces she's going vegan with immediate effect on Christmas morning and doesn't like any vegetables."

Jamie's mouth twitched. He shot down an enemy soldier on screen.

"Eight children under ten, two of them in nappies—"

"Your sister had the baby?"

"Nope." Clodagh smiled. "My sister spent the entire time lying full length on the sofa complaining her back ached and that she thought she was having hyperemesis gravidarium, only I won't try to explain how she pronounced it, and no, she would not accept that this was unlikely to suddenly occur in the eighth month. The eighth child belonged to my brother Scott, who neglected to tell any of us that three years ago he knocked up a girl from Roydon and he's been paying child support on a toddler called Chidi."

Jamie's eyes grew wide. He paused the game.

"I know," Clodagh said. "He was hiding out at my mum's house because the girl's dad had just tracked him down and threatened him with a machete. At least that's what he said. Meanwhile—"

"There's a meanwhile?" Jamie picked up a mince pie and bit into it.

"Two of my nieces got the same doll—one of those ones you feed from a bottle and then it wees into a nappy and poops out little bits of plastic—" she read the horror on his face and grinned manically. "Oh yeah. Cue a lecture on indoctrinated gender roles and why baby poop isn't really made of little colourful bits of plastic. Anyway one doll has two more pieces of plastic poop than the other, so a screaming match ensues which basically goes on for the entirety of Christmas Day. And no, Nevaeh will not give one of her pieces of plastic poop to Keisha to even things out. Nevaeh, in case you're wondering, is 'Heaven' spelt backwards, which maybe gives you some idea of her character."

Mesmerised, Jamie ate another mince pie.

"What else? Oh yes, the tears over the wrong kind of Christmas lights, because flashing emergency-services blue is the only colour to have, unless you can have multicoloured and flashing. Or both. Why not both? The house across the road looked like someone had eaten Christmas and vomited it up all over them."

"Are you making this up now?" said Jamie. He reached for a bottle of port, took a swig then offered it to her.

"Cross my heart and hope to die. Which is more or less the state in which I ended Christmas Day. Didn't even get to watch *Doctor Who*. Would you like me to start on the argument I had with Scott's girlfriend—not the mother of Chidi, the other one—about vaccines and autism?"

"Between which there has been proven beyond a shadow of a doubt to be no link whatsoever?" Jamie said, rolling his eyes.

"Yeah. Apparently that's just what Big Pharma want us to think so they can sell us their vaccines." She took a slug of port, which was richer than she'd expected and went down very nicely. "Anyway. What's the royal goss?"

Jamie held out the tray of mince pies and she took one. The pastry seemed to be mostly butter and it was ridiculously good.

"Aunt Penelope is only and precisely as sick as it suits her to get out of things she doesn't want to do. Annemarie on the other hand can barely walk and has been told to never have another baby. Victoria and Nick still aren't pregnant and will physically attack anyone who asks about it. Someone tried to get into the church with a paintbomb and the security team had to take him down with tranquilliser darts like you use on rhinos, but thankfully the chorus of *Hark! The Herald Angels Sing* drowned out the noise and the only evidence was a pink stain on a gravestone. His Royal Highness Prince Alexander thinks poo jokes are hilarious, as does my grandfather, incidentally, so the two of them get on like a house on fire. And a house on fire is precisely what I'd have preferred to be in after every single one of my relatives asked when I was going to announce my engagement to Olivia."

He held out his hand for the port and Clodagh, her stomach suddenly threatening to reject the buttery pastry, handed it over.

"And? When are you?" she managed to ask.

"Sometime between Never and Not Going To

Happen. That bloody picture, Christ. You should thank your lucky stars you weren't out with us that night or it'd be you Twitter would be storming over."

That didn't help her stomach much.

"I've got Peaseman drafting a statement to the effect that Lady Olivia and I are like siblings and not the kind you get in *Game of Thrones*. No engagement. No marriage. No snu-snu. None of it."

Clodagh looked at the port bottle, which was half empty.

"Snu-snu?"

"You don't watch *Futurama*? They land on a planet where there are no men and they're sentenced to death by snu-snu, which they find out is actually being shagged to death by sex-starved Amazons... it's a geek thing. Never mind. I'm not doing it with Olivia is all that matters."

"Oh," said Clodagh. Jamie held out the bottle and she swigged from it again, warmth spreading through her. "Good to know."

"Isn't it?" He stared at the screen for a moment, where an enemy soldier was frozen at the point of death. "And you? Enjoying your snu-snu with PPO Khan?"

He must be drunk. Clodagh couldn't imagine Jamie asking about anyone's sex life sober.

"Ugh, forget I asked. Sorry. Too much port. None of my business."

Clodagh drank a bit more port and eyed him over the bottle. She must have had too much of it now as well, because she said, "I'm not sleeping with PPO Khan."

Jamie didn't look at her, but she could see his chest rising and falling rapidly. "No?"

"No. No snu-snu."

"Oh." He rolled his head to look at her. "I'm sorry?"

"Try it again without the question mark."

He smiled contritely. "I'm sorry. That was invasive

and I… you can sleep with who you like. I mean, not here, obviously, because violation of security rules…" His attention wandered off, then landed on the present on the table. "Don't you want to open that?"

Clodagh looked at it, then got up to retrieve his. "I was waiting for you."

"Oh."

Jamie moved to sit upright, straightened his glasses and ran a hand through his hair, as if opening presents was a serious business one had to smarten up for. *Probably has a special dress code at Sandringham.*

"Okay, go."

He still waited for her to open hers first. It contained a book, and a print-out. The book was titled *Latin Primer*. The print-out was confirmation of purchase for a course of lessons in Latin.

Clodagh looked up, thoroughly confused.

"For your course," Jamie said. He looked nervous. "They look for an aptitude for languages and Latin opens doors to a lot of them. And it looks good on your application."

Clodagh stared at the book and the paper. Confusion gave way to something warmer, and it spread inside her. "You actually think I have a shot at getting in?"

He blinked. "Of course you do. I've read your blog. You're good. You're engaged and articulate and you have an eye for detail and nuance."

Clodagh stared at the book until the title blurred. "And there's always positive discrimination," she said. "Black girl, state school, no GCSEs, all that."

"Fuck that," said Jamie. "You're getting in on merit."

Clodagh felt tears burn her eyes. She scrambled off her sofa and onto Jamie's and wrapped her arms around him.

"Thank you," she whispered. It wasn't for the book or the course. It was the belief she could do it. Jamie, so clever she didn't even understand his PhD subject title, thought she could get into the same university as him.

I am so into you it scares me.

He put his arms around her, slowly, and she felt his chest move as he breathed. "Coconut," he murmured.

"What?" She straightened away.

"You're a nut. Shall I open mine?"

Clodagh bit her lip. "It isn't as good."

"Hey, as long as it isn't a singing plastic fish I'll be happy." He pulled off the cheap wrapping paper and shook out the garment inside.

She'd had it printed specially from a place online. You could choose the logo and the text and the colour, and she'd sneaked into his room to check the labels on his shirts for the right size.

Jamie took in the royal purple t-shirt with its golden direwolf and the legend HOUSE WINDSOR in the *Game of Thrones* font, and a smile spread across his face.

"Clo, I love it."

"Really?" He was probably really good at pretending he liked presents.

"Yes, really. It's perfect." He hugged her, and she let herself enjoy it. He was so warm, and his arms felt good, like they'd keep her safe, and his hair was soft where it tickled her cheek.

I'm so glad you're not marrying Olivia.

He pulled away as she thought that, and for a moment Clodagh was terrified she'd said it out loud, but all he did was move over the stool she used to keep her ankle elevated so she could stay beside him. He even plunked a cushion on it.

Clodagh smiled warmly at his consideration, and he smiled back innocently, because he'd no idea what his kindness meant to her. He settled back to pick up the TV control, switched the TV inputs and started scanning the listings.

"Now then. Exquisitely acted but depressing historical drama, documentary about polar bears, or *Big Fat Quiz of the Year*?"

"*Big Fat Quiz of the Year*, of course."

"Of course." Jamie switched to Channel Four and glanced critically at the bottle of port. "There's some fizz in the fridge if you want some."

What the hell. Clodagh nodded, Jamie fetched it, and she unwrapped some champagne truffles to go with it as he popped the cork. They drank from that bottle too, getting pissed and giggly. Jamie kissed her on the forehead when she got a stupidly tricky answer right, and left his arm around her.

She woke up some time later, head on his shoulder. The TV was silently talking to itself. Jamie was asleep, head resting against hers. Oh damn.

Oh damn, this felt right.

There was more heat in this simple embrace than there had been in Davood Khan's whole kiss.

"Oh damn," Clodagh whispered.

CHAPTER FOURTEEN

Jamie had his usual arrangements to ski with Olivia and her family over New Year, and Clodagh had her equally usual arrangements to work in the Prince's Arms. He figured she'd got the better choice. He loved Olivia, but her family could be hard work. The one upside was that none of them believed any of the silly tabloid stories about him and Olivia getting married.

He drank champagne and sang Auld Lang Syne while fireworks went off over Verbier, and then he texted Clodagh.

There weren't many days when he didn't text Clodagh.

He thought he'd fallen asleep with her on the sofa on Boxing Day, but she'd gone when he woke in the early hours of the morning. His t-shirt smelled like coconuts though, so maybe he wasn't imagining it.

He wore his House Windsor t-shirt, which confused the Duke and Duchess because there were no wolves on his coat of arms. Olivia's irritating brother tried to make some joke about it being from that "Games of Throwing" TV series which fell flat. Olivia just gave him a knowing look, and said nothing.

"By the way, darling," she said as they took their seats to fly home. "Belated Crimbo pressie. Chap at work does the accounts for a couple of music venues and guess whose name just happened to pop up?"

Jamie had no idea, and told her so.

"Crowded House, darling. And I remembered you're a huge fan even though it's really dorky, so I got you some tickets. They're even in Cambridge. End of the month. Is the Corn Exchange a good venue?"

Jamie stared at her. "I love Crowded House," he said dumbly.

"Yes, I know, that's why I got them for you. Now, I have cleared it with Peaseman. Mentioned it ages ago actually but he couldn't confirm it until now. You have the evening off. It's all arranged. The PPOs can draw straws as to who gets to listen to the mellow stylings of Neil Finn and friends."

She was mocking him, but only lightly. "Are you coming?"

"Alas, I'm in Paris then. Such a shame. Take Clodagh?"

He nearly missed it in his excitement. The slightly over-casual tone would have been missed by someone who didn't know her quite so well.

"Clodagh?"

"Yes." She looked at him expectantly. "Pretty girl. Leg in a cast. Lives with you. You must remember." She peered at him. "Did you hit your head when I wasn't looking?"

He swatted her away. "You're doing this on purpose."

"Doing what?" Her eyes were wide and innocent.

"Setting me up on a date with Clodagh." A date with Clodagh. Who might also be dating Khan but wasn't sleeping with him.

"I have no idea what you mean. I just thought you'd

like to take a friend to see your favourite band. No?"

A friend. Yes. Yes, she was just a friend. Like he and Olivia were just friends. Only not like he and Olivia, because he had zero wish to sleep with her and every wish to with Clodagh…

"My friend," he said deliberately, as the flight attendant came round with flutes of champagne. "I'll take my friend. Who is dating my PPO."

"Anything you say, darling."

Davood had insisted on paying for their first date, so Clodagh insisted on returning the favour. The restaurant wasn't half as fancy, but it was much more in her price range, especially if she just ate a main course and stuck to water. Davood, maybe out of politeness or maybe out of knowledge of her finances—she had no idea how much the PPOs knew but she wouldn't be surprised if they had her bank account number and sort code—did the same.

Thanks to Jamie, the menu was much more comprehensible. She even knew what mooli was now.

How far you've come, Sharday Walsh, said a nasty little voice inside her, and she ignored it and ate some more quinoa.

"Next time we split the bill," she said as they walked slowly home. She'd recently been allowed to take the walking boot off for short periods of exercise, which hurt like hell but made the weakened muscles of her ankle stronger. Jamie had carefully said nothing about her looking daft as she walked on tip-toes or flexed her calf muscles while she stood at the cooker.

"Next time?" said Davood. A small group of men came out of a pub and meandered drunkenly about, and Davood moved to shield her with his body. An automatic instinct, she supposed, but one that still made her smile.

"Yes. Our next date."

There was a pause. They passed the group of men and turned past the Corpus Clock on the corner of King's Parade, with its monstrous grasshopper always gobbling up the passing seconds and minutes.

"I don't think there's going to be a next date," said Davood eventually, and Clodagh paused, leaning on her crutch as she looked up at him.

"You don't?"

He sighed, shoved his hands in his pockets and hunched his shoulders. "Look. I like you—I mean, I really like you, and I really like spending time with you."

"I like spending time with you," said Clodagh, because it was true. He'd become a good friend.

"But be honest with me, Clodagh. You don't see this going anywhere, do you?"

Her gaze skittered away from his face.

"Our mutual friend told me that grasshopper thing," he gestured to the clock, "is meant to represent the inevitable march of time."

"The Chronophage," said Clodagh. "Literally something that eats time."

He smiled. "You see? You're smart. You know things, like Latin—"

"It's Greek. The inscription underneath is Latin." Dammit, Random Fact Girl was back. Jamie was a bad influence on her.

Davood's smile grew wider. "What's it mean?"

Clodagh had asked Jamie, because it was a bit beyond the scope of her Latin primer. "'The world passeth away, and the lust thereof.' From the Bible, apparently."

He nodded, as if thinking about it. "So what it's saying is, time gets gobbled up and we're not getting any of it back?"

"I guess." She shivered, a blast of January wind

whistling down Bene't Street.

"Therefore, we really shouldn't be wasting any of it. That's why I asked you out. Seize the moment and all. But it's not working for you, is it?"

Clodagh didn't know what to say. If she'd met him under any other circumstances, she'd probably have fallen for him. If she hadn't met Jamie.

She'd been silent for too long. Davood nodded, and said, "Come on, it's freezing out here."

Clodagh nodded and walked alongside him back to the gatehouse, where he paused, took her face in his hands and kissed her softly. And it was a pleasant kiss. A kiss that would surely have stirred another woman.

He moved back, an expression on his face that she couldn't read.

"I'm sorry?" she said. *Try it again, without the question mark*.

"Yeah. Tell you what, maybe we'll try again some time."

"Maybe," said Clodagh.

"When you've got over your crush," he said, and she froze guiltily. "I'm very good at reading people," Davood added softly. "It's my job."

"I don't," she began, but she couldn't even convince herself.

He nodded, then sighed. "Just be careful," he said, and opened the door to let her through.

By the time the Crowded House gig came around Jamie was beside himself with anxiety. What if his grandmother or father or someone came up with something else he had to do? What if he couldn't get out of it? What if he missed the gig? The surest way to lose something was to want it too much.

"It'll be fine," Clodagh said to him that morning as he came back to collect the scarf he'd forgotten. "Stop stressing. I'll see you later."

But he was stressing. He really, really wanted to enjoy the concert, and he really wanted Clodagh to, as well. She said she didn't really know the band but liked the few bits she'd heard. Was she being polite? Was it too staid for her?

He was distracted throughout the day, and only stopped worrying about it when Ruchi scurried in, face worryingly tight, after a meeting with her PhD supervisor.

"Are you okay?" asked Zheng.

"Fine."

"What'd he say?"

"Oh, nothing. Just that I have to do it all again." She buried her face in her hands, and the three men in the room looked helplessly at each other.

"Why?" asked Jamie.

"Because he doesn't trust my data! I ran the program three times, it's all sound, but he thinks I've made it up!"

"Well, show him the logs—"

"I did! There was a flaw in one of them which I made corrections for but he said that was sloppy… He just wants me to do it again." She looked up, eyes damp and nose pink. "He never makes any of you rewrite your whole reports."

Hunter and Jamie said nothing. She was right.

"He made me amend mine," Zheng said, "but I had made a mistake in it."

Jamie looked down at his keyboard. He'd made mistakes too, but his supervisor had never made him repeat a whole report. Nor Hunter.

"Do you want me to have a word?" Jamie said.

"No. That will make it worse. Like I've been telling tales. Like I need a big strong man to stand up for me." She blew out a sigh. "All right. Looks like I have work to do."

Jamie felt so bad he offered to take her out for lunch, but she said she was too busy, and he went home that evening feeling angry as well as anxious.

"I mean, I talked to some of the undergrads and apparently it happens all the time," he said to Clodagh as she cooked pasta. "More of the female students get asked to repeat their experiments, or accused of copying someone, than the boys. They waste hours and hours defending themselves, instead of just getting on with their work. And we ask why there aren't more women in science," he snapped.

"Took you that long, did it?"

"You knew about this?"

Clodagh laughed hollowly. "I'm a mixed-race working class woman," she said. "What do you think? Look, they pick on us because it forces us to waste time defending ourselves, or proving ourselves, or proving them wrong, when they know all along we can do it just as well. And it doesn't matter whether 'it' is a degree, or a job, or... just being a human in this world. The more time we're forced to waste, the less time we spend threatening the existence of the privileged white man."

Jamie blinked at her. "Christ, you're right."

"Of course I'm right. Have you heard the one about privileged people feeling discriminated against when all they're facing is equality?"

Jamie leaned against the kitchen table. "Forget history, you should go into politics."

"No bloody fear," she said. "Can you pass me that bacon?"

He did, watching her stir it into the saucepan. He should probably talk to people about this kind of issue. The university, for one. What was the point of being a prince if you couldn't use your voice for good? He wondered if any of the family was involved in a charity or program to address issues like—

217

"Food's ready." Clodagh glanced at the clock. "Did you want to see the support act?"

Jamie shrugged as he sat down opposite her. "No point. According to Geraint the idea is to get in there at the very last minute before the band comes on stage, to minimise contact with the public in the foyer. Apparently the venue's security team will notify him."

"How organised. Do we have to leave the second they go off stage, too?"

He sighed. "I hope not. But probably."

They loitered in the car around the corner until Geraint got the go-ahead, despite the Corn Exchange barely being a ten minute walk from Lady Mathilda even at Clodagh's reduced pace. Either Olivia or Geraint had planned it so well that they could access their seats directly from the side entrance of the building, making for an easy exit too.

The band came on just as they took their seats, flanked on all sides by PPOs. Jamie started to worry they wouldn't share his musical taste, and then thirty seconds into *World Where You Live* he forgot to care. The band joked with each other and with the audience, an easy rapport that spoke of many repeat performances.

"Who came to see us in London?" Half the audience whooped and waved.

"I think I recognise that guy from last time we were here," joked Nick the bassist, peering into a crowd he clearly couldn't see.

"Yeah you do!" someone random shouted back, to general laughter.

Jamie glanced at Clodagh beside him. She was laughing, and once or twice during the better known songs he caught her singing to the choruses.

"Oh my God, I haven't heard this one in ages!" Jamie cried, as they began *English Trees.*

When it ended he leaned close and said in her ear,

"It's possibly about the death of their drummer, Paul Hester. He committed suicide while they were on a UK tour. Well, Neil and his brother were. Nick flew out to be with them and joined them at their Albert Hall gig. A friend of mine was there. They said it was electric."

"They didn't cancel?"

"No. They said Paul's favourite thing was to play music for people who loved it, so that's what they were going to do."

"That's really touching."

More than once, an audience member yelled out an obscure album track, and the band glanced at each other, shrugged, and started playing it. When they brought out the big hits, they played extended versions to let the audience sing along.

At one point, chatting with the audience, Neil said, "Now I hear this place has amazing acoustics, even if you're not using an amp. Shall we try it out?"

"Is he kidding?" Clodagh said, eyeing the massive sound rig.

"Probably not." Jamie watched them unplug their guitars with great flourishes.

"Now you've got to be really quiet," Neil said, and the audience rippled with murmurs before going so silent it was eerie. "Good job."

Then he played an A minor chord and the hairs on the back of Jamie's neck stood up. The sound was small compared to what came out of the amplified speakers, but the domed hall magnified it and the music filled the air.

"Perfect," said Neil, and Jamie had to agree because he knew that chord like he knew his own heartbeat. *Fall At Your Feet* was the song that had made him fall in love with the band, back when he was a kid and modern music was Britpop and trance and grunge and he didn't think he was cut out for it.

And then he'd heard the perfect fall of notes, the minor keys and the unexpected chord changes, and he knew he'd be in love forever.

He didn't realise he had tears in his eyes until Clodagh took his hand, and he gripped it tight as the song floated ethereally around him.

"Will you sing it with me?" said Neil, and the audience, soft but in surprisingly good voice, joined in the last chorus. They even hit the harmonies. And Jamie, anonymous among the crowd, sang along with a bunch of people who didn't even know he was there, a part of a greater thing instead of one focus point in it.

Clodagh leaned against Jamie, her head on his shoulder, probably the only person in the audience not singing. She could feel his voice vibrating through him, a tremor of love and excitement. His eyes shone with worship as he looked up at the stage.

Imagine what it is to be looked at like that by him, she thought, gazing helplessly at his profile, and then the song ended and Jamie turned his head and kissed her.

He'd once tried to explain to her the Crowded House Moment, where a chord changed with such unexpected perfection it took your breath away. This was such a moment.

Clodagh had thought she'd enjoyed kissing before. She thought she'd had chemistry before. But Jamie set her on fire, his lips on hers, one hand cupping the back of her neck, the other clutching hers. Her lips parted and she licked into him and his body yielded against hers and heat followed it. Lightning crackled around them.

I know you. I know you, now, and I always have and I always will.

She breathed him in, the closest thing in the world to herself. There was no one else around.

Then sound washed in around them, thunderous

applause, and Clodagh thought muzzily that they should be applauding because that had been one spectacular kiss, and then she realised she was in a crowd of several hundred people and they hadn't even noticed her kissing Jamie.

She stared up at him, and his face reflected the same shock she felt. Hazel eyes, with a touch of green.

"That was spectacular," said someone into a microphone, and she could only agree.

Jamie didn't let go of her until the concert ended, not even to applaud. She was only half listening, too aware of him beside her, her body turned in against his so she could feel the heat radiating from him.

And when the lights went up after the final encore and the PPO nearest the door opened it and they were shepherded out, shielded from everyone else, directly into the car, she didn't even wait for the door to close before she was kissing him again.

"I am so into you," Jamie breathed, and she'd have agreed but she was too busy kissing him.

When the car door opened again they sprung guiltily apart, and then Jamie grinned and tugged her after him into the garage, towards the door leading to the garden.

Davood Khan stood there, one hand on the car door. His face was expressionless. Clodagh caught his eye stricken with guilt, and the tiniest hint of wryness touched his face. He nodded.

Then Jamie was tugging her across the frosty grass to the front door, and inside he started kissing her again, and she forgot absolutely everyone and everything else in the world.

She held onto her handbag as he led her upstairs, and when it formed a barrier to his removal of her t-shirt she held up one finger for him to wait.

He froze, eager as a hound. She almost expected his ears to quiver.

"Hah!" She held up the packet of condoms triumphantly, and Jamie grinned at her ear to ear.

His bed was huge and plush and they rolled all over it, tossing items of clothing away and arching against each other, kissing and kissing. Jamie, lean and pale in the moonlight, hair wild where she'd clutched at him when he kissed a trail of fire down her body. The way he held her, as if he couldn't get enough of touching her, as if he'd never seen something so lovely or desirable. She felt that way when he looked at her, as if she was perfect and wonderful, and she loved him for it.

Her thigh hitched over his hip as he drove into her and shuddered, lips on her throat, gasping her name. *Yes*, she whispered, and *more*, and he gave it to her, until she was tossing and arching and crying out as she broke apart in his arms.

And afterwards he lay beside her, chest heaving, looking shellshocked.

"Jamie?"

He stared up at the wooden panels of the bed canopy. It was probably as old as the house.

"Yeah?"

"Are you okay?"

He swallowed, and she watched the movement of his lovely throat. "I think you broke me."

Alarm swept her. "Shit. What'd I do?" Had she been too enthusiastic? Had she hurt him? He had gone pretty wild there at the end. Maybe he'd strained something—

"My brain doesn't work. Hang on." He rubbed his hand over his face, then pulled her against him, breathing in her hair as it brushed his face. "Okay that's better."

Clodagh lifted her head to look at him and raised an eyebrow. "Really?"

Jamie cuddled her close. "I've heard the phrase 'mind blowing' before but I've never… I mean…"

She smiled as she snuggled in. "It was good for me too."

"Jesus." He blew out a long breath. "Is it always going to be like that?"

He wants to make this a recurring thing. Clodagh smiled, and said, "Bloody hope so."

Jamie kissed her mouth, then lay back, eyes closed, fingers playing with her hair.

She traced a bead of sweat as it trickled down his chest. She followed further, to his hip with its scrolled tattoo. "You've kept this quiet."

"I'm not in the habit of wandering around naked."

"What's it say?" The script was looped and curled and she wasn't in the mood to read upside down.

"*Nulli Secundus*." He opened one eye. "Sergeant Travers thought that was funny."

"Why? I haven't got that far with my Latin Primer."

"It's the motto of the Coldstream. 'Second to none.'"

Ah. A cruel joke for someone born fourth in line. Because he was a prince, after all, and she'd forgotten that. *Oh Christ, I just had sex with a prince.*

Clodagh kissed Jamie's jaw and said, "It's true as far as I'm concerned."

He squeezed her tight at that, and seemed to relax a little.

"And this?" There was a scar down the front of one thigh.

"Oh. Roadside bomb in Helmand. Small, and badly made, and I was at a distance. Could have been worse."

Clodagh stared at it. About four inches of pale pink, puckered skin on his leg. Much further up and it could have hit his torso. A few inches to the left and he'd have had trouble making sweet love to her just now.

"Jesus," she whispered.

"Hey, I thought chicks dug scars?" he said lightly.

"It could've killed you." She'd known he'd been a

soldier, but somehow the geeky, clever guy she was in bed with didn't match up with a man in camo getting blown up in Afghanistan.

"But it didn't. I only had some stitches and bedrest and orders not to wear shorts in front of a camera. Which, I wouldn't anyway. Hey." He nuzzled her shocked face. "It's okay. I'm not going back. And I tell you what, my dresser was much more scandalised by the tat."

Clodagh pulled herself together. "At least it's a proper tattoo that means something. Mine's just fake Celtic knot garbage. Half the girls on my estate had the same thing."

Jamie stroked the tramp stamp on her lower back. "I like it."

"You don't, but thanks for saying it."

"I like you." Was it her imagination or did he hesitate over the 'like' part?

"I'm pretty into you too."

Jamie smiled, and then he suddenly made a noise halfway between a groan and a laugh.

"What?"

"Olivia. She saw this coming."

"So did Davood." Jamie glanced at her guiltily, and she nodded. "He told me I had a crush on you and I guess…"

"Wish he'd bloody told me," Jamie grumbled, pulling the covers over them both. Clodagh settled back into his arms, which was an extremely pleasant place to be.

"I had no idea you were even interested," she said.

"Really? I've been mooning after you for weeks. You hadn't even noticed?"

Clodagh laughed. "I guess I was too busy trying not to let you see me mooning over you."

Jamie groaned. "Do you ever sometimes stop and wonder if you're not still a teenager and this being a grown-up business is all some terrible mistake?"

"Oh God, all the time."

His hand ran suggestively over her bare back. "Mind you, it does have its compensations. We don't have to get up for school tomorrow."

"You do."

"I am a grown-up doing a PhD and I am a prince of the realm and I'm sure if I get Daddy to give them a call I can go in late."

Clodagh laughed at that, and Jamie grinned, and she fell asleep in his arms, smiling.

CHAPTER FIFTEEN

So I didn't dream it.

Clodagh was still asleep beside him, all that glorious hair spilling over the pillow. He lay for a long moment staring at her, unable to quite believe it had really happened, until his snooze alarm went off and he reluctantly swung out of bed.

The cold morning air woke him up a bit as he crossed the lawn to the gatehouse, where Martins was pulling on a jacket with hi-vis strips over her running gear. "Sir."

"Who else—" He looked up to see Davood Khan standing there in workout clothes, and exhaled uncomfortably. "Khan. Can I have a word?"

His bodyguard nodded and followed him outside to the misty garden.

Jamie stamped his feet and rubbed his hands. "Look. I know you and Clodagh had a… thing."

"Sir." Khan's face gave nothing away.

"I'm really sorry about last night. It was… I didn't mean to rub your face in it. Neither of us did."

"Yes, sir."

Jamie searched the taller man's face. "Is that it?"

Khan appeared to think about it for a moment, then he said, "She was just killing time with me until you figured things out. I don't mind."

He was letting Clodagh go that easily? Was he insane? "Don't *mind*?"

"She was always yours, really. I feel I should be apologising to you."

"Oh God, don't. We'll be here til the crack of doom."

Khan smiled at that. "Do you still want me to walk her home this evening?"

Despite his instincts screaming at him that no one else should be walking her anywhere, Jamie knew what Khan was asking. He and Clodagh shouldn't go public. Not immediately. He didn't want to scare her off immediately, once she found out what it was like to be in the media spotlight. They should take their time. They'd hidden their living arrangements for this long, after all; their sleeping arrangements couldn't be that much harder?

"I'd appreciate it," he said. "But if it's too uncomfortable for you—"

"It's my job, sir," said Khan, and that seemed to be the end of it.

The morning was cold and damp, and by the time they left Midsummer Common to turn for home Jamie was dreaming of being back in his warm, welcoming bed with his warm, welcoming girlfriend…

Girlfriend. Christ, Jamie, slow down. Don't get ahead of yourself. She might wake up and decide it was all a terrible idea and then he'd got the rest of forever to live on the memory of one night.

But when he went back up the stairs and into his room, she was stirring in his bed, opening her eyes and stretching. Oh God, she was gorgeous.

"Hi," he said, probably looking like a moonstruck idiot and not caring in the slightest.

"Hi," she said, and then she grimaced.

"What?" No, not right away, *don't let her change her mind this soon—*

"Argh. Ankle." She sat up and reached under the covers to rub it. "It's fine, just a bit… well I haven't been doing that kind of exercise for a while."

Jamie sat on the edge of the bed and pulled back the duvet to expose her feet. Her right ankle was still a little swollen, although it was hard to tell unless he looked hard. The bruising had gone, however, and from the vigorous way she massaged it he guessed the pain wasn't agonising.

"Can I get you anything for it? Ice pack? Heat pack? Painkillers?"

Clodagh looked up at him and her eyes warmed to amber. "You could get me something. A kiss?"

He did. Oh, he did. He kissed her so long and so thoroughly that forcing himself to get up to shower and change was the hardest thing he'd ever done.

Clodagh followed him downstairs wearing the shirt he'd discarded last night, which was wicked of her because she looked so damn sexy in it he poured tea on his cornflakes and forgot how spoons worked.

"I'm working tonight," she said, as he kissed her goodbye.

"I'll come in to see you."

"Be subtle. I don't—" She broke off, fingers plucking at a shirt button. "I don't know about going public with this."

"Subtlety is my middle name," he promised her.

"No, your middle names are William Frederick Henry," she said, and he went all gooey inside at her taking the time to find out.

He kissed her once more, promised he'd see her later, and whistled all the way to the lab.

"You're in a good mood," said Ruchi.

"I had a good night."

"Oh, the concert was good?"

Concert? Oh, right, the thing he'd been looking forward to for weeks. "Yeah. Really amazing. Blew my mind," he said, grinning.

His smile only dimmed when he saw Ruchi's face darken as Dr Kenyon went past. What the hell. He logged out the system, went to Dr Kenyon's office and knocked on the door. "Can I have a word?"

"Ah, Your Royal Highness. Please, come in."

Kenyon was all smiles for him. He was all smiles for Hunter, too. Funny how he was so much more cheerful when dealing with rich white men.

"I noticed Ruchi Sarkar is rewriting her end of term report," Jamie said.

His supervisor nodded sympathetically. "Yes. I'm afraid it just wasn't up to scratch."

"In what way?" When Kenyon frowned, Jamie explained, "When I make a mistake you allow me to correct it."

"Yes, but Your Highness makes so few mistakes…"

Brownnoser. "His Highness makes plenty," Jamie said. "But Ruchi doesn't."

Kenyon was already shaking his head. "With respect, sir, that girl spends far too much time daydreaming. Always on her phone, texting and playing games—"

"Games?" Jamie played games on his phone all the time. He pretended they were relevant research, but he was totally lying.

"Yes, the thing with the words…"

"I've never seen her do that in the lab. Only at lunch and on breaks."

Kenyon faltered.

"I've noticed that some of the other girls have been punished for not paying enough attention, or have been given lower grades—"

"I can't help it if their work isn't up to scratch," said Kenyon, spreading his hands. "It's not sexism, it's a meritocracy."

Jamie had to employ an awful lot of reserve to keep from rolling his eyes. "It's not sexism if all the girls are outperformed by the boys?"

"It's not my fault men are better suited to-"

"You finish that sentence and you'd better have your CV at the ready," Jamie said sharply. "I'm not in the habit of throwing my weight around, Dr Kenyon, but I have friends in the highest of high places, so maybe don't irritate me by pretending you don't know you're talking bullshit."

"I beg your—"

"It's my grandmother for whose pardon you beg," Jamie said, "not mine. I know for a fact Ruchi doesn't waste nearly as much time as Hunter around the lab. She works diligently and efficiently and you know why? Because she has to, because you keep finding fault with her work. Which forces her to actually waste her time repeating perfectly sound experiments. So when she ends up with inferior results, you can say it's her own fault because you once caught her texting. You can say it's not your fault men are better suited to science. Or computing. Or whatever you were going to say. Face it. Ruchi could run rings around most of the men here, and that scares the life out of you because you don't want to admit she might be equal or maybe even better than you."

"I'm not racist," began Dr Kenyon.

"Funny you should need to defend yourself against something I haven't even accused you of yet."

Dr Kenyon went silent, fuming. Jamie was absolutely certain he'd never been called out like this, or at least not by someone he couldn't overrule.

Finally, something his title was good for!

Jamie stood up. "I'm going to be here for the next three years," he said, and before Kenyon could open his mouth, he added, "Because we both know I'm not going to fail my probationary year, don't we? Neither is Ruchi. If this kind of thing continues, they're going to be a really uncomfortable three years for you, Dr Kenyon. I suggest you research with great haste all possible meanings of the phrase 'check your privilege'."

To his credit, Dr Kenyon didn't bother to splutter that Jamie couldn't talk to him like that.

Jamie walked out, whistling.

Clodagh spent half the day swearing at her hair, which for once she hadn't tied up overnight, and now she was paying the price with snarls and tangles. Desperately hoping Jamie wouldn't come home in the middle of the day, she dosed her whole head with gobs of conditioner and left it in. At least these days she could afford the extra.

Combing it out in front of the mirror reminded her, as it so often did, of her grandmother and the endless pain of having her tight curls yanked about by a brush. Photos of her first few years on this Earth inevitably had her wearing a pink hat or ribbon over her shorn scalp, because neither her Irish grandmother nor her blonde mother had any idea how to deal with 'that terrible frizz'.

It wasn't until Clodagh's grandmother died that she was allowed to get her hair braided, at a salon the other black girls at school had told her about. And it was years after that she finally had the courage to follow the tips she found online and let her curls go natural.

At least Jamie likes them, she thought, and caught herself smiling gooily. Today's haircare was probably a decent price to pay for last night's luxury; although if she spent the night with him again tonight he'd be getting a lesson in why she tied it up at night.

At the pub, everyone told her she looked nice, without specifying why. Clodagh figured it was the secret pleasure they ran through her every time she thought about Jamie's lips caressing her skin, his fingertips trailing fire, his eyes burning with desire for her.

She found herself counting down the minutes until the lab closed and he might be in for a drink, and when she saw Martins walk in, she beamed.

Then she remembered herself, and made her face politely neutral as the student gang filed in and started ordering drinks. Jamie was amongst them, unable to speak to her without anyone overhearing, so it was a torturous half hour before he came up to the bar on a pretense of ordering some crisps.

"I keep thinking about touching you," he said, and Clodagh had to concentrate on breathing. When he came back for the next round of drinks, he murmured, "I keep remembering how you taste," and she was glad she wasn't holding a glass or it might have shattered in her hand.

Everyone else went home after a couple of drinks, but Jamie stayed longer, until she texted him to go home because he was making everyone suspicious. This turned out to be a bad idea, because once he'd got texting into his head he started telling her all the things he'd enjoyed last night and wanted to try tonight.

She practically ran out of the pub after Last Orders.

"Slow down," said Davood, "your ankle isn't ready for that kind of speed yet."

She made herself walk at a sensible measured pace, because he was right, and also because being out with him in the cold night air reminded her she had some apologising to do.

"Look, I'm—"

"Don't," he said. He glanced down at her. "He already spoke to me this morning."

Had he? "What'd he say?"

Davood shrugged. "Oh, you know, that he was open to threesomes—" He grinned as she bashed him. "Look, it's fine. We hardly went out, and it was always pretty clear who you were interested in."

Clodagh chewed her lip. She kind of felt rotten that he'd had to be a front row centre witness to all the wild snogging though.

"A word of advice though? I wouldn't go around dating all your PPOs in future. He might get jealous."

"All my PPOs? Are you expecting me to turn into a global celebrity?" Clodagh said.

Davood just said, as if she was an idiot, "Well, yes."

They'd reached the gatehouse then, so he bid her goodnight and watched her cross the lawn as she tried not to fret too much about what he'd just said.

She wanted this relationship with Jamie. She'd never felt like this about anybody before, such a strong attraction and yet such easy friendship at the same time. She'd never met anyone she felt she knew bone-deep.

And yet. Could they really do this? Keep it secret forever? Of course not. Sooner or later the hiding and the secrets would become all-out lying and denial and she didn't know if she could live like that.

And yet what was the alternative? Going public? Having the world's press focus all of its attention on her? Have her every outfit, hairstyle and facial expression scrutinised? She'd seen what happened to Countess Annemarie, who'd been relatively unknown outside her own country, when she formally became attached to Prince Edward. She'd seen the constant attention focused on Princess Victoria, on every aspect of her appearance, what she said and how she said it, who she was friends with, whether her decision to marry the son of a duke was a good or a bad one, when she'd have children, if she was pregnant already, how thin she was and if it was a sign of anorexia…

And those were two women who'd been groomed for the spotlight their whole lives, who had impeccable reputations and carried no greater scandal than wearing too high a heel or too bright a lipstick.

She let herself in and leaned against the heavy oak door of Jamie's house, closing her eyes. If she was even seen in Jamie's company, if anyone had cause to look her up, to wonder where they'd seen her before or why a half-Jamaican girl used an Irish name…

Her world would still go on turning. But it wouldn't have Jamie in it any more.

"Clo? Is that you?"

She should end it now. Before it could get any worse. Before she got in too deep and it was too hard to get out. Here was Jamie now, padding barefoot over the ancient oak floorboards of the dining room, hair rumpled and glasses smudged and smiling at her like she was the loveliest thing on Earth.

"Hey, I thought I heard you. Are you hungry? I made Spanish tortilla. Won't take long to warm up."

She looked up into his warm hazel eyes as he took her into his arms and kissed her, and she kissed him back and let him lead her to the sofa and feed her and love her and then, coward that she was, she went willingly to his bed and never said a word about why this was all such a terrible idea.

CHAPTER SIXTEEN

February saw Jamie flying out to Spain for a Davis Cup match, cheering Andy Murray on despite never really quite understanding the rules of tennis. Scoring, sure, but when the ball was in and when it was out and quite how one won a point were things he had to be reminded of every time he watched a match. Ed was the sporty one, but Ed was off in Wales visiting one of his pet charities.

He handed his phone over to Geraint so he wouldn't be tempted to text Clodagh during the breaks. This was standard protocol at most events, so he wasn't caught on camera fiddling with his phone—even if he glanced at it for a second during a change of ends, the headlines would proclaim he'd been ignoring the whole match to stare at his phone—but he was so in love with her it was hard to be out of contact for more than minutes at a time.

In love. He might as well admit it now, if only to himself. He didn't want to scare Clodagh, who he sensed was a little overwhelmed at the idea of publicity. On the one hand, this was great, because it meant she wasn't in it just for the fame, and it also lent a rather piquant secrecy to the whole affair; but on the other it really sucked because he wanted to tell the world how amazing it was to be in love with such a wonderful woman.

They'd kept it secret for weeks now. Outside the house, their relationship went no further than barmaid and patron. Sure, some of the guys had teased him about fancying her a bit, and he'd overheard Oz referring to Jamie as Clodagh's friend, but no more than that. Khan was still keeping an eye on her, which meant most people assumed he was seeing her. This was fine by Jamie in a wider sense but also made him want to leap across the table and scream, "She's mine, you fucker," about four times a day.

This was something he had, so far, restrained himself from doing.

For Valentine's Day, he bought champagne and cooked her a meal to be eaten by candlelight at the parquet table in the dining room. He lit a fire in the huge inglenook and for once was glad they hadn't gone out for a meal like normal people, because it would have meant waiting to get home instead of making love to her in the middle of dinner. They ended up eating off plates on the hearthrug, half-dressed and smug with satisfaction.

In March, Annemarie gave birth to a baby boy and Jamie was summoned for various photocalls with the family.

"You will be his godfather?" Annemarie said from the sofa at Kensington Palace, cradling the small bundle.

"Of course. Delighted to."

"Good, because we're naming him after you," said Edward. "Well, middle name. We thought Henry, after Grandpa, then James for you and Willem for Annemarie's uncle."

"I'm touched," said Jamie, and meant it. Of course, they'd named their eldest for the Queen and Prince of Wales, so his was very much a second-tier name, but it was still a nice thought.

He was less touched when his father called him aside and said, "I've been speaking to the Duke of Allendale about Lady Olivia."

Jamie kept his face politely disinterested. "Yes?"

"Yes. He says both of you are adamant you're not getting married."

"Yes?"

Prince Frederick gave his son a knowing look. "We all know what that means."

"Yes, it means we're adamant we're not getting married," said Jamie. "Give it up, Dad. You always told me I didn't have to marry for duty and I should wait until I found someone I truly loved."

"And you don't love Olivia?"

"No more than I love Victoria."

"Victoria is your sister—"

"Yes, exactly."

That, of course, put the idea in his head. He loved Clodagh. He lived with her already, he was sleeping with her and he couldn't wait to get home to see her every minute of the day. He wanted to wake up with her tomorrow, and the day after, and all the tomorrows after that.

He wanted to spend the rest of his life with her.

He was halfway down the stairs when the thought hit him like a lightning bolt. *I want to marry Clodagh.*

It felt right, as right as it had felt to kiss her and to wake up with her beside him, as right as it had felt to hold her hand that morning by the river. He'd waited, and he'd found someone he truly loved, just like his parents had told him to.

Of course, they'd only been together a few weeks, so suddenly declaring his intentions might come across as a little, well, terrifying. He decided to play it as cool as he could.

"How's the baby?" she asked, looking up from her Latin primer as he walked in that evening.

"Baby James, you mean?" He scrolled through his photos to show her. "That's his middle name but you know it's what I'll be calling him. My nephew."

"Your own personal nephew?"

"Yep." He flopped down on the sofa beside her, and she made appropriate noises at the photos. "You should've been there," he added casually. "I know you're great with kids."

She'd gone still, and now she narrowed her eyes at him. "That's not funny. You know, since they announced it was a boy my sister Kylie has been moping because she thought it should be a girl so her son could grow up and marry her. Now she's trying to convince herself that every ultrasound she had was wrong and it's a girl after all."

"Is that likely?"

"No. And besides, like a kid from that estate is ever going to meet royalty, let alone marry it," she said.

Jamie's heart leapt. *Ask her now. That's your cue.*

"So here's a thing, anyway," she said, reaching for her cup of tea. "I was reading that the Romans liked to basically name their kids with numbers. So if your dad was Julius, you'd be Julius Primus, Julius Secundus, and the girls would be Julia Prima, Julia Secunda and so on. Isn't that nuts? To just give your kids numbers?"

"It'd make things a damn sight simpler," Jamie said, letting the opportunity fade away. It wasn't the right time yet. "I could just have been called Quartus when I was born. Mind you they'd have to keep changing it. I'd be Septimus by now."

"Like Snape. No, he was Severus."

"Oh please, I'm a clear Ravenclaw."

She smiled and snuggled against him. Jamie wondered if she knew how much that filled his heart with love. "What am I?"

"Gryffindor," he said straight away. "You can do the Pottermore test but I'm pretty sure you're a solid Gryffindor."

"Ooh, we're like Romeo and Juliet."

"They didn't end all that well."

"No." Clodagh's hand rested on his chest, her fingers fiddling with his shirt pocket. Eventually she said, "If I'd been Roman what would they have called me?"

"You're the oldest, aren't you? What's your dad's name?" He realised he'd never asked her. But then neither had she ever mentioned him.

Clodagh chewed her lip, and then she said, "I have no idea."

Ah. So that was why. Her mother, her sisters and brothers and all the neiflings, sure, but her father? Jamie realised he'd assumed her parents were separated, but this was... well actually, it made sense now he thought about it.

She glanced up at him. "Shocked?"

"No, that is..." He considered what to say. "You've never mentioned him."

"That's because I have no idea who he is." She sighed and laid her head back down on his shoulder. "Mum met him at a party. She thinks it was at this party. She said she hadn't been with a black feller before then. That's how she knows who it was, by the way. If I'd been born white there'd be half a dozen candidates, apparently."

Jamie wasn't sure what to say to that. "She's... is she in touch with him?"

Clodagh snorted. "Of course not. Apparently he'd told her he was going back to Jamaica the next day. You know, like GIs used to tell girls they were shipping out in the morning, I guess. She fell for it. And here I am."

"You've never tried to find him?"

"How? I don't even know his name. Mum couldn't remember. Apparently there were quite a lot of illegal substances at the party. It's a miracle she could even remember sleeping with him in the first place, she used to tell me."

"Christ."

Clodagh laughed hollowly. "No, not him. If my nan was here she'd tell you only God does immaculate conceptions. Wages of sin and all that." She was silent for a while. "Anyway. While the whole country can name your entire family, I don't even know my dad's name."

Jamie put both his arms around her and hugged her close. He wanted to tell her he'd be her family, but he couldn't find a way to do it without sounding weird. Besides...

What would his family say if he told them that instead of the impeccably bred Lady Olivia, he wanted to marry a mixed-race girl from a council estate who didn't know who her father was?

Perhaps if he sort of drip-fed the information. Let them get to know her first. Let them like her and accept her and then casually mention where she was from...

"At least the others do, although in Tony's case it was only after a DNA test." Clodagh's voice came from the region of his chest. "Do you know, I used to be well envious of the twins. They knew their dad. I mean, we lived with him. And they'd always got each other anyway."

"You had a stepdad?"

"Yeah. Well, they weren't married, but we lived with him. He was nice." She hesitated. "Might as well tell you. Duke was Roma. For three years we lived in a traveller camp."

She waited as if expecting a reaction. Jamie pictured the rundown caravan sites he'd seen on the news, usually with some angry local resident trying to hide their racism. He knew what people called them. He expected Clodagh had suffered more than her fair share of it.

"Must've been different."

She snorted. "Yeah. Different is one word. You know how everyone hates gyppos? Well, imagine being the kid who really stands out in the gyppo camp. Duke was really good to me, but he couldn't stop what people said. He told me to ignore it."

Jamie held her a bit tighter. "Did you?"

"I was a kid. What do you think?" She sniffed. "Still he also taught me to throw a punch, so there's that." She sighed. "I miss Duke. He died when I was seven. All Mum's boyfriends after that were dickheads. It's what made me so angry about Lee and Hanna. I could see it coming, just like I had with those men Mum used to bring home, and I couldn't stop it then, either."

I'll kill him. I want to kill him.

She shifted in his grip. "Hey Jamie, I'm going to need to breathe."

He forced himself to loosen his hold on her. Thoughts of Lee Cunningham brought out the snarling beast in him. Sometimes, Jamie entertained violent fantasies of beating seven kinds of hell out of him, kicking and punching until he was just a heap of bloody meat.

Sandhurst had trained him in several forms of armed and unarmed combat, after all, and he did have a few friends in the Forces…

"Sorry," he managed.

Clodagh shrugged. "Don't be. I grew up tough."

That wasn't quite what he'd meant. But she didn't let him explain, sighing in his arms and saying, "Sorry I brought the mood down. My fucked-up family and me, eh?"

"You didn't bring the mood down." The more he learned about her, the more he respected her strength.

"Hey, Clodagh?"

"Yeah?"

"I think you're amazing."

She looked up at him then, and he couldn't read her expression. For a moment she looked almost fearful. Then she rolled her eyes and said, "You going soppy on me, Windsor?"

"Can't a man be soppy with his girlfriend?"

He said it lightly, but Clodagh froze nonetheless. *Dammit. Scared her.*

"I suppose he can," she said, and it was only afterwards that he realised her smile didn't completely meet her eyes.

By April her ankle was as healed as it was going to be, and her heart was near to breaking. The problem was she'd fallen totally in love with Jamie, and he'd made it pretty damn clear he was in love with her.

She'd fallen down the rabbit hole now. She kept furiously researching his family tree to see if there was any sort of precedence to a prince marrying a commoner, but there was precious little to go on. Even the untitled women and men who'd married into the family had been from the very oldest and richest families in the country. None of them were really commoners, not like Clodagh. Not really common.

His great-grandfather, King Edward VIII, had even faced the threat of abdication over his choice of lover: a married woman who'd already been divorced once and had the extra bad taste to be American. Had the family not steered him back towards the widowed Freda Dudley-Ward he'd have been in real trouble. Even Mrs Dudley-Ward had apparently been a risky choice, arriving as she did with two children already in tow, but at least, it had been argued in her favour, this meant she was fertile.

At least Clodagh had never been married, and she was English. Well, half English. Well, a quarter Irish. But she'd been raised in the UK. Had never left it in fact, which wasn't much of a point in her favour.

But the points against her...

At the pub when it was quiet, at home when Jamie was out, at night when she was trying to fall asleep beside him, she turned the facts over and over in her head. His family might be able to accept a girl with no money and lineage, a girl from a council estate. They might be able to accept a girl with no formal qualifications, because at least she was working to change that. They might be able to accept a girl whose grandmother was Irish by way of the East End, and whose father was Jamaican, and whose skin was decidedly not white. They might allow that her parents hadn't been married and she was therefore illegitimate.

But not all of those things, not all at the same time. And they would never accept, she knew, the really big, fundamental things. That her parents hadn't been married because her mother didn't even know who her father was. And that she used her middle name not because it sounded better or to honour her grandmother, but because she wanted to put Sharday Walsh and her horrible, mortifying, pitiable past behind her.

Because if Jamie's family ever found out she'd given up a baby for adoption at the age of fifteen and been filmed doing it on that awful TV show, they wouldn't just keep her away from Jamie, they'd probably have her exiled.

Easter weekend saw Jamie off to Windsor for egg hunts and services in St George's Chapel. He moped for days about going, and on Maundy Thursday he kissed her goodbye so thoroughly she could barely stand.

"I love you," he said. "I don't think I've said it before but I do love you."

I love you too, Clodagh wanted to say, but her throat closed over with tears and she just nodded instead. She watched him leave across the lawn of the Master's Garden, already aching for him.

The pub was empty of students but saw plenty of tourists come in, especially as word seemed to have got around that Prince Jamie drank here. Clodagh was surprised by a face that seemed familiar, if a little out of context.

"Oh my God, Clodagh? It is Clodagh isn't it?" The girl pushed back her sleeve to show Clodagh a scar on her arm. "Becca, remember? From that party? You took me to the hospital."

"Yes, of course." Clodagh peered at the scar, which wasn't half as bad as the gruesome wound had suggested. "How are you?"

"Great!" She turned to the girl beside her. "Julia, remember that time I came home all covered in blood? Clodagh was my knight in shining armour that night. She looked after me so well. Let me buy you a drink, Clodagh!"

Clodagh accepted the tip but not the drink, as was usual, and poured the girls their wines. Becca chattered on, explaining that Julia was her flatmate who was leaving to live with her boyfriend, and did Clodagh know anyone who was looking for a room?

And Clodagh heard herself say, "Yes. Me."

Jamie came home on Easter Monday eager to see Clodagh, but she wasn't in. "Are you at work?" he texted, because her Bank Holiday schedule could be up in the air, but he got no reply. Probably she was at work, and unable to text back, but... come to think of it she'd been quiet all weekend.

He popped down to the gatehouse, where everyone suddenly found an interesting screen to look at, and unease crept over Jamie.

"Hey. Is Clodagh at work?"

No one spoke. Then Geraint said, "I couldn't say, sir,"

The unease grew worse. "What do you mean, you couldn't say?"

Geraint exchanged a look with Khan, which made Jamie's stomach go hollow.

"Tell me," he said.

"She left you a note, sir," Geraint said, and passed him a few sheets of sheets of printer paper, folded over with his name on the outside.

It was her handwriting, the rounded loops of a girl whose education had stalled in her teens. Jamie read the first couple of paragraphs twice, unable to believe it.

"Is this a joke?"

"It wasn't a joke when I helped her move her things out," said Khan.

"Where?"

"She asked me not to say."

Jamie stared at him, appalled. "I order you to."

"I'm sorry, sir." Khan was implacable. "She's a private citizen."

Jamie moved forward, fist in the air. "Tell me—"

Geraint stepped calmly in front of him. Khan hadn't even flinched.

"It's for the best, sir. She said the letter would explain."

Jamie's hands shook. The letter quivered. "Have you read it?"

Their blank faces told him nothing.

"Do you know," he said, thinking of that dossier he'd been too bloody courteous to read, "what she's going to tell me?"

They said nothing, which in itself said everything. Jamie turned and ran back to the house, the big empty silent house. Clodagh's walking boot stood where she'd left it these last few weeks, by the front door. The sight of it burned his eyes.

He slid to the floor and forced himself to read her letter.

Dear Jamie,

I have to end this thing between you and me, and it's breaking my heart but it can't go on. We can't have a future together. There's no world in which it's possible.

I'm sorry. I really am. I'm taking the coward's way out but believe me it's better in the long run. I don't want you coming after me. Please don't ask the PPOs where I've gone. And it's probably best if you don't come to the pub for a while.

You see, Clodagh isn't my real name. That is to say, it's my middle name. I started using it when I left Harlow, so no one would know who I was. Because my real name is Sharday Walsh; the one thing my mum can remember about the night I was conceived was that Smooth Operator by Sade was playing. But she can't spell, so. Sharday.

Google Sharday Walsh. Go on, do it. I know you were too bloody chivalrous to read the dossier on me, because it would have told you all this. You didn't run screaming when I told you I didn't know my real dad or that my stepdad was a gypsy—and if you're making a face at me using the G word then just imagine what the tabloids and the twittersphere will call him—but there's something else you don't know and I was too much of a coward to tell you.

When I was fifteen my mum signed us up for a TV show. It was a docusoap. They were all the rage at the time. This one was sold to us—to her—as a real look at the lives of people living on council estates. She thought it would be even-handed and balanced, that it might show us in a positive light, because why would TV try to hurt her? Of course back then we didn't know about editing and bias. We didn't know they'd deliberately look for drama, stitch bits of footage together to tell the story they wanted to, write a narrative and weave us into it. And the story they wanted was about a lazy, workshy family of chavs who weren't going to get jobs when they could get benefits and free council flats.

They must have been over the moon when they found my mum. Her name was even Sharon, for Christ's sake. Six kids by four fathers, one of whom she said was probably in jail—that's my dad, because she had some vague idea he dealt drugs, which of course is a racist assumption and of course that was duly noted and torn apart by the press.

Oh yes, the press. Of course, they bloody loved it. We were a symbol of Broken Britain. We were the family everyone loved to hate. We were single mothers and graffiti'd tower blocks and benefits cheats and kids with gold earrings. We were barely human.

And do you want to know the coup de grace? The icing on the cake? The YouTube clip that will never die? Well, that would be when the oldest daughter of Britain's Worst Family bursts into tears and tells her mother she's pregnant.

Yep. Fifteen years old, a quick shag in a nightclub, throwing up in the mornings, trip to the pharmacy for a Clear Blue test, and that was my life down the toilet.

My nan had thundered fire and brimstone about abortion being a sin and how dead babies crawled on the floors of hell for all eternity, and it wasn't that I believed her but I didn't not believe her, either, if you know what I mean. Mum thought I should keep it. I tried to get hold of laddo but he was on remand by then, although apparently a social worker did manage to talk to him at one point and he said he didn't give a shit what

I did about the kid, so that was nice.

Having done most of the raising of my siblings I didn't particularly want to be anyone's actual mother, especially not that soon. So I decided to give it for adoption. Everyone thought I'd bottle it as soon as it was born, but I told the nurse to take it away so I didn't have to see it. I'm not sure my willpower would have been strong enough. Mum later said it was a shame I'd never seen him, so I guess it was a boy.

I don't know where he went. I hope he's loved and wanted. I try not to think about him. He's not mine, not really. They said you can go on a register so when the kid is old enough he can decide whether to find you or not, but I didn't want to do that. Clean break seemed best.

Oh, and I haven't told you the best bit yet. They were filming in the hospital. Mum screamed at them not to, but apparently she hadn't read the contract very thoroughly because they did anyway, and it was broadcast. The whole world saw the child I never did.

I'm told it's still on YouTube. Look it up.

So there you go, that's why I'm leaving. Well, I'll have left by the time you read this. You do see why, don't you? Big brain like yours, it won't take you long to get it. Even if your family accepted me with open arms, can you imagine the press? Have you ever seen piranhas in a feeding frenzy? I imagine it'd be something like that. It was bad enough the first time, when I was a nobody.

I won't take you down with me. I won't hurt you like that, or the people you love.

I do love you though. I wasn't going to tell you that, but there it is, I've written it now. I love you, and I'm sorry.

Goodbye.

Sharday Clodagh Walsh.

CHAPTER SEVENTEEN

Royalgossip.com: Engagement imminent, say palace insiders.

It's no secret that Prince Jamie has been spending a lot of time with his oldest friend, Lady Olivia Altringham. According to her friends she's even staying with him at his home in Cambridge. We expect an announcement any day now…

Clodagh hadn't really considered herself to have a lot of friends in Cambridge, but the number of people who asked her if she was all right after she left Jamie was kind of heartening. Oz and Marte at the pub immediately noticed something was wrong, and Ruchi asked in concerned tones what had happened.

On the other hand, not being able to tell them only made her feel worse.

Her new housemates, Becca and her girlfriend Heather, only needed to hear 'I just broke up with my boyfriend' to offer endless sympathy. Becca studied accounting at Anglia Ruskin and Heather was a student nurse, and both were very helpful when it came to university applications and course credits. They were a quiet and obviously contented couple who invited Clodagh to binge watch Netflix with them and talked aimlessly about adopting a rescue dog one day. Their house had a small garden, off-street parking for Becca's car and a downstairs loo in addition to the shared bathroom. The bus into town left from the end of the road.

Six months ago, Clodagh would have been overjoyed to move in. Now, she just felt… desolate.

She spent the first week terrified Jamie would storm into the pub and confront her. The first time she saw Zheng and Ruchi come in she nearly ran away to hide in the cellar. But Jamie had obviously made some excuse not to come, and continued to do so. In snippets from the news and the front pages of the papers she saw that he was undertaking his usual charity work, some of it in place of his brother who was taking time off to spend with the new baby.

God damn the man for being so… decent.

He flew to Africa to visit a conservation trust he was patron of. He was photographed holding his new nephew. He attended the Badminton Horse Trial, the Royal Windsor Horse show, the Chelsea Flower show and all the other events of the Season he'd told her he didn't give two figs about. He smiled, and Clodagh didn't look closely enough to see if it was genuine or not.

The papers were sure he was about to propose to Lady Olivia, who after all had been seen in Cambridge a lot lately and, according to someone called Melissa Featherstonehaugh, was pretty much living with him. Clodagh was torn between her own knowledge that this wasn't likely to be true, and her miserable expectation that it was.

Then, one rainy Wednesday afternoon when not much was happening, a slender woman in a beautiful coat walked into the pub, shaking out her umbrella, and ordered a gin and tonic from Clodagh.

"Lady Olivia."

Olivia brushed her immaculate hair back from her collar and said, "Please don't stand on ceremony with me, Clodagh. I thought we were friends."

Clodagh paused with the bottle of tonic in her hand, closed her eyes for a second, and said, "Please don't play the wounded party with me, Olivia. You're his friend, not mine."

She poured the drink, accepted a too-large note in payment and fixed her attention on the silent TV in the other bar.

"He told me what happened."

"Did he."

"He showed me your letter."

Giving birth had been easy, really, compared to what she'd been told. All the horror stories about three day labours and perineal tearing and breech births, and her baby had been born with no fuss a couple of hours after she arrived at the hospital.

It was afterwards that the real pain started, and it hadn't been physical. Clodgh had spent days in bed, staring at nothing, doing nothing, trying to feel nothing. She'd been offered counselling, and pills, and pamphlets, and it had been the only time in her life when her mother had seemed genuinely concerned for her health.

Giving up Jamie had hurt even more.

"Well then," she said, the TV screen blurring before her eyes.

"It must have been very hard."

"Hardest thing I've ever done," Clodagh said, her throat feeling squeezed.

"Perhaps you could get in touch?"

Every time her phone buzzed her heart exploded. "I don't think that's a good idea."

"He'll be… what, fifteen, sixteen, now? Reaching his majority—"

Clodagh turned to look at her. "What? Oh, you mean… no. I don't want to hear from him either. That's… that's a part of my life that is over. Sealed and done with. Just like… our mutual friend."

Right then Paulie came over for a refill and Olivia fell silent, hanging up her beautiful coat and hitching herself elegantly onto a barstool. She waited until they were alone again before she spoke.

"He loves you."

I know. "Don't say that."

"Why not?"

"What do you mean, why not? Don't you think it's hard enough as it is?" Clodagh dropped her voice so it wouldn't carry. "I love him. All right? I have never loved anyone like that before and I never will again and it makes no bloody difference because we *can't* be together. There's no amount of wishful thinking or fairytales that can change any of it. Do you understand? It won't ever work."

Olivia looked down at her drink. She stirred it once or twice.

"What if it could?"

"Don't be cruel. You and I both know it's never going to happen. The tiniest whiff of a scandal and I'd be packed off to God knows where—"

"You know them that well, do you?"

"And that'd be a picnic compared to what the press would say, and social media, my God. They'd be after that poor kid, you know. A relentless tabloid crusade to ruin his life as well as mine. They'd hunt down his father, even better if he's still in jail. They'd have my family hauled up like circus freaks, let's laugh at the chavs, ten points if she says 'innit'. Those bloody clips would be aired ad infinitum. We'd be memes, and gifs, and punchlines. And my father, remember how we don't even know his name? Bet that'd come out and there's another life to ruin."

Olivia was silent.

"You think I didn't think of all this?" Clodagh said softly. "You think I haven't seen it all, up here? I've been in that media storm before, and that was before Facebook and Twitter and everyone and their grandfathers airing opinions online. And there wasn't a royal involved. There wasn't another family to tear down with us."

"They've weathered worse," Olivia said.

"Really? Yeah, you're probably right. But I don't want to be something to be weathered," Clodagh said. She glanced over to see the regulars watching from their corner, and forced a smile for them. "Now if you don't mind, I have work to do."

She made work for herself, collecting glasses and stacking the dishwasher and cleaning things that didn't need to be cleaned, all the while aware of Lady Olivia's eyes on her.

Eventually, after making very slow work of her drink, the other woman stood up. She was taller than Clodagh, but that might have been her heels. Her hair was glossy and shiny on this damp day that had made Clodagh's frizz. She was so slim, and so pretty, her skin like porcelain and her eyes Delft blue.

She was the kind of woman Jamie should be marrying. She'd look wonderful in photographs and she'd know which fork to use at state banquets and she'd be endlessly polite and sympathetic at charity events.

"I think you were right," said Lady Olivia as she shrugged into her beautiful coat. "I think you are a coward."

And then she was gone, and it was just Clodagh and the pub and the rain.

"And then we have the centenary of the capture of Kirkuk, sir, on 7th May," said Peaseman. "Now. Plans to travel to Iraq were shelved some time ago, and it is intended instead to have a small ceremony at the Imperial War Museum instead."

"Fine," said Jamie.

"There are planned celebrations in Helsinki for the centenary of the end of the Finnish Civil War," said Peaseman. "Originally Princess Victoria had intended to go, but her health currently prohibits it."

"Shame," said Jamie. It was raining outside. He could hear the soft patter of it on the window of his Kensington Palace office.

"Yes… Clarence House is considering an advisory note to the press," said Peaseman. "She has had to cancel a lot of appointments lately."

Jamie dragged his consciousness back into the room. "What's wrong with her?"

Peaseman looked startled. He glanced at his aide, who shrugged. "Sir… the miscarriages. I thought… were you not informed?"

"Miscarriages? Plural?"

"Yes. In November and earlier this month. She called it a stomach bug at the time, I believe. Have you not spoken to her?"

Jamie hadn't. He'd been so absorbed in his love bubble with Clodagh he hadn't even noticed his sister's distress. And now he was so absorbed with his own self-pity he still hadn't paid attention.

"No." Ugh, he was a worm. "And no, obviously I didn't read the memo. I've been… preoccupied."

Peaseman gave his aide a look that sent him from the

room. "Sir. I've been meaning to talk to you about this. The family has noticed. The public have noticed."

"Oh hell. Have they?"

"Yes, sir. I had intended to wait until either you or your father informed me, but… should I begin drafting a press release?"

"Press release?" Oh yeah, he could see it. *Prince James of Wales announces he is officially broken hearted because the woman he loves believes herself unsuitable for him and doesn't want to be torn apart by the press like a fox to the hounds…*

"Perhaps a photocall, sir? A walk in the park, or a casual engagement. There is…" he flipped through his iPad, "a garden party for the children of soldiers who have died during armed combat next week, if you'd like to pencil it in?"

"Sure," said Jamie absently. The busier the better. If he attended every engagement Peaseman suggested, he was forced to fit his studies into what downtime he had left, in the backs of cars and in antechambers and green rooms, over meals eaten by himself in his empty house, in bed when he couldn't sleep. If he was studying he wasn't thinking.

Vincent complained he'd lost weight. Jamie found he'd rather lost interest in cooking when it was only for himself.

"Excellent," said Peaseman, looking pleased. "I shall inform His Highness. Now, about the visit from the Ghanaian ambassador…"

Olivia kept on at him to get rid of 'that smelly old boot' Clodagh had left behind, and he supposed he should probably take it back to the hospital, but it was the only thing he had of her. Her clothes and toiletries and books had all gone, and now Lenka had been round changing sheets and washing towels nothing even smelled like Clodagh any more.

The boot stayed, but Jamie spent less and less time in the Cambridge house. The knowledge she was so close by and so out of reach was unbearable.

He'd been mostly able to avoid his family, Ed and Annemarie busy with the baby and Victoria absent for reasons he'd now been informed of. His parents had been taking up some of the slack and it hadn't been hard to avoid them. Because he could put on a brave face for the cameras but in private it was very hard to do anything but sit around and cry.

He'd even looked up that shitty program, just so he could see her again. It wasn't available in its entirety but the clips on YouTube, those refused to die. Clodagh's mother, barely more than the age Jamie was now, blonde hair yanked back in a Croydon facelift, smoking and boasting how she'd been able to afford a Playstation for the boys this year, unaware that the producers would add in a voiceover about how much of her benefits that would cost. He watched clips of children from toddlers to teenage years, fighting and bickering, the girls in make-up and clothes too grown-up for them, the boys posturing in front of cars they were too young to drive.

Clodagh's mother, Sharon, explaining that her kids had gold hoops in their ears to protect them from evil because that was a Romany tradition from her husband. The voiceover helpfully explained that she'd never been married to Duke, whose travelling community had been evicted from four different sites before he died of lung cancer eight years previously. This particular nugget was shared over footage of Sharon Walsh and her friends sharing a cigarette.

And then Clodagh. Heartbreakingly young, almost unrecognisable with her hair in tight braids, all stilettos and Puffa jackets and frosted lipgloss and bravado, mouthing off in a try-hard 'tough on the streets, innit blud' patois. He watched the clip where she told her mother about the pregnancy test, and the shouting and screaming that ensued, the slammed doors, the tears, the hugs, the 'you can't tell me what to do!', the visits from the social worker.

He didn't watch the clip of the baby being taken away from her. He was appalled it had ever been screened.

A week later, at a garden party full of overexcited children who either didn't know or weren't aware that they were supposed to be in mourning for a parent, he followed Olivia around in a daze and smiled and made appropriate comments.

At least he assumed they were appropriate. If he was honest, he could say and do most of this on such an autopilot he might as well create a robot of himself.

Hah, that was a thought. Maybe he should tell Dr Kenyon he wanted to change his subject to robotics—

"Jamie, smile darling," said Olivia from the corner of her mouth, and he did, switching it on like a light as they were presented with an adorable little poppet who had hair just like Clodagh's. His smile froze, his throat closing over. The camera snapped away happily.

He didn't pay much attention to the papers, but when Peaseman brought them the next day Jamie noticed there was a picture of himself and Olivia with the little girl on the front page of... actually, quite a lot of the papers. In fact most of them.

"At his first official engagement with his girlfriend, Lady Olivia Altringham, Prince Jamie was unable to hide a tear as he met little Kiana Okorie, whose father died in Helmand Province," ran the caption on a broadsheet.

"What?" said Jamie.

"It's official!" screamed a tabloid.

"Finally," said a third, "Prince Jamie admits what we've all known for ages: that he's dating his childhood friend Lady Olivia Altringham."

"Oh what," said Jamie, feeling the blood drain from his face, "the *fuck* is this?"

Peaseman looked confused. "You did approve the press release, sir," he said.

"I did what?" Guiltily, Jamie recalled he'd just signed whatever Peaseman and his flunkies had put under his nose recently. "I—there's been a mistake, I didn't... I need to speak to Olivia."

She took a while to answer, and sounded sleepy when she did. "Jamie, it's the middle of the night."

"It's nine o'clock in the morning and you need to see the papers."

"Mmm? Who looks at papers any more, darling. I get my news from Twitter, like a normal person." A male voice murmured something in the background and Jamie's eyes nearly rolled themselves out of his head.

"Is there someone with you? Did you hook up last night? You might need to get rid of him," he said, pacing the floor of his Kensington Palace bedroom, "because according to the world's press you and I are now a couple."

"We're what?"

"A couple. Dating. Shagging. I don't know. Is that why Oll was invited?" he said to Peaseman.

"Well, yes, sir... but I told you all this..."

"Clearly I wasn't listening." He waved his personal secretary out and shut the door. "Oll, this is a disaster."

"Hang on." He could hear a murmur and slight sound of surprise as she and her gentleman friend evidently looked up the news. "Oh dear. Where has that come from? Did someone approve it?"

"Yes, me, apparently. I don't know what I'm doing, Oll," Jamie wailed, flopping onto his bed. "I didn't even read any of the stuff Peaseman gave me. I can't concentrate on anything. I can't do this."

"Oh, darling." She sighed. "All right, I'll come round. We'll figure something out. Damage limitation. If all else fails we'll just keep quiet until it goes away—"

"Goes away? When does this stuff ever go away?"

"I could always Instagram me and Hugo in bed right now if that would help?" she said, and Jamie heard a growling noise come from his own throat. "All right, I'll come round."

He'd no sooner rung off than his phone rang again. This time it was his brother.

"You and Oll, finally!" he crowed.

"Yeah, no," said Jamie wearily. "It's not happening. It's a mistake. Wrong end of the stick."

"But there's an official release—"

"It's a misunderstanding," Jamie growled. "I'm not seeing Olivia. I'm not dating Olivia. I'm not sleeping with her, I'm not living with her or engaged to her or marrying her or anything. For the last fucking time, we are just friends!"

Realising he'd yelled that last bit, Jamie forced himself to take a breath.

"All right, little brother, if you say so," said Edward. "Look, got to go, the chopper's waiting."

"Chopper? Where are you?" Edward had been around yesterday afternoon. Annemarie was still in situ.

"Oh, just popped over to see a friend. Shh, don't tell anyone I brought the bird. See you later."

"Right," said Jamie, and ended that call. He ran his hands through his hair and caught a glimpse of himself in the mirror.

Vincent was right, he had lost weight. And it wasn't just that, it was misery weighing him down. His eyes were hollow, and if he didn't plaster on a smile every minute of the day his face kept falling into despair.

He stood up and stretched out some of the aches of a bad night's sleep. Then he took himself off for a shower and a shave, because there was no point facing a crisis looking like a scruff.

"Oho, so that's why we haven't seen him!" said Stevo, tapping the paper.

"Too busy shagging," leered Paulie.

They scrutinised the picture of Jamie and Olivia, both smiling down at an adorable small child wearing her father's military medals. They made a handsome couple, and it wasn't hard at all to imagine them smiling down at a child of their own.

At least it's Olivia, Clodagh thought distantly, gazing blindly at the TV. Olivia, who was kind and considerate and loved Jamie. She would make him happy, and she'd always be... appropriate.

"The Queen is said to be pleased with the news. She has always regarded the Duke of Allendale, Lady Olivia's father, to be a close friend," read Paulie. "Another royal wedding then?"

"We should start a pool," said John the Milk. "Where are we now, May? I reckon... October."

"Nah. They'll do it in the summer."

"Too soon, mate."

"Date for a while, announce the engagement in autumn, yeah, then get married in the spring," said Stevo. "That's what the last one did."

"Oh, you been keeping track, have you?"

Clodagh paid them little attention. Friday, the Computer Science students tended to come in early, especially since it was a Bank Holiday weekend, and every time the door opened she got tense. Jamie had been disappointingly good about avoiding the pub, but there would surely come a day when he couldn't avoid it any more.

Here they came, the crowd much smaller now Jamie and his PPOs weren't part of it. Clodagh told herself she was relieved about this. "Have you seen?" Ruchi said, waving at the newspapers. "He's got a new girlfriend!"

"That's why we haven't seen much of him," said Hunter. "The dog!"

"He has been pretty distracted," said Zheng.

"Did you know?" said Ruchi, and Clodagh shook her head so fast she made herself dizzy.

"Nope. No. Why would I know?"

"I thought you guys were buddies," said Hunter.

"Oh. No. Not really. No more than you are. Hardly know the guy. A Carlsberg, is it, Hunter?"

Great. Not only did she have to get over Jamie without being able to talk to anyone about it, now she had his happiness thrown in her face too.

Or was it his happiness? Was he actually dating Olivia, or was this another media invention? No, it couldn't be. All the papers at the same time? Statement from Clarence House? This was real. Jamie was going out with Olivia.

"I'm sure they'll be very happy together," she said, and the boys took their drinks to the table.

Ruchi laid her hand on Clodagh's arm. "I know you liked him," she said.

"What? No, I… I mean he…"

"He's a handsome prince," Ruchi said simply. "Who wouldn't like him?"

A handsome prince. Yes, she supposed he was. It was so easy, when she thought about Jamie's kind eyes and his amazing mind and his passionate kisses, to forget that he was a prince. If he was just Jamie, this student she'd met in the pub, how different would it have been?

"Oh, hang about," said Paulie. "What's this?"

"Breaking news? Turn it up," said Stevo, as heads started to turn towards the TV. "Who's got the…?"

Clodagh looked around for the control, and because she was doing that she missed the news ticker flicking

263

across the bottom of the screen. She heard the gasps, the sudden, disbelieving silence, and then she turned it up as her eyes caught up with her ears.

"…around ten o'clock this morning. The cause of the crash is not known. It is believed His Highness was accompanied by members of household staff, whose bodies have not been recovered."

Ice clutched at Clodagh's heart. There was footage of some kind of wreckage, the twisted metal remains of some kind of aircraft maybe, flames erupting from it as emergency services battled to get close.

"The helicopter was travelling from Caernarfon on the Welsh coast to London, according to the flight plan." The newsreader looked shellshocked. "Prince Edward himself filed the flight plan, as he is an experienced helicopter pilot. We do not have confirmation, but it is likely he was piloting the aircraft as it came down."

Edward. Not Jamie. It wasn't Jamie.

Clodagh realised she was trembling.

"If you've just joined us," the newsreader said, as if she was parroting words she couldn't believe, "the breaking news is that Prince Edward, the Queen's oldest grandson, has been killed in a helicopter crash in the Chiltern Hills. The Prince, who was 36 years old, has—had—three children, including one-month-old Prince Henry, with his wife Annemarie…"

Her words faded into a weird blur. Clodagh kept staring at the ticker. *Prince Edward is dead. Prince Edward is dead.*

Jamie's brother is dead.

"It can't be," someone said.

"It's awful," said someone else.

"Jeez, on such a happy day," said someone.

I have to call him, Clodagh told herself desperately, and somehow had the presence of mind to stumble into the cellar before stabbing with shaking fingers at her phone. It took several tries, and she didn't know what to say, but it went straight to voicemail anyway. Not even his voice on the recording but some automated woman asking her to leave a message.

Clodagh hung up.

KATE JOHNSON

CHAPTER EIGHTEEN

Jamie walked behind the gun carriage with his grandfather, father and brother-in-law. He read the piece that had been selected for him in the Abbey. He probably sang along with the hymns. If a gun were to be pressed against his head he couldn't have recalled any of the details.

Edward was interred at St George's Chapel in the Lower Ward of Windsor Castle, in the same side chapel as his great-grandparents. Someone told Jamie the plan they'd used for the funeral was the one they'd been rehearsing for the Queen.

Olivia was allowed to attend the funeral, but not at Jamie's side. That honour was reserved for spouses and immediate family members. His parents kept close to each other, Victoria clung to Nicholas, and Annemarie to her bewildered children.

London was draped in black. The only colour came from Edward's personal standard, differenced from the Monarch's by the three-pointed white label with its single blue caltrop. It hung wonky and weirdly irritating for the whole journey.

Jamie kept his eyes on that standard. Twelve years ago, when he turned eighteen, Garter King of Arms had presented him with his own arms, differenced from Ed's by having five points on the label and three caltrops. "When you become the son or brother of the king, it will be altered to three points," he'd been told. Only he'd never be the brother of the king, would he? He'd be the grandson, the son, and then the uncle. Little Alexander should be the one with the three-pointed label now, only he'd probably never get his because by the time he turned eighteen he'd likely already be the Prince of Wales, inheriting his grandfather's arms.

When they arrived at St George's Chapel there was a gap in the Quire where Edward's standard used to hang, and whoever took his place in the Order of the Garter, the change would be a permanent reminder. *It wasn't supposed to look like this.*

There were people everywhere. Outside Buckingham Palace the flowers were laid ten metres deep. People left teddy bears and balloons, as if Ed had been a child and not a full-grown man with a military career and children of his own. They sobbed publicly about how he'd changed their lives. People who'd never met him, appropriating the family's private grief, stealing it, making it about themselves.

His anger grew, every time he looked at that damn standard, every time he saw the flowers, the people bowing their heads—without removing their bloody hats, because why bother to get the etiquette right?—as the cars passed, every time he took his place behind his cousins and ahead of Annemarie, walking alone with only his suffocating grief for company.

Olivia broke with protocol and took his arm as they left the chapel to head into Windsor Castle. Her presence was a comfort, but it wasn't the one he wanted.

"I hate all this," he said to her as they escaped inside.

"I hate not having…"

Clodagh. *I wish Clodagh were here.* She'd make it bearable.

"She wouldn't be allowed to be here anyway," Olivia said quietly.

"Christ, this *family*. And that lot," he jerked his chin at the window, at the ever-present cameras, the weeping crowds, the masses desperate to show they were mourning the most and the best. "Bloody voyeurs."

"He lived his life in public," Annemarie said. "Why should his death be any different?"

"Do you have to be so… Dutch?" he said, struggling to keep in the tears his anger kept feeding him.

"There'll probably be more people watching this than the wedding," said Victoria. She looked pale, thin, tired. She really wasn't well enough for this. Jamie hated himself for not even realising it.

"You should be resting," said Nicholas. "Come on. It's been a long day."

He escorted his wife away, out of the room they'd all gathered in. It wasn't a wake, exactly. Ceremonial funerals didn't have wakes. Royal families didn't attend wakes. They just stood around Windsor Castle clutching glasses of whiskey and trying not to cry.

"Jamie," said Annemarie, who had been cuddling baby Henry since the moment they left the Abbey, "may I speak to you?"

Jamie shrugged, preparing for a bollocking about his attitude. She took him into an antechamber and checked the door was securely closed.

"It's about Dai."

"Die?" Was her English failing her. "Dying?"

"No. Dai. Edward's boyfriend."

The wind abruptly vanished from his sails.

Jamie blinked, blinked again, and waited for her to continue. He hadn't known, exactly, but… it just wasn't exactly a surprise. Ed had always been raised to marry a woman and have babies with her, but that wasn't the same as actually wanting to.

Duty before everything.

Tiny little bits and pieces fell into place. Jamie felt like an idiot for not realising it sooner.

"You're not shocked," Annemarie said.

"I… not really." Ever since Ed's helicopter had come down, Jamie didn't think anything could shock him any more. "Neither are you."

"I always knew," she said calmly. "Edward was never allowed to come out, to be himself, but he confided in me." She shrugged. "Plenty of people have complicated marriages, Jamie. And people like us, we don't have the luxury of marrying for love, do we?"

A bitter laugh escaped Jamie. "That's not what my parents told me." They'd lied, because what was the whole family if not a series of lies and half trues and confidence tricks?

"You're lucky. You get to marry Olivia. She is appropriate, and you love her."

Jamie said nothing. He hadn't spoken much to Olivia this week, not about their supposed relationship, anyway. She'd stayed with him, comforted him, supplied him with alcohol and helped him answer the endless questions people kept asking. He did love her, he realised, but she was his best friend. The old cliché of seeking to validate life after a death didn't ring true.

If there had ever been a time he might have got naked with Olivia, this last week would have been it.

Instead, he'd wished, so desperately, that it was Clodagh by his side. Clodagh who held his hand and let him cry in her arms. Clodagh who listened to his stories about Ed, Clodagh who helped him decide between readings and hymns, Clodagh who told his staff to piss off when he was too overwhelmed.

"Edward loved Dai," said Annemarie. "They met when he was working on the Search and Rescue team out there. Do you remember him? Handsome boy, red hair, nice smile."

Jamie shrugged. He'd probably met the guy. What did it matter now?

"Hah," he said, suddenly realising. "All those trips to see his old colleagues."

"Yes, exactly. I don't know what I should do about him," she went on. "I can mourn publicly, I can visit Edward's grave, I can do all the things one does. He can't. I will always have a place here, with your family and the people who knew him and loved him. What does he have? They were both so careful I don't think there's even a photo or a text message to remember him by."

Jamie couldn't stand up any more. His body felt like a puppet with the strings cut. He collapsed into a Queen Anne chair and said, "I'm buggered if I know."

Annemarie looked down at the baby for a moment, jiggling him a little.

"Are they his?"

"The children? Oh, yes. Definitely. Can't you see, they're perfect little Windsors." She gave Jamie an old-fashioned look. "I told you. It was a complicated marriage."

"Why are you telling me all this?"

Annemarie shrugged. "I had to tell someone. Victoria wouldn't understand, I think, and she has enough to worry about now anyway. My own family... no, this is not their problem. Besides, we are Dutch, we have different ideas about this kind of thing."

"You figured I'd be a sympathetic ear?"

"You always have been before." She sighed. "I'm sorry. I should not have burdened you—"

"No, you should. It's fine." Why not? Wasn't that his role in life, to come second to his brother, to support the family? "You want something for this Dai to remember Ed by? A legacy? A recognition?"

She nodded. "Recognition could be dangerous though. You Brits still have sticks up your asses about this kind of thing."

Jamie snorted in a most unroyal way. "Yeah. Yeah, we do." He tried to think. Dai had loved Ed but would never be able to tell anyone. He'd never be able to mourn publicly. Never be able to explain what had been taken from him. His grief had to be private…

Jamie straightened.

"Yes?" said Annemarie.

"You should," Jamie began, and narrowed his eyes at the distance as he thought. "You should go to him. You should tell him you know how much he loved Ed. You should share your grief with him. Let him meet the children. Be a part of his life."

"How? Move back to Wales?"

"Maybe." His gaze suddenly focused on her again. "Annemarie, when you heard the news who was the first person you turned to? Who was the person you needed to be with, more than anyone else?"

She looked nonplussed. "The children, of course."

"There's no one else?"

She shrugged. "Edward was my best friend."

"Just like Olivia is mine," said Jamie, standing up. "And you know what, if I marry her then someday one of us is going to be having this exact same conversation. She's my best friend, not the woman I love."

"I don't understand?" said Annemarie.

Jamie went over and kissed her and the baby both on the cheek. "I love someone else and I've been miserable without her and you know what, time passeth away and the lust thereof, so I'm going to bloody find her."

He walked into Olivia on his way out. She looked livid.

"Where have you been? I'm putting out fires here. Your grandmother just asked me when we're going to announce our engagement."

"Never."

"Well, that's what I said, but she said the country needs some good news. *Panem et circuses* and all that."

He paused. "Oll, I love you, but it'll be a cold day in hell when I marry you."

"I know," she said, exasperated. "Will you slow down? Where are you going?"

She hurried to keep up with him as he dodged out of sight and along a back corridor.

"I'm going to find Clodagh."

"What? But—she said she didn't want to hear from you—"

"She also said she loved me, so fuck that. Where the hell is my phone? Who has it?"

Geraint caught up with him as he flew out of the castle into the inappropriately pleasant sunshine. "Sir, I'd advise against—"

"Shut up and give me my phone. And if you tell one person where I'm going I will have your job, your rank and your pension, do you understand?"

"Sir."

Jamie kept running until he was in the back of a car and Olivia had given up trying to follow. She called him as the car set off.

"Don't you dare tell me not to."

"I won't." She hesitated. "Everyone's leaving. Annemarie says she's going to Wales tomorrow."

"Good for her. Don't tell anyone where I'm going."

She sighed as if he was being impossible. "I won't, but—"

He cut her off, and tried to find Clodagh's number on his phone. But someone—bloody Peaseman or someone, probably—had erased it. Great. Well, then, this was

273

going to be a surprise.

"Strange day," said Oz, glancing back at the TV as if pulled by an invisible thread.

Clodagh just nodded. She couldn't get the images out of her head: the coffin draped in the Royal Standard, the endless crowds, thousands of people lining up to pay their respects, the oceans of flowers, the procession of princes walking behind the coffin, sober in black…

…Jamie's face, drawn and bleak, the only time she'd seen him unsmiling in public. The camera—the damned camera!—zooming in to catch his damp eyes. She hated the cameras for invading his grief like that, but at the same time she was greedy for every shot of him.

His voice had stayed steady as he'd read from the Bible. The TV said it was 1 Corinthians 13, a passage that was vaguely familiar. "When I became a man, I put away childish things," he said, and his voice broke, and everyone held their breath, and Clodagh didn't even pretend she wasn't crying as he faltered through the next couple of sentences.

But then he looked up, and finished, "And now abideth faith, hope, love, but the greatest of these is love," and his eyes were more green than hazel and Clodagh had to leave the room.

Oz found her in the cellar, leaning against the wall and weeping into her hands.

"Jesus," he said, and she startled, swiping frantically at her eyes in a manner that didn't fool anyone, "I thought it was just a crush."

She sniffed. "What?"

"Come on, Clodagh. You were walking on sunshine when he was around and you've had a face like a wet weekend since he left." He broke open a packet of serviettes and handed her some. "Nice going with Davood, by the way. You had me fooled at first."

She thought about denying it, but there was no strength left in her. She shrugged and blew her nose.

"Is it really obvious?"

"It is right now. Look, everyone's upset, it's a weird day, no one will judge you for crying a bit. Why don't you go home early and I'll cover for you?"

Clodagh was tempted, but Becca had announced her intention to watch the whole of the royal funeral with a big bar of chocolate to hand. There'd be no escaping it, and at least here she had things to do.

"No," she said, and swiped at her nose with a serviette. "I'll stay. That was probably the worst part."

But it wasn't. Because the cameras stayed on the coffin as it was loaded into the hearse that would take it to Windsor, and whilst they didn't follow it inside, the presenters chatted sombrely to various people who had some claim to knowing Prince Edward while they waited for the family to emerge from the chapel. The patrons of the Prince's Arms grew bored at that point, and Clodagh busied herself fetching their drinks and collecting their empties.

And just as she walked past the TV the announcer said in stentorian tones, "And now the family emerge from the chapel. His Royal Highness Prince Edward of Wales has finally been laid to rest…"

And there was Jamie, walking out alone as the rest of his family followed, hand in hand with spouses or children. His face was bleak, those kind, intelligent eyes blank, and Clodagh stood stricken, aching for him.

Then someone walked up beside him, took his hand, bussed his cheek, and he gave a ghost of his former smile to Lady Olivia as he walked with her into the castle.

"Oh, they're gonna be having funeral sex," said someone, maybe Hunter, and it was only Paulie grabbing her wrist that kept her from smashing the glass she was carrying into her face.

"Ignore him, girl," he said softly, and there was knowing in his eyes. Clodagh realised she didn't know the first thing about this man she served beer to every day, but here he was, being kind to her.

She nodded and took the glasses back to the bar.

After the TV coverage ended and some dull, inoffensive antiques programme began, a lot of the crowd dispersed, but the lull didn't last long. The early evening crowd came in sooner rather than later, some of them with the distinct air of having cracked open the gin whilst watching the royal funeral at home.

Pouring a gin and watching it all in HD, like it's entertainment and not the last resting place of a man who was going to be king one day, all laid out for your viewing pleasure. They were no better than a crowd at Tyburn.

Clodagh was finding it hard to keep a civil tongue in her head.

And here they were, picking over it all like vultures, deciding whether they liked this frock or that hat or whether she should be wearing those shoes. If everyone had looked suitably sombre. If the cousin who accidentally smiled would be cast out forever. If Edward's children really should be in attendance.

They decided, one after the other, that Annemarie's parents hadn't looked bereaved enough, but that Prince Jamie shouldn't have nearly cried like that.

"Probably been told to," said some woman, nodding sagely. "You know, to make it look sadder."

Oz wheeled Clodagh away before she could even open her mouth.

"I know," he said. "Go and serve in the other bar."

Spitting like a cat, Clodagh bit out, "She—"

"Go and serve in the other bar," he repeated, and she snarled at him but did as she was told. Which meant that when the top bar went suddenly quiet she didn't know why, and when she walked through to find out the crowds parted like the Red Sea and there was Jamie.

There was Jamie, striding towards her and meeting her mouth to mouth, kissing her as if he'd die if he didn't, and she kissed him back, tears pouring from her in sheer relief that he was here, he was here with her and she could finally touch him, hold him, grieve with him.

Her hands went into his hair, grabbing it by the handful as her body moulded against his, and he shuddered as he sank against her, arms tight around her body.

"Clo," he breathed against her mouth, and she tasted salt because both of them had tears streaming from their eyes. "Oh God, I need you."

"Yes," she said, kissing his face.

"You—I've just needed—all this time, I can't—"

"Whatever you need," she promised, fingers going under his collar, needing to touch his skin.

"Come with me. Please."

And Clodagh said, "Yes," and followed him out to the car.

CHAPTER NINETEEN

Jamie woke, exhausted, in an unfamiliar bed, and spent a moment frowning at the ceiling. It failing to yield any clues, he put on his glasses and looked around.

Wherever he was, he was alone. That dream he'd had of Clodagh, of walking out on his family to be with her, of that amazing kiss, had been just that, a dream. He closed his eyes, took a deep breath to keep the tears at bay, then wondered why he was bothering.

He sat up in the bed, which was comfortable enough and had carved wooden posts at each corner. The room wasn't large, and it was oddly shaped, as if each of the four corners had an extra, rounded chamber plonked on them. One seemed to contain a bathtub.

The windows were leaded, but all he could see was sky and a bit of tree. Wait a minute…

The Hunting Tower. Of course, yes, he'd come up here with Olivia when they were kids, and then he remembered her telling him they were having it renovated into a holiday cottage. The round chambers were turrets, one of them containing a tightly wound spiral staircase. A room on each floor. She'd called last night while they were on the M11 and told him the place was free this week if he wanted somewhere to hide out. The housekeeper would drop off some supplies…

But if Olivia had called then it meant he hadn't dreamt escaping and if he hadn't dreamt that—

The door in the staircase turret opened and there she was, his Clodagh, wearing a t-shirt with the Prince's Arms embroidered on it and carrying two mugs of tea.

"Hey," she said. "I didn't mean to wake you."

"You didn't." He rubbed his eyes, and she was still there. Oh, she was a goddess.

She put the mugs down on his nightstand and sat down on the edge of the bed. "Did you sleep?" she asked.

"Yes," he said, surprised at the answer. Better than he had in weeks, in fact.

"Good. Grief is exhausting."

He'd slept in the car, he remembered now. He'd clutched at Clodagh and sobbed and cried for half the journey, and she'd held him and soothed him and cried a bit, too, and then he was waking up with a crick in his neck and being guided inside the darkened tower, where Clodagh had cuddled him close as he fell asleep.

"I'm sorry," he said.

"What for?"

"Well, for crying all over you last night—"

She waved that away. "Don't be silly."

"And for kind of kidnapping you."

She raised an eyebrow. "Asking someone politely and getting an answer in the affirmative is kidnapping where you come from? I said I'd come with you," she said, her hand covering his, "and I did. Although I will add I'm bloody glad one of the PPOs had the presence of mind to get my bag and my jacket. May in Derbyshire: not that warm."

She reached for a mug, which he noticed had the

Allendale crest on it, and took a sip, brushing her springy hair out of her eyes.

"There's enough food downstairs to last us for weeks," she explained, "and clothes and toiletries too. All with this crest on, strangely enough. Wherever could we be?" she said with mock confusion.

And Jamie said, "I love you."

He didn't know why. Well, he did, he said it because it was true, but he didn't know why he said it just then.

Clodagh calmly put down her mug, and then she threw herself at him and buried her face in his neck and said, "I love you too. Oh God, Jamie, I really do."

He held her, hardly able to believe it was real.

"And I don't know what the fuck we're going to do," she said, lifting her head, "because any chances of yesterday not going public are pretty much slim to none."

"Yesterday?" Jamie said. Ed's funeral had been broadcast to the world, what did she—

"You walked into the pub and snogged my face off in front of all those people," she said, and Jamie lost his breath. "You in your black with your bodyguards, everyone would have recognised you, snogging someone else when you're supposed to be seeing the lady whose tea we're drinking."

"What? Oh." Allendale. "I'm not. I'm really not. I don't even know what happened with that. We were trying to figure it out when…"

She nodded, and rearranged herself more comfortably beside him. Her arm went around his waist, bare skin to bare skin, and he wished she wasn't fully dressed.

"I am not seeing Olivia," Jamie said firmly, just to reiterate it. "I'm not engaged to her, or going to marry her or anything. The only person I want to—"

He broke off before he said the embarrassing thing.

"The only person you want to… what?" said Clodagh

softly.

"Um. See. Date. Be with." He cleared his throat. "Is you."

Her hand touched his bare chest. Her thumb stroked thoughtfully and his heart beat in time with it.

"And then what?" she said.

"What do you mean, and then what?"

"Jamie, love, I've kind of gone all in on this. You know all my… you've seen all the skeletons in my closet. And they're all going to come out to play now, whether we like it or not. And I strongly suspect not. So… I guess what I'm saying is… finish that damn sentence, will you?"

His mouth went dry. He couldn't speak. He managed, "Seriously?"

"Yes. Either we're in the shit together, or separately. And if it's together…"

"*Semper in excretia sumus, solum profundum variat*," he murmured.

"Always… we are always…" she frowned up at him.

"We're always in the shit. Only the depth varies."

"Right," she said, clearly confused.

"And, and…" Argh, proposals weren't supposed to include conversations about shit! "Look, what I was going to say before my brain stopped working was, there's only one person I want to marry, and that's you."

Her hand found his, fingers twining together. "Really?"

"Really. So, will you? Will you marry me?"

Clodagh smiled, and then she laughed, and said, "Oh God, this is the worst idea in the world." But she didn't look like she was going to say no, especially not when she climbed on top of him and kissed him long and hard and said, "Yes, I'll marry you. I love you."

"Even if it's the worst idea in the world?"

She considered this as she combed her fingers

through his hair. "I mean, it's not 'getting married in Westeros' bad, but..."

"Is it worse than wearing a red shirt on Away missions from the Enterprise?"

"Mmm. It's just about possible to survive that. We have an analogy."

I am so into you. "We'll survive it. I promise."

She cuddled him close for a long moment before settling back down by his side. "I know we will."

"I think what I was trying to say," he said as they lay side by side, fingers playing together, "was that if we're going to be in the shit we might as well make it worth it."

"So romantic," she said. "That's a quote for the ages."

"A story to tell on the news. When we make the announcement," he added, and she sighed.

"Oh yeah. That. Ugh. Jamie, why do you have to be a prince?"

"A question I ask myself every day. I could quit," he said wistfully. "Renounce the title. Remove myself from the succession."

"Thus making yourself an even bigger object of fascination," Clodagh said.

"And depriving you of a title and a tiara…"

"Ooh, there's a tiara?"

"There are always tiaras," Jamie said, gathering her close to him. She wore jeans and t-shirt, where he was only in his underwear, and the feel of her clothes against his bare skin was kind of a turn-on.

He forced himself to think logically. If—and it was one hell of an if—they could ride out the inevitable media storm Clodagh's background would cause, he'd have to ask the Queen's permission to marry. She'd never said no before, but then none of her descendants had wanted to marry anyone she disapproved of.

"Regrets already?" Clodagh said softly, and he shook his head vigorously.

"No. Never. Not one moment with you have I ever regretted," he said. "I love you. That's not going to change."

"With you, bread and onions," she said.

Jamie leaned in close and whispered, "That's because you know what I can do with bread and onions."

Clodagh laughed, and squirmed closer, and said, "You know what I found in the bags of stuff downstairs? There's Allendale soap, and Allendale socks, and Allendale eggs… and there's one thing that's not made on the Allendale Estate."

"Yeah?" said Jamie, wondering where this was going.

"Yeah. Unless they lease land to Durex."

Jamie groaned and kissed her and it wasn't long before he was racing downstairs to find them himself.

At Geraint's firm suggestion, they'd handed over their phones last night to the security team, who had settled in an annexe behind the Hunting Tower. Clodagh shuddered to think how many messages would be on it now, from Oz and Marte at the pub, from Becca and Heather wondering where she was, and from her mum and her siblings even, if the news had broken.

She didn't want to find out. If she stayed in this place with Jamie, then she never had to know if the story had broken. Like the rest of the world was Schrödinger's box and they alone stood outside it.

The large, glossy carrier bags of supplies on the kitchen table seemed to have come almost exclusively from the Allendale gift shop, which appeared to sell everything under the sun. There were toiletries of all kinds, made in the local town and scented with herbs and florals 'traditionally grown in our kitchen garden.'

"Must be a hell of a garden," she said to Jamie,

unpacking a shampoo and conditioner set made with local honey.

"I'm kind of disappointed the toothpaste isn't made with their own spearmint," he replied, holding up an ordinary tube of Colgate.

"Okay, you get points for the toothpaste and I get them for the condoms. Anything else they don't stick their own label on?"

They made a game of it, unpacking local cheese and bread and vegetables. Jamie won points for supermarket pasta, and Clodagh for teabags. The Duke of Allendale was apparently very proud of his sheep, and the estate produced sweaters and socks and even lanolin soap. Clodagh expected to win the game by unpacking this bag, but there appeared to be a 'country shop' selling eye-wateringly expensive clothing of the sort worn by people who carried shotguns broken over their arms and were permanently followed by Labradors.

"That doesn't count, they sell them here," Jamie said as she held up some walking boots.

"You can't just make up the rules as you go along," she complained.

"Course I can, I'm a prince."

"And I'm a… what am I going to be?" she asked, slightly delirious.

"Uh…" he was sorting through a bag of cheerfully coloured shirts and didn't look up, "probably a duchess. It's usual to grant a title upon marriage, so we'd be the Duke and Duchess of somewhere. You could be Clodagh, Princess James of Wales, but probably not since Annemarie didn't take that and anyway, it's—Clo?"

She grabbed at a chair and sat down abruptly. "A duchess?"

"Yeah." Jamie put down the shirt he was holding. "One of the extinct titles, I expect. Cumberland? Sussex?

Um… probably don't want Albany, he was a traitor in the First World War. Are you all right?"

"Duchess," Clodagh said. She took a deep breath and let it out, and there was Jamie, crouching in front of her. He took her hands.

"You don't have to be," he said. "We could ask not to be."

"Prince Jamie and Mrs Windsor?"

"Mrs Wales, or—yep, right, shut up Jamie. Hey." His eyes were kind. "It doesn't mean anything. It's just a title."

"Says the prince. 'Clodagh the Duchess.' Oh God, my mum will do her nut." She screwed her face up. "Ugh. I'm going to have to call her, aren't I?"

Jamie nodded reluctantly. "And I've got to call… I don't know. Peaseman probably." He got to his feet. "Breakfast, and then we'll go and see what the damage is, okay? Can't face all this on an empty stomach."

They had eggs and bacon and orange juice. "Points to me," said Clodagh, taking it out of the fridge, and Jamie grinned mischievously.

"Nope. Orangery, my dear Clodagh. Check the label."

She did. "Are you kidding? Oranges in Derbyshire?"

"The glasshouses are really impressive. I'll show you… one day," he finished lamely. They both knew there wasn't going to be much opportunity for that any time soon.

They hadn't quite finished eating when there was a knock at the door. Exchanging glances, Clodagh said, "I'll go."

It was Geraint, sober-faced. "Sorry to interrupt, but there have been a few developments."

"What kind of developments?"

He had a pile of newspapers under his arm. Clodagh's appetite abruptly vanished. She took her plate to the sink, and Jamie's followed shortly after.

"Well. To start with, Lady Olivia has been running interference for you, sir. I have had some... vehement phone calls from Her Majesty's office."

Jamie winced. "I'll bet."

"We have kept your location secret for now," Geraint said, and the last couple of words sounded heavy to Clodagh. "However, there has been..." he paused, "heavy media speculation about your... actions yesterday."

Jamie ran his hands through his hair, which made it stick out all over the place, and sighed. He held out his hand to Clodagh, who took it and went to sit beside him. "Okay. Go."

Geraint plonked down the sheaf of newspapers. Most of the headlines were about the funeral, most of the main pictures the Royal Standard-draped coffin. But the teasers up by the mastheads, they were all about Jamie and his 'mystery woman'.

Mystery woman. Well, that bought her some time—

"Online versions have since been updated," Geraint said, bring out his iPad and showing them a broadsheet website. Jamie flinched. Clodagh squeezed his hand hard, and made herself look.

"Prince Jamie's 'Mystery Woman' Revealed," it said, and underneath was a picture of Clodagh from sixteen years ago. A headshot of her from the publicity stills the TV company had done at the start of filming, and then a larger, fuzzier shot of her from the show itself. She was probably seven or eight months pregnant, hair scraped back into a pineapple style, ears full of gold rings, face full of make-up. She had the total chav uniform, too, the velour tracksuit and the cropped t-shirt showing her belly.

Clodagh exhaled slowly.

"Teenage mum identified as Prince Jamie's secret

squeeze," said the subheading.

She turned away. "I don't want to read it. Who... was it my family?"

Jamie put his arm around her as she turned her face to his chest. "It looks like your mum. Wait... no, a friend saw the footage online—"

"Footage?"

"There were photos from the pub and a short video clip," said Geraint. "It went viral."

"Of course it did," said Jamie pessimistically. "A friend saw it online and texted her that it looked a lot like you, and... she remembered the name of the pub you worked at because, of course... well, long story short she seems to have put two and two together and made four. Locals at the pub would only identify you as 'Clodagh who works behind the bar' but no more than that, so that's loyalty, I suppose," he added, trying to sound encouraging.

"But my mum dropped me in it."

"I'm sure it wasn't on purpose. I mean, I'm sure she didn't mean to..."

Clodagh sighed. Well, this had been nice while it lasted. "She never means to. I can see it, she'll have got all excited and called one of those 'do you have a story' lines they have in the tabloids and told them." She lifted her head and looked at Jamie, all sympathy, and Geraint, stoically blank.

"She won't have thought about what it actually means for me, or you, or even herself. Was there a payout? Bet there was a payout."

"Estimates in the region of six figures," Geraint murmured. "For a tabloid exclusive."

"Really? Jesus. Well, no wonder. That'd buy half of Harlow." She'd never really looked at property prices there. It wasn't like anyone in her family could afford to buy anything. But even at the bottom end of the six figure scale, "That's more money than anyone in my family—on my whole estate—has ever seen in their entire lives. All put together. You'd sell your own grandma for that. You'd sure as hell sell your daughter," she added, looking sadly at the iPad.

"How much of the story do they have?" Jamie asked.

"Most of it, from what we can tell. Sold it to one of the tabloids as an exclusive. Everyone else has picked it up from there. It had spread before we could block it," he added apologetically.

"Not your job," Jamie said crisply. He seemed to straighten. "Right. You've spoken to Peaseman?"

"Many times," said Geraint, with just a hint of suffering. "He was most insistent he spoke directly to you. We have also taken calls from your mother's press secretary, your father's, your sister's and your sister-in-law's, as well as Her Majesty's. Lady Olivia has drafted a statement she wishes you to look over."

He flicked to something else on the iPad.

Jamie kissed Clodagh on the cheek and said, "Never explain, never complain, never apologise."

"Easy for you to say," she said miserably.

Geraint handed over the iPad with Olivia's press release.

"*His Royal Highness Prince Jamie is aware that there has been significant speculation about his private life in recent weeks but asks for respect and privacy at this difficult time.*"

"That's it?" Clodagh said.

"Her ladyship wondered if an additional few statements might be added," Geraint said. He scrolled up.

"*Clarence House can confirm that an erroneous statement was released describing His Royal Highness as 'in a relationship' with his childhood friend Lady Olivia Altringham. Whilst Lady Olivia has been of significant comfort to Prince Jamie during the recent tragic events, His Highness and Her Ladyship wish to clarify that their relationship has never moved beyond close friendship.*"

"I see we're bringing out all the titles," Jamie muttered.

Under this statement was another one, framed with question marks.

"*Clarence House is pleased to confirm that Prince Jamie is in a relationship with Miss Clodagh Walsh. The couple met in Cambridge last year as His Royal Highness began his PhD studies.*"

It was succinct, to say the least. Clodagh supposed the less was said, the less there was to be misinterpreted.

"Kind of playing is fast and loose with their use of the word 'pleased'," she said.

"How much do they know?" Jamie asked.

"I can't say, sir." Geraint looked pained. "I really think you ought to talk to Major Peaseman, sir."

Jamie groaned, buried his head in his hands, and then straightened and held out his hand for the phone.

"Major—yes, I'm fine, I—well, of course I've heard —yes, I was *there*, for God's sake—no, of course I know —because I wanted to get away from this bloody circus, that's why!"

He leapt to his feet, free hand rumpling his hair. Clodagh watched him pace as Peaseman evidently gave him an earful.

"Ma'am?" said Geraint, and Clodagh looked up. "Lady Olivia wished to speak with you."

"She did?" Clodagh felt a bit sick. "About?"

To his credit, Geraint didn't roll his eyes. He just held out a phone—her own, Clodagh realised, seeing a horrific number of missed calls and a collection of texts whose number seemed to be updating rapidly.

"I'll be outside," he said, and made his escape.

Clodagh took a deep breath and scrolled to Olivia's number.

"Darling! Oh my God, I thought you'd never call. Bear with," she said to someone else. "No, shut up, this is very important. Darling, are you all right?"

"Me darling?" Clodagh said.

"Yes, you, darling. Everyone has ears around here," Olivia muttered. "What's going on? Have you seen? It's everywhere! I knew he was… but not that he'd… well. I mean the cat's out of the bag now, isn't it?"

"Yes," said Clodagh. When she closed her eyes she saw that picture of herself.

"Right, now, hang on… all right. That's better." The background noise faded away. "Now. I assume you know the whole story has broken? All the gory details. That dreadful YouTube clip has… goodness me, the counter is still going up. Have you seen the coverage?"

"Some of it." Clodagh looked out of the window, where only trees and sky were visible.

"Right. Don't look at any more. That's the first rule, don't read what they're saying about you. Get someone else to do it and summarise. Is that Jamie I can hear?"

"He's talking to his private secretary."

"Ah. Yes. The good old Major. We've had several somewhat terse conversations this morning. I won't bore you with the details. He's going to need his own press secretary at this rate. Now. I've drafted a couple of statements, so have a look for me and we can see if HM's press secretary approves. They're all writing their own, of course, but it never hurts to get one's oar in first. Has Geraint shown you?"

"Yes. They look fine to me, but what do I know?"

"Poor darling, you're having quite the crash course, aren't you? Now. Are the two of you happy to say you're in a relationship? Takes the bloody heat off me, but then I'm just being selfish."

"I—" Clodagh glanced at Jamie, who was leaning against the Aga, listening to his phone and looking fed up. "I don't know. I—we—"

"Right. Yes. Well, I'll need to speak to him. Now. Damage limitation. We need a strategy. Do you have any ideas?"

"Um," began Clodagh, who didn't. *Damn, and I turned down Media Studies GCSE.*

"Because what I was thinking was… we just say nothing."

She paused for effect. Clodagh stared at the trees and sky.

"Nothing?"

"Yes. Let the whole frenzy just play out. All the clips and the reruns. The Palace can probably suppress some of them, but injunctions always make the news and it all ends up being counter productive anyway. What's out there is out there. We draw a line beneath it, and move on."

"Move on?" echoed Clodagh, disbelieving. Nothing was ever that simple.

"Yes. Never explain, never complain, never apologise. You see—look, there's one important question I have to ask you. Should have asked it first, really. How serious are you about him?"

Clodagh looked back at Jamie, who caught her eye and made a chattering motion with his hand. He looked tired, and bored, and the smudges of grief weren't going to leave his eyes any time soon, but he was her Jamie, and she loved him completely.

"I love him," she said. She said it into the phone, but she was looking at Jamie, and his smile widened. "I love him to the height and depth my soul can reach."

"Oh," breathed Olivia, but Clodagh wasn't listening. She set down the phone on the table and went across to Jamie, putting her arms around his waist and laying her head on his chest.

"Actually, Major, can I interrupt you for a minute there?" Jamie said into his phone. He didn't wait for an answer, but tilted Clodagh's face up and kissed her.

"Shall I tell him?" he murmured.

"Olivia wants to know how serious we are," Clodagh said. Stretching up, she whispered in his ear, "I think we should tell them."

Jamie's fingers caressed her neck. "And let them figure out the details?"

"Yes. So much yes."

He nodded, and straightened away from her. "Okay. Is she still live? Just a…"

He took Clodagh's phone, ignored Olivia's squawking, and did something that linked both lines. Clodagh grinned. Sexy, clever man.

"All right, Major, Olivia, you're both on speaker phone. Shut up and listen a minute."

He waited while they both protested, and drew Clodagh into his arms.

"Do you have a pen? Take this down. 'His Royal Highness Prince James of Wales is delighted to formally announce that he is in a serious relationship with Miss Clodagh Walsh. His Royal Highness met Miss Walsh last year in Cambridge. The couple request your respect and privacy at this time.' Got that?"

He glanced at Clodagh as both phones erupted with questions.

"Also, we're getting married," Clodagh murmured, as if either of them could hear.

"I think we'll keep that quiet for now, don't you?" he said, and Clodagh nodded. "I've got to speak to Granny anyway."

"Release that statement," Jamie told the phones. "Put it on Twitter, and my website, send it to the papers, do what you like. Easel outside the palace, I don't care.

That's the official statement. No more until I've spoken to my family. Goodbye."

With that he ended both calls, and exhaled hard, finding a smile from somewhere for Clodagh.

"Well done."

"Yeah." He put his arms around her and she let herself enjoy the feel of his body against hers. "That's the easy part. I'm afraid," he sighed, "we can't put it off very long."

"Your family?"

"My family." He held her a bit longer, the two of them standing close and quiet in the kitchen of the Hunting Tower, and then Jamie sighed and reached for his phone. "Major. Did Her Majesty give an indication of when I was to be summoned? Right. Okay, let me know."

He fiddled with his phone a moment, then did the same with hers. Clodagh stayed still, listening to his heart beat.

"Should be getting calls from Peaseman, Olivia, and the PPOs only," he said, tossing her phone on the table. "Otherwise they'll never shut up." He hesitated. "You want to call your mum?"

No. "What can she possibly say?"

Jamie gently lifted her chin and made her look at him. "Maybe she's worried about you."

"First time for everything." She eyed her phone as if it might sprout legs and teeth and attack her. "Urgh, I don't wanna," she groaned, but Jamie picked up the phone and held it out to her. "You're mean."

He quirked an eyebrow at her and sat down to watch. Clodagh took the seat katy-corner from him and dialled her mum, praying for voicemail.

"Shar? Oh my God, it's Sharday! Everyone! Shar why didn't you tell us! Oh my God we have champagne here! Well, Mr Singh didn't have any so we've got prosecco but it's the same thing anyway. Are you, like wall-to-wall champers there, babes? Shar?"

Clodagh closed her eyes. "Hi Mum."

"Are you okay, babe? You don't sound very happy for someone who's just totally snagged a prince. A prince!" she cried, and people cheered in the background.

"Well, his brother did just die so we're not all rainbows and puppies around here," Clodagh reminded her.

"Oh. Oh, yeah. My condolences to him, yeah? Is he there? Can I talk to him?"

Clodagh could absolutely see her, fluffing up her hair as she talked on the phone.

"Yeah, no he's really busy," she said, making a face at Jamie. "We've got a lot to sort out, what with you outing me like that."

"Outing you? What you on about?"

"Well," said Clodagh. "How can I put this? Remember how we got slaughtered by the press sixteen years ago? It's about to get a lot worse."

"Oh, no one even remembers that, babe," said her mother, but her cheer wavered.

"No. No one did remember it. But there's this thing called Google." Clodagh suddenly felt terribly tired. "Soon as they got my name they looked me up."

"It ain't in the papers," her mum said uncertainly.

"It's online. It'll be on the front page tomorrow. Gossip loves a scandal, Mum, and you've just handed them one."

"Oh, yeah… but…" Sharon Walsh faltered. "Yeah, but there's like…"

Across the table, Jamie mouthed, "Tell her you're talking to Granny," and winked.

"I have to go, Mum. There's a lot to do here. I have to talk to…" She couldn't lie, not outright, "some very important people, so we can decide how to respond to all this."

"Ooh, well get you, all fancy," said her mother, clearly stung. "Don't you forget where you came from, missy."

"Believe me, Mum, I don't think that's going to happen," Clodagh said, and rung off.

She dropped the phone on the table, feeling the need to wash her hands. And her ear.

Jamie hitched his chair closer and put his arm around her. "Well done. That's the worst of it, for now."

"I thought the worst of it was talking to your family."

"Well, that's why I said 'for now'," he said sheepishly. "Until Her Majesty decides when she wants to see us, we're at leisure." He tucked a bit of hair behind her ear, from whence it sprang back immediately. "What do you fancy? Nice walk in the parkland? Board game?" His eyes went warm. "Try out the bathtub?"

It was a *big* tub. "What if Peaseman calls when we're in the bath?"

"I'm not intending to put him on Facetime."

Clodagh pretended to think about it as he nuzzled her neck. "Well, if there's nothing else to do…"

Jamie grinned, and led her upstairs.

CHAPTER TWENTY

"And you call her…"

"Your Majesty in the first instance, and then ma'am, rhymes with jam," Clodagh said obediently, wondering how much this was costing in data usage. The car sped smoothly down the M1, every minute bringing her a little bit closer to the most terrifying thing she'd ever had to face.

Having a baby was a fucking picnic compared to this.

Olivia nodded on the iPad screen. "Right. And only shake her hand if she offers it. Do not touch her in any other manner. Wait for her to sit before you do, and stand when she does. Wait for her to speak first. Can't stress that enough."

"And don't be freaked out if I stay silent," Jamie said. "She might only address you, which means I won't have permission to speak. I'm not ignoring you."

"You need permission to speak to your own grandmother?" Clodagh said, appalled.

"In formal situations, yes. She is the Queen, after all."

"Right," Clodagh said. She took a deep breath and let

it out. She'd been doing that all day and it wasn't helping at all. "What about the walking backwards thing? Is that just Hollywood?"

"Try not to turn your back," Jamie said. "A couple of steps backwards, then turn to the side, that usually works."

"For God's sake don't put me in heels," Clodagh said, panicked. She hadn't worn heels for ages and certainly not since her ankle had been broken.

"But all the outfit choices I've got look better with— all right, I'll find you something flat. This would have been so much easier in the winter," Olivia grumbled. She glanced at the rack of clothes by her desk, which all looked the same to Clodagh. "You did shave your legs and underarms?" she demanded.

"What, now my personal grooming is public knowledge?" Clodagh muttered, as Jamie said, "She did."

A short pause, during which Clodagh felt her face burn, then Olivia said, "Very good."

"By the way, what's in that conditioner?" Clodagh said desperately. "The Allendale honey one?"

"I have no idea, darling. Why? Is it good or bad?"

"It's amazing. It just says honey on it, so I was a bit leery…" but there had been no other choice at hand, without calling the housekeeper or someone to find the right stuff, "but it's brilliant."

"Ooh." Olivia perked right up. "As recommended by the future Duchess of… any ideas, Jamie?"

Clodagh froze, because they'd decided not to mention their engagement to anyone yet, but Jamie just said easily, "One thing at a time, Oll." He glanced at his watch. "Look, I think we need a bit of downtime."

"Some Crowded House would be good around now," admitted Clodagh.

"You see? A convert," said Jamie, smiling warmly at

her.

"You two," said Olivia, but she said goodbye and signed off. Jamie dialled up some music and they sat quietly for a moment, holding hands. Clodagh calmed down a bit, until she remembered she was going to meet the freaking Queen, and then the panic came back again.

"You'll be fine," Jamie said, his thumb stroking her hand. "Just be polite, and respectful, and everything will be fine."

"What if she asks me about…" Oh God, where to start? "My dad, and the baby, and…"

"Then be honest. She'd rather that than you lied."

"Says someone with nothing to be ashamed of."

Jamie was silent a moment, and then he said, "There's stuff she doesn't know."

"Like?"

"Well, she wasn't terribly pleased to find out I'd had a live-in girlfriend for weeks," he said drily.

"Is that all?"

"Well, I don't think Victoria has been entirely upfront about the number of miscarriages she's had."

Clodagh's gaze flew to him. "Really?"

"She's going to have some tests run, apparently. What makes it worse is all the speculation about when she's going to start having babies."

"Oh God. Poor thing."

"And then there's Ed," he said, and his fingers tensed.

"What about him?" Clodagh asked gently. Jamie had talked about his brother a bit over the last couple of days, but mostly it had been the happier recollections.

Jamie blew out a long sigh. "He… the reason he was in Wales," he said, and stalled.

"Visiting friends and old colleagues?" That was what the news had said.

"No. Well, yes. One particular, very special

299

colleague," Jamie said, rolling his head to look meaningfully at her.

Clodagh felt her eyes go wide. "No. Seriously?"

"Yep." He hesitated again, then squeezed her hand and said, "This really goes no further, you understand? Not ever. If Annemarie chooses to make it public some day that's one thing, but otherwise you take this to your grave, you hear?"

Clodagh nodded. "Trust me, I'm good at secrets."

"I know you are." He took a deep breath, then said, "Ed's lover was a man."

For a second Clodagh could only blink at him. "What?"

"Yep. Apparently it'd been going on for ages. Annemarie knew about it. I did not," he added, "ask for the specifics of their relationship. She assures me the children are his."

Clodagh stared at nothing. "Whoa."

"Yep."

"Your poor brother."

Jamie looked surprised.

"Having to live a lie like that. Never being able to publicly be with the person he loved. Having to lie about it all the time. It must have been…"

"Yeah," said Jamie shortly. She realised his eyes were damp, and squeezed his hand.

"I'm sorry. This whole thing is awful."

"I'm never going to do that," Jamie said fiercely.

Clodagh tried to keep her tone light. "What, take a male lover?"

"Live a lie like that. Do you know," he said, turning to her, "after Ed died, I was so… I didn't care. If I couldn't have you, I didn't care."

"Jamie." She leaned over the centre console to hug him.

"If Olivia had said she'd marry me I'd probably have

said yes. And then one day it'd have been me in that helicopter, flying off to see you instead. Lying to the public, to my family, making us all unhappy. I won't do it. It's you and me and we're not doing any more polite fictions. Agreed?"

"Agreed," said Clodagh, wondering what the hell she was letting herself in for.

"Oh Christ," she muttered as they drove under the archway and into the quadrangle. Jamie had done this hundreds of times, and usually he was too busy or distracted to think about where he really was, but he looked out at the palace and realised how intimidating it must be.

The car took them to the portico where the Queen was usually filmed boarding her golden carriage for state occasions. Clodagh's hand shook as he took it and led her inside, following a footman in his impeccable livery.

"Do you wonder if they ever spill their lunch on their uniforms?" he murmured to Clodagh, who gave a shaky laugh. That was better.

They'd gone straight to Olivia's office, where a bewildering array of demure black dresses had awaited. Jamie had given Oll the length of time it took for him to change into the black suit and tie Vincent had brought, in order to make a decision on what Clodagh should wear. Five minutes more for a make-up girl to do something with powder and eyeliner. Clodagh never wore much make-up and he didn't want her to feel any more overwhelmed than she already was.

To his relief they weren't taken to the State Apartments, which were so intimidatingly grand they might have given Clodagh a heart attack, but to the private apartments where the Queen received the Prime Minister and other government officials. His parents were already there, and so were Victoria and Nick and

Annemarie, every one of them still in mourning black and none of them smiling.

Jamie kept hold of Clodagh's hand as the doors at the other end of the room opened and his grandparents entered. Everyone bowed and curtseyed, and Clodagh managed just fine at his side. Her fingers held his in a death grip.

"James," said the Queen, unsmiling.

Well, if that was the way she was going to play it… "Your Majesty," he said. "May I present Miss Clodagh Walsh."

His grandmother was in her late eighties now, but her eyes had lost none of their shrewdness. She looked them over, then said, "Miss Walsh."

It was a command. Jamie let go of her and urged her gently forward. For an awful second he thought she might not go, and then she did, stopping a few feet away as he and Olivia had coached her, and giving another little curtsey. At least Oll paid attention about the flat shoes, Jamie thought as he went to stand near his sister.

The Queen remained standing, and said nothing for an excruciatingly long time. Jamie saw Clodagh's fingers go white as she pinched a fold of her skirt. She kept her gaze pitched low. Her breathing was rapid.

A clock ticked loudly.

"I understand you are from Harlow," said the Queen eventually.

"Uh, yes, Your Majesty," said Clodagh, looking up in confusion.

"Such an interesting idea, these new towns. All with some innovation. Gardens and cycleways and the like. Sculpture, I believe, in Harlow."

"Yes, ma'am, Henry Moore," said Clodagh, as if she couldn't believe she was having this conversation.

"Indeed. Do you enjoy modern art?"

"Um. Well, I… to be honest ma'am, most of the time

it was covered in graffiti and bits of chewing gum, so I never really… got to appreciating it."

Her accent sounded more Essex than he'd ever heard it, or maybe that was just because Granny sounded posher than usual. Jamie was too anxious to tell.

"They used to call it Pram Town, I recall," the Queen said. Her face gave nothing away.

"Really?" Clodagh said, in something of a strangled voice.

"Yes. On account of the baby boom after the war."

She didn't elaborate on that, but decided to take a seat instead, and gestured for Clodagh to take the sofa opposite. She perched there, looking terrified.

"You are the eldest of six?"

"Yes, ma'am."

"And your father?"

Clodagh licked her lips. "I never knew him, ma'am."

Jamie knew the Queen knew this. "Indeed. Perhaps that should be rectified. Or perhaps he will come forward of his own accord, given all the publicity?"

Oh God. This was horrible. Jamie forced himself to keep his expression neutral when all he wanted to do was yell, "Stop it!"

"I couldn't say," said Clodagh.

"No. Of course not. We are, of course, aware of several details of your past, courtesy of your mother. Is there anything you'd like to add to her story?"

Clodagh looked down, and he saw her take a couple of breaths. And just when he thought she'd say no, she lifted her head and said, "Yes. There is something. I know you probably think it's terrible my mother sold me out like that for a few quid, but the thing is that's more money than she's ever seen in her whole life. It's not greed that did it. It wasn't greed sixteen years ago. It's short-termism. Why think very far ahead? It's just going to get more bleak and miserable. You grasp anything shiny with both hands whenever you can.

"Your Majesty, that kind of life is so...small, and so mean and so hopeless, you do what you can to make any of it better, even if it's just for a minute or two. Any kind of escape you can get from the squalor of the real world, whether it's junk food or lipstick or five minutes with a stranger in a nightclub toilet, you go for it. There's no prospect of life ever actually getting better. You can't get out. It's a crab bucket.

"And I know we're all supposed to work hard and strive to improve, but if that worked then we'd all be rich. 'Cos the thing is, it costs money to get better, to go to a good school and get good grades and go to university, and money's the thing none of us ever had. I have worked like a dog to even get to a point where I even have the qualifications to apply to university, and even then I have no idea how I'm actually going to afford it. And then someone comes along and offers my mum six figures, just for identifying her daughter to the press? She'd have been mad not to."

There was a sudden silence. Nobody dared move. Jamie wasn't sure he dared breathe.

"And the... adoption?"

Clodagh's chin came up, as if she knew she'd blown it already. "Was a terrible period of my life and I never want to revisit it," she said. "But since we're here, yeah, okay. Five minutes in a nightclub with a stranger when I was fifteen, and boy did I pay the price for that particular moment of escapism. Yeah, I shouldn't have let myself get into that situation and yeah, I'd have done it differently given half the chance, and no, I don't regret the adoption and no, I don't want anything to do with that kid. I hope he's happy and that's the end of it."

"I see," said the Queen after a moment. "Well, Miss Walsh."

That was all she said, but Jamie got the feeling

volumes were being spoken as she looked Clodagh over.

She inclined her head slightly in his direction. "Jamie."

He went forward, gave her a quick head bow, and sat beside Clodagh when she gestured him to.

Defiantly, he took Clodagh's hand in his. It was ice cold.

"This is the woman you have chosen?"

"It is, ma'am."

She regarded the two of them for an excruciatingly long while. Everyone in the room was utterly still.

"It will not be easy, becoming part of this family," his grandmother said to Clodagh. "You must be very, very certain this is what you want."

"I am," Clodagh said.

"So am I," Jamie said, hope coursing through him.

"So I see." The Queen rose, and so did they. "Perhaps December, for the wedding. Windsor is picturesque in the snow."

And with that she departed. Jamie's grandfather, who'd stayed standing and silent throughout, winked at him and followed her.

Wedding. *Wedding*. Sweet Jesus.

As the doors shut behind them Clodagh turned to Jamie and kind of collapsed into his arms. "Oh my God," she breathed.

"It's okay. You did it." He started smiling. A December wedding. At Windsor. That was as good as a blessing. He'd do the formal thing, of course, but she'd approved. Of course she'd approved, Clodagh was amazing. "Christ, I love you."

Clodagh looked up, and her smile was shaky.

"Come and meet my parents."

After that, meeting the Prince and Princess of Wales was a cinch. Clodagh had no idea what she said to them, or to the younger royals, but no one seemed to take offence so she assumed it had all been okay.

"Of course, we have weathered worse," said Jamie's dad, Prince Frederick, the man who was going to be king one day. "Grandpa, of course, hellbent on ruining the whole family with unsuitable women."

"And Cousin Margaret," said Jamie's mother, the Princess of Wales. "Never met an unsuitable man she couldn't fall in love with."

"Not that Clodagh is unsuitable," Jamie said, with warning in his voice.

"Oh no, of course. But press speculation, you know. We must close ranks."

"The history of royalty is absorbing incomers and repackaging them as something acceptable," said Jamie's sister, Princess Victoria. "I think it's marvellous," she went on, with some determination. "We could use some fresh blood. It's only in the last century we stopped marrying our cousins."

Fresh blood. Oh, great. Like a vampire.

"Don't worry, when we first met she spent the entire conversation talking about the training methods my father's shepherds use on their sheepdogs," said Princess Victoria's husband Nicholas, who was actually Lord Nicholas of somewhere. He was thinning on top and had a prominent Adam's apple, and the press liked to make a game of forgetting who he was since he wasn't a senior member of the family. But Clodagh saw the way he and Victoria looked at each other, and liked him on sight.

"Yes, and with me it was my teenage years in Botswana," said Annemarie. "My father works in the diamond trade," she added, and Clodagh's eyes dropped to the gigantic rock still on the third finger of her left hand.

Victoria had a ring of similar magnitude, and the Princess of Wales wore a cluster of rubies that had once belonged to Queen Victoria.

Oh Christ, I'll be getting one of those, she thought hysterically. I'll have to do hand-strenthening exercises. What if Jamie chooses something incredibly ugly?

She managed to smile and chat politely, until the Prince and Princess of Wales departed and Annemarie said she needed to go back to the children and Victoria excused herself with an appointment.

The whole conversation had lasted about five minutes. The inference was clear: once the Queen goes, we clear out. The room they were in was apparently a private audience chamber, not part of the State Apartments, but it was stuffed to the gills with grand features, paintings and little statues and finely carved fireplaces. The furniture was so fancy Clodagh was glad she'd only been seated for a minute or two.

Jamie held her back until everyone else had gone, which she supposed was a precedence thing, and then as the footman held the door open he led her out, down a corridor and to an antechamber at the top of a staircase, where he turned to her with his eyes shining.

"You," he said, "were bloody magnificent."

"I was?" Adrenaline seemed to drain from her. Clodagh felt herself tremble as Jamie took her in his arms.

"I am so in love with you," he said, and kissed her long and deep. Clodagh worried that there might be a footman or a butler or whoever wandering around the place watching, but Jamie had that way of kissing her that made the entire world go away.

Eventually someone cleared their throat, and Clodagh felt her face burn as Jamie glanced away from her without letting go.

"Sir, your car is ready."

He rested his forehead against Clodagh's and groaned. "I suppose it is. Come on, then. I have to go and see Peaseman and relate all this and get his people to talk to Granny's people and all that."

Clodagh should have been flushed with jubilation when she got back into the car, but instead she trembled in the throes of an adrenaline crash. Jamie glanced over and, wordless, got an energy drink and a chocolate bar from a cooler hidden in the centre console.

"There. Listen, when I'm done with Peaseman do you want to go back to Derbyshire? Cottage is ours for the week. Or home? Back to Cambridge?"

Home. Clodagh still couldn't quite take in the magnitude of what she'd let herself in for. Home would mean living with Jamie, which was fine except for Jamie was a prince. And living with him meant that she'd be announcing their engagement soon, which would be a big thing except that it would actually be a huge thing, because he was a prince. And then there would be the wedding, which would be a huge thing except that it would be a ginormous thing, *because he was a prince.*

Edward and Annemarie's wedding had been televised from the moment Annemarie left Kensington Palace, all through the ceremony, the kiss on the balcony of Buckingham Palace, right up to their final drive away from the palace to spend their first night together as a married couple. Coverage of Victoria and Nicholas's wedding had hardly been less excitable, with cameras following the first Princess to be married in the twenty-first century from the second she emerged that day.

Every detail had been pored over by glossy magazines and trashy ones, by respectful BBC commentators and American talk show hosts, by people in fashionable circles and people in the pub. Bookies placed bets on the dress designer, the colour of the bridesmaids' frocks, who would cry. Clodagh had been upset enough by the coverage of Edward's funeral. How was she going to cope when it was herself in the spotlight?

"Clo?"

"Um." She brought herself back to the present. "Derbyshire, I think. I'd like to… have some downtime."

"Downtime it is. I'll get someone to fetch some things from home… do you need anything? Where are you staying, anyway?"

"Staying? I *live* with a couple of friends in Cherry Hinton."

"I beg your pardon. Would you consider," he took her hand, "moving back in with me? Since we're going to be spending the rest of our lives together and all that."

Clodagh pretended to think about it. Truth was, that little house cloistered away in Cambridge seemed like a wonderful haven right now.

"I probably could, yeah," she said, and he grinned and called Peaseman. Then he got out his tablet and called up a few images.

"Okay, not that I've been thinking about this or anything," he gave her a sheepish look, "but let's talk about engagement rings."

Warmth spread throughout Clodagh. Generations of social conditioning, she told herself, but still couldn't help getting madly excited about the prospect of a giant sparkler.

"There will be a lot of focus on it, so it needs to be something you're really happy with. Take it off because you don't like it, and be prepared for the country to have declared us practically divorced already. Now. Stop me and buy one," he said, and began scrolling through images.

Oh God.

Clusters of yellow diamonds, coloured metals, spiky square things, something that looked like a skin disease…

Jamie stifled a giggle.

"You just Googled 'ugliest engagement rings', didn't you?" she said, relief pouring through her. She bashed his arm.

"Some people love these!"

Clodagh peered in fascination. "Yeah, well, I am not walking around with a Star Fleet badge on my finger, even if it is made out of...what even is niobium?"

"Hypo-allergenic," Jamie said helpfully. He gave her a contrite look, then opened some new images. Oh yes. Art Deco sapphires, emeralds and diamonds, yellow and white gold, clean simple designs that showed off the magnitude of the stones they contained.

"Anything?" he said, as she scrolled on.

"Well, all of them, obviously. Would it be unacceptable to have a coloured stone?"

Jamie looked nonplussed. "Well, so long as it's not one of those hideous chocolate diamonds then I think you can have anything you want. This is literally the only time it's acceptable to go as big and sparkly as you like. Bling it up. Get whatever you want."

Clodagh stared longingly at an emerald and diamond ring. "I'd be afraid of losing it."

"Trust me, there'd be enough eyes on you to stop that happening. We can go to the royal vaults, if you like, and look for something there? Or would you like something new? The family owns plenty of rocks. I could have one of them made. Or something entirely new. Go to Annemarie's mine and buy something. Anything you want."

Clodagh gazed at the emerald. "That's a dangerous thing to say."

"I mean it though." He took her hand and smiled. "From here on out, Clo. Anything you want at all."

PART THREE

CHAPTER TWENTY-ONE

"All right. We're down to two. The blue, or the cream."

Ugh, when had she ever been excited about this? Clodagh stared unseeing at the two dresses hanging on the rail. Lately, life was one endless round of questions and orders. Questions about stuff she really didn't care about—like which of these two dresses to wear, or which lipstick she should choose, or which presenter should do the engagement interview—and orders about stuff she'd rather have a say in, such as when and where and how she was going to marry Jamie.

"Blue," she said. "And the red shoes." Not because they looked any better than the others, but because they were the most comfortable she'd tried on. Apparently, there was only so long you could milk a broken ankle.

"But—" began the stylist.

"Blue and red," Clodagh said firmly. "Next?"

"Jewellery. Now. The focus should of course be on the ring, so nothing too bold. We have this, and this…"

An endless progression of gold necklaces was parades before her. They were all discreet and elegant and there was little to tell them apart. Clodagh picked one at random, then spent ten minutes pretending to listen to the stylist persuade her that another was better.

"Okay, that one. Next?"

"Earrings, ma'am." The stylist hesitated and glanced at the jeweller.

"Hope you brought a lot." Clodagh gave them a merciless smile. "There's more hole than lobe in my ears. Come on. Tiny row of studs. I'll even go nuts and have a diamond in the first hole."

Pretty much every stylist and dresser and random hanger-on—and there had been a lot—Clodagh had met since she'd first been brought to the Palace had tried to persuade her to lose the earrings. She'd agreed to the manicures and facials and the personal trainer, whom she hated with a vicious passion, and to the heels and the laser hair treatment and the specially selected controlling underwear.

She'd been introduced to a skinny white guy who was supposed to be her hairdresser, and laughed for ten minutes straight before they got the message and sent for a black girl instead.

"No offence, but the only white hands coming near this are Jamie's," she said as the skinny guy departed in a huff.

When she appeared at official events she had weights sewn into the hems of her skirts so the wind didn't blow them up and reveal her Spanx to the world. Her clothes had been carefully chosen to progress from black to dark colours, through to subtle, conservative shades but nothing too bright, which was irritating in summer. She'd been handed over to a bunch of very posh women who taught her how to talk elegantly, and sit elegantly, and get in and out of a car elegantly. Her curtsey had been branded a disaster and she'd had daily lessons until she'd flatly refused any more.

"Here's the thing," she said. "The earrings stay."

"But—"

"Do you want me to call the prince? Because I'll call him," Clodagh threatened, getting her phone out.

"But, ma'am, it's not… traditional… to have so many piercings."

"I look like a traditional royal bride to you? If he wanted traditional he'd be marrying Olivia." Clodagh picked up her phone. "Siri, call J—"

"All right, the earrings stay," said the stylist, and Clodagh grinned, because she'd switched off voice recognition on her phone anyway, after an unfortunate event when she'd been in bed with Jamie and her phone had fallen under the pillow and, well, it turned out that "Oh Jamie" sounded a lot like "Call Jamie" and his calls were being diverted to Peaseman…

Clodagh allowed them to choose more plain gold studs to replace the ones she was already wearing, and endured a debate about whether the main earring should be an emerald stud or an emerald drop.

Everything had to match her ring for the big day. Clodagh stretched out her manicured hand and admired the large green stone. She'd let Jamie choose, and he'd chosen well, noting her Art Deco preferences and having royal emeralds and diamonds set into a simple design. Simple, but still huge, heavy, and surprisingly flashy compared to the 'understated elegance' she was supposed to be radiating at all times.

"Are you kidding? Have you seen the Crown Jewels?" Jamie laughed when she put this to him. "Granny had to do neck-strengthening exercises to keep the crown on. She said if she looked down her neck would snap."

"I don't have to wear a crown, do I?"

"No, love, you get a tiara. Well, she might lend you one. I could buy you one?" he offered, and Clodagh, appalled by the sheer cost of the rock on her finger, shook her head rapidly.

"All right." The stylist looked over her list, muttering to herself. Clodagh wasn't sure what else there was to decide on. She'd even had her stockings picked out for her.

"Are we done? Can I go?"

"Yes," said the stylist.

"No," said the assistant Peaseman had deputised, "wait, the questions for Thursday…"

"I have them." She and Jamie were supposed to rehearse answers.

"No, they've been revised…"

Clodagh took the list from Sarah, the only one of the coterie of professionals who didn't issue orders or ask stupid questions, and made an effort to smile. "Are there any major differences?"

"Mostly phraseology. It's been approved by the Palace, so…"

"And we all know the Palace must never be crossed. All right, now can I go?"

It was allowed that she could. Clodagh was escorted back out of the anonymous set of offices somewhere in St James and into one of the Range Rovers, which took her to Kensington Palace, where she was informed His Highness was still busy with his own arrangements for Thursday. Clodagh, who hadn't seen him for two days, rolled her eyes and said, "How industrious of him. Can I go see him?"

She didn't wait for a reply, but set off along the route she'd come to know quite well, down a series of unflashy corridors to Peaseman's domain. Trotting along behind her was Martins, who had been seconded to her personal security until she was allowed a team of her own. *Thursday…*

Clodagh's reflection in a picture glass caught her eye. She still looked like herself, but… somehow smoother and glossier. Her new hairdresser had done amazing things to the curls Clodagh had always been proud of keeping in good condition, and she'd had her teeth whitened and skin smoothed, and even though she was in civvies she looked somehow a bit more expensive.

Best not tell them these jeans came from New Look, she thought drily as she tapped on the open door and went in.

"… yes, of course I can tell the difference, I just don't care."

Jamie was pacing, hair all over the place, shirt creased and untucked, his jaw shadowed with stubble. Hung around the office were various suits, shirts and ties. An array of shoes and socks covered an assistant's desk. Peaseman leaned against one desk, tie loosened in a manner Clodagh hadn't seen before. Even Vincent looked exasperated. This must have been some session.

"And I thought it was just me," she said, and they looked up in surprise.

"Clo!" Jamie's face lit up. "God, sorry, is it that late?" He looked at his watch. "Quick, pick a tie."

She pointed to one at random.

"But, ma'am, does it entirely match your dress?" asked Vincent fretfully.

"Perfectly," Clodagh lied. "Now, I'm going to steal His Highness. We have a very important appointment."

"But—"

"That suit," Jamie said, pointing, "that shirt, that tie, those shoes, and frankly if you ask my opinion on socks again I'll do the whole thing in a *Big Bang Theory* t-shirt." He grabbed his iPad. "Let's go."

"You're such a rebel," Clodagh teased as they made their way out of the back rooms of the palace.

"Oh yeah. You know what I'm going to do on Thursday? Not wear a tie pin." Clodagh gasped in mock outrage. "I know, right?"

They got into the car, with its leather and luxury that Clodagh almost didn't notice any more, and he leaned across to kiss her.

"You smell nice."

She laughed. "You want to hear something funny? They've been testing perfumes on me for Thursday."

Jamie opened his mouth, shut it, then frowned at her. "Er... for a TV appearance?"

"Right? Go figure. Apparently I must be 'fragrant at all times' so there go the curries and sweaty socks. Where are you taking me?"

"Windsor. Couple of things I wanted to show you."

Clodagh hadn't been to Windsor yet. She'd had become slightly familiar with Buckingham Palace since her first trip there two months ago, and even more familiar with Jamie's official residence of Kensington Palace. As an unmarried girlfriend, she wasn't allowed to stay the night with Jamie, and the one time she'd been allocated a room it had been so far away from his they'd have needed GPS to find each other.

Everyone in the family knew she was living with Jamie, but for the sake of maintaining a polite fiction her address was still listed as Becca and Heather's house in Cherry Hinton. She'd been more or less obliged to quit her job at the Prince's Arms, which made her panic somewhat until Jamie quietly explained that for the sake of the same polite fiction she'd been given a titular job as Victoria's advisor, which meant a salary being paid into her account until she came under his own household officially, after the wedding.

"It's not a total lie," he said. "You have advised her."

"Once," Clodagh said. Victoria had, very tentatively, asked her about the adoption process. Clodagh didn't have much to tell her, but it turned out Victoria just really needed to talk, and to cry, and much to Clodagh's surprise, she'd cried too.

Sixteen years of keeping it in, and that's when it comes out: in the company of a princess.

Windsor was about forty five minutes away, and they were interrupted more than once by Peaseman and his minions fretting over details for Thursday.

"Christ's sake, Clo, do you care about flowers?"

"Flowers?" she said, bewildered. "I didn't even know there would be flowers."

"There are always flowers. Look, whatever you think is appropriate. You've been advising my family for years, Major, you know what's... yes, I know this is your first time organising a... well, then ask Annemarie's people. She probably has a flower person."

He rang off, rolling his eyes at Clodagh. "Who knew royal weddings were so complicated," he said, as if that was still funny any more, and she took his hand.

"Gretna Green isn't that far away. I mean I could run to a suitcase and a ladder, if you buy the train tickets."

He kissed her fingers. "I love you."

It was a damn good job, Clodagh thought. She'd stopped even looking at the papers, after one glance the day after the story broke, and she daren't even go online where, she'd been informed, the vitriol got even worse. Everyone had an opinion, from the benign to the patronising to the downright hateful. Petitions had been started to 'get the gyppo out' after her mother's relationship with Duke had been revealed. Far Right groups had shrieked about the pollution of the royal line with 'negro blood'. People called her ugly, fat, and common. Her hair was too big and too messy, her clothes too bright, and yet she was also too conservative in her dress and had abandoned her black roots by dressing like a white girl.

When Clodagh stayed publicly silent, they called her aloof, and out of touch with her roots. When her mother or siblings spoke up—as they did frequently, somehow blissfully unaware that every friendly stranger they spoke to was a reporter—they were greeted with derision. The names her mother and her sisters had chosen for their offspring were ridiculed. Comedians did sketches about them. Cartoonists drew her as Vicky Pollard from *Little Britain*.

Every single person in the country seemed to have an opinion on the decisions she'd made as a scared fifteen-year-old. And not just in the country; politicians and lobbyists and advocacy groups all weighed in on what she'd done right and what she'd done wrong; mostly what she'd done wrong. Tabloids and clickbait sites all over the place kept offering rewards for information about the baby she'd 'abandoned'.

There were days when she went out of her way to avoid it all, and still got smacked in the face with it. Days when she came home from whatever beautifying exercise had occupied her time, and wept in Jamie's arms.

And then she straightened up, wiped the tears away, and told herself to be a fucking grown-up about it all.

Jamie checked his watch as they turned off towards Windsor, and pressed the intercom button. "Frogmore first," he said, and got a reply in the affirmative.

"Frogmore?"

"One of the homes in the Home Park," Jamie said.

"Ah yes. Why have one royal residence in the grounds when you can have several, all within an easy few hours of each other?"

"This was the dower house for Victoria's mother. It's only open for a few private tours in the spring. The mausoleum is where half the family are buried."

"Oh, lovely."

"It was bought by George III for Queen Charlotte. Shall we check for portraits?"

She'd been expecting something modest. Well,

modest by royal standards. But Frogmore House turned out to be just as palatial as everything else.

"Don't you people have small houses?" she said, as she craned her neck to see it all.

"However would we fit our egos inside?"

He led her inside, and Clodagh tried not to be shocked anew at the grandeur and scale of the place. She'd thought she was used to all the splendour now, but every time she saw something new a fresh sense of wonder, mixed with terror, settled over her.

"The family uses it for events sometimes," said Jamie, leading her through rooms painted with flowers. The early evening sunshine glinted off the gilt accents present in several of the rooms—hell, present in every royal room Clodagh had been in. "But the public don't come here often. I thought," he said, coming to a halt in a gallery draped in red and taking her in his arms, "you could spend the night before the wedding here."

"Here?" She looked around at the high windows giving out onto the picturesque lake and gardens. "I mean I suppose I could sleep in a chair…"

He kissed her ear. "Silly. I mean in one of the bedrooms. You could have one, and Oll could have one, and your mum could…" He paused as she winced, "… stay in a hotel in town."

"Good, yes, I like that idea. Or the whole thing will be derailed by her insisting on a diamanté manicure because it looks well classy, and using my veil to wipe a toddler's nose."

Jamie laughed softly. He and Clodagh had made very polite excuses about being busy whenever Clodagh's mum had offered to visit, and in the end scheduled a visit somewhere they could meet on somewhat neutral ground. None of her family knew about the wedding. Clodagh had begun idly wondering if they'd fall for an all-expenses paid holiday somewhere exotic for the whole duration.

"Are you sure you want Oll as your maid of honour?" Jamie asked her. "Shouldn't it be one of your sisters?"

"No. No, no way, and never, which is incidentally what I might start calling them," she said, resting her face against his neck. "Oh God, Jamie, they're going to be a nightmare."

"They'll be fine. I mean, mad clothes and too much bling and incomprehensible accents are more or less what my family do, so yours will be no different."

"Hah. That old cliché that common people and posh people are the same? You're still in for a helluva shock."

He stroked her face. "Good job I'm marrying you, then, and not them." He kissed her softly. "Come on. Let's go try out the bedrooms."

They were grand, even the ones not kept roped off for the public tours. The beds were large and, Clodagh was pleased to discover, at least one of them was particularly bouncy.

"You are a wicked man," she said as she lay beside Jamie, trying to get her breath back. Sweat cooled on her skin. It was a warm July day and the royal family didn't seem to believe in air conditioning.

"You seemed to think I was quite good about five minutes ago," he replied. He propped himself up on one elbow and traced a line with one finger between her breasts.

"Please tell me you locked the door."

"There's no one else here. Unless…" He cupped his ear as if listening. "Oh yes, that'll be the WI private tour."

Clodagh walked her fingers over his hip. "And here we have the Crown Jewels…"

"Now who's wicked?" He captured her fingers for a kiss. "Just think, night before the wedding, you'll have some good memories of this room."

She smiled and pulled him towards her for a kiss, but they were interrupted by the buzzing of his phone.

"Yeah? Okay. Just… give us ten minutes, yeah?"

He cast her a sheepish glance. "It's okay, there's no public around."

"Are you telling me I look a mess?" She sat up and groaned at her reflection. "Jamie!"

"You don't look a mess, you look…" His gaze travelled her bare body, and he grinned.

"Yes, exactly. I'm not turning up at a royal palace, regardless of the public, looking like I've just been shagged."

Jamie stretched luxuriously, then swung to his feet. "It's a good look on you."

At least these days she had enough make-up—and decent stuff, at that—in her bag to do a repair job. Olivia was on at her to get her underarms Botoxed to prevent sweating, and on a day like this Clodagh could almost see her point.

A rushed ten minutes later, she was dressed and presentable, and Jamie was taking her back to the car, which thankfully did have air conditioning and let her cool down enough for the next thing.

"What is the next thing?" she said, as the car drove through the streets of Windsor.

Jamie motioned out of the window.

"I'm going to show you where we're getting married."

There were signs everywhere warning them that Windsor Castle was closed to visitors and that St George's Chapel was holding no further services that day. The Range Rover, of course, ignored all that and drove straight in, clearly expected.

Clodagh stared around. It wasn't what she'd expected, resembling more of a village green than a castle. Around it were crenelated cottages, arched cloisters and a herringbone redbrick house not unlike their own in Cambridge. And then there was a huge edifice with stained glass windows. Part of the castle, she supposed. These residences were huge.

"Your Royal Highness," greeted a man in the robes of the clergy. "Miss Walsh. If you'll follow me…"

He led them to a door in the castle. "We'd prefer not to be disturbed," Jamie said, and the man hesitated. "This has been cleared by my security team and private secretary?"

He phrased it as a question, but it was clearly intended as a statement. The clergyman backed down, and Jamie winked at her as he led her inside.

"Welcome to St George's Chapel," he said, and Clodagh looked at him in confusion.

"Chapel? But this place is…"

She stepped inside and looked around the cathedral-like space. A soaring, vaulted ceiling. Side chapels gated off from the main nave. One entire wall made up of individual stained glass panels, through which the last of the evening light flooded. Marble sculptures of astonishing size and beauty.

"…huge," she finished, eyes wide. "You said it was a chapel!"

"It's a large chapel," Jamie allowed, striding out into the middle of the massive space as if he owned the place. Which he nearly did. "Look, the West Window, the third largest in England apparently. Fifteen by five panels, that's seventy-five. Are you still impressed by my maths skills?" he joked, as Clodagh stood with her mouth open.

Her eyes tried to calculate the distance from the doors beneath the West Window to the altar. "It's a long aisle."

"Um," said Jamie.

Clodagh narrowed her eyes, and he gave her a charming grin before towing her forward, behind what she'd taken to be the altar.

"Are we supposed to—oh, okay," she said, as he tugged her under an elaborately carved archway into a whole new section of chapel beyond.

"That was just the nave," he told her. "This," he walked backwards and spread his arms, "is the Quire."

Clodagh looked around. Dammit, she really should have looked all this up online before she said yes. Not that there was much alternative. The Queen had said Windsor, so Windsor it would be; and besides, it wasn't as if Westminster Abbey or St Pauls were precisely small and intimate.

There's a church just up the road from my mum. It's not the ugliest Brutalist church you ever saw and some days it doesn't even get vandalised. Let's get married there.

There were carved wooden stalls either side of the black and white chequered aisle. Fashioned into seats, they were softly lit by little lamps. Beyond them was the proper altar, huge and impressive, backed with yet more exquisite carving and stained glass.

"What d'you think?" said Jamie.

Clodagh managed to close her mouth, swallow, and said, "I think I'm really not posh enough for this."

He came back to her and put an arm around her shoulder. "Nonsense. You deserve it. My wife deserves it."

Clodagh took another deep breath and let it out. "Your wife." *I will be his wife. Jamie's wife.* If she thought about it like that, and didn't think about the whole duchess bit, it was okay.

"Yep. That's what happens after we get married," he explained helpfully. "You become my wife."

"Hah."

"And I become your husband. We belong to each other, you see."

Clodagh laid her head on his shoulder and he pressed

his cheek against her hair. *I belong to you anyway.*

Jamie began pointing with the arm not holding her. "Up there is the Oriole window built for Catherine of Aragon to observe services. Of course, that's when the place was run by filthy Catholics and not good clean Church of England like what we are."

Clodagh, whose grandmother had been a filthy Catholic, dealt him a look. She'd had to promise she didn't adhere to that faith before wedding plans could go ahead; apparently it was fine if she had no particular faith, or if she was Jewish or Muslim or Jedi, so long as she wasn't Catholic. Not for the first time, she considered that the Royal Family was utterly mad.

"Those are the crests of the members of the Order of the Garter, which is the—"

"Highest order of chivalry that can be bestowed," said Clodagh, who had done some of her homework. "And the oldest."

"Absolutely. See the crests, mounted on helms? That's the King of Norway, and that's the Emperor of Japan, and that's Annemarie's uncle. On the wall, see those plaques?Behind the stalls? Those represent the previous incumbents of that stall. The Order is for life, you see, and there are can only be twenty-four of them, plus supernumeraries for the family. So those plates there hold the crests of previous Knights. And a couple of ladies, too."

"You're an excellent tour guide," said Clodagh, who knew he was doing it to relax her. Hiding in history always made her feel better.

"Behind us," he swivelled her around, "is Granny's box, all in royal blue, of course, and that is where my Dad traditionally sits." He pointed at the banners hanging above them, the Royal Standard and the Prince of Wales's Standard, and then at the versions flanking them, each differenced by a white label, its small symbols identifying it much as Jamie's identified him. "Grandpa, Uncle Charles next to him, then I think that's Great Aunt Elizabeth, and…"

He broke off, and slightly abruptly turned to the other side of the entrance. "Aunt Penelope, Great Aunt Georgina, Great Aunt Mary. Edward VIII appointed all his children, and then Granny appointed hers, and then there wasn't much space so it was just…"

Clodagh looked at him, and realised there was a gap in the banners on one side that wasn't there on the other.

"It was just Ed," Jamie said. "Vicky and I used to joke we'd have to wait for someone to die before either of us got appointed. I, ah…"

Clodagh turned and put her arms around him, and Jamie pressed his face against her hair and sighed.

"Two months and it still hasn't… I still keep thinking of him. Like a joke I want to share or some memory I want to ask him about and then I remember…"

Clodagh stroked his hair. There wasn't much she could say that hadn't already been said.

"Come with me," Jamie said, and marched her out of the Quire, through the Nave and towards one of the side chapels, gated and locked. He pointed to a starkly fresh tomb. *Prince Edward of Wales 1982-2018.*

Clodagh stood with Jamie, looking at the tomb of his brother, which was supposed to have been kept for his grandparents and been used too early.

"It's just so weird how he's in there."

"It's always weird when someone's gone. There's something left but it's not them any more," Clodagh said. She hadn't been allowed to see her nan after she'd died, but they'd been taken to see Duke, laid out and looking like a waxwork version of himself. Clodagh had cried when the coffin was lowered, because even though she'd understood he wasn't coming back, the burial seemed so… final.

"I keep thinking he'd hate to be in a stone box. He was always so active, so unrestricted. Had to be moving and doing, hated being still. He could never understand how I could spend so many hours reading or playing games."

"One of those people who enjoys exercise," Clodagh said, in tones of faint wonder.

"Yeah." He cuddled Clodagh close. "He'd have liked you, I think. He'd be glad I'm marrying someone I love, because God knows he couldn't."

Clodagh kissed his tears away. "Did Annemarie bring Dai here?"

"Yes. She says… she says one day, when the children are older, when the dust has settled, she's going to tell the truth."

"No more secrets."

"No more secrets."

The sound of a door opening made them both turn. The same clergyman from before stood in the darkened doorway of the chapel.

"Your Highness?"

"Yes." Jamie swiped at his eyes. "Yes, we're ready. Thank you. Oh—no, one more thing."

He walked Clodagh down to a monument by the West Door. It depicted mourners draped in veils at the bedside of a shrouded corpse, one frighteningly realistic hand just showing under the sheet. Above it soared three angels, one of them carrying an infant.

"Princess Charlotte," Jamie said. "Daughter of—"

"George IV. Died in childbirth. And the baby too. The doctor killed himself out of guilt, so I've read," Clodagh said. She studied the veiled mourners, so real she expected them to get up and move, and the figure lying under the shroud, not neatly set out but sprawled as if at the moment of death.

"We don't go in for that kind of thing any more,"

Jamie said, taking her hand, but she could see the sadness in his face at the difference between this and Edward's stark white box.

"Your Highness?" said the voice behind them again, and Jamie squeezed Clodagh's hand and led her away.

CHAPTER TWENTY-TWO

The photos were mildly excruciating. Clodagh had never been good at smiling for the camera, and all the pictures of her that had appeared in the press so far had her looking mildly constipated.

They'd been offered various royal locations, but Cambridge seemed the most logical and, with the whole family obsessed with symbolism, the most appropriate. The photographer was so fashionable Clodagh had never heard of him. Stylists descended on the rose garden of the Master's House, and her new assistant Sarah was dispatched to spread rumours it was for an outdoor Shakespeare production.

Photos were taken in the Lady Mathilda library and in King's College Chapel, which after all did bear a certain resemblance to St George's. All of them felt stiff and posed, her wrist at a weird angle as she attempted to display her ring. As Clodagh was changing into yet another outfit, Jamie got a thoughtful look on his face and disappeared.

"New location," he said when he came back, and the photographer, frustrated with Clodagh's apparent lack of natural ease in front of the camera, threw up his hands and agreed.

They got in the car, drove about fifty yards round the corner, and stopped. "Um?" said Clodagh, and Jamie grinned.

Outside, the PPO's sheltered them from curious onlookers as Jamie led her into—

"Are you kidding me?" Clodagh said, looking up at the faded pub sign of the Prince's Arms.

Jamie winked. "Why would I be kidding? This is where I fell in love with you."

The pub had evidently been closed in a hurry. Oz and Marte were still clearing up glasses, and in the other bar the extra security drafted in for the day were patting down regulars.

"Ooh, yeah, I like this, it's edgy and atmospheric," said the photographer, who was a terrible hipster. "Horse brasses, look at them. And conkers! Brilliant."

Drinks were poured for them to pose with. "This is so cheesy," Clodagh said as they sat in the conkers corner.

"Making you smile, though," he said, and she shoved him playfully.

That was one of the shots they used. Clodagh grinning, pint of lager at her elbow, as she reached out to a laughing Jamie. There were others, of her pulling a pint while Jamie held the glass, and of the two of them laughing at a terrible joke Stevo was telling Paulie. The regulars and the bar staff populated the background of the photos, the mementos of generations of drinkers surrounding them.

"There," said Jamie, looking at the photos as they were emailed through that evening for their approval. "That looks like us."

The interview was recorded the next day at Kensington Palace. Jamie had wanted the Master's Garden at Lady Mathilda College, but Clodagh had vetoed it as a private space and far too easy to locate with a bit of Google-fu.

"Am I not studying for a PhD in computer science?" Jamie complained. "I could totally obscure it."

"Still no," Clodagh said. "Besides, we should probably do something your family approves of."

"Incidentally," he said in a low voice, as people fussed with light meters and boom mics, "have you tried looking up that footage from your old TV show recently?"

Clodagh's face evidently gave him the answer he required.

"Well, if you did, you wouldn't find it." He looked very pleased with himself. "It keeps... accidentally disappearing."

"Jamie," she said warningly.

"What? I didn't do a thing! But if some grad students I happen to know, let's say invented a program that could track down a certain video clip and destroy it whenever it was uploaded, well then I couldn't possibly comment."

Clodagh couldn't help smiling, even as she said, "Isn't that illegal?"

"Is it? Well, good job I know nothing about it then, eh?"

The interview, by an old hand at the BBC, wasn't as bad as she'd feared. The questions had all been carefully vetted to eliminate any traces of controversy, and she spent it all with her hand firmly holding Jamie's.

This wasn't a detail the media ignored. The Palace press department had been working overtime to emphasise the incredible love story that had Prince Jamie falling in love with a barmaid. "It only works if you're in love," someone had said, and Jamie had given them one of his 'descended from thousands of years of royalty' looks.

He told the story about the boathouse and the bacon

sandwich, leaving out the way Clodagh had harangued him but keeping in the magical hand-holding. She told the story of Jamie rushing to her side in the hospital, but left out the part where she'd been thrown down the stairs by a man now in jail.

The photocall immediately afterwards had Clodagh aiming her ring at the sea of cameras like it was a magic weapon. Later, she was told her blue silk kimono-style dress had sold out in seconds, with the red shoes close behind it. Various media outlets proclaimed her choice of colour 'an official end to royal mourning,' which would probably irritate the Queen.

They were taken straight to Buckingham Palace afterwards, where the Queen informed them she had chosen their new title.

"The last holder of this title married a commoner for love," she informed them.

You don't get much commoner than me, Clodagh wanted to say, but didn't. The Queen still scared the bejeesus out of her.

"And given your fondness for the university it seemed only appropriate to grant you the title of Duke and Duchess of Cambridge," the monarch went on. "This will of course be kept quiet for now and only used after the wedding. Miss Walsh, I have arranged a visit from Garter King of Arms to create a coat of arms for you so that it can be impaled with Jamie's. Please consider carefully which symbols you would like to include on it. May I suggest details from the flag or arms of Jamaica?"

"Jamaica, ma'am?"

"Yes. Perhaps a pineapple. And have you given any thought to who will design your dress? I would suggest a British house. And consider your Something Borrowed, *et cetera*. Annemarie had a tiara, and Victoria a necklace." Her gaze wandered to Clodagh's earrings.

"I'm sure we'll think of something."

She rose, and so did Clodagh and Jamie, because by now she knew a sign of dismissal when she saw one.

"So is this the one time I'm allowed to wear a tiara before I'm married?" she asked.

"If you like. If it goes with the dress and the veil…"

He left that hanging, and Clodagh pretended it was all a secret and not like she had no idea what she was doing on that front.

Her phone started ringing before the car had even passed the Victoria Memorial. It was her mother.

"Well, that peace was fun while it lasted," she said, and had the presence of mind to hold the phone away from her ear as she answered.

Jamie winced as the sound of the screaming echoed around the car.

"You're gonna marry a prince!" her mother hollered. Clodagh figured she could have saved herself the phone call and just shouted it out of the window.

"Yes," she began, and got overridden by whooping and screaming.

"Oh my God, Whitney is so jealous, she reckoned once he met her he'd fall totally in love with her," her mother said, when she was finally capable of putting a sentence together.

"That's weird," Clodagh said.

"So where's your dress from? There's this place up near Aldi, it's well classy…"

Clodagh covered her mouth with her hand. Jamie gave her a questioning look, and she put the phone on speaker.

"…got hers from there, it had this diamanté all over the boobs, no what's that word? Like your cleavage?"

Wide-eyed, Jamie murmured, "Décolletage?"

"Oh my God is that him!" Sharon screamed in a pitch approaching ultrasonic.

335

"Do we have to go and see her?" Clodagh mouthed, and he nodded, grinning.

A visit had been on the cards for a while with the Harlow Council, although the details had been kept deliberately vague for fear of spilling the beans. Clodagh explained when her mother paused for breath, that they'd be over at the weekend to visit the hospital and that a reception had been planned afterwards with the mayor.

She rung off quickly. "I just don't know what they're going to do on the big day." She hesitated. "We do have to invite them, don't we?"

"They're your family," Jamie said warmly, "it'll be fine."

Clodagh fixed her gaze on her ten carat emerald engagement ring and tried to persuade herself she agreed with him.

As usual with hospital visits, only the most photogenic patients were wheeled out to see them. Jamie shook hands and kissed cheeks and laughed at feeble jokes, and Clodagh did a decent attempt at the same.

He noticed her gaze straying to the maternity wing more than once, and realised with a shot of 'Christ you're an idiot, Jamie' that this would have been where she gave birth all those years ago.

"Changed a bit, has it?" said one of the nurses, and Clodagh's smile froze.

"Everything changes," Jamie said easily, and led her away.

"I'm sorry," he murmured, "I didn't think—"

"It's fine. Don't worry about it."

But a tour of the maternity ward was offered and hard to turn down, and Jamie was incredibly proud of Clodagh for squaring her shoulders and getting on with it. She cooed over new babies, offered sympathy to overdue mothers, chatted to the nurses and generally did what she'd been trained to do since that day in May when he'd first taken her to the Palace.

He watched her crouch down to talk to a small child, her skirts spilling over her knees and onto the floor. She'd favoured 1950s style summer dresses in bright silks and cottons ever since the Palace had decreed they could move away from grey and navy. He knew the media had been cruel about the effect of such dull, dark colours on her complexion, but what the hell did they expect? She'd turn up dressed like Jessica Rabbit and screw mourning protocol?

"Excuse me, Your, er, Highness?" said a woman cradling a newborn. Clodagh straightened and smiled at her.

"I'm not a Highness yet. It's just Clodagh."

"Yes, um. Look, I wanted to say thank you." At Clodagh's mystified look, the woman went on. "I had a baby when I was seventeen. My family persuaded me to give her up. I never stopped thinking about her but I was supposed to pretend like it never happened and…" She sniffed back tears. "I never even told my husband about it til after your story came out. We've gone on the register. You know, so she can find us if she wants to."

Clodagh was getting better at hiding her reactions, but Jamie knew her well. Her smile was a little rigid as she said, "That's wonderful. I'm glad it's helped you. And who's this?" she went on, diverting attention to the baby.

"Nicely done," Jamie murmured as they were shuttled off to some conference room for tea and cakes with the town's dignitaries.

"Yeah, well. That was one of the nicer ones. Sometimes it's all vitriol."

Jamie squeezed her hand with its massive emerald ring. "I get people telling me about their dead siblings all the time. People like to take your tragedy and make it their own. Made me angry when Ed died but I guess… at least they're empathising."

"I've been thinking," Clodagh said, sotto voce. "It's not the first time that's happened. Your family's been making noises about me choosing charities and the like. There must be something I—oh, good, there's my mum."

It seemed the whole Walsh clan had come out for the occasion. There were hundreds of them, all descending in a wave of decibels and hairspray to hug Clodagh and himself. He wasn't even entirely sure which one was Clodagh's mum. All the women were fake-tanned and dressed in the same kind of outfit of tight dress and high heels, and they all had the same ironed, bleached hair and the sort of make-up Clodagh had explained was meant to shape and highlight the face but in reality kind of made them look… stripey.

The staff who'd been babysitting them looked slightly shell-shocked.

There were also dozens of children rushing around the place, two of the girls wearing Disney princess dresses and one of the boys dressed as Spiderman.

"Jamie, this is my mum, Sharon Walsh. My sisters Whitney, Kylie, and Charlene, and my brothers Scott and Tony. The kids are…" She looked around helplessly. Two of them were fighting over an iPad. One had got hold of a marker and was scribbling on the wall. "Well, they're all here. I think."

She took a deep breath and linked her arm with his as if they were soldiers forming a shield wall.

"Everyone, this is my fiancé, Jamie."

An awful lot of eyes stared back at him. Then Sharon —the one in the pink dress with the blingy necklace— hissed, "Curtsey," and they did some variation of it. The younger brother, Tony, swept an elaborate kind of courtly bow.

"It's nice to meet you," Jamie said politely. "Clodagh's told me so much about you."

"Only good stuff, I hope!"

"Of course," Jamie lied. He cast about for something else to say, but there was no need. Clodagh was fallen upon and dragged away from him by her left hand.

"Oh my God look at that ring! Is that like a hundred carats?"

"Is it a real emerald?"

"Can I try it on?"

"Yeah 'cos my mate Megan, she's got one like that only hers is fake, obvs."

"Hey mate, ain't it suppose to be three months salary?" said one of the boys. "How much d'you make?"

"State secret," Jamie said. The ring had been made from an emerald in the royal collection, with diamonds from Annemarie's family mine. He'd paid close attention to the rings she liked and didn't, and carefully designed this one to suit her tastes. She'd professed herself delighted with it, although she had added that it was so impressive her family would probably assume it was fake.

"We're the royal family," he'd told her, "we don't do fakes."

Glancing around the room, he could see what she meant. Jamie wasn't much interested in fashion but he knew good workmanship when he saw it, and if that handbag was real Chanel and those diamonds were real then he was the Queen of Sheba.

Clodagh shot him a desperate look, and he reached for her arm, pulling her back out of the clutches of her family. *Crab bucket.*

"Ah, I believe there was a presentation?" he said.

There was always a presentation. This time it was a long-service award. He and Clodagh smiled and posed for pictures, and then inevitably her family wanted pictures too.

At least they'll brighten the place up, he thought as they bickered and fought for position.

All right, so they were loud, and they were brassy, and there had been some serious lapses of judgement when it came to a couple of outfit choices and the appropriate amount of perfume to wear, but at least they were genuine. Everyone in Jamie's family was so terrified of expressing an opinion or having a personality that sometimes he had trouble telling some of them apart.

Clodagh's mother tried to get them to go for a drink afterwards—"I mean you met in a pub, yeah?" but Clodagh invented an excuse to leave. They were on their way back to the car when Sharon slowed and faltered, staring off ahead.

"Mum?"

They all turned to look where she was looking. Jamie could see hospital staff and his own security team, although he didn't recognise that one guy in a suit behind Geraint…

Just as he was about to hustle Clodagh out of the way of the stranger, her mother said, "Oh my God, it's you." Her face went drip white under her make-up.

The PPOs weren't doing anything. Who was this guy? Was he dangerous?

"Sir, perhaps we should go somewhere private?" said Geraint.

Jamie glanced at Clodagh, who looked as puzzled as he felt. And then she looked at her mother, and the stranger, and he saw realisation dawn.

"A friend sent me this on Facebook," said the stranger, who had introduced himself as Kingston Clarke. He was a tall black man of around fifty, broad-shouldered, smartly dressed in what Clodagh could now tell was a very good suit, and he had a head of gloriously incongruous dreadlocks that fell halfway down his back.

He showed them a photo on his tablet. It was of a party some time in the mid-eighties by the style of clothes and hair, and it was full of slightly drunk-looking people with beer cans and cigarettes in hand. Some of the cigarettes, on closer inspection, were probably spliffs.

"That's the photo I sent the paper," Clodagh's mum said. "They asked about your dad and I said I didn't know but I thought it had been at this party."

The photo had done the rounds ever since Sharon first sold the story. They all peered at it anyway as it was displayed there in its digital glory, on the conference table they'd returned to. Her siblings and the kids were milling about outside. Clodagh didn't need them all here for this. It was just her mum and Kingston, Jamie and Geraint. The chief PPO had vouched personally for Kingston.

Clodagh made herself look at the photo she'd been avoiding for two months. Yes, there was her mum in the middle of the photo, done up like Madonna in *Desperately Seeking Susan,* and there was a bunch of other girls and guys. They were all white.

"None of those people are my dad," she said. She felt like a wire someone had wound so tight it trembled. She knew where this was going.

"That guy there," Kingston pointed to a man on the right of the photo, "is my friend David. He recognised the picture and sent it to a bunch of us who were all at uni together. There's four of us in that picture. I might have been the one taking it." He shrugged. "It was thirty-two years ago."

"Probably thirty-three now," said Clodagh. It had been her birthday in that bleak, dark period after she'd left Jamie. She hadn't celebrated it. "That must have been... what, June? July?"

"July, 1985. I'd finished my first year at UCL and I was going off to Jamaica for the summer to see my family. I was born in England," he explained, in his South London accent, "my parents came over with the Windrush generation. Anyway. Dave sent me the picture, jokingly I think, and I realised I recognised that girl. And I did some maths, and... well."

"Well," said Clodagh dumbly.

"I mean I might be way off, but... anyway, one of my summer jobs at uni was nightclub security with a guy who'd gone on to do personal protection." He glanced at Geraint, who gave a slight nod. "So I got into contact. Long shot, but I remembered that girl. You, Sharon."

He looked up at Clodagh's mum, who'd been uncharacteristically silent.

"We," she cleared her throat and started again. "We'd gone up to London for the night. Met some guys in a pub. Went on to a student party. Thought we was well fine. There was a guy... I remembered 'cos I'd never been with a black feller before. *Smooth Operator* was playing, d'you remember?"

He clearly didn't, but he said, "Hence Sharday?"

"Yeah." Sharon fell silent again. "I didn't know, you see... I didn't know how to get back in touch with you. If it even was yours. 'Cos I had to... um, I mean I..."

"She didn't know what colour I'd come out," said Clodagh. "By then it was a bit too late and you were..." she looked him over, an outwardly respectable man, "away."

"I'd have been back in the country by then," said Kingston. "In my second year."

"Second year of what?" Clodagh asked bluntly, and he looked surprised.

"My degree. PPE. I teach it now, at SOAS."

Clodagh and her mum stared at him.

"But I thought you was a drug dealer," Sharon blurted. "You said you was going away. I thought you was going to jail."

"Jail?" Kingston looked shocked. "No! I've never been to jail. One parking ticket to my name, I swear. Why did you think I was a drug dealer?"

There was a sticky silence.

"Right." His voice was heavy. "Why else would a black guy be at a student party."

"There were drugs there," Sharon said defensively.

"I didn't bring them!"

Silence fell again. Clodagh felt for Jamie's hand as she studied the man who might be her father. She hadn't inherited his height, that was for sure, and her skin was much lighter, but then her mum was pretty white. His eyes, though, they were the same light brown, almost amber, as her own.

"You teach at SOAS?" Jamie said into the silence. Force of habit, she supposed. Next he'd be asking her maybe-dad if he'd come far.

"Yes. I worked in the City for a while, then went back to school and got my doctorate. Still do some consultancy. Brings in the pay." He hesitated. "I have two kids to put through university."

"You do?" Clodagh said. Oh great. More siblings.

He nodded and swiped through a few pictures. "There. Rose, she's at Aberdeen studying pharmacology. And Andrew, he's just got a conditional offer from Oxford. History of Art."

She stared at the two smiling faces. Andrew had eyes like her, and Rose had her mouth.

"Their mum?"

"We divorced five years ago. Fairly amicable. I, uh. I understand you're applying to Cambridge?"

Clodagh nodded vaguely. It had once seemed like the

most important thing in the world, and now she hadn't even been able to pick up her Access to HE diploma in person.

"Yes, when applications open in September," Jamie said, as Clodagh continued to stare at her half brother and sister. "Clodagh just got her diploma."

"That's great. Well done. We get quite a few students entering with Access diplomas,"said Kingston, leaning forward. "What's your subject?"

"History," mumbled Clodagh.

"Oh, you'll get on well with Andrew. It was a toss-up for him whether to do history or art, but in the end he split the difference."

Clodagh looked up at him, and then at her mum, as if she could blur their faces into one to make her own.

Kingston cleared his throat. "I, uh. I understand this is probably a shock. It was for me, too. I haven't told the kids. That is…"

"Oh Christ," Clodagh found herself suddenly laughing. "That means I'm one of eight!"

"Maybe," said Jamie. He straightened up. "Not that I doubt anyone's story here, but I'm sure you'll understand this is an unusual position we're in. As we're currently in a hospital, would you—both of you—mind giving a blood sample? I'm sure we can get the results back fairly soon. I'll pull some strings. Where's Sarah —?"

Geraint went to find Peaseman's assistant, Sharon started flirting with Kingston, and Jamie peered at Clodagh's face. He frowned, then said quietly, "It won't take long, I'm sure, and then we're back in the car and heading home. Lasagne for tea tonight?"

She blinked at him. "Wait a minute," she said.

"What?"

Perhaps a pineapple. "She knew. Your grandmother, she knew."

344

"How could—" He glanced in the direction Geraint had gone. "For crying out loud. No secrets," he said in exasperation.

"Crest of Jamaica," Clodagh said. "She told me, didn't she?"

Jamie started laughing. "She's probably already had it designed."

As it turned out, he wasn't far off. At some point during the full time job that planning her wedding had become, Clodagh found herself being driven to the College of Arms near St Pauls. Slightly to her disappointment, Garter King of Arms turned out to be an ordinary man in a suit, but he was polite and friendly and explained the decisions behind the drafted coat of arms she was to be granted.

Clodagh fiddled with one earring and tried not to giggle with sheer incredulity. A coat of arms. It was insane.

"The pineapple, ma'am, to represent your father's heritage." He didn't actually say the words 'now that the DNA results have come back' but Clodagh figured it wasn't a coincidence her appointment was for the day after.

Garter gestured to a rather excitable-looking display where the shield was flanked by a man and woman wearing little grass skirts and not much more. "As you can see, the pineapple features on the arms of Jamaica."

"So do bare breasts," Clodagh said. "And an alligator."

"A crocodile, as it happens. Now, we have also incorporated the seax—"

"I know that one!" Clodagh said, because they'd done a school project about it when she was a kid. "The Saxon knife. From the Essex flag."

Garter looked pleased. "Yes. It's quite an ancient coat of arms, you know. Very rare to have no supporters, crest or motto. Very recognisable."

He unveiled a painted oval divided into four with some knives and pineapples on it. "Accordingly, your blazon shall be: Quarterly, first and fourth Azure a pineapple, second and third Gules three seaxes in pale to sinister."

He looked at her expectantly, as if this wasn't gobbledegook. Clodagh felt her gaze sliding to Sarah, who gave her a helpless look.

"His Royal Highness has been sent a copy, of course."

"Of course," she said. "Has Her Majesty seen it?"

"Yes, ma'am, the pineapples were her idea. Now. This shall only be your arms until your marriage to His Royal Highness, of course—"

"Of course." She could almost do this with a straight face now.

"—when it shall be impaled with his."

"Impaled?"

"A heraldic term, ma'am, for combining the two. It will look something like this."

The simple quartered oval with its two plain devices vanished, to be replaced with an insanely busy coat of arms. It had lions and unicorns wearing crowns, and feathery flourishes at the top, and a lion wearing a crown on top of another crown.

If she looked closely enough she could make out her seaxes and pineapples squished into one half of the shield, which itself seemed lost in the middle of all that finery.

"Ma'am?"

Clodagh realised she was staring. This was it. The symbol of this whole mad thing, this drunken daydream she'd been living in since she'd looked up and seen Jamie there asking for a pint of Carlsberg. The three knives of Essex next to the three lions of England. The

Royal Standard, nestling cosily beside Jamaican pineapples.

She pinched herself. Nope, it was still there.

The Royal Standard, and some Essex knives, welded together. Jamie and Clodagh, side by side.

"Ma'am?"

"Yes." Clodagh tried to sound like she was paying attention. "That all seems... very... good." She glanced at Sarah. "Can I get a copy of that?"

"It has already been sent to your private secretary, ma'am."

"Jolly good," said Clodagh, and then wondered when she'd become the sort of person who said 'jolly good'.

She thanked Garter King of Arms, shook his hand, smoothed down her pretty expensive dress and picked up her tiny expensive handbag to walk out on her beautiful expensive heels.

She patted her expensive hair as Khan opened the car door for her.

"Ma'am?"

"Didn't I used to be Miss?"

He shrugged. "You're a Ma'am now."

"I was Clodagh once upon a time," she said, and he smiled at her and ushered her into the car.

She had a meeting with a textile designer next, to go over fabric choices for The Dress. Probably there would be pineapples. Or banana leaves. *Christ, what do they have in Jamaica? Am I going to have a lace design incorporating Usain Bolt?*

When Annemarie got married, she had a tulip design worked into the lace on her veil, as well as white tulips in her bouquet. She'd worn jewellery belonging to the Dutch royal family. Part of her dress incorporated lace from her own mother's wedding dress, which was something Princess Victoria had also done. At least four people had begun to suggest this to Clodagh, before pausing awkwardly as they realised her mother had never been married.

Victoria, the only daughter of the Prince of Wales, had a fleur-de-lys design incorporated into her gown. She wore a tiara belonging to her grandmother the Queen. Her bouquet had included white roses for England and thistles, from Nicholas's family coat of arms.

Clodagh had been told that all royal brides carried a sprig of myrtle in their bouquets, from the tree Queen Victoria had got hers from. Personally, she figured following the wedding traditions of a woman who spent most of her life as a widow was a bit of a daft idea, but the Family were firm about this.

There was a text waiting from Jamie. "*Pineapples, huh?*"

"*And knives,*" she texted back. "*The arms of the royal pina colada maker.*"

"What flowers are native to Jamaica?" she asked Sarah, who began googling.

"Er, the lignum vitae. It's a sort of bluish purple."

Well, that was out, as she'd been told royal brides had white bouquets. White dress, white flowers, white white white. "Anything white?"

"Hibiscus can be white. They grow in Jamaica."

"Hibiscus. Good." Clodagh made a note, as they were taken towards the converted warehouse in Shoreditch being used as a secret HQ for The Dress.

The basic design of the dress had been approved, from a list of designs approved by the Palace by a group of designers chosen by the Palace. White, with a big skirt and something to cover the shoulders and upper arms. Apparently strapless wasn't the order of the day. Clodagh, who was still a normal adult human shape and not a fatless wonder like her sisters-in-law-to-be, didn't mind that development so much. She'd naively asked about wearing a proper bra and been told, somewhat patronisingly, that corsetry would take care of all that.

"So my choice of fabric is white lace, white lace, or a different kind of white lace," she said, looking at the samples.

"No, no, ma'am, they're very different…"

Olivia had taken one look at her and proclaimed that if anyone put her in ivory she'd have their hides. "White, with your skintone, darling. You'll dazzle. Poor Victoria should have had something warmer, bless her, but dear old Mummy was calling the shots on that one…"

She wished Olivia was here now, instead of finalising bridesmaid choices. They had at least agreed that having Clodagh's sisters would be a car crash, and that her nieces couldn't be relied upon to do anything other than throw a tantrum. Jamie's godchildren were being carefully sorted through for well-behaved and photogenic poppets instead.

I should probably tell Oll she's the maid of honour, Clodagh thought idly, staring in utter boredom at the white lace.

This wedding was getting away from her.

No one was even really paying attention any more, the dress designer and the textile designer in deep conversation about technicalities. Sarah was making notes.

Clodagh, the reason they were all there, got her phone out and wondered if anyone would notice.

"*Does everything have to be white?*" she texted Jamie.

"*That's the tradition. Oll says white would suit you?*"

Clodagh tried to think back over her life and wondered if she'd ever worn white voluntarily. It wasn't flattering and it wasn't practical, so she doubted it. "*The only non-white thing in this wedding is me*," she texted him glumly.

And Jamie, the dear sweet man that he was, texted back, "*Then wear mustard yellow if it makes you happy. There are lots of shades.*"

The mustard choice. Oh God, she'd thought that was extravagant once.

A few seconds later he added, "*I could wear my House Windsor t-shirt. It'll be awesome. Look, it's your damn dress. Don't let them push you around.*"

She frowned at that. He was right. It *was* her damn dress.

She straightened. *For fuck's sake, Clodagh, you're going to be a duchess soon. You've got a coat of arms. You've just begun proceedings to set up a charity to give advice to pregnant teenagers. You're applying to Cambridge. Don't let your own bloody wedding get away from you.*

She thought about the gypsy weddings she'd been to as a kid. Brides drowning in acres of frothy meringue, flowers in their hair and riots of colour all over. They'd been brash and loud and glorious, their one shot at being a princess for the day. Clodagh used to think that was what she'd look like when she grew up and got married.

"I don't like any of these," she said, and the room suddenly went silent. "It's boring and it's not me."

"But ma'am, it's traditional—"

"Yeah, you know what's traditional in my family? A bridal boutique next to Aldi where diamanté is considered classy, and that's if you actually get married. Look, I grew up in a Romany camp and a council estate, and everyone knows it. Why are we trying to pretend I was born a lady?"

There was an embarrassed silence.

She squared her shoulders. "Right. Where are those sketches? This bodice needs to be more streamlined. No lace all over it. I don't actually like lace. It's like wearing a doily. What's that stuff where it's sheer netting with stuff embroidered on it?"

"Illusion lace?" murmured the textile designer's minion.

"Yes. That. The same colour as my skin, so have fun making that. We'll have that for the sleeves and shoulders with little flowers here and there, and how about some gold? I'm from Essex after all. Bling it up for me."

The dress designer, an intimidatingly middle class woman, gave her a patronising look. "Ma'am, gold is not trad—"

"Still don't care. The Roma consider it lucky."

"Ma'am—" began the textile designer.

"Who's going to be a royal duchess here? Me or you?"

Their gazes dropped away. Clodagh drew herself up in satisfaction. "Gimme a pencil. Look. Gold here, maybe, and a bit on the skirt. Around the hem. I like the big skirt and the scalloped hem," she said, as their faces few more and more alarmed, "but instead of little white flowers scattered, make them golden. And make some of them hibiscus flowers."

The designers glowered. Their minions nodded.

Clodagh grinned.

"Yes. Good. Oh, and make sure that netting is silk, or it'll play merry hell with my hair and I'll be caught on camera detangling it in front of the whole country. What else?"

"The train?" asked the designer dangerously.

Clodagh checked the notes on the sketch. "How long is cathedral length, again?"

"Three metres."

She considered. "It'll do. Now, the veil—"

"The designs are here," she was told sulkily.

All of them were sketched on a bride with an elegant updo. Clodagh's hair didn't do elegant updos. It did wild curls.

"We will of course wait and see which tiara Her Majesty lends you."

Clodagh thought about Annemarie and Victoria. She thought about the gypsy brides with their riots of colour. She thought about hibiscus flowers.

"No," she said. "No tiara. Sarah, how many colours do hibiscus flowers come in?"

CHAPTER TWENTY-THREE

"I still look like a macaw," Jamie said, as the mirror showed him in all his glory. The red jacket of the Coldstream and the blue riband of the Royal Victorian Order, the medals and stars, the braiding. He was only lucky he'd escaped aguillettes.

"You look splendid, sir, if I may say so."

Jamie glanced at Vincent's reflection and smiled, relaxing his shoulders a bit. "I do. Thank you, Vincent. You manage the impossible every time you turn me out."

He shook the man's hand, to his surprise.

"Has it stopped snowing?"

"I believe so, sir. The paths are being cleared. It's very picturesque."

Jamie looked out the window at the unbroken white expanse of the Long Walk. It was unspeakably beautiful, if one didn't have a wedding to get to. "Does the Glass Coach have snow chains?"

"Stop worrying."

That sounded like Annemarie. She stood in the doorway, elegant in pale pink, wearing the same blue riband Jamie had.

"That's what Edward would have said," she added, coming into the room.

Jamie looked at himself. There was a space beside him where Edward should have been, as Jamie had been beside him on his wedding day. "I know." He cleared his throat. "She wanted the landau, but in this weather?"

"It will be fine. You look very handsome."

Jamie tugged at his jacket. "Is it too much? I feel like a peacock. Clodagh gets to wear white."

"Trust me, no woman finds white the easy option." She hesitated, eyeing the medals pinned in their proper places on his chest and riband. "I hear you're to be appointed to the Garter."

"That's supposed to be a secret."

She raised her hands. "I heard nothing. But listen, there was one thing… I hope I didn't overstep any bounds."

Jamie narrowed his eyes. "What did you do?"

"I gave Edward's garter to Clodagh. For her 'something borrowed'. It felt like the right thing to do."

Jamie felt tears come to his eyes. "Annemarie, that's… it's perfect. Thank you." He took her hands, and then figured what the hell and hugged her. "Did you get Dai on the invites?"

"Yes. He will be with some of Edward's other colleagues. I've promised he can visit the side chapel."

"Good. That's good." He hugged her again, then straightened and let Vincent readjust his trimmings. "Right then, enough of this sentiment. We have a chapel to get to."

They met Nicholas on the way, standing as Jamie's supporter. He clasped Jamie on the shoulder, and they went to get in the Bentley taking them the short distance to the chapel. Usually, the Family would enter the Chapel through the Gilebertus door near the altar, but it had been decided that today Jamie would get his maximum exposure to the crowd, so they were driven round to the West Door.

The Lower Ward was filled with cameras and reporters and crowds of well-wishers. Jamie smiled as he remembered Clodagh sending him a text the night before. "*Is there any mulled wine? Spare blankets? I don't want people dying of frostbite on my wedding day.*"

He'd arranged for a cart to be taken out dispensing hot drinks and checking on people, and made sure everyone knew it was Clodagh's idea.

The crowds cheered as he emerged from the car and waved at them. The chapel looked magnificent in the snow, sunlight just breaking through. It was freezing, but Jamie was far too nervous to be cold.

"How did you do it?" Nicholas said. "It rained when I got married."

"Nick, Nick, Nick," said Jamie. "Haven't you figured it out yet?"

It was Olivia who had pointed it out. "Come on, Jamie, she's a put-upon maid with a family who take her for granted and an absentee father, and for heaven's sake, she's near as dammit got the footman—"

"Not a footman…"

"—who's in love with her—"

"I think he fancies you more," Jamie said, because Davood Khan had taken to working more shifts with Clodagh when he knew Olivia was going to be around.

"That's for me to know and you to find out," she said pertly. "And look—she even left a shoe behind at your house."

"It was an ankle cast. What are you trying to say?"

Olivia just gave him a knowing look. "It's a fairytale, that's all."

"Shut up, Oll."

"What haven't I figured out?" Nick wanted to know as they went up the West Steps and into the chapel. It was wreathed in winter greens and heavy with the scent of flowers, and people turned to look at him as he made his way to the front of the nave, the better to smile and wave to the VIPs as they entered.

The pageantry started here, with various European royals arriving. Jamie nodded to Annemarie's relatives as they took a seat on the right hand side of the chapel.

"Here we go," he murmured, as they were followed by an explosion of sound and colour. Several gigantic hats appeared in the doorway, and underneath them was Clodagh's family. Her brothers wore morning suits with cummerbunds. One of the little girls was dressed like Queen Elsa from *Frozen*.

"I can't look," said Nicholas.

"Oh my god, innit grand!" said one of Clodagh's sisters.

"Oi, be dignified, like Clo said," admonished another.

"Ooh, I don't like that," said the third, peering at Princess Charlotte's tomb.

"Where is he? Innee gorgeous," said Sharon Walsh, waving extravagantly at Jamie, who waved back to everyone's amusement.

A footman guided them to their seats, heroically keeping a straight face.

Cousins and aunts began to arrive, the tiara count going up rapidly. Jamie glanced up at the Garter banners hanging in the Quire as various relatives took their places. He'd be up there soon.

Ed's place still stood empty. *I wish you were here so I didn't have to fill your place.*

Then he reminded himself that Clodagh wore Ed's garter, and that Annemarie and Dai and the children were here. And so was Ed, if he got sentimental about things.

Annemarie and Victoria arrived with baby James. Alexander and Georgina were part of Clodagh's band of miniature attendants. Soon after his parents entered, and then the National Anthem was playing and his grandparents walked in.

Jamie bowed his head to the Queen, who smiled back at him, and he and Nicholas moved forward to the front of the Quire, where the ornate organ screen prevented him from seeing most of the Nave.

And then there was a wait, an agonising wait, as he fantasised grimly about the Glass Coach overturning in the snow, before the roar of noise outside told him Clodagh had arrived. According to his watch she was right on time, but he was pretty sure time was moving more slowly today.

He wasn't sure he'd survive the wait to see her.

Clodagh's phone buzzed again, with her mother's number. She'd already sent a million texts and called her at Oh God O'Clock in the morning. She'd called again when the hair and make-up people Clodagh had sent round appeared at the hotel, and then again to complain they were making her look old and boring.

"You can't hardly tell I'm even wearing lippy, babes," she said, and Clodagh had pretended her phone was being confiscated by a royal flunkie before her mother frazzled the last nerve she had.

"It's stopped snowing," said Olivia, peering out of the window.

"Has it? Good. Is that good? Do we want it to snow?"

"No, darling. Makes a mess of your hair and then there are all the well-wishers and journalists freezing to death like little match girls, which is frightfully bad press."

"You mean bad luck," Clodagh said, as the hairdresser fussed over one particular strand.

"I mean bad press, darling. We make our own luck." Olivia submitted to the attentions of the make-up artist attempting to improve upon perfection. Clodagh had been somewhat annoyed to find that Olivia still had an immaculate complexion even after her make-up was taken off.

"It's very pretty out there," said Sarah. "The photographers have been going mad. Um," she added, "Er, we might need to be ready just a smidge earlier so they can take some more pictures outside..."

Clodagh met her own panicked gaze in the mirror. "Earlier?" They still had an hour to go, and that didn't seem nearly enough to accomplish every task on Sarah's frighteningly comprehensive list.

"It will all be fine, darling. Have some 'poo," said Olivia, and waved at someone to open a bottle of champagne.

"I do wish you wouldn't call it that," Clodagh muttered, but she accepted a glass. Jamie had teased her gently about how much she'd taken to champagne after trying the good stuff; at least, he had until she'd bought a bottle of the cheap fizz she'd been used to for special occasions, and he'd experienced first-hand why she'd never liked it.

Her phone buzzed. *Christ, not Mum again.* But it was Jamie, and she felt her heartbeat calm a little at just the sight of his name.

A few more hours, and then you'll be married and all this will have been worth it.

She batted away Sarah's hand and picked up her own phone. "*Question: would you mind if I ditched Nick and had Ghost the direwolf as my attendant?*"

She laughed at that. Her first thought on seeing the snow this morning had been that Windsor looked like something out of *Game of Thrones*. She searched for an image of the Night King with his crown of ice, and sent it to him. "*So long as I can dress like this.*"

"*Dammit, Clo, you're not supposed to show me what you look like! You've just cursed us to ten feet more snow!*"

She texted back that there was probably a dragon hanging around somewhere to melt it—after all, his father was the Prince of Wales—before Sarah confiscated her phone.

Oll shimmied into her dress, a slinky beaded affair that made her look like a cross between Daisy Buchanan and an Oscar statuette, allowed herself to be sprayed with another layer of make-up fixative, and nodded to the dresser in charge of Clodagh's dress.

"Come on then," she said, and Clodagh clutched at her dressing gown. "Or you'll have to get married in that."

"Like the *Vicar of Dibley*," Clodagh said in panic. The dress—*The* Dress—was so beautiful, shimmering and floating like a dream. She couldn't wear it. It was too perfect.

"She had pyjamas. Now then. Another swig of 'poo, and off with that robe."

She already had a corset on. And stockings, and the blue garter Annemarie had brought round that morning. She'd kept her own knickers, though. Primark's finest. Something old, she'd explained firmly, and been grudgingly allowed.

Her dress was allowed to be the something new. The something borrowed was a diamond necklace of the Queen's. A man from the Jewel Tower had brought it this morning. It weighed far more than its real mass on her collarbone and Clodagh was aware of it with every breath.

Olivia removed the champagne to a safe distance, and The Dress was lowered over Clodagh's head by three attendants. The designer herself fastened the laces at the back, fussing over the exact fit for longer than Clodagh could bear.

She couldn't quite look at herself in the mirror, not

until it was all finished, and Olivia took hold of her chin gently but firmly and made her.

"Oh," she said, because the woman looking back at her was a princess. Diamonds winking at her throat, her silk dress glowing, gold embroidery shimmering with every breath.

And the princess started to smile.

She smiled all through the photos that were staged in one of Frogmore's beautiful unused bedrooms, the make-up and hair people pretending to attend to her, the dress designer making sure she was photographed straightening a seam, the florist handing over the bouquet.

She smiled as she was photographed on the stairs, her train arranged carefully behind her, and in front of various fireplaces and vases and portraits, including one of Queen Charlotte.

She smiled as her father appeared in the drawing room, handsome in morning dress, and the camera clicked away as he took her arm.

She smiled as she and Olivia posed in the frigid air beside a snowy holly tree, and then outside the Glass Coach before climbing carefully in as she'd rehearsed.The coach, its body tiny compared to the huge painted wheels, dipped and swayed alarmingly.

"I think it was made for tiny dainty Victorians," said Kingston, who hadn't had as much practice as Clodagh had.

"Actually it was first used for the coronation of George V in 1911," said Clodagh, who didn't think Random Facts Girl was going to go away when she became a duchess.

He gave her a grimace of a smile as the coach lurched into movement, but it had turned into something less seasick and more camera-friendly by the time they rode through the streets of Windsor. The coach probably wasn't that warm, but adrenaline was keeping Clodagh fueled. She grinned and waved like a maniac.

People lined the streets, cheering and waving behind crowd-control barriers. Banners were hoisted, congratulating Our Clo on landing a prince.

"They love you," said Kingston.

"I better not fuck up then," she said, and he laughed.

All too soon the coach stopped and the red-liveried footman opened the door. Clodagh beamed when she saw it was Davood Khan, just as it had been all those times she'd rehearsed. He winked at her as he helped out her father and then herself, and she was grateful for his steadying hand as she took the three rickety steps down to the pavement. The noise of the crowd nearly overwhelmed her.

"Smile," he said.

"Wave," Oll said.

"Oh Christ," Clodagh said, grinning through clenched teeth and shaking her bouquet at them. There was bunting with her face on it.

Kingston gave her his arm to walk up the West Steps, which seemed to be at least thirty feet higher than last time she'd done this, and only faltered a little at the top.

"What is she doing?" he muttered, as her mother hurried down the aisle towards them.

"Mum!" Clodagh hissed. "Get back in your seat!"

"Oh, I will babes, I just needed to see you." She beamed at someone standing near the exit. "This nice young lady said it'd be all right."

Clodagh glanced at the woman, who ought to know better if she was really a member of the wedding party, and saw only a hand slipping inside a fur coat and coming out with—

"Shit!"

That was Kingston, rapidly turning Clodagh away and shielding her with his body. Khan swung forward,

Olivia gasped silently, and over her father's shoulder Clodagh saw the woman tackled to the floor, covered in red.

Oh God, he'd shot her! There was a death at her wedding! This wasn't what she'd meant by *Game of Thrones*—

Wait, no shots had been fired. As various security personnel blocked the view from the nave, Khan handed a small canister to an attendant.

"Paint?" said Clodagh's father, as the girl tried to sit up, glowering at them all.

"You were going to throw paint on her?" said Olivia, aghast.

"You fucking cow!" snapped Sharon Walsh, and punched the girl in the face.

Clodagh, Essex to her core, couldn't help a small victory cheer.

"Was that you last Christmas?" Khan demanded.

The girl on the ground, her fur coat ruined by the paint, glared up at them. "I love Jamie!" she said.

"Melissa, for God's sake," said Olivia, folding her arms. "A one night stand, and a year later you're trying to ruin his wedding?"

"He loves me!"

"No, he loves Clodagh," said Olivia in disgust. "He's marrying Clodagh. Davood, be a lamb and get this miserable creature out of here, darling? Now, then. No paint spatters anywhere? Help me with this train, will you?"

Olivia bossed them all into order, someone came forward with a mop—what the hell, did Oll have a mopper on standby?—and Clodagh found herself arranged like a dolly, as if nothing had happened.

There wasn't even any paint on the floor.

"Right babes, while I'm here," said her mum, and got out her phone, turning on the front-facing camera.

"Really, Mum, a selfie?"

"Who else gets a selfie like this?" said Sharon, and the picture was taken with Clodagh laughing.

Her father took her arm. Her mother kissed her cheek and said, "It ain't a wedding without a punch-up, babes," and took her seat.

And then the music changed and Clodagh began the very long walk up the aisle.

With Annemarie, whose train was a full five metres long, the post-arrival primping of her gown had taken some damn time. Victoria had needed four attendants to organise her veil. Had Clodagh gone for something even more extravagant? Jamie, his back properly turned, told himself he was the product of centuries of breeding and thirty-one years of training and he could damn well stand still and wait a few more minutes.

Oh Christ, no he couldn't...

Last week they'd rehearsed the ceremony for the umpteenth time, and Clodagh had innocently said to the Archbishop, "Are you sure we can't have *Helpless* from the Hamilton soundtrack to walk down the aisle?"

"It's even got *Here Comes The Bride* incorporated into it," Jamie added helpfully. "Hey, we could even dance down the aisle."

"Or some nice Crowded House? I think *Seven Worlds Collide* would be very appropriate," Clodagh added, and it had taken a distressingly long time for anyone to work out she was joking.

They'd agreed on *The Arrival of the Queen of Sheba*, which was appropriately regal and might just last long enough for Clodagh to cover the vast length of the aisle.

And now it was striking up, which meant she was on her way, and he had to be calm. And wait.

Keeping his back turned nearly killed him, especially when Nicholas peeked over his shoulder and whispered,

"Oh my God."

"Oh my God good?" Jamie said out of the corner of his mouth.

"Yes. I think yes. Yes, definitely."

Why the hell had they picked a chapel with such a long aisle?

Oh, fuck it. At the halfway point he turned, to see her walk into the Quire on the arm of her father.

Jamie stared. His mouth dropped open. And then he laughed in sheer joy.

Clodagh looked *perfect*.

Small white and gold flowers clustered around her seemingly-bare shoulders. The white silk bodice of her gown was plain, more petals scattering lower on the full skirt, collecting six inches deep at the hem. Instead of a veil she wore a cloak of gossamer white silk which fluttered as she came to stand beside him and leaned over to kiss her father on the cheek. Olivia carefully arranged the hood to fall back over Clodagh's shoulders, revealing her hair in all its curly glory, crowned with a wreath of creamy white roses, the traditional green myrtle, and hibiscus in a glorious riot of colours.

She handed the matching bouquet to Olivia and smiled up at Jamie.

"I am so into you," she whispered, and his heart turned over.

"I'm pretty into you too, Cinderella."

"I am not your Cinderella," she said, and then the Dean cleared his throat, and the ceremony began.

Royalgossip.com

We can't believe it's been five years since the wedding of the century: Prince Jamie and Clodagh Walsh! Sorry, other royal brides, but nothing gets the Cinderella factor quite like Our Clo, who proved that you don't have to have blue blood to marry a prince.

Remember that gorgeous wedding, which sparked a trend for wedding cloaks? When Clodagh and Jamie posed on the Great West Steps of St George's Church and Lady Olivia Altringham brought her a white velvet cloak to wear for the processional journey around Windsor, every bride in the country turned to her fiancé and said, "I want one of those!"

Of course, the Duchess has been pretty hard at work setting up the Clodagh Walsh Foundation, which helps and advises pregnant teenagers, as well as providing childcare bursaries for young mothers who want to go to university. She's also been active in campaigning against domestic violence and offering support to victims, and along with her sister-in-law Princess Victoria has become a patron of one of the country's foremost adoption charities. Check out this adorable picture of Princess Victoria with her adopted son, Edward!

Let's not forget Prince Jamie's graduation from Cambridge, making him the first royal to ever attain a PhD. Here he is looking gorgeous in his traditional academical gown with the red-lined hood. We can't wait to see if he wears the Scarlet gown and Doctor's Bonnet when he takes up his Fellowship this autumn. We bet he can pull it off, even if it is a style that went out with Henry VIII.

Of course, the most stylish royal is still Our Clo. At Jamie's graduation she wore an amazing dress in the exact blue and green of Lady Mathilda College. This was especially appropriate since she'd just finished her first year of study at the college, reading History. Now she's graduated to an MPhil and we all want to know if she'll be the second Royal to gain a PhD. We know she's the only one who can rap all the lyrics to Hamilton: check out this video of her keeping up with the London cast at a Buckingham Palace Dinner.

And finally, for those of you awaiting the patter of little royal feet, Their Royal Highnesses The Duke and Duchess of Cambridge were this week very pleased to announce the arrival of twins: a pair of kittens called Alexander and Angelica. The Palace confirmed that they won't be added to the line of royal succession...

AUTHOR'S NOTE

The branch of the royal family in this book is, obviously, fictional (please read on for a family tree). It's a guess at what might have happened if Edward VIII had married someone his family and government approved of, and therefore hadn't been required to abdicate in favour of his brother, so setting in motion the royal family we know today. Jamie's grandmother would be the first cousin of our Queen Elizabeth (the great aunt he mentions in St George's Chapel). Freda Dudley Ward was one of Edward's girlfriends before he met Wallis Simpson, so the supposition isn't that outrageous. Maybe.

The Cambridge college Jamie attends, Lady Mathilda, is likewise fictional, but aspects of it, like its location and the Master's Garden are based on Corpus Christi, on Free School Lane. The Prince's Arms is not based on a real pub, but its location is roughly that of the Eagle or the Bath House on Bene't Street. The Watson & Crick and Franklin plaques are in the middle room of the Eagle; there's a beer called DNA in their honour.

The Corn Exchange is a brilliant live venue. I don't believe Crowded House were playing there in January 2018, but I've seen Neil Finn live there more than once. I hope he forgives the dialogue I've put into his mouth. The Royal Albert Hall concert Jamie describes was real, however, and the events surrounding it more or less as he tells them. That was the incident with the unplugged version of Fall At Your Feet. For real.

Harlow isn't quite as bleak as I made it out to be. Mostly. Sorry, Harlow. But those emergency-services blue flashing Christmas lights really do my head in.

The sharper-eyed amongst you might notice Jamie and Edward's coats of arms are based upon a certain pair

367

of real-life princes. The Prince of Wales has a very different coat of arms (until he becomes King, upon which he inherits the Royal Standard of the monach and his son takes up the PoW arms), but the Queen's other children and grandchildren bear some version of the Royal Standard.

Heraldry, like royalty, is an arcane world with very precise rules that can also be changed on the spot. And yes, the man in charge of it really is called Garter King of Arms.

Those of you who've visited Chatsworth will probably find Lady Olivia's family estate of Allendale to be strikingly familiar. The Hunting Tower is certainly a real place and you can actually rent it for a week.

Royal brides have a very strong tradition of wearing all white (set by Queen Victoria), with a white bouquet. Clodagh might not have been allowed to get away with the ensemble she chooses in real life... ah but then she's not your usual royal bride, is she?

Here's a weird note to leave you on, however: I first made notes on this book in 2006, a full 11 years before I actually decided to write it. The fictional royal family was mapped out at that stage, and the oldest son of the Prince of Wales had two children, called George and Charlotte (I changed their names for obvious reasons!), with a third unnamed child on the way. I'd intended it to be a boy called James. We'll see...

Kate, February 2018

FAMILY TREE

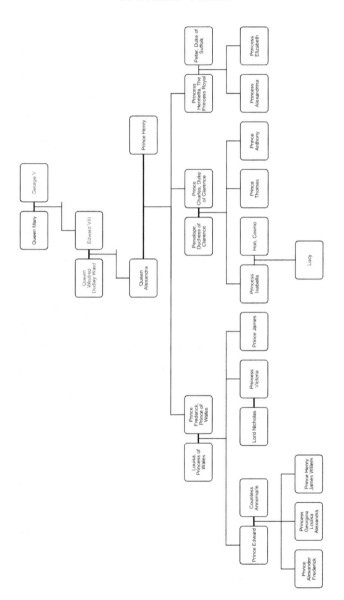

ABOUT THE AUTHOR

Kate has a second cousin who held a Guinness World Record for brewing the strongest beer, and once ran over herself with a Segway scooter. She misspent her youth watching lots of Joss Whedon and reading even more Terry Pratchett, which made it kind of inevitable that when she grew up to write romance novels, they'd be the weird ones around the edges. A few years later, she lives with her cats who are only partially named after Whedon characters, and a dog who is only partially evil, in the south of England. She still loves Joss Whedon and Terry Pratchett.

In 2017 Kate became the first author to win a Paranormal Romantic Novel of the Year Award from the Romantic Novelists Association, with *Max Seventeen*, which was also the first self-published book to win in any category. She has been shortlisted twice more, for *The Untied Kingdom* and *Max Seventeen: Firebrand*.

You can follow Kate online:
www.twitter.com/K8JohnsonAuthor
www.facebook.com/K8JohnsonAuthor
https://www.pinterest.co.uk/k8johnsonauthor/not-your-cinderella/
or find out more on www.KateJohnson.co.uk

Want to be first to hear about new releases? Sign up here: http://etaknosnhoj.blogspot.co.uk/p/newsletter.html

ALSO AVAILABLE

All books: http://author.to/KateJohnsonAuthor

Max Seventeen: Paranormal Romantic Novel of the Year 2017. Sci-fi action romance
http://mybook.to/Max17
Max Seventeen: Firebrand. Sci-fi sequel
http://mybook.to/Max17Firebrand

The Sophie Green Mysteries: chick-lit mystery
http://mybook.to/ISpy
The Untied Kingdom: alternate history romance
http://mybook.to/UntiedKingdom
Impossible Things: fantasy romance
http://mybook.to/ImpossibleThings

For more information please visit
www.KateJohnson.co.uk

Keep reading for an excerpt from *Max Seventeen*...

EXCERPT FROM MAX SEVENTEEN
Paranormal Romantic Novel of the Year 2017

Max was running.

The day was hot and bright, because days were always hot and bright on this crappy planet at the arse-end of the universe. Cheaply terraformed, barely able to support the dreg ends of life, farted at by the sun on a regular basis. Nobody lived here if they didn't have to.

At this moment, Max was sincerely considering how much 'have to' there was about living on Zeta Secunda, a planet so shitty it didn't even have a proper name. There was a spaceport a few clicks away, but spaceports required ID and security, and Max was fresh out of both. Well. Fresh out might be a stretch. Probably that last ID had ended up in the same place as that last decent pair of boots: inside those fecking sand-beasts. Ten feet long, and that was just the jaw. Max had been lucky to get out alive.

For a given value of luck, anyway. That bunch of culchies were still mad at Max for something. Hard to figure out what. Might've been the card sharping. Might've been the fake money. Might've been that fella left with his pants hanging out the window.

Either way, Max was running.

Sand fountained up ahead, and a whine whistled past. Grand, so they'd found their guns. At least here in the badlands they were the cheap old kind with bullets, which required aiming and accuracy, neither of which this lot seemed to have. Quite probably they were hungover. Possibly also still drunk. Not that Max could judge, brain still throbbing with last night's poteen.

Max was running on empty.

"I see you, kid!"

Max ignored that, and leapt over some low rocks to the sand below. Ahead, there was nothing but more rocks and more sand. So much more sand.

"Ain't nowhere to hide!"

Yeah, *obvs*. Sand, rocks, more sand. Max was dark with dirt and sun and vaguely sand coloured, but not nearly enough. There was nowhere to go, no shelter, no respite. Sooner or later they'd catch up.

Another smash. Another whine. Closer this time.

Max stumbled, foot rolling on a stone, knee thudding into the sand. Hell of a day to have fallen out the window with no clothes on.

The sun was fierce punishing. The desultory government advisories for Zeta Secunda included not going outside without solar protection. They meant proper pharma grade sunscreen. They didn't mention the fucking sand. Max didn't even have a shirt.

"Run, punk, run!" Those yahoos were getting closer. Some terrible little land buggies, or maybe horses. They used both around here, and it wasn't as if the wind was giving away any clues. No bugger was rich enough for a heavy-air vehicle. The HAVs and the HAV-nots, Max thought hysterically, stumbling on.

Smash, whine. Closer together. Sound and sand hitting at the same time.

Shit, not this time, don't let me die like this! I've got no fucking pants on!

The ground shook with the vehicles, pounded with the hooves of the horses. Closer, closer. Max kept on running. The sand gave way, shelving and sliding. Burned like the lava it once had been, grinding and grating, raw against raw skin. Max slid, the sand like waves made out of grit, desperate not to scream.

Sand fountained, the herald of impeding doom, and Max scrambled to bleeding feet, limping on over unforgiving dunes. The shadows closed in.

Max kept on running.

The engines of the Dauntless hummed smoothly, at a frequency that seemed perfectly calculated to grate on Riley's nerves.

Just four more years, then you can quit this fascist popsicle stand.

Fantasies of ripping out that Service chip they'd implanted and hurling it at the captain made up quite a lot of Riley's downtime.

"Sir?"

The captain gave no indication she'd heard.

"Sir, it's about Pherick. Pherick Green, the coolant engineer? It's just, he's been gone three standard weeks now, and—"

The captain tapped something on her tablet and didn't look up. "Green is on personal leave."

"Yes, sir, I know. But we're not allowed personal leave longer than—"

"The Service is capable of making exceptions," said the captain coolly.

Really? thought Riley. In whose favour? Eleven bloody years I've been committed to the Service, and when was the last time I got any leave?

The dark thought occurred that on Sigma Prime, you could commit murder and still get out of jail in less than eleven years.

"I understand you are friends," said the captain, and there was something in the way she said it that made Riley uneasy.

"We work together."

"I see. And Ensign…" she tapped her tablet, "Yakira is not an acceptable substitute?"

"Ensign Yakira is doing a fine job."

"Then what is the problem?"

The problem? Riley wanted to say. The problem is

that Pherick just disappeared one day, barely a few hours after telling me he'd uncovered something really disturbing but he couldn't tell me what. The problem is that his brother Jameson went AWOL on an away mission three months ago and he's not even supposed to be part of away missions. The problem is I think something very strange is going on here and I'm kind of scared that if I start asking questions about it, I'll be the next one to disappear.

Out loud, Riley said, "I just wondered when Pherick would be back, sir. I owe him a drink."

"I'm sure you'll be buying it soon. Was there anything else?"

You'll be watching every single thing I do on this ship from now on, won't you? thought Riley, but said, "No, sir. Thank you, sir."

The cool, neutral corridors of the ship closed in like a jail as Riley strode away, plotting escape.

Max Seventeen is available in ebook and paperback: http://mybook.to/Max17

Did you enjoy this book? Please consider leaving a review!

This book is enrolled in Kindle's Matchbook program. For more information, see Amazon.com

Printed in Poland
by Amazon Fulfillment
Poland Sp. z o.o., Wrocław